**WINNER OF THE 1991
SOUTHERN BOOK AWARD FOR FICTION
FROM THE SOUTHERN BOOK CRITICS CIRCLE**

**Critics everywhere love the stories in WHITE PEOPLE.
Here's what they had to say about some of their favorites.**

MINOR HEROISM: *Something About My Father*
"The first story examines a boy's relationship with his war-hero father, a deeply cruel man. It is a complex and poignant story, one of the most moving I have ever read, funny and heartbreaking. And as in the other stories, high-voltage emotion is accompanied and countered by a thorough intelligence that shapes and directs at every point.... Gurganus *knows* the South—with the intimate knowledge of someone who has grown up in it and has never stopped watching it for details.... A glorious collection, quite different from 'Widow' yet equally brilliant."

JOSEPHINE HUMPHREYS
Atlanta Journal & Constitution

BREATHING ROOM: *Something About My Brother*
"Dramatizes the growing split between Bryan and his younger brother, Brad. From an asthmatic child for whom protective brother Bryan feels complete responsibility, Brad turns into his father's favorite boy, sports-loving, model-building, goal-oriented.... I suspect many readers will feel as I often do about Walt Whitman: that Allan Gurganus' considerable skills as a storyteller and comic writer and his sympathy for a variety of white (and black) characters are pearls he has grown at great price."

JEFFREY RICHARDS
The Raleigh News & Observer

*Please turn the page
for more reviews....*

A HOG LOVES ITS LIFE:
Something About My Grandfather
"When her senile father-in-law makes a grotesque incursion into the bridge tournament she is throwing for 88 clubbable women, the hostess in 'A Hog Loves Its Life' grimaces and dithers momentarily but then remembers her manners—and her soul. . . . Love and guilt commingle in an uneasy blend that inspired speech can barely hold in equilibrium. . . . Gurganus seems to have taken such care in getting them all down right that one thinks of Mark Twain."

DENNIS DRABELLE
The Washington Post Book World

NATIVITY, CAUCASIAN
"A brilliant, brilliant story, [it] recalls Bryan's birth at a neighborhood contract-bridge tournament: His mother finds herself in her hostess' kitchen, stretched out on one of those post-war counters stuck in the middle of the room, having her baby in a jungle of smashed dinner mints and half-smoked cigarettes. . . . Gurganus introduces ourselves to ourselves; lovingly, tenderly. . . . A major achievement: more appealing [and] more loving than his earlier novel, OLDEST LIVING CONFEDERATE WIDOW TELLS ALL."

CAROLYN SEE
Newsday

REASSURANCE

" 'Reassurance' is in the form of two letters, one an actual letter by Walt Whitman, the other a ghostly or dreamed or, anyway, imagined letter from a dead Union soldier, Frank H. Irwin of company E, 93rd Pennsylvania, to his mother, both from the early summer of 1865. . . . It is very hard to be ample and accessible these days and to sound smart at the same time. In his novel and now in the eleven stories gathered together in WHITE PEOPLE, Mr. Gurganus manages to do that gracefully and skillfully. . . . Trust these tales and through them you will come to know and enjoy the teller."

GEORGE GARRETT
The New York Times Book Review

BLESSED ASSURANCE: a moral tale

"The true jewel in this collection . . . a novella with the weight of a much longer work. Jerry, a 19-year-old white boy who is putting himself through college, gets a job collecting funeral insurance payments from black customers who live in an area of town known as 'Baby Africa'. . . . [Gurganus] is a fine writer . . . in love with the language."

JUDITH FREEMAN
Los Angeles Times Book Review

*Please turn the page
for more reviews. . . .*

ADULT ART

"The conflict between human sexuality and social convention is dramatized ... in 'Adult Art,' [in which] a married, middle-aged father describes his erotic attraction to a younger man whom he meets by chance in his office building.... WHITE PEOPLE is shaped by a singular storytelling energy, and it proves as well that [Gurganus] is a remarkably versatile writer. Ranging from family memoirs to historical pieces, from satire to surrealism, WHITE PEOPLE celebrates American culture in all its humanistic vibrancy and grotesque contradictions. Blending trenchant satire with outrageous humor, Gurganus' stories recall both Mark Twain and Flannery O'Connor."

GREG JOHNSON
Chicago Tribune

AMERICA COMPETES

"Many of the stories are quite humorous, and 'America Competes,' an attack on the 'National Fundament of the Arts,' is one of these. Here the central character, besieged by human mediocrity and need, concludes 'We are one big unhappy family, and poor, aren't we?' 'Stories,' another character remarks, 'maybe offer us a little deal-making revenge on Time.' But we are left with his final lament over the passing of those he has loved: 'Where've they all gone?' This question haunts the stories in this disturbing collection, fine and sensitive studies that solidify Gurganus' position as a chronicler of America's nostalgic hankering after happiness—and immortality."

JOHN C. HAWLEY
San Francisco Chronicle

ART HISTORY

"[A] story about desire and spectatorship, 'Art History' tells of a schoolteacher and 'respected gentleman' (his daughter's description) and his own search for sublimity. But the reality is riskier here and Gurganus fragments it through a contrapuntal structure, shunting between the gentleman, his daughter and the arresting officer.... Gurganus writes without a safety net; no precautions are taken against pathos, bathos, authorial indignity. As a result, his best stories command a sort of sublimity of the mundane; they locate the dangerous glamour in ordinariness."

HENRY LOUIS GATES, JR.
The Nation

"The work of the very best writers leaves a taste in the mouth.... Critics and fans keep trying to stick Allan Gurganus in [the] kitchen with Flannery and Bill [Faulkner] and Miss Welty. Like Faulkner, Gurganus is concerned with myth and memory; like Welty, he strip-mines layers of Southern manners to get at the naked truth; like O'Connor, his characters' actions always imply a larger scheme to the world than mortals can understand. But Gurganus' work has its own distinct flavor. WHITE PEOPLE overflows with the buttermilk of human kindness. The velvety sentences just come rolling out, smoothly folding and lapping over at the ends, but it's more than a matter of sentences. It's a hundred tiny moments of kindness bestowed and withheld, and keenly observed. It's a writer reminding you that sweet good writing can even make you feel better about your own existence.... Allan Gurganus has been an important writer for a while now. It's just taken the world a while to catch on."

MARK CHILDRESS
Los Angeles Times Book Review

Also By Allan Gurganus
Published by Ivy Books

OLDEST LIVING CONFEDERATE WIDOW TELLS ALL

WHITE PEOPLE

Allan Gurganus

IVY BOOKS • NEW YORK

For my friends,

especially for Daisy Thorp

and for Paul Nagano

Ivy Books
Published by Ballantine Books
Copyright © 1990 by Allan Gurganus

All rights reserved under International and Pan-American Copyright Conventions. Published in the United States by Ballantine Books, a division of Random House, Inc., New York, and simultaneously in Canada by Random House of Canada Limited, Toronto.

All the stories and novellas in this volume have been previously published. Grateful acknowledgment is due to the following:

   The New Yorker: "Minor Heroism." *The New American Review*: "Condolences to Every One of Us." *The Paris Review*: "Art History" and "It Had Wings" (reprinted in *Harper's*). North Carolina Wesleyan College Press, which published the opening of "Breathing Room" and "Blessed Assurance" as limited edition chapbooks. *Harper's*: "America Competes," "Reassurance," and "Nativity, Caucasian." New American Library, which published "Adult Art" in *Men on Men II: Best New Gay Fiction*, edited by George Stambolian. *The Quarterly*: "A Hog Loves Its Life." *GRANTA*: "Blessed Assurance."

   The author wishes to thank the editors of these magazines, anthologies, and small publishing houses for their early encouragement and sustaining belief.

Library of Congress Catalog Card Number 90-52943

ISBN 0-8041-0851-X

This edition published by arrangement with Alfred A. Knopf, Inc.

Manufactured in the United States of America

First Ballantine Books Edition: April 1992

There is a kind of success that is indistinguishable from panic.
EDGAR DEGAS,
as quoted in Daniel Halévy, *My Friend Degas*

One inexorable rule of etiquette is that you must talk to your next-door neighbor at a dinner table. You MUST, that is all there is about it! . . . At dinner once, Mrs. Toplofty, finding herself next to a man she quite openly despised, said to him with apparent placidity, "I shall not talk to you—because I don't care to. But for the sake of my hostess, I shall say my multiplication tables. Twice one are two, twice two are four—" and she continued through the tables, making him alternate with her. As soon as she politely could, she turned again to her other companion.
EMILY POST (Mrs. Price Post),
Etiquette: The Blue Book of Social Usage,
illustrated with private photographs and
facsimiles of social forms, 1922 edition

Very late that fall, my grandfather and my father and a great many more went down to the Humboldt River to fish. . . . When they came back, they brought us more news. They said there were white people at the Humboldt Sink. They were the first ones that my father had seen face to face. He said they were not like 'humans'. They were more like owls than like anything else. They had hair on their faces, and had white eyes. My father said they looked very beautiful. . . .
PRINCESS SARAH WINNEMUCCA HOPKINS,
in *Life Among the Paiutes* as quoted by Joanne
Meschery in *Truckee, California: A History*

Contents

Acknowledgments

Thanking people is my favorite vice. The following friends have been especially kind in reading my work fast, always with honesty and empathy. I owe much to Jane Holding, Mitchell Eil, Danny Kaiser, Amanda Urban, Elisabeth Sifton, Peter Andersen, Steven Burke, Thomas Emerson Link, George Andreou, Marie Behan, Connie Brothers, Doris Grumbach, Andrea Simon, Claire Whittaker, Jane Cooper, my former students, and so many other fellow believers. Thanks, friends.

Minor Heroism
Something About My Father

For William Maxwell

1. AT WAR, AT HOME

*I*MAGINE HIM IN HIS PRIME. *A FAIRLY RICH AND* large-eared farm boy newly cured of being a farm boy by what he called Th' War, meaning the second one. He'd signed up in Charlottesville when most of his fraternity had done it as a group, and up till then he had been somewhat humorlessly typical. He had been hung up with the rest of them in the fraternity of the university that Jefferson designed, and he was as lean and carefully prepared as all the very best Virginia hams. And it would seem to follow that, in 1942, my father began being made more valuable by several years of smoke. But this smoke was not the curative Virginia kind; it was the high-flying smoke of German cities burning. My father was a bombardier. He became a minor hero in the Second World War and a major hero in Virginia/Carolina. He was photographed as Betty Grable stood on tiptoe to kiss him. He was tall. He still is. But his height meant most when he was dressed as an officer in our Army Air Corps. Today, in civvies, he is just another mildly handsome businessman. It was in uniform that Father looked most like himself.

Heroes should have looks. His were better than most,

better than wholesome. It was one of those faces that fit handsomely into photographs and under a brimmed cap. It seemed to know in every pose that captions would be under it eventually. His profile, nearly as good as a Barrymore's, was better for being blunted slightly by boarding-school boxing. With very combed blond hair waving back in the way hair did then, his was a face that even from the front told much about itself in silhouette. Many of the photos still exist.

When I was a child in the years just after that war, people cornered me with accounts of my father's valor. They told me in front of other children how, though everybody's father had certainly helped with it, mine had done more than most to insure that the Nazi plot to rule the world—to rule the very ground on which this birthday party was now taking place—had been crushed by the Americans. They mentioned the Freedoms, four in all, and promised that the whole white world was now capable of worshiping in whichever ways it chose. They said to me, "Do you know what your father did?" I was told how people had printed "Welcome Richard!" on broad banners made of sheets that stretched all the way across Main Street.

But before the war was won and he came home, there was the business about what they made my grandmother do. Though bossy when alone with family, she was a remarkably shy woman, even for then. In North Carolina, in 1942, shyness was less unusual than it is today. Both her parents' families had been equally distinguished and austere, and, as if to commemorate this, she parted her hair impartially down the middle and most always wore the same rare brooch at the exact center of her collar and throat. I once saw her hiding in the dark back hallway of her house; eyes opened very wide, she stood against a wall, as unwanted guests on the front porch repeatedly rang the door chimes.

She had been reared at home with her three sisters, on a Raleigh side street in a house cool most of the year with the amount of marble in it: veined tabletops, hearths arched and white as tombs, classical statuary, athletic and luminous in dark corners. The marble hearths and statues floated upright in the house's murk. Tabletops rode the gloom like oval rafts. It seemed the marble objects were the rooms' true residents, directing every household current into eddies split around themselves and cooling off whatever drifted past them.

But Grandmother's wish for the stillness of 1909 was inappropriate in 1942. There was a war going on and her son, they told her, was crucial to the local view of it. They put much unnecessary pressure on a lady so easily swayed. All it took was one unscrupulous question about how much patriotism she really felt as, after all, a longtime member of the DAR. At this, she said that yes, yes, she would do it, but only if they did not ask her to speak. Of course, those present assured her, she wouldn't have to utter one syllable she didn't rightly feel she could or should utter. But no one believed she would stay silent once she got up there and got the feel of it from all the bunting hung around. They forced her, in this way, to sit on public platforms. When the speaker selling war bonds acknowledged her, seated there as formal as her central brooch, she winced in recognition of her name and nodded back to him and tried to smile out at the audience like a mother, but she looked like a potentially bereaved one.

Mrs. Roosevelt herself came through on a decorated train and got off and walked over to the platform they'd set up outside the station, and not even then would my grandmother speak a public sentence to those gathered on the street and hanging out the windows of the Bank and those who dangled legs like extra letters over the sign usually spelling Ekstein's Finer Men's Apparel. Suspended from four lampposts were giant photos of my father in uniform, in profile. When Mrs. Roosevelt came over as the ceremony ended and said how handsome my father must be, to judge from his pictures over there, my grandmother finally spoke. She was nodding and thanking Eleanor Roosevelt as an equal when she noticed Mrs. Roosevelt wore no hat, which seemed odd in one of her station. What she was wearing, its weight tugging at the fabric of one shoulder, was a huge pale, wide-mouthed orchid which, some suggested afterwards, had looked much like her.

But Mrs. Roosevelt had won them over nonetheless, and it was lucky that others overheard what she said to Grandmother about my father's good looks. Grandmother would never have repeated it to anyone. Though she acknowledged things graciously, she never started them. In this way, she had become an adult and then a wife and, quite soon after that, a mother. Some were annoyed by this belief of hers that silence was always in good taste, but most people felt it was probably fine the way she was; that somehow it was more patriotic for a wife and mother not to say too much—except, of course, for Mrs. Roosevelt, and some people even felt that way about Mrs. Roosevelt.

The photograph of Betty Grable kissing my father's flat cheek seemed to hold the house up. I was born in 1947 and, as far as I knew, it had always been there. People who did not come often to the house would sometimes ask to see it. They were led back to the den, where it was hung with the medals. Smiling, they stooped to get the picture window's reflection off of it, and they'd shake their heads and nod appreciatively. I remember someone's saying that when you were young during a war it is hard to know later if you liked being young during a war or liked just being young or maybe even the war itself, who knows?

In the picture, he does not return her kiss but stands there; a statuesque soldier, newly decorated for minor heroism, accepts the homage of a distant voluptuous country. He is enjoying it probably, but he does not smile, for at that moment the fate of the Western world as we now know it still hung in the balance. But Betty Grable could smile. It was all right if she did, and the official Army photographer, whose job it was to photograph the wake of morale she left behind, snapped an Army camera, and there it was—on most front pages in either Carolina and with practically the whole page to itself in our local *Falls Herald Traveler*. And though manliness and the national moment forbade he show it, yes, certainly my father was enjoying the kiss synchronized with flashbulbs, just as local boys too young to go themselves were not too young to go at themselves several times a day upon finding this hometown representative in a favorite national fantasy with a Grable whose legs were here not even photographed to advantage, though the boys knew them well enough from other pictures. The local boys looked over at the grainy photograph they'd cut out and pinned up to the wallpaper beside their beds, and for a while there, several times a day, any number of them were replacing my father in his uniform, with Grable breathing right there beside them in her WAC's outfit shortened way beyond regulations. And after the ceremony, as the dots of flashbulbs were still dying out of their vision, there the boys were, there he was, the local high-school valedictorian, in the south of England, wearing my father's

uniform and medals and walking across a muddy camp
with Grable on his arm. He was looking down at her
little WAC's cap pinned to the blond hair swept up on
top. Pulling back the tent flap, she goes in first; he
waits, takes a few more drags from the Camel he is
smoking, then flips it smoothly into a nearby puddle
and goes in himself. She is right there, patriotically
spread-eagled on the tent floor, waiting for more minor
heroism. In the flexed nostrils of the class valedictorian,
the stink of weatherproofed canvas combines with the
scent of Betty Grable's own perfume, a perfume that
all the factories at home are working overtime to make
available for her to bolster soldiers' morale, perfume
that all the smokestacks smoke for hours to make one
ounce of, perfume that all the factory girls at home
helped make with skilled fingers, factory girls waiting
up in their little rooms for men, disheveled healthy girls
with their own skilled factory hands working up themselves with thoughts of soldierhood and regulation bay-
oneting and, oh, how crucial my own father was to
local high-school boys behind closed doors in the early
spring of 1945.

But when I was eight years old, some adult would
take me aside and say, "Bryan, do you know what your
father did before you were even born? Has he told you
about what he did?" I said I didn't know for sure but
that they used to paint little German planes on their
bombers every time they shot a real one down, and my
daddy's score was very high. They said no, not that.
Not exactly. It was Dresden, the terrible and decisive
firebombing of Dresden, that had been his real moment.

I nodded and always imagined a city of plate and
saucer monuments and crockery apartments and wartime's smoking smokestacks made of stacked white bot-

tomless coffee cups. And in the center of the shining
city was an oil depot, looking very like a soup tureen
of Mother's—a white one too large for just us to use but
brought out for dinner parties and reunions and once, I
remembered, filled with vegetable alphabet soup. I'd
stood, amazed to see the very spindly alphabet I was
then learning to draw between blue lines fattened up
and floating on the top of something I and all my family, even my illiterate younger brother, could drink down
like reading. But the tureen I imagined there in Dresden
was a million gallons high and filled to the top with the
crudest, blackest German oil that fueled the deadly
U-boats. A remarkable target for my father in his clear air
over the heart of gleaming Dresden. In my conception,
the black bomb wobbles toward the very shadow of it
growing on the glossy upper disc of all those gallons.
The life-sized shadow meets the real bomb falling in
and going off down at the very bottom. Such beautiful
war-movie slow motion now allows a perfect view of
all the damage as the tank pops jaggedly open and out
the gallons gush into the tranquil city. Black oil gluts
the sewers of the sanitation system. The overflow is
fingering up and out into the gutters and makes a black
street map of the white municipality. Borne along in the
dark gloss are clusters of diced carrots and chopped
celery from my mother's kitchen, and there come the
fat paste letters of the alphabet, movable type sucked
down with the black into the gasping manholes. The
level rises—filling, incidentally, the holes, which are
the handles of the chaste white coffee cups. Darkness
crawls about and then above the town and finally de-
fines a surface that a cup or saucer may float along on
briefly, till tilting, then filling viscously, they sink in,
one by one, until they all are underneath. Now everything is underneath. All the quaintness of Germany, all

the cuckoo clocks are under, all the perfect German sheet music played by countless amateurs on Sundays, and, worst for me, all the inedible lost letters of my mother's English alphabet have become one glossy black deluge which now shows just the tiny moving shadow of my father's bomber, speeding back to England, back to the USO show, which will not begin till he is there in a seat being saved for him.

The photographers are smoking at the airport now; they are awaiting him. They are men also in the Army. Their job is to photograph the bombardiers like my handsome father, crawling from the cockpit, less exerted than excited by the damage he has done, looking clean and highly combed as when he left some hours ago.

But by the time I was imagining the bombing of Dresden, my father was done with all that. The war had been won. Dresden's place setting was being sorted out. With Germany having an Occupation forced upon it, it was time my father settled into a job himself. His fading local glamour at least proved useful in helping him choose a career. Cashing in on people's memories of him, he became an insurance salesman. It was not hard, selling insurance, and with his law degree, with the certificates Grandfather had given him, with the smattering of rents collected from the colored-tenant houses—the only remnants of Grandmother's "fortune"—Father felt he could more than make do. He married a clever girl he'd met at a deb party before the war. He brought her south from Richmond and carried her into a thirty-thousand-dollar house already paid for in advance by his cashing in certificates in companies making aluminum and small-screened televisions—all companies on the brink of booming when he sold their stocks. But though he was without much business sense, still there was the thirty-thousand-dollar house, much larger than what one could buy oneself today for that amount of money. So my father and my mother moved into a house that echoed slightly because it had more rooms than furniture. Sometimes the guest room was occupied by a recurrent itinerant aunt; but when she was gone the doors were closed, the heating ducts turned off, and three bedrooms, now accommodating only boxes full of unused wedding gifts, again stood very vacant.

My father still wrote to war buddies. They often passed through town en route to Florida, howling in through the front door to hug him. A lot of them were dark men, hairy in a way my father and his fair Carolina friends were not. It seemed that all New Yorkers were brown-eyed and sooty from the city; they looked odd here in the clear to amber light of our Tidewater. Mentioning their wives waiting out in the car, they lifted eyebrows suggestively, as in the old days—as if that were some notorious and easy girl out there. Mother never liked their wives much, and when they'd left, Father told her she was a snob. "War buddies' wives are not necessarily war buddies themselves," she quipped. Once, when he insisted, after hanging up the phone, that they drive two hundred miles to a motel where someone from his squadron was staying on the way to Miami, Mother mentioned a bridge tournament; she said, "Show him my picture," and settled luxuriously back onto the couch with the latest novel by Daphne du Maurier. "He already saw your picture and he's heard more about you than you'd ever guess!" my father shouted as he stormed out with the car keys and an unopened bottle of Jack Daniel's and, slamming the door, rattled the china cabinet. Very early the next morning, he came in drunk and in a loud voice over the telephone canceled an afternoon appointment to sell Group Life. My mother wandered down to breakfast in her quilted yellow housecoat, and noticed a broken headlight on the Packard parked at the wrong angle outside. When they'd settled at the table, coffee poured, she offered him the usual tirade about his egotism, her suffering, and their marriage, which she liked to say was "crumbling, Richard, crumbling!" I sat eating scrambled eggs with a big round training spoon, and my younger brother dropped his baby bottle on the floor, then looked down at it till I picked it up. "Oh yeah?" my father said. And then she said, "Don't you use that trashy New York slang around your children." "Oh yeah?" he said.

But when you are definitely home from the European Theater, which is dead now, and war buddies you'd have given your life for now phone less and less, are more and more just Christmas cards with photos of new children, cards signed in a woman's hand, when insurance (fire, burglary, auto, and life) is now what people think of when they think of you, when Marilyn Monroe is filling the shoes of Betty Grable, who's retired, what do you do then?

You find that the headaches are because you suddenly need reading glasses. You resign yourself to buying bourbon by the case because it is cheaper and you now have room to store that much, and you have no doubt that it will somehow get drunk up. You call your two sons soldiers when they submit stiff-faced, thin-armed, to Jonas Salk's discovery. You pay someone to keep the yard worthy of your wartime aerial-photo vision of its symmetry and shape from overhead. You take your wife to the occasions you count on the country club to invent, and there, with friends who have become clients and friends who have not become clients and with clients who want to become your friends, the two of you get more than genteelly drunk, even by Eastern Carolina's lubricated standards. And afterward, after the baby-sitter has been overpaid to cover your tardiness and the fact that the front of your jacket is dark from some accidental spillage and to cover the expense of the cab that must be called to get her home, in the silence after that, of the house becoming increasingly more valuable as the boxwoods expand themselves outside, with the hint of dawn coming on, you both manage to know what a prime moment in the history of your physiques this is.

Otherwise, you learn to make do, and when some threat arises you are soldierly in disposing of it. Almost, there are not enough threats anymore. Here you are, among the most successful of the bombardiers, now grounded, in the awful safety of this decade, in its suburbs. You do what you can around the house and grounds to re-create some of that drama you remember from the forties. All the events that made one's life eventful: The Axis. Roosevelt Dead. Hiroshima.

The furnace explodes early one morning. You carry Helen outside, dump her onto a lawn chair, rush back for the sleeping boys, dash across the street and pull the fire alarm. Later the fire chief emerges from the basement of the house and ambles around the engine and out toward your family group, huddled in pajamas among the neighbors, who have brought blankets, coffee, garden hoses. "Nothing serious," he says. "The furnace sort of exploded. A little soot, but nothing serious."

"What do you mean, 'nothing serious'? You should have heard it. I thought we were being attacked or something."

"Noisy," the fire chief admits, scratching his head, trying to be both tactful and professional, "but nothing serious."

The next day, you order a fire-alarm system for the house. While the children grumble, while a siren howls and neighbors watch over fences, you stage your first weekly fire drill. After two of these, the drills are discontinued.

It is a personal affront when tent caterpillars invade four of the yard's eleven trees. A neighbor says you'll have to burn them out; only thing they understand. The yardman prepares to do it, till you curtly give him the day off. This job, worthy of you, will require a little strategy. There are moments when a father and his boys must work together. Standing in the back door, you shout, "Now is the time for all good boys to come to the aid of their father and their yard!" *"What?"* Helen asks.

You put a torch together—a broom handle, rags, some kerosene. You ignite it with your wartime Zippo. Up into the infested tree nearest the house you crawl. This is a mission; for once, in peacetime, you know exactly what you're going to do. The boys watch idly from the ground as you sear the first lumps of worms out of the plum tree. Smoke suddenly everywhere and such a smell. "You two down there, don't just stand around. Stomp on the ones getting away." Clusters of black caterpillars, pounds of them, are toppling from their webs, falling to the ground and steaming.

Making girlish noises, your sons start hopping on the smoldering worms. Bradley jogs about, eyes straight ahead; he lifts his knees and makes a calisthenic game of it. Feeling dizzy, Bryan shuts his eyes, holds out his arms for balance, and earnestly pretends he's dancing, though his tennis shoes keep slipping out from under him.

In the tree, you find you've started muttering almost

forgotten, complicated curses from the war as, one by one, you solemnly eradicate these black colonies of pests. Your sons' whimpering infuriates you suddenly. "Shut up down there, you two. You'll do your job and keep your mouths closed. These things are going to get to other trees. They'll get over into the Bennetts' yard if we don't kill them now. This is no game here, this is an emergency, so quit squealing like sissies and stomp on them. That clear?"

Your two children look up at the orange glow inside the tree, at a single wing-tip shoe visible among the leaves. In unison, they say, "Yes sir."

2. MY ELDER SON

I'm not as young as I used to be and it follows that my sons aren't either. Bradley, our baby, is twenty-five now and makes a hundred and twenty thousand dollars a year. He graduated third in his class from the law school of the University of Virginia. He's now with a fine corporation-law firm working out of Georgetown. Brad married Elaine last May at a garden wedding that was rained out but that was nice anyway. The brides-maids' dresses were made of some thin material that got transparent when wet. Elaine is from a fine old Maryland family. Her father served as attorney general of the state a few administrations back. Now Brad and Elaine are renovating a town house in Washington, do-ing most of the work themselves. What with Elaine's small private income and her looks and taste, and with Brad's salary, my wife and I feel good about their prog-ress in life. Elaine always remembers us with little cards and gifts on birthdays and anniversaries. It's a comfort.

Bryan is our elder son. He's twenty-seven and a mys-tery to me. Two years ago he gave up a fairly good job as a designer of furniture. He decided to become a writer. When he was home last Christmas, we heard him typing a few times, but he never offered to show us anything he'd written. I have no doubt that it's good. He has always had a real flair for the arts. But if you've never read a word your son has written and if you understand the kind of money a writer can expect to make, it's hard to work up any real enthusiasm for this occupation.

To support himself, Bryan does articles for a magazine called *Dance World*. When people ask me what he's doing, I tell them he writes for a magazine in New York. If they ask me which one, then I'm forced to level with them. I'd have to be a writer myself to describe the sinking feeling I get when I tell this about my elder son. Helen says that my attitude in the matter is unreasonable. All I know is, the first year he worked for the magazine he sent us a free subscription, and it got so I couldn't even stand to see copies on the coffee table. I could hardly believe some of the pictures of the men. Looking at them, you didn't know whether to laugh or cry or get angry or what.

My wife also informs me that there are two kinds of dance, ballet and modern, and that Bryan's specialty is modern. Helen says, with lots of enthusiasm, that modern is less costumed but just as athletic as ballet. Somehow, knowing this doesn't help.

You might say Bryan and I have never really seen eye to eye. He has always had certain mannerisms and his talents are unlike my own. When he was younger he stayed pale from spending too much time indoors. I kept telling Helen that one day he'd discover the world outside. I said, "Now he keeps a diary, he paints still lifes, he reads French like a Frenchman, but believe you me, one day he'll come around. You watch."

I see I might have been wrong. He's twenty-seven

years old and I think the only women he ever talks to are waitresses. He lives with some actor-model roommate. We had lunch with them in New York. The roommate met us at the restaurant. I was expecting somebody thin who looked pretty much like Bryan. In walks this big, broad-shouldered kid, taller than me and with a suntan and a jaw like a lifeguard's. For a second, I was ashamed of myself for having jumped to certain conclusions. Then the first thing I noticed was his handshake. One of those dead fish. Second thing I noticed was, he'd smashed his thumbnail in something; it was black. Third thing was that all his fingernails were black. Nail polish. I could hardly understand what this meant. I thought it must be for medicinal purposes, because how could anybody do that for decoration? Helen was staring so hard I had to nudge her under the table. Usually she's the one nudging me. Afterwards she said she wouldn't have been so startled if it had been red polish, but black?

Now that we've met Jacques, he seems to be everywhere we look. Helen never forgets a face, and she keeps finding his picture in magazine ads—mostly for whiskey and shirts, once for soap. In these ads his nails are never black. I won't get over that. The kid looked like he should be on the U.S. Olympic team carrying a torch—and then the handshake, the nails, and his trying to talk all during lunch about the music of the forties. He kept asking Helen and me about Kay Kayser and his Kollege of Musical Knowledge, and about the Andrews Sisters. Helen surprised me by remembering the name of each Andrews Sister and knowing the order in which some'd died. She entered right into the discussion. He asked her how it felt to have heard "Tangerine" when it was new, and Helen was sitting right there telling him. Jacques kept saying over and over again, "What a period, what a period!'' For a person like myself, who loved the forties, the silliness of this kind of conversation made me sick. As if anybody like that could ever understand what it meant to be alive then.

You send your sons to the best schools possible, and you hope that their friends will be bright kids from similar backgrounds. Sometimes I wonder what my son and this type of person have in common. Then I take a guess, and right away I'm wishing I could forget my own conclusions.

I was not going to mention it, but as long as I've built up this much steam I might as well. Last spring, Bryan came down to his brother's wedding in Baltimore. We were glad he came. It was right that he should be there, but I won't even begin to describe the person, the creature, he brought along with him. Everyone who saw this particular person immediately got very disturbed. This particular person somehow managed to get into and spoil about half of Bradley and Elaine's wedding pictures. Elaine's parents were obliged to find a place for Bryan and his guest to stay during the weekend of the wedding. They were certainly very gracious about it and never said one word about this person's appearance. But Helen was so upset and embarrassed she cried most of the nights we were there. Because of the strain, she looked terrible at the wedding.

Of course, it was Helen who was always telling Bryan he was gifted. She was enrolling him in adult art classes with nude models when he was twelve damn years old, buying him thirty-dollar picture books full of abstract paintings, driving him fifteen miles to the next town because our local barbers couldn't ''cut with the curl.'' I told her she was spoiling him, but beyond that what could I do? I'd always said that the boys should have nothing but the best. No, I'm definitely not blaming

Helen. After all, that's one reason you make your money, so you can spoil your kids in ways you weren't.

You start off with a child, a son, and for the first six years he's on your side. It's clear there's nothing wrong with him. He's healthy, and you're relieved. He's pretty much like all the others. Not quite as noisy, maybe not quite as tough, but that might be a good sign, too. Then things somehow get off the track. He's coming in with a bloodied nose once a week, and you know damned well that nothing happened to the kid that did it. He's inside listening to records when he ought to be outside playing with the others. His face starts looking unlike yours and hers. You come home from a hard day's work and find him sitting in a high-backed chair cutting shapes out of colored paper and spreading them on the rug. You wonder for a moment if this white-skinned kid can be fourteen years old; can he be half your responsibility, half your fault? Of course, there are times when everything seems well enough. He takes out girls. He learns to drive. His tenor comes and goes, then comes to stay. One day you see he's nicked himself while shaving, and all the time you feel you should be grooming an heir he grows paler, taller, and more peculiar. He locks doors behind himself and startles you in the dark hallways of your own house. You're afraid of his next phase—afraid how the finished product will compare with the block's other boys, with his own kid brother who plays on the junior varsity and mows other people's lawns for money.

At the PTA open house a teacher pulls you aside and tells you, all excited, "Bryan can do anything he likes in the world. How few of us can do absolutely anything we like. He's among the chosen few, and I thought you both should know." His mother beams all evening, but afterwards you find him in the kitchen, at the table, dripping candle wax on black paper. "An experiment," he mumbles as you walk into the room toward the refrigerator. You feel clumsy and you try with your expression to apologize for having barged in like this through the swinging door. But, after all, you tell yourself, it *is* your kitchen and your table, that is your son. The "anything" his sad teacher promised gives you more distress than comfort.

He drops calling you just Dad and changes you to Father. One night you turn on the television and hear him say, "Television is for fools," and dash out of the room, offended by your need to see the news. You expect more from him as he gets older, but the distance grows. He reminds you of a thin, peculiar fellow you knew slightly in the Army, a bookworm nobody spoke to.

Till last New Year's Eve, I felt I'd had a pretty good track record as a father. I mean, I knew I'd made some mistakes, but somehow, over the years, you forget specifically what they've been. Bryan had come south for Christmas for the first time in two years. Helen and I got home from a party at the Club. We were slightly drunk. Bryan was sitting up reading when we got in. He was curled on the living-room couch in a floor-length maroon bathrobe he'd worn most of his visit. He was reading something he'd brought down from New York. He laughs at our books and magazines, picks up Helen's novels and giggles at them and puts them down again.

Charlie Fentress had announced his daughter's engagement at the New Year's Eve party. The band played a few bars of the Wedding March. Bradley and Elaine weren't married yet and Brad had decided to spend Christmas with his college roommate on St. Thomas. Only Bryan was home. Edward and Mildred Fox took Helen and me aside at the party to say they just wanted to let us know they were going to be grandparents. They were hugging each other and they both had tears in their eyes. The band played "Auld Lang Syne." It seemed everyone was being honored and rewarded by their children but us. Bryan had laughed at our suggestion that he come to the party and see his old friends. "What would I talk to them about?" he asked. "The pill, kindergarten car pools?" His quickness with words has made him all the more upsetting. But we got home and there was our son on the couch. There he was. His hair cut in a shaggy expensive way, and wearing a silk bathrobe. He looked over his shoulder at us as we stood in the foyer taking off our coats and rubbers with a little drunken difficulty.

"How was the prom, kids?" he asked and turned back to his book. I walked into the living room. On the coffee table before the couch I saw a bottle of cognac I'd paid forty bucks for, three years earlier. A snifter was beside it and a lot of wet rings, some of the cognac spilled on the tabletop.

"Who told you you could open that bottle?" I asked him.

"Father, it's New Year's Eve. Let up a little." The back of his head was still toward me.

"Look what you've done to that table. Your mother breaks her back keeping this place decent and you act like you're at the goddamned Holiday Inn."

It's easy enough now to say I shouldn't have cuffed him. But I felt like doing it, and I was just drunk enough to do what I felt like doing. He hadn't even bothered to turn around while I was talking. I took a backswing while he was reading. Helen said, "Richard!" in a warning tone of voice, but, like me, she really didn't think I'd do it. I smacked him with my best golfer's swing right across his fashionable haircut, and knocked him off the couch onto the floor. It scared me as much as it seemed to scare him. For a minute he lay blinking up at me, mouth open, on the carpet. We were like that for a second. His mouth open, mine open, and Helen with both hands pressed over hers. Then she was all over me, trying to hold my arms like I was going to kill him. He got up, straightened his robe, and marched upstairs. The whole thing was so sloppy it made me sick. Even with all I'd drunk I couldn't sleep.

The next morning there was to be a New Year's Day church service at Trinity Episcopal. Helen had asked Bryan to come with us, but we didn't think he'd get up, since it was before his usual rising time, which was anywhere from noon till three. Helen and I were eating breakfast. We were dressed for church, eating without talking, trying not to think about the night before, but thinking about it anyway.

We were both staring at our eggs and coffee when Bryan came downstairs, all dressed for church. His head was bound up in a professional-looking gauze-and-tape bandage that covered most of his hair and forehead. The tanned ears stuck up over the white cap. He looked like someone recovering from brain surgery. Helen was drinking her coffee as he came in. In the middle of swallowing, she went into a genteel coughing fit. Bryan poured himself a cup. As he was adding cream and sugar, he said cheerfully, "Father, when people at church ask what happened to me—and inevitably they will ask—I intend to tell them exactly who's responsible for this."

I sat staring down the table at him. We were squared off, me at my usual place, he at his. I started chewing on my back molars in a way I hadn't done since the War. He went on drinking his coffee. Once in a while, he'd glance up at me over his cup. He seemed pleased with himself. Helen was staring at him with her mouth half open. She would look from him to me, her face all strained, as if she wanted me to explain him to her. So this is it, I thought. That one over there with the bandages, that's my elder son and heir. I had to decide then whether I would really break his head or if I'd let things go. At some point, you have to decide with children whether you're going to kill them or let them go.

I thought of those foreign-exchange students we sometimes had to dinner when they passed through our town. Odd-looking kids with funny-shaped glasses, sometimes bad teeth, and accents half the time Helen and I couldn't understand. But we always pretended we did. You could tell when they had asked a question, and even though you hadn't really caught it, you still nodded and said, "Yes." And when it turned out that the question couldn't be answered with a simple Yes, when they stared at us, at least we'd shown that we had wanted to agree. In the long run, that was all Helen and myself could do for International Good Will.

So at this breakfast I decided to give Bryan the benefit of the doubt. I told myself I'd treat him at least as well as we treated these nonwhite foreign students who come to dinner for just one night. You didn't even expect thank-you notes from them. These kids' customs were so different, their homes so far from us here. But we were always kind to them, thinking of American kids who'd be in their country someday. So I told myself there at the table, if not as a father then at least as a host and an American, I should treat Bryan at least as well as one of them. After all, a foreigner is mostly what he's been to us.

Helen didn't want him to go out bandaged like that, but you have to take your own kid to church. Besides, if we hadn't taken him he'd have called a cab and how would that have looked? I'm sure he told whoever asked about his head whatever it was he'd decided to tell.

He left for New York that very afternoon, still
wrapped up like somebody with amnesia. Except for
Bradley's wedding, we haven't seen him since. I suspect
that he's in secret correspondence with his mother, and
that's fine and natural, I suppose. Some days she's more
tearful than others. In the middle of a meal, she'll fold
her napkin, place it on the table, leave the room.

Someday he'll probably publish a story or a whole
book about what a tyrant I've been. I can imagine a chap-
ter listing all the times I ever raised my voice or hit him.
Of course, people always believe what's down in black
and white before they'll listen to just one man's word
about what happened. I have made some mistakes, I
know. But I won't accept his verdict of me. I'm not a
villain. If anything, I've wanted too much for him, and,
considering all the ways you can go wrong with a son,
it seems the one he would be quickest to forgive.

3. ADDENDUM

In this drawing I am doing, a tall red man holds the
hand of a small white boy. The man wears a decorative
uniform: policeman, soldier, milkman. He is much
taller than the child, but his right arm has been conve-
niently elongated, elasticized like a sling or bandage so
it easily supports the boy's white hand.

My art teacher called me out into the hallway on the
last day of school and whispered, "You mustn't tell the
other children, but you're the best drawer I have ever
taught in eighteen years. The most imaginative. Of your
age group, I mean." Now, deciding to place the man
and boy before a doorway just like that one there, with
a similar selection of Mother's houseplants sprouting all
around them, I recall Miss Whipple's compliment. I feel
fully capable of adding exactly what I intend. When I'm

done, people will say, "Look. He's drawn a man, a boy, a doorway, and some plants in pots." There is a comfort in knowing you can make things recognizable.

I have lots of room on this table we inherited early from my farmer grandfather and his shy-in-public wife. It was built to seat a family of ten, plus guests. I am alone here at my usual end. Mother, Daddy, Bradley, and I each have a whole side to ourselves and must speak up to be heard by everyone. Venetian blinds cross the dining-room window, and sunshine throws a laddered shadow straight across the walnut surface of the table. The round-ended bars of light rest there in a row, like giant versions of my own crayons.

My brother and his friends are playing baseball in the front yard. They chant their jeers to various Episcopalian cadences. A few minutes back, a foul ball rattled off the roof. The grandfather clock in the foyer musically commemorates each and every fifteen minutes, however uneventful, and my crayon seems responsible for every drowsy sound.

The surface of the table gives a sudden jerk, and the crayoned frond of the potted palm I'm drawing takes an unexpected twist. I look up and watch my handsome father seat himself at the far end of the table and spread his mail like a game of solitare. Crosshatched with sunlight, his white shirt is dazzling and reflected in the tabletop. From his favorite coffee cup, steam climbs. It twists and plaits itself up through the alternating stripes of sun and slatted shadow. He holds an envelope to the light and rips into it with one finger. With that same hand, he slapped me two days ago. It burned across my face and swiveled my whole head in that direction. I go back to my control of crayons. Maybe he'll take his bills into the study and leave me here to excel privately at drawing.

His voice startles me. "Why don't you go outside

and play with the others? It would do you some good."
I continue drawing. Indoor clouds rain blue and purple
pellets on the houseplants. "Did you hear me down
there?" "Yes sir." "What don't you like about baseball? Are you afraid you'll get hurt or what?" I know
I must say something. "I like drawing." A pause. Still
watching me, he drinks from his coffee cup. "But it's
summer, Bryan. It's a beautiful summer morning and
you're seven years old and when—" "Eight," I say,
not looking up. "What?" "Eight years old." "All
right, then, eight, all the more reason. If you've got to
draw on a day like this, what's in here that you can't
draw just as well outside?" All the floating clumps of
leaves have sprouted pots. "I asked you a question.
What do you find to draw, sitting in here like this?" A
challenge. He thinks I don't know. Most Imaginative of
My Age, and he thinks I don't even know what I'm
drawing. Tell him an airplane, tell him an airplane.
"You," I say, despite myself. "Drawing me?" Why
did I tell? Now he'll want to see it. Casually, he glances
again through his mail. "So, you're drawing your dad,
huh? Well, let's have a look." I note that he's forgotten
all about the baseball game. After slapping me two
times in one week, he's crazy if he thinks I'll spend all
morning drawing him and then get up and walk to the
far end of the table and deliver it. He only notices my
drawing when he wants to show that it's a waste of time.
I won't let him see this. Absolutely not. Unless it's that
or getting slapped again.

"It's really not any good," I assure him.

"Let me see it."

"You won't think it's any good. You'll get mad 'cause
it's not the way you really look."

"Bring it here."

"Well, I drew in the door and plants behind you, and

I think you really have to see it from down here at this end, because this is where I drew it from.''

''I can turn around and see those,'' he says, peeved at conceding this. ''Bring it here, Bryan.''

I concentrate on the black crayon in my damp right fist. I study the picture itself. ''Daddy,'' I begin, definite. ''I just don't feel like you would . . . I don't want you . . . to see it . . . **yet**. I'll show you later, in a minute, later on.''

''This is getting ridiculous, young man. I'm asking you to bring that to me. Are you going to bring it or aren't you? It's that simple.''

I have included him here, but that makes the drawing even more mine, less his. It's the one thing in this house of his that's really mine right now. The man's mouth is a single horizontal line. The boy's a silly U-shape. ''It's mine,'' I say quietly.

''You said it was a picture of me.''

''It is, but I'm the one that did it. Please Daddy, don't make me this time.''

A long silence from the far end of the table. ''I'm waiting, Bryan. Bring that down here right this second.''

Almost before I think of it, the crayon is scribbling. In tight black loops it traps and then eclipses half the page. I choose one figure. The face and hands are lost forever underneath an oily whorl. There is the chanting from the front yard, the scratchy circling of my crayon, less loud as black wax accumulates. My exertion delicately clinks his coffee cup against its saucer. As I scrawl, feeling sick and elated at this solution, I grind my teeth and stare straight at my enormous father, smaller than usual at the far end of the table. He seems to be sitting for a portrait as I furiously describe a neat black cyclone on the page. His jaw is set. I can hear his breathing. I know the signs. Any second he will lunge down here, grab me by the shirt, lift and shake me, slap me once with a hand the full size of my head; he'll shove me, stumbling, toward my room, shrieking in my own defense. Now, just as he places both palms on the table to come for me, I stand. I lift the drawing by its upper corners and carry the page as if wet.

I move toward his chair, the only chair with arms. He is waiting there to punish me for drawing during summer, for drawing anything but him all day, for then un-drawing him without permission. I stare between his eyes at the faint inch making two eyebrows one grim horizontal line.

I warily approach him in my acolyte's gait. I hold up the drawing, a white flag, between his body and mine. I am now beside his chair. Seated, he is just as tall as I am standing. On his forehead there are rows of pores, and over that the teeth marks where the comb passed through his hair. His back is pressed straight against the chair, hands still tense on the table's edge. Over his business mail I place my artwork. One flimsy piece of white paper with some colored markings on it. His eyes move from my face down to my drawing. He sees the figure there. I hear him quietly exhale. His solid hands reach out and pick the paper up. I am very conscious of the hands. There I am, that's me, I feel him thinking. He has recognized himself. I release my breath and gratefully inhale some of Miss Whipple's wonder at my own imagination. Good for something, it has just spared me a whipping. I've sketched an image of him for himself, while I am permanently off the page, and saved. He is not asking why the uniformed gentleman's longer arm is weighed with this bristling black cancellation. He is now responding to the easy magic of a drawing of a uniform on a tall figure, the horizontal mouth, the buttons and braid.

"So, there I am . . . ," he says, relaxing. "Why'd you do this crossing out? What was that under there?"

I have lost interest in the drawing. I stare out the window at the summer lawn where my brother and six neighbor kids are climbing a young evergreen, tilting it almost to the ground. "Nothing," I say.

"So, there I am. Those are sure some ears you gave me. What are these round things here on front? Are those medals? Medals for what?" He hesitates to risk a guess. I look back from the venetian blinds and stare at him. He sits studying the drawing, his face rosy, jovial now. More than anything, I want suddenly to hug him, to move forward and throw my arms around his neck. I want to cry and have him hold me. Lift me off the floor and up into the air and hold me. Instead, there seems to be a layer of electricity around him. I know I will be shocked for touching him with no reason. Somewhere in the house an alarm will sound, the grandfather clock will gong all out of sequence, the door chimes will go wild, sirens will howl out of the heating ducts, and foul balls will crash through every window in the place. I look at him and, in answer to his question, shrug.

He holds the drawing out for me to take. He's done with it. Slipping past his chair, I saunter to the back door and, on my way outside, turn around. I see him seated in stripes of light at the vacant family table. Sad, he holds my own drawing out to me as if offering a gift or an apology or some artwork of his own. Something changes in me, seeing him like this, but as I pass into the sunlight I fight to keep my voice quite cool and formal and call back, "I'm finished, Daddy. You may keep it now. It's yours."

1972–73

Condolences to Every One of Us

*For Brett Singer
and for Marianne Gingher*

Dear Mrs. Whiston,

I was in Africa on Father Flannagan's Tour of the World with your parents when they were killed. I want to tell you how it happened. My son-in-law is a doctor (eye, ear, nose and throat) at Our Lady of Perpetual Help outside Toledo, and he says I should write down all I know, the sooner the better, to get it out of my system. I am a woman of sixty-seven years. I have a whole box of stationery here. If this doesn't turn out so hot, I'm sorry. My mind is better than ever but sometimes my writing hand gets cramped. I'll take breaks when I need to. I've got all morning.

I blame the tour organizers. They should be informed about the chances of a revolution happening while one of their buses is visiting some place. When I first looked at Father Flannagan's literature, I got bad feelings about Tongaville. I'd never even heard of it, but on these package deals you just go where the bus goes. You take the bad cities with the good.

Your parents were the most popular couple on our tour. They always had a kind word for everyone.

They'd made several other world trips, so your mother knew to be ready for the worst. She shared her Kaopectate with me when I most needed it outside Alexandria. I'm sending along a picture I took with my new camera at the Sphinx. It's not as sharp as I expected but here it is. Your mother is the one in the saddle and your father's holding his baseball-type cap out like he's feeding her camel. He really stood about ten feet in front of it because we were told they bite. The woman off to the right is Miss Ada McMillan, a retired librarian just full of energy and from Winnetka, Ill. She is laughing here because your father was such a card, always in high spirits, always cheering us up, keeping the ball rolling in ways our tour guide should have. I hope knowing more about your parents' death will be better for you than remaining in the dark. I think I'd want the whole truth. What I've read in American papers and magazines about the revolution is just plain wrong, and I believe that using the photograph of your poor parents lying in the street was totally indecent and unforgivable. I pray you have been spared seeing it. That started as a Polaroid snapshot taken by my neighbor and ex-friend Cora White. She was along on the African tour. I hear she sold the picture to a wire service for 175 dollars. I will never speak to her again, I can promise you that, Mrs. Whiston.

I'm rambling already, so I will begin to sketch out what I remember. If you choose to stop reading here, I can understand that. But I'm going on anyway. If I don't get this Africa business laid out in the open, I know my dreams and housework will stay like they are now, a big mess.

My memory is one thing I've always been proud of. I can rattle off restaurant menus from lunches I

ate with my late husband in 1926. Till now, the only
good this ability has done me is not needing to keep
grocery lists and never forgetting any family member's birthday.

The bus had to wait for sheep to cross the road just
outside the capital city. I was putting on my lipstick
when we heard the explosion. Tongaville is made of
mud walls like what's known as stucco in America.
The town was far off, all one color on a flat desert
so it looked like a toy fort. One round tower blew
into a thousand pieces. The shock waves were so
strong that sheep fell against the front of our bus.
They got terrified and were climbing up on each
other. They don't look like our American sheep but
are black and have very skinny legs. Their coats are
thick as powder puffs, only greasy. Seeing how scared
they were scared me.

Some of us tried talking sense to our tour guide.
He wasn't any Father Flannagan. We'd all expected a
priest, even though the brochure didn't come right
out and promise one. This guide was not even Cath-
olic, but some Arab with a mustache. He spoke English so badly you had to keep asking him to repeat
and sometimes even to spell things out. We told him
it would be a mistake, driving into a town where this
type of thing was happening. But he said our hotel
rooms were already paid for—otherwise, we'd just
have to sleep on the bus and miss the Game Preserve
the next morning. We were so tired. Half of us were
sick. Somebody asked for a show of hands. Majority
ruled that we go in and take our chances. But my
instinct told me, definitely no.

Mrs. Whiston, we'd been in Egypt earlier. It is dry
and outstandingly beautiful but as far as a place to
live and work, it lags way behind Ohio. But, maybe

that's just me. Thanks to Egypt, I had the worst case
of diarrhea I have ever heard of or read about. You
cannot believe how low a case of diarrhea can bring
a person's spirits and better judgment. Because of it,
I voted Yes, enter Tongaville. In my condition, a bus
parked on the desert, where there's not one blade of
grass much less a bush for fifty miles, was just no
place to spend the night. So, like a pack of fools, we
drove into Tongaville, right into the middle of it.

The bus was air-conditioned, and we couldn't exactly hear what all of them were shouting at us. Then
Miss McMillan, who's in your parents' snapshot and
at seventy-nine is still sharp as a tack, she said,
"CIA, they're yelling CIA," and she was right. First
it sounded like some native word but that was because they were saying it wrong. Miss McMillan was
on target as usual. The only ones who'd voted to skip
Tongaville were her and the three Canadian teachers
who often acted afraid of us Americans, especially
the Texans, and who wore light sweaters, even in
Egypt. "Father Flannagan's World Tours" was
spelled out in English all over the bus. Some of our
people said it had probably tipped off the natives
about our being Americans. But after three weeks
with this group, I knew we weren't that hard to spot.
I never thought I'd be ashamed of my home country,
but certain know-it-all attitudes and rudenesses toward Africans had embarrassed me more than once.
This might have been my first world trip, but wher-
ever I am I can usually tell right from wrong. The
Texans especially were pushy beyond belief.

Hotel workers came out and joined hands and made
two lines for protection, a kind of alley from the door
of our bus to the lobby of the Hotel Alpha, which
was no great shakes but, by this time, looked pretty

good to me. Your father, I remember, was the last to get off because he kept photographing rebels through the big tinted back window. They had already started rocking the bus and he was still inside it running up and down the aisle taking pictures of their angry faces near the glass. Your mother just plain told him to come out of there this minute and he finally did. I made it upstairs to my room and looked out the balcony window. The crowd had climbed up on our bus and pried open the door. They swarmed all over it, about a hundred half-dressed people, so skinny it hurt you to look at them. The bus's sunroof was glass and I could see them in there scrambling over every seat. The street in front of our hotel was just crawling with people. One group waved brooms. A few boys had found golf clubs somewhere and were throwing these up then catching them like majorettes would. A naked man and a woman danced around, holding a vacuum cleaner over their heads. He lifted the body of it and she'd slung the hose over her shoulder and kept shaking the wand part at people. Even from the second floor, I could tell it was an Electrolux. The crowd didn't seem to know what a vacuum cleaner was. They kept staring up at the thing. Seeing this scared me more than anything so far. Then our bus drove off. Most of the Africans ran after it, all cheering. I stood there at the window thinking, Well, there our only hope goes. This is probably it, what could be worse for us? That's when I noticed our tour guide. He went sneaking across the street, looking left and right, guilt written all over him, and carrying a red Samsonite makeup case exactly like Mimi Martinson's, a rich divorcee's from St. Pete. That little Arab turned a corner. I knew then we were on our own, with this mess out of our control.

I decided to build a barricade in front of my door but realized that the rest room was out in the hall. We had to share. Father Flannagan's leaflet said in big printing, "Rooms with private baths at the best of the earth's four-star hotels." I went to find the bathroom but somebody was in there and four more of our people were waiting in line.

Old Mr. McGuane, one of the Texans, stood around, real casual, holding a pistol. He was telling the others how he'd brought it along just in case, and somebody asked how he'd gotten it through customs and the hijack inspections and he said he didn't know, it had been right there in his bag all along, but he could tell them one thing, he was mighty glad to have it with him now. Other people asked, just in case, what his room number was. I had to use the bathroom so much but I knew it was going to take forever. Seeing people from our tour had depressed me even more. So I walked back, locked my door, and just sat down on the bed and went ahead and had a good cry. I thought of Teddy and Lorraine, my son-in-law and daughter, who'd given me this trip to get my mind off my husband's death. I couldn't help believing that I'd never see Toledo again. I kept remembering a new Early American spice rack I'd hung in my kitchen just before leaving. It's funny, the kind of thing that gives you comfort when you're scared.

I told myself that if I just lived through this, if I got to go one more time to the Towne and Country restaurant near my home, and order their fantastic blue-cheese dressing, and then drive over to the Old Mill Little Theater and see another production of *Jacques Brel Is Alive and Well*, I'd give five thousand dollars to the Little Sisters of Mercy Orphanage. I vowed this and said a quick prayer to seal it. I found some hotel stationery and sat down and wrote out my will. I already had a legal one back in our safe deposit box, but it soothed my mind so much to write: I leave all my earthly goods to Teddy and Lorraine. I leave all my earthly goods to Teddy and Lorraine. Sitting there, I fell asleep.

I know I'm rambling worse than ever. But in emergencies like this, little things bunch up and get to seem important as the big facts. So I'm putting most everything in.

I woke up and at first didn't know where I was, then I remembered, Africa, and I thought, Oh Lord. Even in Ohio, sometimes this feeling comes over me and I wonder, What exactly am I doing here? In Tongaville, it was that same question but about five hundred times as strong. I crawled to the end of my bed and looked out the balcony window and that's when I saw your mother and father wandering around down on the street. Frankly, Mrs. Whiston, I thought they were pretty foolish to be out there. When our bus was hijacked, its spare fell off, and now the street was totally empty except for your parents and the tire and a beggar who was propped up in a doorway down the block. I think he was only there because the mob had carried off his crutches as two more things to wave around.

Your dad was taking a picture of the tire and your poor mother was looking at the light meter. You probably know how your father asked her to help by testing the brightness of the light. He pretended to include her in his hobby but, in my opinion, he never really listened to Lily. Many times I'd hear her say, "Fred, it's way too bright out here. Without some filters, every shot is going to be way overexposed. This is Africa, Fred." He'd nod and go on clicking away. She acted like she didn't notice this, but after forty years of a thing, you notice. It made me remember my own marriage to one basically good man. I wondered, Is it wise or crazy to put up with so much for so long. Your dad was mostly kind to her and he didn't mean any harm, but this once I wish he'd told her not to bother, to just go on upstairs and take a nap or something. Instead, there Lily was, two stories down, the poor thing holding out a light meter of no earthly good to anybody, squinting at it and wearing her pretty yellow pantsuit. I should have called to them. If it had been just her I definitely would have, but when a woman's husband is along, you often act different.

Then they both looked down the street. By leaning out the window, I could see a whole parade, this whole mass of people carrying signs painted on sheets stretched between green bamboo poles. The writing was a foreign language, foreign to me, at least. Groups came down the street and sidewalks, pushing, waving scrap lumber and garden tools. They all moved together. They looked organized and almost noble, like they knew just what they wanted and deserved, and, right now, were headed there to get it. I expected your parents to run straight back into our hotel. They had time. But instead, your father changed cameras. He wore about three looped around his neck and he crouched down like a professional and started taking pictures. The Africans were shouting something hard to understand except I think the CIA part was still in there. The chants got louder and echoed between buildings. Your dad stayed put. Lily looked confused but tried to make herself useful anyway and held out that light meter toward the crowd, like she was offering it to them. Lily kept glancing at the hotel doorway. Somebody must have been signaling for her to come inside. But she didn't budge, she stuck out there in the open with your dad. He hunched down facing them. I just stood upstairs and watched. I kept believing he knew things I didn't.

His camera had a long black lens and this was pressed up against his face, and I don't know if people thought it was a gun or what, but along with their chant, I heard this one pop, no louder than a firecracker, and your poor father fell right back. It was as fast and simple as that. It seemed like he did a backflip he'd been planning all along, or got more interested in the sky between buildings than the crowd, because he was lying there staring right up at the sun. He tried to toss the camera to your mother, like the camera mattered most. She caught it and looked down at the thing for a minute. Then she seemed to wake up and she took two shaky steps toward him. But that moment the people shoved past our hotel. There were hundreds of them and they were running fast. Some were banging on pots and garbage-can lids. They carried things along over their heads. A phone pole on its side, people hanging onto the loose wires like these were leashes. Along came what looked like a huge snake held up by dozens of black hands, but it was just the vacuum hose. I could see flashes of her yellow suit down there. The last of the parade went rushing by, women, children, and some bony dogs hurrying to catch up. Your mother was facedown on the street, way beyond your dad. People had taken her blouse off. All the cameras were gone but one that had been trampled. They'd carried off the tire, and your poor mother's yellow blouse.

I just fixed myself a cup of coffee, Mrs. Whiston, and ran cold water over my writing hand. I'm in such a state trying to get this down. I plan to start forgetting just as soon as this letter is done. But I think it's important to face the hard facts at the time, and not let yourself off easy.

My Willard died at the cement works where he'd been their employee for thirty-five years. I drove out a week or so after the funeral and talked to the boys he'd worked with on his last morning alive. They told me little things they remembered from that day. One man, a colored fellow named Roy, he'd been with Diamond Cement as long as my husband. He said Willard told a joke just before lunch hour, which is when he passed away. His heart went. The joke was about the three priests trying to catch a train to Pittsburgh. Willard must of told that one about five thousand times. He'd got it down to an art, this priest joke and some other favorites. I asked Roy, Which joke? like I'd never heard it. He probably guessed that in the twenty years Willard had been telling that corny thing, I'd have to know it by now. But he started up anyway, understanding that I needed it. Roy went through the whole thing, waiting in the right places, adding all Willard's extra touches. When he finished, I laughed out loud like it was new to me, and not just for show but from the heart. Hearing it helped me so much. I'm not sure why I started telling this. I think it's to show why I'm not holding one thing back, not sparing you anything, no matter how bad it sounds.

I tore the sheets off my bed and unlocked the door. People had stacked their luggage as a barricade across the stair landing. I shoved through this, and some fell down the stairwell but I didn't care. I ran into the lobby. A black bellhop tried to stop me but I got past him through the revolving door. Out in the sun and heat, seeing them stunned me all over again. I bent down beside your father and felt him. One camera had been stepped on, lens glass was shining all around his shoulder. Then I ran down the street to your mother and put my hand on the side of her face. Both your folks were dead. Her back looked so bare and white, and the bra strap seemed to be cutting her. I spread the sheet over Lily and then I lifted it up and undid the clip of her strap. The beggar had leaned out of his doorway to stare at me. For some reason, this made me feel guilty, like I could have saved them or was stealing their watches. I stood up dizzy but made it back and called the bellboy to come out here and help me carry your folks inside. I kept waving but he'd just press up against the glass and shake his head no. Then he crooked his finger for me to come back in. I saw something move upstairs and I looked up there, and it astonished me. There were three guests in every balcony window, our whole bus-load all lined up in rows and staring down at me with your poor parents.

Cora White peeped over the grillework on the third floor. When she saw me looking up, her head jerked back. But one of her arms stayed there holding the Polaroid, then her other hand came out and poked the button. Many people were taking pictures. The whole group from Texas was, every last one of them. I put a hand over my eyes for shade and called, "Come help us, come help us. The Madisons are dead," and I pointed to your folks. But nobody budged. It was a scary and terrible sight, Mrs. Whiston. Most windows were closed, so I called louder. Some of the women would look at each other and back at me, but not one soul up there moved. So then, when I saw what was going on, I started screaming names. I'm not a young woman, Mrs. Whiston, but with all my might I hollered upstairs, especially to my friends who, like me, had signed up for this at Holy Assumption. "Deborah Schmidt, Cora White, LaVerne and May Stimson, I see you, and I know you, so you all come right down here and help us." But as I called their names, they'd ease back into the rooms or let the drapes fall over their faces. I was out in the sun, feeling totally lost. I was starting to shake. People weren't even looking at me or your folks any more but along the street in the other direction, and when I saw a crowd headed here even bigger than before, I stooped down and ran right back inside. The bellboy jammed a baggage cart half into the revolving door, then the two of us ducked under the front desk and we stayed there.

I'd turned into just as big a coward as the rest, so who am I to point the finger? All the same, I won't forget how it is to be the person who needs help, and to look up and see your group, your people, lined up like in a department-store window, and every one refusing you. Your dearest friends on earth doing that.

I never figured out how the Marines from the U.S. Embassy knew where we were, but all of a sudden they showed up in a truck, carrying rifles. I was so concerned for my own safety I hardly gave your parents' bodies another thought, Mrs. Whiston. The Marines looked very young, like they couldn't be old enough to drive, and here they were rescuing us. I asked if the Embassy had maybe picked up your parents, because by this time, they were both gone, nothing left but broken glass on the pavement. The Marine said, "No, Ma'am." I wish you could have heard him say that. He was tall and had a sweet pink healthy face. Like all of them, he seemed to talk in a Southern accent, and when this boy told me, "No, Ma'am," it was so full of politeness, so old-fashioned and American in the good way that after what our busload had just done, I broke right down in the lobby. Nobody on our tour would come near me now they'd gathered downstairs, all shy to see me still alive. The Marine looked embarrassed. I thought if he would just put his arm around me for a minute, I'd be all right. And I'm sure he was going to, but when he saw that no one else was rushing over to help, not even one of our women, he said, "Excuse me," and hurried off. He was just shy, a man's body and this little boy's face.

Up drove the Embassy's four black cars to rush us to the airport. American soldiers and government secretaries were driving anything they could lay hands on. They said to leave all the luggage we couldn't carry in our laps. Mimi Martinson asked everyone but me if they'd seen her precious makeup bag, so why should I have told her where it went? More officials arrived, two sports cars and a Buick that looked bigger than ones at home but was a lot like Teddy and Lorraine's, only yellow. For one second, I really thought it was them come for me. That's how crazy I'd turned. By this time, I didn't know Africa from around the block.

A Volkswagen camper with Delaware plates pulled up in front. I rode in that. It belonged to the Ambassador's daughter. We unloaded food from the little refrigerator to take on the plane with us. The freezer was full of Stouffer's Lobster Newburg dinners, and more of these were waiting at the airport in ice chests from the Embassy Commissary.

We'd started for the plane when we heard the biggest explosion yet. An oil refinery, this row of tanks went off like bombs and in one minute the entire sky got black. We had to keep low in the camper, but at an intersection near the refinery I heard something and looked out and saw two sheep running through the empty streets. I think oil had spilled on them and their coats were on fire, Mrs. Whiston. They both ran down the center of the road right along the dotted line. Smoke came blowing off their backs and real flames and they were making noises so human, so terrible I cannot describe it. When I was a child, I was sick a lot and had nightmares full of horrible sights, and this was like some dream from then but worse.

The Embassy man tried to tell me that these sheep were headed toward some river and would be all right. But, if there was a river through the desert, how could it stay a desert and dry? We flew to Athens then to Brussels then home to Kennedy. We were treated like royalty, except by the reporters, who were rude. The Ambassador and his wife acted just like everybody else and weren't a bit stuck up. He said he'd known there was some trouble brewing, but as for a revolution, he guessed he'd been caught napping.

Now, I am home. I'm safe and sound at my own kitchen table. When I walked in here for the first time last week, my new maple spice rack looked like an altar to me. I'm tired and never plan to leave the security of Toledo again.

Mrs. Whiston, it's hard for me to believe that our earth has gotten this bad this quick. I'm not saying your dad was right in doing what he did, rushing outside without understanding how dangerous things are now. He just forgot his place and took way too much for granted. He thought all people on earth were as good-natured as himself, and with as much free time, and would pose for him. But he overlooked hunger. That is bound to make terrible changes in people's dispositions. White or black, people are more miserable and less willing to be scenery than the *National Geographic* would like us to think. Every fact I once held dear has swung around and turned into something else.

As one example, Teddy says there probably *is* no Father Flannagan. It's just a name somebody thought up to suck people in. Anyway, I contributed a gift in honor of your folks and my late husband to the Little Sisters of Mercy Orphanage. I found I had less of a nest egg thanks to the bite the money crunch has made in our economy, so I only gave half of what I promised, but the Sisters seemed happy and Teddy told me I was crazy to do it.

I feel that knowing what I know now, I should start life over. If you asked what Africa taught me, I couldn't spell it out with words but in my heart, I think, something serious has switched. Chances are, my life is too far along for any last-minute change in plans. However, I've been thinking. Maybe we should give up what we own to feed the hungry? But at my age, an old white woman and spoiled like this, I wonder how much I could do without. It shocks me to understand how greedy I am. Really, I've learned so little.

As a result of being long-winded like this, I am very tired. So listen, across the miles, Mrs. Whiston, I just offer you a hug. I do hate to hit the end of this letter. I would like to buck you up in your time of sorrow but my place, I think, is still here in Toledo in the old neighborhood. This afternoon I'm tending my grandchildren who are way ahead of others their age. They're final stars in whatever crown I'm going to get on earth.

Oh well, so long. We all do what we can, don't we? We just hope that in the end it's worth the hard daily efforts and has been mostly for the best. We are really the lucky ones. The rest think they are outside looking in at happiness. If they only knew. When the highs and lows are so far apart, it's hard to stay in the middle and think of yourself as a good person. But I'm trying.

Teddy and Lorraine said to send their regards. I pass on my deep sympathy to you and, as far as that goes, to every one of us. I'll just sign this as coming from

Yours truly,

Mrs. Willard Gracie (Maria)

P.S. If you write back, wonderful. I don't get much mail.

1974

Art History

For Joanne Meschery
and for Robert Chibka

IN THE SHADY NORTHEAST CORNER OF THE PARK, where vines have overcome the water fountains, and evergreens grow, rangy and unkempt as in the depths of the Vronsky Forest, I came upon two children doing something very naughty. I had wandered to this most rustic corner of the Common seeking quietude and relief from the dogs recently permitted by a foolish ordinance to run free without leashes in the park. Their barking had annoyed me, a man of modest but fixed habits, and I strolled in this new direction.

I turned onto a footpath between fir trees. A terracotta sculpture stood there, its color soapy and golden: Cupid, mounted on a marble block little taller than I. The children had just scrambled up onto the pedestal. One broken branch of the spruce beside it still swung back and forth. I stopped, appalled at what these urchins were already doing. Cupid's weight rested poised upon one tiptoe. The other chubby leg swung behind him in the illusion of flight and forward motion. The girl squatted underneath the sculpture, hooking her thin arm over its uplifted leg. She laughed, calling for the boy to watch, then pulled matted hair back from her forehead, craned her neck, and began licking at the statue's bulbous little underparts. I stood there, astonished.

In the rosy light that fell across the sculpture at this hour, her head moved like a suckling calf's. The boy locked arms around the Cupid's neck and shouted something I did not understand. He then eased his weight back between the two arched wings and hung there, as from a bicycle. I saw that he had pulled his plaid shorts down. Now, swinging forward, he wrapped skinny legs around the statue's hips and began rutting vigorously at the plump sculpted buttocks. In street argot, he called obscenely to the girl. She leaned beyond the terra-cotta belly, squinted up at him, gave a sharp cynical laugh.

With a slight breeze, the sun intensified. I was startled at how long I had watched all this, and with what detachment. I told myself, these are not simians climbing about their artificial island at the National Zoo; these are human beings defiling a human monument. My abdomen registered a tremor: nausea and some preposterous sexual desire. Gripping the paper, I saw how sweat had smudged the evening news across my palm. I could not bear to look at the Cupid again but turned and hurried to the concession booth, where a policeman had been chatting with the boy behind the counter. As I passed the fountain, I saw the uniform, still there. I approached and observed the officer bent into the booth, examining a medal around the neck of the concessioner. I asked the policeman to come with me at once. I was afraid to tell what I had seen. I requested that he please follow me quickly. Others there, twin brothers with bottled lemonade, a plain girl eating an apple, stared at my face, my clothing. The gypsy boy behind the counter toyed with the gold medallion at his throat and smirked at me. I beckoned the officer along a brick path, beyond the broken fountain, four stranded bronze swans, an apple core set cruelly upon the head of one. A nurse watched me lead the policeman. I felt like Charlie Chaplin followed by an enormous constable. I hoped none of my pupils or colleagues might chance past. I was already pointing toward the Cupid when it came into view beyond the spruce. The children were gone.

The sun had moved higher on the statue so only its head and wings now showed golden in the light. "They have run away," I said and walked forward, feeling ridiculous. I had to be certain and, standing on my tiptoes, I pressed fingers to the genitals, still darker than the rest, and damp. At least I knew. The policeman stood beside me, watching my examination of the Cupid.

"Perhaps," I stammered, settling back onto both heels, "I will not bother you with what I just saw at this spot." He laughed once, good-naturedly, and easing me back against the marble pedestal, continued grinning as he reached down and gently cupped his hand between my legs.

Since Mother's death, my father has become a great heartache to us. Soon after she died of food poisoning on a seaside outing, it was announced that Father would be retired from the Academy where he has taught since I was born. This puzzled my husband and me. Father had always been well liked at the school. When I was a child, he invited the poorer boys to our home on holidays. He was an athletic gentleman and played sports with them on the mowed side yard. He devised complicated scavenger hunts which lasted until evening. I would sometimes help wrap the little presents he gave them. He wrote out each boy's full name in his beautiful old-fashioned script. Often he copied mine and let me keep the slip of paper.

I sent Ernest, my husband, to investigate Father's dismissal. When Ernest came home, he looked in through the doorway, shaking his head with disgust. He said that Father had been fortunate, being dismissed so quietly. My own father, Ernest told me bitterly, had taken boys from the school to a hotel room on a holiday trip to the seashore. Their parents believed the Academy sponsored this outing. Afterward, one boy reported my father's misconduct. When this happened, others came forward to confess. How I cried when Ernest told me this so coldly. How this soured all memories of Father tussling with the boys on our side yard in those perfect early evenings.

Watching such games through the cottage window, Mother once wept. "Oh," she sobbed, stroking the cat, Mitzi, who always slept there on the windowsill beside the potted geraniums and herbs, "you should have a little brother, Hedwig. How your father needs a real son."

She pressed the long embroidered apron to her face. I reached for her skirt and leaned my forehead against her strong leg.

After Father's forced retirement, he again concentrated on his book, a work of art history he had been rewriting since I was a baby. Ernest and I hoped Father would be happier, retired. He owned the cottage, he had a small pension and the remains of Mother's land, the yearly rents from her two dairy farms in the South.

Three evenings ago, I read in the newspaper of my own father's arrest. He had not called or notified us. Ernest says that shame was the reason. One paper printed Father's photograph, an out-of-date portrait from his brilliant days at the University. The trial is next week. Ernest says I must not go, but, of course, I shall.

I am only glad my mother never lived to see so respected a gentleman fall to such public disgrace. His book was with a publishing company. Ernest says they will not print it now.

The mother of one boy my father took to the ocean resort wrote me a terrible letter. Ernest read it, then tore it up before I ever saw it. He will not tell me what it was about. He only says he can understand why a mother wronged in this way would write such dreadful things. Every hour of the day, I am ashamed.

The defendant approached me in front of the concession stand at Ney Park that afternoon. He seemed distressed and asked me to accompany him. He was a distinguished-looking older gentleman and I thought perhaps an elderly companion of his had fallen or was sick somewhere in the park. This had happened to me last summer; an old woman said nothing but gestured me to follow and there her friend was, holding her hat, crying beside a bush, her hip broken. I asked no questions of the defendant but followed him to the northeastern edge of the park, the corner near the War Memorial. He led me down a narrow path between trees to a statue of a baby angel. Once there, he said we were now alone. He stood on his tiptoes and touched the private parts of the baby angel. Then he held his hand up to the light and examined his fingers. He smiled slightly, turning to face me. It was at this moment that he leaned against the base of the statue, seized my right hand and pulled it over against his privates. As a result, I then arrested him.

* * *

"Your grandsons?" the desk clerk asked, smiling sentimentally. "Oh, yes," I lied to simplify matters, "an outing with them." I signed my last name and their firsts. The boys, each holding a small pasteboard suitcase, stood across the lobby near the French doors. Felix quietly read aloud the Latin names of shells. Both boys' legs were edged with light, the down—ankle to upper thigh—glowed, an incandescent fringe. Their long shadows angled across the marble parquetry to where the desk clerk and I stood watching. My students were suffused, without seeming to notice, in a pink and golden light as pure as the vivid glazes on the conch shell they now held between themselves. They listened intently, both heads tilted toward it, as to a telephone receiver.

"Karl, Felix," I called them. Karl carefully replaced the shell and they both came quickly over. Neither had ever stayed at a hotel before. Both were observant, obedient children. The desk clerk smiled sadly, admiring them. "Sir, I envy you," he said, "being as I am myself, a bachelor and getting older." I gave him a coin, took up my satchel, then led the boys to a small lift. The three of us crowded into the wrought-iron cage, ascending.

After they had tested all the plumbing, after every dresser drawer had been checked, after samples of the hotel stationery and soap had been packed away for their parents and sisters, the boys stretched out on the big beds. Felix yawned once and flexed his long pale arms.

"Before you both fall to sleep listening to the ocean, is it not time to bathe?" I asked.

"Yes, before supper," Karl said and, standing in his socks, bouncing on the old bed, he pulled the shirt over his head and tossed it down at Felix, who was feigning sleep. What good boys, I thought, remembering some chocolate I had bought for them at the train depot. Hoping it had not melted, I unbuckled my bag. Karl stepped off the bed and, now wearing only his white undershorts, opened the glass doors of the balcony and walked out into the breeze. The long lace curtains rose from the floor, lifted straight into the room, then bellied out and dropped, first one then the other, settling as in sighs upon Karl's bed. He stood leaning out over the balcony, pointing to a freighter trailing orange smoke across the horizon of violently streaked pastels.

"Karl," Felix called through the open doors, "Do you like your bathwater very hot, or in between?"

This pleased me, made me smile. I unfastened my valise and fumbled around inside for the candy. It had warmed and, in its gold foil wrapper, felt quite pliant.

"And did he"—the headmaster leaned into the brilliance of the one desk lamp, daubing his forehead with a folded handkerchief—"offer any rewards if you would . . . co-operate and keep silent?"

"Chocolate," the boy replied, looking down at the blond hair on his forearm, "chocolate and a copy of that statue, the statue in Brussels of the small boy . . . urinating. And a seashell, he bought each of us a conch shell at the shop in the train station."

"I see," the headmaster said, pulling his shirt cuffs out of the sleeves of his jacket and standing all in one lurch as if his whole body were spans, tabs, and joints of crisp overstarched linen. With a curt nod, he repeated, "Thank you. You have acted wisely to tell us this." The boy bowed and left. The office door snapped closed, then the latch of the antechamber was heard.

Pinching his trousers' creases into proper alignment, the headmaster eased down onto the edge of the desktop. He then unfastened his still shirt front and, snatching handkerchief from jacket pocket, reached in and violently daubed each armpit. He slapped at his pallid chest as if powdering it, all while envisioning the gentleman in question wheezing around a cheap hotel room, like some satyr in pursuit of two thin white boys, giggling, dripping wet. The headmaster, drying neck and forehead, now imagined the ocean, thunderous then silent then thunderous again outside, as the gentleman eased across the floral carpet on his knees—toward the corner where two smiling panting boys had stopped at last. Sliding nearer them, the man balanced a silver tray on either palm. The seashells rattled, rocking hard against their own pink reflected undersides; the brass statuettes stared down at themselves upended; there seemed exactly twice as much milk chocolate. The boys watched, interested, as the trinkets wobbled closer. Shivering slightly, droplets from the interrupted bath eased over each visible rib then down their long tanned legs. Chocolate, a statuette, a seashell. A set for you, and a set for you. For years and very quietly, giving boy after boy these inexpensive appreciated gifts. Chocolate, a statuette, a seashell.

The headmaster bit down on his folded handkerchief, then bit again.

As a cellmate, they have assigned me a burglar, a would-be jewel thief. He has a connoisseur's love of gems, a child's idea of how to steal them. He is agile, blond, casually corrupted, seventeen years old. His mind is tender and lurid as his scar. This mark begins at the center of his throat, twists up one side of his face, and narrows to a crescent which falls just short of hooking his childish mouth. Its almost perfect C-shape connects an adult's throat to the indolent choirboy mouth. His scar complicates and redeems his commonplace good looks. When he is feverish or angry, I see the mark grow crimson, *scar*let actually. Like a thermometer, it colors from the bottom upward.

He bathes himself with great care, with a jewel thief's intelligent fingers. I lie on the bottom bunk, hands behind head, watching him. There is nothing else to look at in this cell and my staring seems acceptable. As he bathes, he whistles quite beautifully, warbling popular songs through his front teeth. In sunlight from the barred window, he soaps himself vigorously. Sections of his lathered back gleam in stripes. He whistles an accompaniment of chirps and complicated trills. Holding his long arms straight out, one at a time, he rubs soap along them. I glimpse the sheen and smooth translucence of certain marble Pietàs. His ribs, under tight shifting skin, curve one way, while lines of sun fall in quite another, so, as he moves, these stripes smoothly chafe each other, a crisscrossing matrix like plaid or basketry, till I see his whole torso light up, a radiant sieve.

In prison, I am trying to teach myself factual thinking. I am comforted in recalling how once at University, for a final examination, the great art historian, K. Blenheim, strode into the conference room where we, his favorite class, sat waiting. On the central revolving pedestal, he placed a homely object.

"Gentlemen," he said, "please describe this. Leave your test booklets here when you are done. I have enjoyed associating with you for these three years."

He turned and left; an outside door slammed, echoed down the hallway. We looked at one another, then the object, then again at one another. It was a copper float, part of a toilet's workings. Ovoid, little larger than an orange, a serrated seam bound its center. During our three years of intense work with him, Blenheim had daily placed different sorts of relics on this pedestal: Persian enamels, a small beautifully preserved Greek vase, an eighteenth-century miniature of an English squire's favorite spaniel, an Egyptian footstool. Now, several of my classmates, some of the most brilliant, pushed back their chairs, creased their examination booklets and stalked out, singly and in groups, some muttering, most silent.

"Art History?" a thin mustached man called over his shoulder in a breaking voice. "The history of art?" Others stayed seated, chuckling, bitter. As I watched, the boy beside me massaged the thin bridge of his nose and laughed quietly, eyes pressed shut. "Three years of my life," he whispered. Still another fellow snapped his pencil, once then twice. He cupped the pieces in his fist, rattling these like dice as he left.

Some of us sat here looking at the pedestal and its toilet fixture. From the street came sounds of morning traffic, a man selling newspapers. Finally I opened my test booklet. I simply tried to describe the thing. As Blenheim had taught us in his reedy rational voice, I energetically looked and looked at it. I mentioned no implied plumbing. I did not assume that this was part of anything larger, mechanically or historically. I treated it as an object whole unto itself, and not without certain peculiar beauties all its own.

In just this way, in this unlikely setting, I now try to see myself.

Before sleep, I exercise my memory, recalling seating charts of favorite classes I taught at the Academy. From these I lift my choice of thirty years of boys. All that character, all those eyes. I place each child at his original desk. When I finally survey this composite class of best-loved pupils, I am amused sometimes to find two or even three boys from different years, whole different generations, now stacked, smiling, all one age, in the same desk chair. I imagine my cellmate seated there on the front row, not wearing a school uniform like the others, not in his coarse prison garb, but instead luminous and shirtless, and—I note—shiny, still soapy from some bath. There are no books, no pen staffs before him. Only jewels on his desktop, a great mound of them glittering as in some children's tale of treasure. The gems refract the morning classroom's sunlight; they cast prismatic shapes on floor and ceiling. Purest spectral hues dance all across the room. A winking angle comes and goes above the murky lithograph of Goethe. One corner of the green aquarium is spotlit and clouds of emerald algae, glints of fish, drift through it.

The wall map of America is flecked with coin-sized lozenges like ghostly hints at coming capitals or miracles or future battles with Red Indians. And, seated at the center of this blurry constellation, my latest favorite shines. Gems' light rests upon his glossy chest, the chin, his garnet scar. Suddenly, he lifts the jewels like an armful of harvest or sea life and our classroom is tattooed with rainbow stripes, tremulous octagons and arcs. Other students laugh and dip their hands into these pools of light. They start to sing, in three-part harmony, one song I taught them all in different years. My cellmate holds treasure out to me, and voices of my best-loved children tremble up into a sweet assured crescendo.

Decades of favorites, a class of masterpieces, comrades, all harmonious.

1975

Nativity, Caucasian

For Ethel Mae Morris

("**W**HAT'S WRONG WITH YOU?" MY WIFE ASKS. She already knows. I tell her anyway.)

I was born at a bridge party.

This explains certain frills and soft spots in my character. I sometimes picture my own genes as so many crustless multicolored canapés spread upon a silver oval tray.

Mother'd just turned thirty and was eight-and-one-half months gone. A colonel's daughter, she could boast a laudable IQ plus a smallish independent income. She loved gardening but, pregnant, couldn't stoop or weed. She loved swimming but felt too modest to appear at the Club in a bathing suit. "I walk like a duck," she told her husband, laughing. "Like six ducks trying to keep in line. I *hate* ducks."

Her best friend, Chloe, local grand master, tournament organizer, was a perfect whiz at stuffing compatible women into borrowed seaside cottages for marathon contract bridge.

"Helen precious?" Chloe phoned. "I know you're incommoded, but listen, dear. We're short a person over here at my house. Saundra Harper Briggs finally checked into Duke for that radical rice diet? And not

55

one minute too soon. They say her husband had to drive the poor thing up there in the station wagon, in the *back* of the station wagon. I refuse to discriminate against you because of your condition. We keep talking about you, still ga-ga over that grand slam of yours in Hilton Head. I could send somebody around to fetch you in, say, fifteen minutes? No, yes? Will that be time enough to throw-something on? Unless, of course, you feel too shaky.''

Hobbyists often leap at compliments with an eagerness unknown to pros. And Helen Larkin Grafton was the classic amateur, product of a Richmond that deftly and early on espaliers, topiaries, and bonsais its young ladies, pruning this and that, preparing them for decorative root-bound existences either in or very near the home. Helen, unmistakably a white girl, a postdeb, was most accustomed to kind comments concerning clothes or looks or her special ability to foxtrot. And any talk about the mind itself, even mention of her well-known flair for cards, delighted her. So, dodging natural duty, bored with being treated as if pregnancy were some debilitating terminal disease, she said, ''I'd adore to come. See you shortly, Chloe. And God love you for thinking of me. I've been sitting here feeling like . . . well, like one great big mudpie.''

The other women applauded when she strolled in wearing a loose-cut frock of unbleached linen, hands thrust into front patch pockets piped with chocolate brown. (All this I have on hearsay from my godmother, Irma Stythe, a fashion-conscious former war nurse and sometime movie critic for the local paper.)

With much hoopla, two velvet pillows were placed on a folding chair, the new guest settled. They dealt her in. Young Helen Larkin Grafton. Phrases floated into the smoky air: Darling girl. Somewhat birdlike. Miscarried her first two, you know? Oh yes. Wonderful organizer—good with a garden. School up north but it didn't spoil her outlook or even her accent: pure Richmond. Good bones. Fine little game player. Looking fresh as a bride.

These women liked each other, mostly. At least they *knew* each other, which maybe matters more. Their children carried family secrets, cross-pollinating, house to house. Their husbands owned shares of the same things and golfed in groups. If the women knew about each other first, *then* either liked one another or not, husbands liked each other (till proven wrong) but didn't always *know* each other deeply. Anyway, it was a community. Shelter, shared maids, assured Christmas cards, to be greeted on the street by your full name.

One yard above the Persian and Caucasian rugs, temporary tabletops paved a whole new level. Surfaces glided along halls and on the second-story landing. Women huddled from four edges toward each other. That season's mandatory pastels, shoulder padding. Handbags propped on every level ledge. Mantels, banisters. Cloisonné ashtrays glutted with half-smoked cigarettes. Refreshments—aspics, watercress, cucumber— waiting in the kitchen. The serving lady late, Chloe, our hostess, a plumpish blond woman, discreetly glancing at her watch. Such nice chatting. Exclamations over bad hands and good. Forty belles and semi-belles. Junior guilded. All rooms musical with voices, the great gift of Southern women, knowing how to coax out sounds, all ringing like this. Queen Anne furniture, ancestral portraits, actual Audubon prints thanks to forebears who underwrote the project actually, Moroccan-bound books, maroon and gilt. Williamsburgy knickknacks, beiges, muted olive greens. A charming house chock full of lovely noise, and smokers not inhaling but hooked anyway.

Chloe's prize Pekingese, Mikado, snorted under card

tables as through a tunnel ridged with nyloned columns. He edged, grimly interested, toward this new arrival's scent. An ancient wheezy male animal, Mikado took the liberty en route of sniffing up as high on women's limbs as he could reach, of rubbing languidly against the swishy silk and hazy shins of every woman there. Chloe had tied a yellow bow around his topknot; he tolerated this on bridge days, a fair trade for the cozy sense of being underneath a long playhouse of gaming tables, cards fatly snapping overhead. His path lay strewn with kicked-off shoes. Dainty aromatic feet to nudge. Mikado, the Blankenships' cranky one time ribbon winner, is only mentioned here because he suspected—before any other living creature in this murmurous house—that something was about to give.

He sauntered to a halt, stood under her table, stared—proprietary and enraptured—up at the area (dare I go through with this grisly sequence and its raunchy aftermath, my life?) between the young Helen's barely opened knees.

Mikado's flat face was mostly nose, very wet, chill as the jellyish aspic now gleaming on a kitchen counter. Cataracts had silvered over both his popping goldfish eyes. Smell, swollen to exciting new dimensions, remained the one great jolt and consolation left him. He nuzzled near enough and quite almost against the silk to get a better sample scent of something rich and decidedly awry here. The placing of his wide cool snout upon her shinbone made Helen, who'd just spread her cards, shudder with a little flinch. The subtlest sort of pelvic twist, then a serene smile of recognition: "Oh, Mikado," she whispered to her geisha fan of cards. For this was a society where ladies knew the names of other ladies' gardeners and maids and lapdogs.

Next . . . into this party cubicle of china shop small

talk and play-it-safe decor, Nature lunged fairly bull-
ishly. Intent on clobbering mere taste, it went right for
a trigger spot and let loose one deep-seated wallop. It
happened Now.

The Peke got hit by falling waters, about a bucket's
worth. He yelped and scrambled down the hallway
through a grove of table legs and female feet, skidding
to safety under a favorite sideboard's shadow. Once
there, Mikado collapsed and was panting when Helen,
mouth a perfect O, bellowed forth in some voice totally
unladylike and three full octaves deeper then her usual
musical lilt, "Oh my Gawd, I've stawrted!"

Cards scattered atop the table, some teetered onto her
steep lap, fell to dampened Persians. Her three table-
mates stood, overturned the Samsonite. With it went a
coaster full of lipsticked butts. Table to table, downstairs then up, news darted at the speed of sound. Three
women moved to help Helen stand but she'd stretched
out all her limbs. She was less seated on the chair than
propped against it, semi-rigid as a starfish, muttering
some Latin from her convent days.

First they dragged her toward the velvet chair. But
Chloe, who'd just spent a fortune having that piece re-
upholstered, dissuaded them by backing, beckoning,
through the kitchen's swinging portholed door. The
cluster veered in there and, for want of a better spot,
laid Helen on the central counter, under a panel of humming fluorescent tubes. Her shoulder bumped a wooden
salad bowl filled with party mix (pretzel sticks, nuts,
crackers, sprinkled salts, and Worcestershire sauce) and
sent this shooting across linoleum's fake brick. Other
dishes toppled, too. Pink and green mints rattled everywhere, the silver compote clanged toward a corner.
One red aspic fell, splitting to sheeny smithereens before the Spicer twins took charge and set the other party

foods along shelves or on the floor around the waist-high counter where Helen lay, distended.

Friends bustled to hold her hands, trying to dry her skirt with paper toweling. Pat Smiley quickly phoned the hospital for advice, forgetting to request an ambulance. Others listened in on two upstairs extensions, scolding her when she hung up. Then someone just as flustered dialed the fire department. Irma, my godmother, the movie reviewer, a short sensible woman who'd seen more films more times than practically anyone, now did what they would do in movies at such moments, on sea voyages, at Western waystations: she put water on to boil and fetched some string plus a bottle of Jack Daniel's (still in last year's Christmas gift box). She spread what seemed to be a sheet under my poor mother, rocking her from side to side. Helen, chewing knuckles, apologized to Chloe. "Really ruined your party. If I'd only guessed . . . Richard will be absolutely livid. Oh, this is so *unlike* me."

"Hush," Chloe said. "You couldn't know. It's Nature's doing, darling. Keep calm. Help's coming. We all love you."

Others, timing her contractions by the kitchen's sunburst wall clock, mumbled Yes, they did. They patted her wrist, pressed cool terry cloth scented with wintergreen across her dead-white forehead. Irma said, "Forgive me, dear. I hate to, but—" and boldly flapped back Helen's dress, took a look, mumbled, "Uh-oh. Somebody did call someone, an ambulance or something, right?" Others gathered behind Irma, stooped, shook heads sideways, held onto one another. Mavis DeWitt gave an empathetic moan, recalling her twins' forty-nine-hour delivery. She whispered, "I think I'm going home. I feel . . . I feel . : . Good-bye."

* * *

At the corner of Elm Avenue and Country Club Drive, the ambulance, ignoring a stoplight, overcome by the power of its siren and right of way, bisected the route of a northbound fire truck headed to the same address, and each vehicle, similarly entranced and headstrong with mission-of-mercy noise, mistook the other for its potent echo. They collided. Nobody was hurt but the vehicles got pretty well smashed up. A medic shunted about applying first aid to firemen all in black rubber raincoats and seated on someone's lawn. The assistant fire chief lifted the ambulance's hood and sniffed for smoldering.

Women fought to peek through the kitchen door's porthole. Helen was thrashing now and Irma, a squat level-headed person, ordered all potential fainters to the living room. Then Pat Smiley barged in with news that sirens had been heard from an upstairs window and, grinning at her own alertness, saw my mother laid upon the work counter, legs apart, surrounded by floored platters of party foods set like offerings around some sacrificial altar—my demure mother spread-eagled where the light refreshments should be, now writhing, gasping rhythmically, some heady severance already evident—and Pat, usually so stalwart, tottered toward the sink, blacking out en route, grabbing a hanging split-leaf philodendron, taking this down and falling in a ripe blur of store-bought dirt and looping greenery. Irma promptly shooed the others out, all but the hostess and the reliable Spicer twins, who, for twenty-nine years, had locally team-taught Home Ec. These lanky sisters hoisted Pat from either end and crunched toward the living room, shuffling through broken crockery, vines, aspic scattered here and there like wobbly carnage. They'd revived her when Mikado waddled in, having licked himself clean of perfectly respectable waters. He sniffed at the damp towels blotting Chloe's rug. A beast, wet to the size of a rat, white in the eyes, still licking his dark chops, sent poor Pat Smiley out again with one sleepy shriek. The Spicers simply lifted her legs back onto the furniture.

"Where *are* those ambulances?" Chloe got out ice tongs, any tool that looked silvery and surgical. "Sirens have been at it for ten darn minutes." Mother's wails now filled the house. Thirty acquaintances took up handbags, met at the front door, faces wary as if Helen's fate had befallen each and all of them. They told one another in lowered voices, "We'll only be underfoot," and, once assured of their basic good sense, fled.

Young Helen pleaded, between quickening seizures, to be gagged for decency's sake. She kept screeching personal charges against her husband, saying this mess was all his fault, his fault, his fault. Irma cradled Mother's head, lifted a water tumbler of Jack Daniel's, tried to tip some between the victim's lips. But Helen kept choking. So instead they doubled over a tulip-shaped potholder and simply stuffed this between chattery teeth. "Bite down," Irma told her. "It's risky to move you, dear. We hear them, hold on tight."

At the phone, Chloe was barking orders to the manager of the country club two blocks away. "Preston, listen and listen good: you get into a cart right now. You ride out and grab any doctor on the course. A dentist, a vet, anybody. But, Preston? Hurry. The poor little thing's head is out already."

A fringe-topped golf cart wobbled into the driveway. Two young doctors, one podiatrist plus everybody's dermatologist, wearing three-toned golf shoes and flashy shirts, barged in without knocking, found a fainted woman sprawled on the living-room chaise, hurried over, peeled back her skirt, yanked down panties. Elvyra Spicer, unmarried and long aware of men's baser drives, flew enraged across the room, slapped Dr. Kenilworth's head and sports cap, shrilling, "Not her. Not her, you. In there!"

The kitchen was an epic mess. Cereal, pretzels, soils, shards of aspic, stepped-on mints both pink and green—all this litter split and crackled under their spiked shoes, which sent Chloe swooping through the kitchen door to check on her inherited Orientals. But the kitchen did smell wonderful: good bourbon. Someone with nothing better to do perked coffee.

A wet Pekingese sat on hind legs in the pantry doorway, panting, a soggy yellow ribbon draped across its head. The doctors' caddy, a handsome black kid of fourteen, now jangled in from the cart, heaving forward two golf bags. In his excitement, he stood braced, as if expecting players to choose a proper putter for this situation.

Young doctors studied the event with an old amazement, some wonder missing from their hospital routine. They studied the committee of busy improvising women, studied a red rabbit-sized and wholly uninvited little wriggler aim out toward fluorescent light, looped to a pink cord that spiraled downward. Irma Stythe (God bless her sane and civil heart) guided the creature, eased it—still trailing slick residues and varnishes—up into general view. Just now, Irma, recognizing the doctors, grinned wanly over at them, said, "You want to slap it?" proferring the ankles.

"No." Kenilworth shook his head, took his cap off, modest at the sight of women in such complete control. "No. Please. You—" and he lifted one hand as if offering the option of a waltz.

So Irma hauled off and smacked it smartly. She did this again. And once more, until It squalled into Me. They all smiled to hear a new human voice in the room. As recognition, the caddy clapped. Applause, but just a smattering.

The ambulance driver, nose bloodied, rushed in to explain the delay, chatted with a doctor who dabbed at the guy's upper lip. Pattie Smiley, coming to, hearing the cries, insisted on getting up. The door swung open just long enough for the company to see her grin, glimpse the coral-colored cord, blanch of human coloration and drop backward to the carpet as the door fell closed. They wrapped the baby in monogrammed towels and laid him in his mother's arms. Helen's face was puffed, glossy with tears. Her bun had come undone some time ago, brown hair a wooly pagan mess. She gazed down at the purplish child, still bawling, his fists already pounding air in spastic if determined blows, the infant's flop-eared ugliness a final indignity in a series of such. Helen really sobbed now. Concerned, Elmira Spicer tugged the potholder from the sudden mother's mouth but she groaned, "You put that back."

A new siren, then the fire chief lumbered in, wearing full regalia. Helen and the infant, both wailing in different registers, were carried past the card tables, borne over the prone Pattie Smiley and her attendant, Elvyra, who bent across her, pressing down the hem, sure the men had come back for a second try.

Irma phoned Richard's insurance office to make sure he knew. Somehow, no one had thought to call him. His best business voice: "Yes Irma? Actually I'm in the middle of a group life conference. But what can I do for you?"

She gave one croupy giggle, then leaned against the wall, fatigued. Irma, midwife, clamped a hand over the receiver as if to smother, told Chloe, "Richard's asking what *he* can do for *me*."

Chloe was wandering around, palms pressed to her cheeks, surveying the remains of her model kitchen.

"You heard right. Go to her, Richard, take flowers.

She was so brave. The baby has real lung power. No, have your *secretary* send the flowers. You get moving.''

Chloe stumbled into the front room and collapsed on the beleaguered chaise. Irma followed, stood looking down at today's hostess, Grand Master Chloe, rubbing her neck and shoulders, eyes mashed shut.

The twins had dragged Pat Smiley home a few doors down. Abandoned handbags lay scattered under chairs. Cards and party favors, a set of keys, one ashtray smoldering.

"Irma." Chloe lifted her head. "You're still standing? Could I ask you for one more thing? That damask tablecloth on the counter, the one that was under her? Would you just maybe toss it into the washer? Put in about a pound of Oxydol. I can clean up the rest later. I'll just call Fatima and her sister and their whole neighborhood to come over here and work for a solid week. But I don't think I can quite abide the sight of that cloth just yet.''

"You mean the sheet?"

"Yes, it was a tablecloth, actually. Damask. You couldn't have known, Irma. It was Grandmother Halsey's, 1870 or so. Not to fret, darling.''

Irma Stythe leaned back into the kitchen. Cloth's pattern of wheat sheaves, bounty, harvest home, was now spread with urgent gloss and gore. Mikado trotted after her toward the laundry room. Upstaged all afternoon, antsy for attention, he now rolled over, played dead dog, sat on his haunches, then—tentatively—pranced.

Irma held a tumbler full of bourbon above the chaise. Chloe sniffed, opened one eye. The big house was oddly silent now. A few yards away, some lawn mower hissed and yammered, reassuring. Chloe sat up, took the glass in both hands as a child might, and tossed back three adult swallows. Mikado circled the heaped towels, smelling them. "No," Chloe called, halfhearted, "bad dog." But the animal climbed onto the pile, gave a huffy sigh and, head resting on crossed paws, closed his eyes.

"How about a toast?" Irma retrieved the glass. "Here's to it, to the baby. To the neighborhood's newest. Some start, hunh? And here's to our dear ole alcoholic neighborhood, God help us all."

Then both of them glanced at the closed kitchen door. They'd just decided without words, to go back in and start the cleaning job themselves. It would be wrong to burden the maid and her sister. Those two women had lives and troubles of their own. Besides, this was probably some sort of tribal duty, a task too ludicrous and personal to inflict on anybody else.

Chloe stood with difficulty, then stretched a bit, seemed steadied. "Well, my dear, are you ready?"

Irma nodded, then punched open the swinging door and lightly draped one arm around her friend's shoulder. They lingered here on the threshold for a moment, two well-meaning white women, childhood friends, lots nearer their deaths than their births. They studied the whole mess realistically.

"You know?" Irma cheered herself. "It's not nearly so bad as I remembered."

Then they scuffed straight into ankle-deep debris, waded toward the broom closet, got boldly back to it, got on with it, with life as it is practiced on this particular handsome side street in this particular dwindling country, ladies getting on with business as usual.

World without end. Amen.

1975–76

Breathing Room
Something About My Brother

For Bruce Fraser Gurganus
Craig Morris Gurganus
and Gary Thomas Gurganus

A STHMA RATTLED IN MY BABY BROTHER. ONE wooden wall kept his bed from mine. Upstairs and at the far end of the hall, our rooms were democratically identical. Mother read books on ways to reinforce a child's creative nature. These told how individuality blooms best in private, how the locks on children's doors should work.

Draperies matched my bedspread: the locomotive's evolution from its early toylike phases to solid modern-day models. Charts showed the silhouette of every name-brand dinosaur. Collections weighed the bookcase I'd spent five days sanding, then enameled red. Bird feathers I found were crammed into the narrow necks of jars. From one milk-of-magnesia bottle, very blue, mementoes of a bobolink, a swan, goldfinch, and crow all sprouted into one unlikely fan. Quartz rested, solid at eye level—some pink or bluish, others clear— and faceted as randomly as ice. Our mother had survived a convent education. She believed true knowledge always involved Latin. So, to the undersides of everything I owned from nature, I taped labels, carefully inscribed with chubby script. The holy names of local things: "Tailfeather (May 5, Crystal Lake). genus: Passer/family: Ploceidae. English Sparrow. Male, I think."

Our house's outer walls were very thick. Quilted silver stuffing sandwiched between well-made slats. Each joint and corner carpentered to keep out weather, pollen, noise, and moths that might make lace of adult tweeds.

But walls inside, ones that showed where rooms would start and stop, these divided only space from space, us from us, and were appropriately flimsy. So after midnight, when outdoor birds and insects settled into thin brief sleep, when the chugging laundry room and Mother's wailing hair dryer and Father's baritone electric razor rested, as I hid chin-deep under quilts and printed trains, my brother's troubled breathing lifted up out of the darkness. It stayed the leading sound all night as I lay listening.

Breaths must be consecutive to work. Bradley's seemed to forget this, then at the last moment, recall. Breathing, when it's sick, is such a sound . . . it causes you to reconsider everything. I inhaled quietly. I was older, with an eighteen-month head start in atmosphere he seemed allergic to. I vowed I'd listen till the other sounds revived at dawn. I thought of how, come morning, they might find him, quiet finally and cool under his bedspread's clipper ships.

Mother's books said, Kids need secrets, secrets thrive on privacy. But my bed was totally unfortified. Breath zigzagged through our mutual wall. It claimed and sectioned off my private space, tore into my territory surely as if ripping strips out of a paper map.

Brother's sicknesss riffled through my shelves, puzzled why I was so healthy, all tucked in and still. An inside job, his sickness snooped through everything I owned. It counted shoes and sandals on the closet floor. It overturned quartz, read Latin names, guessed which collected things were favorites. It poked into all hiding places, found the fossiled rock I'd stolen from Bradley then slipped inside a box under my bed. That rock, with its sketchy prehistoric minnow, grew incandescent now, glowed through tissues wrapping it, shone along the seams of the cigar box I'd taped shut.

Sometimes safety, in the blockish silhouette of our real father, stumbled up the stairs when I most needed help and living company. He'd arrived home slightly drunk and sentimental now at three a.m., tiptoed to my room, his arms out, feeling for the desk chair he'd once tripped over. Father leaned against my bed's far end; it creaked as he stared down, as I played dead, arms wrapped around myself to keep from shaking—with the privilege and jitters of pretending. If I woke up now, would I get hugged or lectured? I knew he didn't want to talk. He just came upstairs to stand here, to appreciate my safety in a bed he'd bought. Once I'd heard him call me his "little soldier." So now I couldn't flinch and disappoint.

But when he got this close, this far into the morning, I wished I were the baby. Then I could whimper, fake a nightmare, cry aloud so he'd bend down and tell me, There there. That everything was fine, that he was here, our house was locked, the war was done, and not to worry. But Father turned, stalked out of mine and into Bradley's room. The door unlatched and brother's standard noises sounded new to me and worse than usual. I opened my eyes, shivered wildly as I wanted, counted to sixty, slowly, once then twice. I timed his visit. I had to know if brother's sickness held our father longer than my unintentional good health.

Early next morning, sunlight woke me. I sat up, frightened, then heard Bradley peeing in our sunny bathroom: music, and a credit to my vigil. I thanked myself. No one else would. My attention alone had kept him rasping on till breakfast. Then other sounds resumed responsibility. Over eggs, we again became good-natured enemies.

He didn't seem to understand he was a sickly child, attuned to perils as a lightning rod. He let others worry for him. He wanted to do everything and at the regular pace. His enthusiasm seemed a simple eagerness to die, but he was four years old and wholly ignorant of how, at any moment, it might happen. Privately, adults told me that along with other things, Bradley was allergic to the sting of bees. As for fiercer sharper wasps, those went without saying: one bad bite might do him in.

Did I remember how he swole all up last spring when he'd tried collecting bees in a glass jar? Remember how his eyes were piggy little slits for days and how he had to drink through a clear curving straw, like a thermometer with liquid ups and downs, and how the doctor came and everybody said that this was really serious? I nodded. After all, who was his one brother and self-appointed keeper?

Sunlight had been stanched and smothered behind the draperies' blue clipper ships. Bradley's door stood half open. Downstairs in the foyer, Dr. Satterfield mumbled technicalities to Mother. I stepped over, tilted into the shadows, "Hey, Bradley?"

"Huh?"

"Can I come in?"

"Uh-huh."

I could hear myself talking too loud but couldn't help it. ''I've been trying to see you. She wouldn't let me. Boy, you sure are puffed up. Does it hurt?''

''Uh-huh.''

''You can't say words, can you?''

''Uh-uh.''

''Momma just told the doctor that your face has gone down some. How big *was* it?''

From under the covers, his swollen hands lifted. Ten white fingers stubby as toes stopped inches beyond either cheek: *This* big. Above quilts, a head large as Father's, features creased within deep folds. His rounded face and neck gave off a sheen in this blue light, looked brittle as some vase propped among the pillows. I thought of a piñata we'd ceremoniously shattered at school. A painted ram, papier-mâché. Its belly dented, then cracked jaggedly, and out like gore leapt candy, trinkets, drenching other kids who laughed and jigged under this downpour. I hid behind my desk.

I'd been hoarding news for him. So much can happen in a week outdoors. But seeing Bradley, fat with poison—one bee's worth—I forgot my gossip. I only recalled how vast our woods seemed with just me in it. On trees, new blobs of amber sap made me think of him. Through our undergrowth, heavy-bodied rodents scuttled toward their burrows.

Nothing to say. Brother couldn't ask a question, his throat swollen shut. So I edged toward the bright door. ''Oh. You remember your fossil, that missing one? Well, I think I can get it. I'm sure I know the kid that stole it. He heard you were sick and all and he thought it might help cheer you up to have that back, for keeps.''

Bradley lifted one hand off the nautical bedspread and held it out to me. I eased over.

Light from our hall showed his true color, white as roots.

"Viie," Bradley moaned.

"Bye," I told him quickly, pleased to understand. I touched his cool palm, ashamed of fearing it and him. I grabbed his plump fingers. I gripped, in proof of loving him, and tried to press right through this bloat and underneath.

He hissed. That hand slowly pulled away from me. It fisted and slipped under coverlets. I hadn't meant to hurt him. I backed toward the door. But just then his face did something, jack-o'-lantern slits widened. I'm sure he hoped to make me feel better. I went over and leaned across his bed, looked eye-to-eye right at him. The puckered folds all stretched, tightening.

"You're smiling, aren't you?"

He nodded, still doing it.

"Okay. Well, good. Get better, all right? Bye, Bradley." I hurried to my room next door. Fully dressed, I crawled under my covers. In this muffling tent of quilts stitched by Grandmother's own dead mother, I could think about him and even cry, but quietly. He mustn't hear. If he just lived, I swore to God, cross my heart and hope to die, I'd guard him so much better than before.

Somehow he shrank back to regular, to the way he used to look. Then everybody said with new conviction, He's a beautiful beautiful child—and silently I began to notice what they meant. Adults told me, Bryan, when you're out with him, outdoors, keep bugs away, son. You must. All kinds, or he may die. We can't know what he's allergic to until it bites him. We must look after him, and carefully. "We" meant "me." I nodded, solemn with the seriousness of my brother's complete condition.

* * *

From our thick-walled house, I heard and saw the waiting choirs and chorus lines of danger. Huddled in the thorny twigs of every hedge, lumped under the eaves of each garage we passed, hidden hives buzzed, thrumming with malevolence. Bugs. Brittle and mobile and every one rigged with a stinger. Bradley, here beside me now in June, wore just a short seersucker sunsuit.

I led him quickly past the clover, its sweet lethal scent banked into damp corners where hornets and bees convened. In summer air, I waved away the merest mayfly. I even snatched at gnats, hovering—mid-evening—in granular atomic clots. Bradley hardly noticed. Being but a baby, and wanting to do everything like anybody else, he forgot their scary lectures. I remembered for him. For myself. Till the two of us, crossing a weedy field, seemed an entire group, an entire kindergarten outing, disorganized and all in danger. Vigilance is exhausting. Finally, I ached to simply arch right over him, to settle like a jar with air holes and enough floor space so he'd not be bored. Then he could see out but be immune from bad things. I scanned the woods we walked through, hand in hand. I saw only a diagram of pitfalls, harmful nests, occasions for the artificial respiration I'd memorized from charts.

Bradley failed to grow tough like others. He wasn't even tough as me. He had only his ringlets to protect him. He was just a precious substance peeled and left exposed for air to darken, for any flying thing to find and fret. I watched the way his elbows bent in two deep doughy folds, the way his neck was plump and met his shoulders all at once. And how, instead of knuckles, his fist dimpled five times, like a newly poked and planted garden row.

It made you doubt he'd make it. So many things not

even fully pressed yet into view: thick catalogs of threats awaiting each. Nature ought to pass a law against so much susceptibility in a single creature. Bradley made me think of damage as the world's one constant. Even bees, which some consider lyrical, are really martial in their readiness for anything. So all the honey in the world, dense amber vats of it, is balanced and offset by one microscopic duct of poison.

I carried a leafy twig and, like attendant to a dauphin, brushed off any stone he might perch on, wiped the wooden swing seat with my shirttail, scoured away a ridge of piny sap a bee might glue itself to and then sting straight up, through summer seersucker and into one white buttock.

I imagined how we'd be quite far from home, in our best tunnel and deepest hidden camp, in the one cool fringe of woods the suburbs had not eaten yet. And how Bradley would reach up to grab a coffee can we kept club dues in, and how the Bee would be there, sunning on the warm tin rim. Bradley would howl and hold his hand and fall back into our cave, not knowing what was what. And then he'd simply say, "A bee, Bryan, a bee again." And I would haul him from the hole we'd dug together, I'd drag him quickly as I could through weeds neck-deep, back toward where our smooth lawn started suddenly. He would be swelling up with what I knew the poison did to him, and I'd be calling out for help, expecting none, but pulling home my younger only brother. Blaming myself and hauling him by two chubby wrists, his weight snapping a trail of weeds. I would be wailing, head back, as the softer of us puffed and maybe died. Nothing I could do about it now. Wailing for our mother so she'd greet us where the weeds ended, wailing to prepare her for the sight of what happened when, for one selfish second, I had looked the other way.

* * *

Here at the big kitchen table, my favorite artist's studio, I control a piece of vast white paper; in easy reach enough peeled crayons to map a war. I am ready to commit myself to the drawing of those persons I know best, I know too well. Today each will get not a color—because white people are not, colored, or are they?—but, one shape apiece:

My ringleted brother is a small choice circle, like a target made of palest tissue paper, drawn drum-tight, and waiting.

My mother, Helen, our mother, lover of contract bridge and needlework and Daphne du Maurier's many books, Mom says "actually" often. That must make her oval. "Actually" sounds oval. Mother wears her hair pulled back at her neck's fair nape, pulled no-nonsense to the usual oval. Her face is shaped Pilgrimishly upright but can go so suddenly friendly, it stops your air, her beauty. The face is dear as good new round-edged hand soap, guest soap, scented, "not for every day, boys." Yes, the perfect ample oval, doodled solemn on my page. So ripe and forlorn in her lonely madonna kind of geometry. Makes me sad but good-sad, sitting here, to see the shape I drew for being her.

My father, son of the brooched socialite, son of the big-eared sun-cured farmer that this socialite so unaccountably adores, my father is the medal-plated minor hero of a major foreign war. This makes Father a rectangle mostly, but one set, disciplinary and royal, on its tallest end. He is a shape you must look up to, sheer rockfacing, you must look it up as you'd look up a number over and over in the phone book, say, forgetting it between. The head end of the former pilot swims so far up in air. Shortstuff, go ahead and signal so he'll see you—and consider landing—even consider landing on you, way here far below.

Oh, and Ardelia, our lifelong helper, cook, and company, who's right across the kitchen scribbling steam over on her ironing board as I work at drawing here. Ardelia, humming, is bottom-heavy among her (our) laundry, the face of her forever ready at my eye level. She is a brown (colored) triangle, she is a sweet dark tent.

And I am, what?—maybe a wax crayon line, improving, underscoring other things, a good clear line connecting, I'm beneath them, around and for them so. Tense. Fine. Sick of being cooperative in keeping them created on a page they barely notice how darn kindly I control. —What is more alone than a single line on so white a page?

Without much accuracy, with strangely little love at all, your family will decide for you exactly who you are, and they'll keep nudging, coaxing, poking you until you've changed into that very simple shape. They'll choose it lazily. Only when it suits them. Maybe one summer morning. You could, for instance, be seated in a wicker chair that your mother, stirred up for six weeks by a crafts class, spray-painted a lurid apple green. Why? You could be slouched on the porch reading, at age ten, page sixty of some Tom Swifty adventure full of selflessness, abandoned lighthouses, adult crooks, plus one loyal and incredibly intelligent beagle puppy. And because you're curled up, engrossed, chewing on one index finger, book pressed near your face, because at just this moment your father, bringing home a business partner to lunch, trudges up the backstairs, nods toward you and boasts, "Our family brain," because of this one moment, you will go on laboring under that half-slanderous heading for a lifetime. Bryan=Brain.

And even if you somehow sensed the phrase's branding-iron finality and whined a protest, it wouldn't help. This name has already "taken," in the way a smallpox vaccination takes precisely because it ends up as a scar.

You were hardly reading Hegel. But the more you deny the title, the truer they'll believe it is. Hey, they'll think, We've really hit on something here. So, that is that. That is you. And, two weeks later, the family doctor, who must have somehow heard, says your eyes are tired because they're very very weak and overworked eyes and need help; he claims you'll go on wearing glasses at least until it's time for college and maybe later, maybe all your life. Glasses make you even more what they said, what your father said, that name he gave—as families give everything—in passing but for keeps.

"Candlelight dinner tonight," Mother would sometimes call aloud and musically. She opened a drawer, lifted out two pronged lumps of protective esoteric fabric. These coverlets were husked off and you'd see silver, unblackened by air: two big twisty candelabra. Into each, a dozen white candles got jammed. For lighting these she used a specialized pencil-thin taper, very long. She touched flame to every upright wick.

Pyromaniacs, we watched. Then we pretended to be blind boys holding out tin cups.

"Very funny. Have you two ever heard of 'atmosphere'? It's actually quite rare in this section of North

Carolina, but that just makes me try harder, for your sakes. You turn up your noses at eggplant, crabmeat, even artichokes. You don't want finger bowls on the table, even at Easter dinner. Well, you boys cannot discourage me.''

''Yeah,'' Bradley said, ''but with just candles, you can't see what you're eating. The peas look like all one thing.''

She was in a good mood. After dinner, she'd rush off to preside over some civic meeting downtown. Now she chanted at him, ''Well, sticks and stones . . .''

''All right, children of all ages. Enough.'' Father hastily muttered Grace.

Your eyes soon got used to the light. Thanks to it, people looked healthier than they really were. Even our salt shaker gleamed like something faceted and valuable. Mother apologized for leaving early. It was her year to chair the Heart Drive, and three nights a week she would scurry out, officious, her blouse freshly pressed, carrying a clipboard she had bought at Woolworth's then sprayed matte beige to complement her conservative suits. Now we sat in her atmospheric aftermath, listening to the station wagon grind around the drive. Her exit's back-door breeze got here tardily, tilting all twenty-four flames.

When left alone with us, Father formally pretended to relax. His face now glowed, a steep stretch of angles, shadows, dents, and fullnesses. ''Yep,'' he said, stirring his coffee. ''Yep'' what?

Brother and I sat, silent, staring at our emptied dessert plates. Bradley toyed with the candle snuffer, holding it to his nose, then one eye. It was a tarnished wedding gift we'd found in a closet. He was allowed to smother one candelabrum's worth. I got the other. If you could dip the snuffer into your water glass when neither parent looked, then flames hissed out louder and made much more smoke.

"Well, so . . . tell me, Bradley, old boy. What'd you say you were going to be when you grow up?"

It saddened me, Dad's waiting—glum—for Bradley's occupation. You'd think your own father could come up with something more personal than this. He wanted to be chummy but was so bad at it. If only I could tell him: Dad, it's just us here. Don't get nervous. What can go wrong? We're already yours.

After dinner, when we were alone upstairs, Bradley always made fun of Father's stiffness. But face-to-face, I bet he'd definitely answer.

"Lawyer probably."

"Well. A lawyer, huh? I guess you changed your mind from last time. Lawyer. Great. Bound to make a lot of money, that's for sure. Yeah, a first-rate lawyer can just about write his own ticket."

"Plus," Bradley added, eyes wide, "when people get caught in a house where some guy's been murdered and the police say they did it, lawyers can show they didn't and get them off."

"That's right. It's good for people and it's a comfortable living, too. Well, if you really want that, I guess law school could be arranged eventually. Of course, both my brothers went to U. Va., but your mother's father and yours truly put in time at Harvard, their law school there, so it's just a matter of visiting the places and deciding which—"

"Hey, Dad?" I butted in. "Well, Bradley is just nine years old and, I mean, he could change his mind about four hundred times before then, right? We shouldn't make him think he *has* to do anything, right, Dad?"

There was a pause. Candles sputtered. On wallpaper

behind him, Father's shadow wavered, his edges wobbling.

"Bryan, I know how old your brother is. Also, I keep telling myself, son, that you're almost what, eleven? and that you should probably understand by now, it's fairly aggravating when you cut into other people's conversations. As for law school, you can never start planning a thing too early. At least that's how I see it. And how about you, your plans? Somebody as smart as you, with grades and all like yours, I guess, really, the sky's the limit. Person like you could do just about anything he sets his mind to, am I right?"

He knew that I took even rhetorical questions to heart, that I'd need at least a minute to choose my life's work; so, with an unexpected tenderness, even with a measure of respect, Father stalled, "You know, Bryan, I think you inherited the Larkins' kind of reasoning, instead of the Graftons' way of acting first, thinking later. The way I operate, for instance."

I sat looking right at him. He had this whole theory about me and my mind. Now I just wanted to please him. I sat poking at warm tallow on the lowest silver stem. Butcher, thief, Indian chief. It didn't matter what I said. Anything would satisfy. I'd seen Bradley watching a Perry Mason rerun this afternoon; he was so easy to figure. Father noisily stirred his coffee which was cold by now and didn't need stirring. My time was running out. I didn't want a job, mine would be a calling, something with a mission to it. Well, explain *that* to him, anything. Go ahead, just spit out, "Doctor."

But I couldn't do it. I honestly didn't know. It was a silly question even if it was the best he could manage. Uncles, salesmen asked such things. Have you got a little girlfriend? Oh, I bet you do, too. Come on, who, who?

"Well? What are you going to be, Bryan? I guess you heard me."

Bradley turned his face this way, the rat, smirking so Father couldn't see; he understood exactly how I felt. I decided: I love Father three times more than Bradley does with his quick cutesy answers.

"I don't know." I stared at my hands. "It probably sounds sassy but it's true." I looked up at him. "I really don't know, Dad. I could say something but I wouldn't mean it. And you want me to *mean* what I tell you. Right?"

He let out a slow elaborate sigh. "Mr. Seriousness, huh? Okay. Have it your way." Then he turned back to Bradley and, stretching long legs under the table, "So— Corporation or Criminal law?"

I studied the two of them, cozy in the orange glow at their end of the table. "May I be excused?" I asked quietly.

Father tilted this way and around the candlesticks to get a full view of me. His eyes showed: clear, fierce, handsome, glinting with an orange speck for every flame. Then he swung right back to his relaxed and manly pose, smiling at Bradley.

"So," he said, upbeat. "Corporation or Criminal?"

I was loaded down with naturalist's equipment, bound outdoors to bird-watch when I spotted a whole new month of magazines on the foyer mail table. Walking over, I startled myself in the hall mirror. Today I wore my croupier's visor to relieve the squinty glare of binoculars plus eyeglasses. This sunshield arched just above my eyebrows and tinted my face a cheerful green. I'd stuffed a notebook and a yellow pencil into my shirt pocket. Binoculars hung from a neck strap. Grandmother had brought this high-powered set from Switzerland, especially for me. I admired myself: Bermuda shorts, argyle knee socks and the brand-new hiking boots I'd got with my own Christmas money.

Mother subscribed to lots of glossy bulletins about good looks for home and self. I stood flipping though these, studying this month's styles: women with hollowed ideal faces, whitish houses like Museums of Comfort. I turned to a picture of a room almost exactly like Bradley's, only tidier. The photograph was an ad for linoleum; its caption read "Positively Boy-Proof." On invisible wires, model biplanes dangled from the ceiling, frozen in nosedives. Pennants praising Trojans, Steelers, Bulldogs triangulated all across the paneled wooden walls. Traffic signs were nailed and tilted everywhere, conflicting demands, just like Bradley's collection.

Mother had caught him sneaking a red stop sign into our house. "Aren't you ashamed, young man? You turn right around and take that back. Think of all the accidents you might be causing this very minute." "Hey," he said, face lifting, brightening with his own consequences. "Neat-o."

How did Bradley know just which things to collect? What about my horde of quartz, fossils, file cards on local birds, my Latin labels? Where did all that fit in? Brother must share traits with the kid whose bedroom they showed here. Even if a decorator made the whole thing up, imagine all the boys' rooms in the USA that must be just like this. Birds, state to state, look enough alike to be identified as members of the same genus. Maybe ideal standard boys shared such habits or markings, nesting patterns.

I postponed bird-watching. He was somewhere in this house right now, no one else at home. I'd just go say hello. I wandered room to room. The binoculars, snug

and Swiss in their horsehide case, slapped amiably
against my frontside. Hiking boots glided noiseless on
our carpeting and Persian rugs. I traced him to his hideaway upstairs. The door stood half open. I peeked in.
He lay there on the oak floor, belly-down, on newspapers. He was arranging countless components from his
new and biggest model. He had lined these up as a
miser might. Vital parts of the USS *Enterprise*. Ardelia
insisted on the papers, claiming that this glue was just
impossible to scrub up. Now, between two tennis shoes,
he'd cleverly propped the square magnifying lens. Grandmother had given Bradley this, her reading glass, when
he'd resented my expensive binoculars. He got this, plus
the lederhosen she'd brought him.

With the silver beak of Mother's versatile eyebrow
tweezers, he pinched up a tiny antiaircraft gun. He held
it beyond the prism-edged glass and, head tilted,
frowned in the lens. Then, magnified as in a fishbowl,
something pink appeared from one side, an hors
d'oeuvre toothpick, the kind Father bought to jab at
baby onions in guests' martinis. This one was laden
with a dewdrop of clear glue. It scumbled against the
khaki-colored gun no larger than an insect's leg. Bradley knew I stood watching. He could hear the leather
of my neck strap creak a I leaned on his doorjamb. But
he couldn't glance up just yet. I understood the reason.
That glue dried so darn fast.

I scanned his room. Boy-Proof. For once, it looked
significant and enviable, nationally advertised. I speed-
read left to right: Raiders. Yield. Visit Orton Plantation. Wolverines. Harvard. Go Back, Wrong Way.
Luther Hodges for Governor. Shoplifters Prosecuted.
Love Those Tarheels. See Castle of Reptiles, a educa-
tional must for kids visiting Florida. God Bless This

Mess. No Shirt, No Shoes, No Food. Dr. Ornstein Dentist Patient Parking. Wolfpack. So, I thought.

Just then he looked up. I felt awkward, sneaky. He never came to my room unless invited. Half in his doorway, half in our hall, I stood, eager for some quick sign of approval despite our differences. I needed just one word, a nod from him, then I'd leave. I smiled, uneasy. I said, "Hi."

In his magnifying lens, the toothpick tipped with glue stayed poised just opposite the tweezer prongs. Propped on elbows, he lay watching me, awaiting what I'd say next. I couldn't think of a thing, not a single thing that might concern or interest or amuse him. I just grinned. His eyes, in one downward sweep, sped across my visor, binoculars, notebook, knee socks, new tan boots. His vision scraped across these and me, like the downward opening swipe of some surgical instrument made specially for that. As I hung here, smarting in the doorway, he leisurely turned back, a blond boy as in magazines; his whole concentration swerved around and fell again upon that useless plastic USS *Enterprise* and, quietly, still poking half-dried glue, he mumbled one word, "Weird."

Four days later, the family brain was taking a shortcut across the school ground, hurrying home with three new public library books tucked under his arm, walking in a pompous almost military step, having just read something really great about a drummer boy, twelve years old, who'd saved the day at an African fort. Since school let out, only pigeons huddled here in daily attendance, chalking up the windowsills and bas-reliefs. All season, there'd been an epidemic among pigeons at Gorham Elementary. You'd see one lose its footing on a third-floor gutter, then fall, flapping spastic out into the sunlight, hooting for its friends and family. But, nested in brick niches, the others never seemed to notice. I asked my teacher what we could do about this, about our school's birds being so sick, and Miss Whipple said, "Not one thing, Bryan. It's nice that you're tender-hearted. But pigeons just aren't like our friends the bluebirds and cardinals. I say, good riddance." That spring a pair of pigeons, still healthy enough, had chosen our windowsill as the perfect sunny spot to mate. Miss Whipple busily pretended not to hear our class tittering. Then she dropped her spelling book, lunged madly shrieking toward the window, slapped the glass so hard we thought she'd slashed her hand to spite the springtime, to punish us for underestimating phonics, for noticing the world itself.

Soldiers at a tribal outpost get pounced by local Africans. Way outnumbered, the whole English regiment is blow-gunned, speared, or hit hard by fever; all but the drummer boy. He sets up rifles in the fort's lookout towers, then pulls the strings attached to far-flung triggers, making natives think that seven able-bodied men still stand—not just one thin resourceful boy. Two days later, owing to hunger and blow darts, he begins seeing things. But just then, reinforcements announce themselves, a whinny of bagpipes eddies far across the veldt, terrifying superstitious villages. Into the fort thunder drums, tartan kilts, and muskets. All congratulations for the boy. When he sees his comrades propped up, revived, attended to, the hero keels right over, dead asleep after weeks of perfect duty. The soldiers carry him upstairs and tuck him into the big bed of a valiant general, speared earlier. Clean silk sheets, it said. "A stout-hearted lad, and true." Stirring to think of days when that old brand of bravery still held . . . held on just long enough to get a person appreciated by a person's replacements.

Miss Whipple, the librarian part-time, had said, Your reading speed is really picking up again, and I'd said, Yes, ma'am, I think it is. The eaves of Gorham Elementary hummed and cooed and crackled pigeon life. I turned a corner briskly: now, to practice speeding up my stride with the rudder-true trajectory of a fast-reading eye. I passed some shadows, heard a groan, and stopped. Four kids there, two holding the arms of one, another lifting a white pigeon into the face of the middle kid, and Bradley's eyes and mouth were pressed totally shut. He cringed just beyond Jimmy Otis's fat fist where the bird was shuddering, sick. I took three steps into the shade and stood right alongside, simply watching. My being there changed nothing. Two boys Bradley's own age kept wrenching his arms, lifting these straight up behind, so he now stood almost daintily on tiptoe. Brother's head strained as far to one side as it would twist, neck muscles bulged, the bird's scarlet beak nearly touching a tense spot just beneath his earlobe. It seemed some peculiar injection.

"All right," I said. Otis looked squarely at me and winked. He was famous even among sixth graders for his innovative meanness. Rumor claimed he'd given his own mother a black eye; she was just twelve years his senior, and tragically she just looked like him. Now Otis jammed the pale bird closer, crushing its soft breast against my brother's right ear and rigid neck.

"All right." I cleared my throat, tried to age my voice, imitating the austere if kindly Miss Whipple. "I guess you guys couldn't know it, but, see, Bradley's got allergies. At least he used to have some, to bees, things like that. And this might be fun and all for you, but it could be kind of dangerous for him. You probably didn't

even know that, right? So let's just break this up, okay?''
Enthusiastically, I answered myself, ''Okay.''

''Yeah?'' whined a bony kid hoisting Bradley's left
wrist even higher. ''You and who else's army?''

''Hey, Leo,'' Otis snapped, ''un-lax your mouth, why
don't you?'' The whole group, still in their odd pose,
now shuffled around to get a better view of me. They
rotated Bradley who did a little jig because of pain. Otis
turned, his freckled cheeks tensed fat, half smile, half
not. He aimed the pigeon headfirst at me, as if he held
a flashlight or a raygun beaming sickness. They all
looked me over. I wished I were carrying a basketball.
Actually these reading glasses should be in my pocket
probably.

Across the pigeon's amber eyes, a bluish film eased
up in tugs, then lowered, shuddering. Even healthy
white pigeons can look quite sickly. This bird's bill
seemed polished, a cheerful red, waxy as red licorice,
but in the nostril dents, each breath rattled two small
crescents of foam, then sucked these back.

''Know what we got here? This here's what you call
a dead duck,'' Otis told me as I studied it, my sadness
undisguised. ''It's going to croak in about one minute.
Might as well get some use out of it now, right?'' Grinning evenly at me, he lifted the bird, pinched its head
between two yellow fingers and, using the steadied
beak, scratched one side of his close-cropped scalp. A
sound like coarse sandpaper's I glared at Bradley, my
signal for him to run. I'd told him not to play with this
pack of kids. I'd told him.

Brother's face observed me; his neck had relaxed, but
the chest, I saw, still heaved in a striped shirt I'd outgrown. Cars passed, other pigeons flapped in gutters
overhead. Then Bradley jerked free. The two kids
reached for him, but Otis waved them back. Instead of

running home, brother took a single step toward me. Otis, interested, put hands on hips, one fist bunched around white feathers that kept rustling in spasms.

Bradley's eyes showed me the clear familiar blue of mine, but his seemed brighter, set inside a better tan. Now everybody glumly faced me. Things had somehow switched around. How? Bradley lifted both his hands and placed these on my shoulders, fingertips and just the weight of wrists. It felt odd, like some Indian greeting from the movies. Otis squinted. The other two, knowing we were brothers, seemed embarrassed, witnessing this peculiar embrace.

"Hey," I asked my brother, "you all right?" But, looking down at him, I couldn't quite remember why I'd interrupted. And, for an instant, it seemed that Bradley had stepped in, was saving me.

One strong simple shove, no harder than necessary. It knocked me straight back. My glasses dropped into my lap, books skidded through dust. After a moment of just sky, green copper gutters, I sat, eyes lifted toward his. The others stooped, eager to see us fight, their fists raised automatically. They stared from him to me, but mostly now at Bradley, and with new regard. I sat aimed at brother's plump brown face, the fringe of ringlets. His chubby fingers balled to fists. We'd hardly ever looked so squarely at each other. Usually before, it was side by side, his curly hair and shoulders lower than me, or I'd been peering out ahead for small dangers in our way. Now, unwilling to cry or ask questions, I stayed where he had pushed me. They were standing. I was here, down here.

"Okay," Otis said, "let's us go someplace else, guys."

He turned. They all did. Bradley, too. Over one shoulder, Otis tossed the pigeon. It scrambled in a crazy arc, then thudded, landing on its breast, left wing fanned out complicatedly, right pinned underneath. The crew shambled away, and one of his tormentors now gave Bradley's upper arm a playful jab, and murmured, ''I'd of done that harder but I'd of done that.''

''Shut your trap, Leo,'' Otis told him, then glanced back at me, a look too casual to even show contempt. I crouched and started gathering my books, not wanting to seem dazed. Then I stood and brushed myself off. No harm done, happens all the time. But they'd passed toward the jungle gym, beyond the school.

I squatted now, stacked the books, evening their lower edges with a few jaunty taps on my knee. I'm not hurt. And Bradley's not hurt. So everything's all right. I noticed my summer shorts, the bare legs. They didn't seem mine, just shapes in the corner of a picture. I sat back down. The bird, with one exerted twist, righted itself and hobbled, zigzagging into the building's shadow. Its white turned a strong blue. The pigeon listed, shuddering, but its arched iridescent head pulled along the body, and with this pathetic dignity. It tipped into a dry cement drainage trench beside the wall and scuttled over debris till, finally settling, it tilted against mossy bricks. I watched the bird's back fill and shrink, quick croupy breaths.

One side in shadow, one side out, my own sunny half was warm. Dust clung softly to the under edge of both my legs. I felt groggy, troubled but relieved. It seemed I'd been hurrying past this spot, bound on a vague urgent errand, aware as in a dream of some crucial appointment or deadline. I'd been moving briskly, pompous with a compliment the librarian had paid, thinking about African heroics; and now, my unstated mission felt abruptly canceled or accomplished. I could sit here as long as I wanted. I could read all these books right here, or sleep, anything.

> *The Art of Japanese Gardening*
> *How to Increase Your Word Power*
> *Gunnar, A Boy of the Frozen Lap Tundra*

I lifted my new glasses from the dust, wiped these on my shirt, slipped them into my pocket, patted it. I did feel tired.

Let him take care of his own self. Or maybe one of those southside river rats would do it for him. Let them stuff dying birds down his throat for all I cared. Or force those fat hands into jars of wasps, even scorpions. Let earthquakes, Mack trucks, jungle fever, let anything that wants him have him. Good riddance. Sleepily and out loud, I said, "Okay, Bradley."

To walk five blocks home seemed an ordeal just now. I needed time to think what I'd do next. Evening was here, a chill. Shadows had wheeled around and over me already. I neatly piled the books, then lay down for a minute, my head resting on them, dusty legs pulled neatly up against my chest.

Illegally, a car drove onto the school yard. Its lights shone just above me. A huge shape bent down now, wouldn't stop this shaking, my head wobbling side to side. Someone leapt from the front seat, came flapping over, and I was down among their legs, a grove of adult legs cutting through the light, throwing vertical shadows long as walls.

"What has happened, baby? What has actually happened, here, darling?"

He stopped shaking me so I could answer her. "I fell asleep, I think. I got so sleepy." And I tried to stand, but he didn't believe I could and he picked me up, off the ground, for the first time in years. His voice: "Are those your books, Bryan?" I nodded, "The library's," and I put my arms around his solid neck. The car's back door flipped open and a short person got out and walked around and stood in front between the headlights, hands on hips, all silhouette. Who's that? Mother got the books and she came running alongside. "Are you sick, darling? Here, let me feel," and her hand tried resting on my forehead, but I kept bouncing toward the car in Father's arms, and her warm fingers clamped over my eyes, my mouth. She wrapped me in the itchy tartan football blanket. She propped me on the backseat and climbed in front, but leaned over, her beautiful hands so good at needlework and bridge. Father gunned the engine; then that squatty other person crawled through the back door, slammed it, sat right across from me. Father drove slowly and Mother spoke in bursts, "We didn't know. The sun had set. I called the library. I even phoned poor Harriet Whipple at home. She loves you. Oh, Bryan mine, we were so unbelievably worried."

Over there in one corner. Back pressed to the door. Some little man. His arms crossed. Looking over here at me. Some midget in a striped shirt. Face all shadowed. Mother still yammering. I knew her. I knew Father. But who was this one watching me? Father almost stopped when, purely terrified, I dove over the seat and nestled between their sides, keeping low to hide from that one in back, a little man, a little midget gangster, midget monster midget.

"Richard, see how he's shaking? Poor thing is scared to death. Bryan, sit up. Bryan mine, now listen to me. You can tell us. Tell Mother, did some grown-up try to do something to you? Did some man *do* something to you, Bry?"

I sobbed and sobbed. "Oh my God," she said, "a

man.'' They carried me to bed. Father did. He bent
over and said to keep that extra blanket, anything I
wanted, and to sleep, just sleep. That would mend me
fine. He gave me two kisses, one over each eye, and a
big one in the middle of my forehead. Sleep, he said.
He propped the door half open using my desk chair. He
left. Then I heard it. Odd noises. Someone opening and
closing drawers. Some stranger in the next room moving all the furniture around. I lay listening, too frightened to call for help, but trying very hard to. Call. For.
That. With all my strength, I wished for sleep.

Morning, and my room looked the same as ever, collections nicely organized, but I got up feeling bruised,
timid, humiliated. I leaned into the hall, saw into the
bathroom. The little man stood brushing his own teeth.
But it was not a real man. Nothing to be scared of, just
Bradley more or less. At breakfast, they fought to be
polite. They didn't mention what had happened but took
turns watching me, like at any moment I might drop
out of the breakfast nook, fall to the linoleum, me kicking, hissing, in some wild blind lavish fit.

I planned it like a bank robbery. To the minute. I'd
been waiting. Only today might I get away with it.
Jimmy Otis was moving out of town. His dad worked
at the Du Pont plant and they'd transferred him to Mem-
phis. For the last three months, Bradley and Jimmy had
been best friends. Our parents disapproved. So did I.
They were pleased to see the friendship broken up so
easily. So was I. Mother said, ''He is just the grubbiest
little red-headed thing.''

''He can't help it, Momma,'' Bradley told her. ''He's
poor.''

''Listen, young man, anybody can afford soap and
water.''

One afternoon, I looked into Bradley's room and saw Otis, visiting. He reached up and with grimy fingers tapped a suspended model plane. It spun in circles. "Are these that hard to make?" he asked, almost shy.

"Not too," Bradley said. "Haven't you ever done a model?"

"Unh-unh. It always seemed like kind of a waste. Who painted the camouflage on it?"

"I did. I do all my own paint jobs. That's the important part."

I sat on my bike, just across the street from the Otises' stucco house. I sat studying the van, the moving men. A rusted De Soto was parked in the yard. Lampshades were stacked on its backseat. Everything seemed ready to roll. Jimmy came down the front stairs carrying a vinyl footstool. He saw me. I pushed off and, feeling elated, waved back over my shoulder without looking, good-bye Idiot, good-bye School Bully and Bradley's Best Friend. Good riddance.

On the way home, I biked near Bradley's Little League game and heard some competitive shouts and whistling. It was a beautiful spring afternoon, steep and brassy. Nobody at home but Ardelia, humming hymns and some of Mother's show tunes as she ironed. I went up to my room to collect the supplies. A cardboard box, and in it a pair of scissors borrowed from Mother's needlepoint basket, a can of charcoal lighter fluid from the garage, and matches out of Father's pipe rack.

Wearing the hiking boots Bradley'd made such fun of, I padded quietly across the hall, closed his door behind me, locked it. I took the scissors, stepped up onto his desk chair and, feeling some stage fright but no regret, cut down the first suspended model plane, tossed it into the box on his bed. I could have just yanked them down, tack and thread and all . . . but

somehow it appealed to me, leaving a fringe of long
colorless strings bearding the whole ceiling. My move-
ment stirred the dangling plane just like Daddy's war
one. That went too. Me, up here among them, snip-
ping. Cut threads, relieved of weight, curled and looped
or spun in lazy twists. I stripped his room of every
single model: seventeen big ones and twenty smaller
designs. I stacked ships and airplanes, crisscrossed in
an apple crate, sweet-smelling, rotten-smelling. On my
way down the back stairs, I heard Ardelia talking church
gossip by phone to her best friend over the steam iron's
slosh and whisper.

I cut across the weedy field behind our house and
broke into a run. Plastic jiggled, brittle in the big box.
I breathed funny, knowing I was up to something really
mean and downright wrong and very hurtful. Bullies
must feel like this, day-in day-out. How could their
hearts stand it?

At our camp, I stopped. We'd dug this hole together.
We called it the Cave. It had once seemed very deep
and private but I'd grown, and now it was just an over-
sized puddle at the wood's edge. I stood on the brink,
panting, quick shallow breaths. I dumped all Bradley's
models into the hollow. My palms sweated as I fumbled
with the lighter fluid's complicated cap. Printed along
the red plastic nozzle: CHILD-RESISTANT. I felt personally affronted till I recalled how Father himself had
cursed it a few nights earlier. The spout snapped up. I
looked guiltily around. I squirted out half the can. The
whole heap down there looked varnished. The flagship
Santa Maria was carefully rigged with tiny sails Bradley
had stitched himself, while Mother advised. The dye already spread, bleeding as fabric soaked up fluid. With
his small jars of candy-bright enamels, Bradley had
worked on these for hours: all the wing-tip stars, insig-

nias, and camouflage. I pressed the can's flat sides until its spout wheezed, gasping.

In an hour, he would wander home from his game, wearing that natty pin-striped uniform, the green felt cap, number 17. A real plane buzzed overhead. I felt almost sad, striking this match, tossing it into the crater. Flames leapt even higher than I'd hoped. I jumped back, then touched my bangs, singed a little. I brushed away scorched hairs, then hunkered down to watch the damage. The fronts of my legs warmed as things below began to snap, like delicate bones popping in quick series. Jet wings merged with the bulbous undersides of boats. Blue-black smoke, stinky curling stuff, trailed out over the high weeds. On the tilted flight deck of the *Enterprise*, planes no bigger than bees softened to tear-shaped blobs and slid downward, hissing. Plastic rudders and propellers whined, frying to one leaden shape. I found a branch and prodded the debris. Pockets of air snapped loud in toxic farts. When most flames stopped, I shoved the stick into the soft center and lifted the whole solidified mass up out of the hole. I stood supporting this at arm's length. It smoldered, still creaking, complaining; strings of plastic looped across hulls and blubbery fuselages, all crusted with sand and drooped around my stick like lava. It stunk and clicked like something newly dead, something accidentally deformed in a horror picture: "The Manta Ray from Hiroshima." Something you could pity.

He ambled in from Little League, forty-five minutes late. I'd been seated for an hour at the kitchen table, drawing, Ardelia as my witness. I'd brought one of my better finished crayon drawings downstairs so it would seem I'd been here longer. Now he was tardy and I'd ruined it. I sat recoloring a dark sky for the fourth time.

He sauntered past, pounding the palm of his orange pitcher's glove. "You all win?" Ardelia asked, half-interested at best.

"Sure did. That First Presbyterian is a bunch of nothings. I struck out three of those guys in a row."

He strode past this table without speaking. Just as he pushed through the dining room's swinging door, I said, "Oh, Jimmy Otis came over to say good-bye. I thought you were home. I told him you'd probably be in your room."

"He was supposed to move this afternoon. I *already* said good-bye."

"Well . . ." I shrugged, going back to coloring. "He was up there looking for you."

I listened to his every step. Turning down the hall. Hopping up two stairs at a time. I wished Ardelia would hum less loudly. It took about a minute. I heard him coming back down. Not hurrying. His sneakers on the staircase carpeting. I pressed my damp palms to the waxy drawing and leaned over it so he couldn't see my face. He sat at the opposite end of the table, Father's usual spot. I counted to sixty two times. Finally, I risked it. I glanced up. Bradley'd taken his cap off, his yellow curls were matted on the sides. His face totally blank, drained of character and color, all that pug-nosed male-animal confidence vanished. "My models are gone."

I slowly chose a new color from the shoe boxful. "Wha?"

"All my models . . . somebody's stole all my models."

I looked down the tabletop at him. Notice this, I told myself. One minute ago he was bragging about pulverizing sissies. Look at him now. But the sight gave me no pleasure at all; it distressed me. I even considered confessing, then got dizzy at the thought and decided I would never admit to this. Ever. How could I have done it, anyway, and why?

"Otis knew I was at Little League. He came over here and took every one, then he goddamn moved to Tennessee." Bradley hurried to the wall phone, dialed a number. I kept my crayon moving, but felt blind, lightheadedness. The longer he stood there gripping the receiver, saying nothing, the more deeply I could breathe. "They're gone already. Ardelia, this is important. Did you see a red-headed—well, you know who Jimmy Otis is—did you see him carrying my models out of here? All my models?"

"Ain't nobody been here this afternoon but us chickens. Just me. And Bryan."

Bradley's head snapped my way.

This crayon sliding back and forth, I managed to say quietly, "Otis came to the back door. He wouldn't leave through *here*."

Bradley studied me, his jaw working. I saw him considering, then his face relaxed to its original frown. He came over, sat again. Some Perry Mason!

"And I gave him a good-bye present. I gave him a model to make. That rat. I'm calling the police right now." My brother stood.

"Ain't nobody calling no police till your momma gets back from clothes shopping. And don't you be saying no 'goddamn' around me, neither."

"That Otis was so jealous of me," Bradley mumbled. "He was even jealous of you, said you were probably smart underneath—Otis, you'd have to be a pretty rotten kid to do something like this."

For the first time in years, Bradley was about to cry. I watched, mesmerized. He still can, I thought; he's really going to. Brother kept shaking his head side to side. "Boy," he said breathily. "Boy."

"Bradley. He knew what you liked most. And he took it. I *told* you Otis was bad."

"Yeah, but my models, Bryan. My models." He put his head down on the table. The way he'd said my name, without any joke in it, without being bossy, made me think of how things used to be when he was little, when he lived in trouble and I looked out for him.

Ardelia wandered over, a potato peeler now in one hand. She wiped the other palm dry on her apron, then patted his shoulder, stood there absently fluffing out his flattened ringlets. "Your daddy'll buy you some more models."

"Not like those, Dee. Those were *my* models."

I needed an activity. I went back to coloring but kept glancing down the table. Her hand, dark on back, ivory-colored underneath, pinched at his curls. Bradley's pin-striped shoulders bucked and his sobs kept cracking, filling this room, all wild and unrestrained, two years' worth of not crying, packed and condensed in him, now leaping out.

"You buck up, champ. Hear?" Dee said. And he did start quieting. Relieved, I went back to coloring with a Crayola nubbin. That Otis, I thought. That sneak of an Otis. Tears beaded on the layered wax of what, an hour ago, had been a landscape: a smoking chimney, a stream, a horse, a house. Someone had done something really mean to my kid brother. I got furious, so furious I yelled, "*I'm* calling the police."

"Ain't nobody calling no police till your momma gets back from clothes shopping."

Bradley looked up, appreciative, his face all blurred. I sketched, furious. I drew a long curling tail, mint green. I wrote across the blotched colors: I AM A RAT. I AM A TRUE AND REAL RAT. A ROTTEN ONE. I LOVE MY BROTHER REALLY. I LOVE MY OWN BROTHER. BASICALLY.

* * *

"Why Did Dinosaurs Die Out So?" Thus ran the name of my searching papier-mâché Science Fair Project, a runner-up locally. As I recognized the lapdogs of Summit Avenue, I knew the shape of each beast unseen for so many thousand years. When I put the question of why group extinction to Miss Whipple, my unmarried appreciative art-and-science teacher, she said, "Because, my Bryan of Bryans" (there were seven in sixth grade), "because they could not change." "Oh," I said, and worried.

My head replaced those lumbering and peaceable and mostly grass-eating monuments I adored almost as pets, replaced them with nearer and more recent loved ones. I pictured my born-poor grandfather, ears very large, coming into Falls from deep weedy countryside, wanting not to be so country, wanting to evolve into being one of the old families who seemed least capable of that. Of change. And marrying into one of the old extinct-almost, almost-rottenly-old families. And that was called upgrading. Why Do Dinos Die? Maybe Bradley's allergies proved some weakness in us whites? "You will be tested on this. Regarding their extinction, regarding anything's extinction, boys and girls, it's simply: If a group cannot bend, it fails to grow—it loses out to heartier and therefore worthier life forms. To quote Darwin, 'In Nature, there is no equality, only adaptation.' Any questions? This *will* be on your final."

Quite easy to confuse the long spiny silhouettes of the missing titan-lizards with those shapes I had awarded, via Crayola, my co-householders, my species and my genus too. The local names of holy things extinct. And could we grow and bend? And did we want to? Did we *have* to want to?

Maybe other looser quicker ones would find us, years

from now, stuck in our swamps of Packards, patios, soup tureens, needlepoint pillows, model planes? What might reduce us to the palest possible fossils? Fossils that children of some future might collect and swap among themselves? What shifty, limber, and way-more-colorful life form will nail us first?

Puberty's disadvantages can hardly be exaggerated. Thirteen years old. I'd got there, somehow. Like on vacation in the car, falling to sleep in North Carolina and waking up, rubbing your eyes, to ask, "Are we halfway yet?" And being told, "Oh, you've been asleep. We didn't want to wake you. This is Florida already. We're here!"

Bradley had been born nearly two years after me. Suddenly, when he reached the same thirteen, his physique forgot this. Things are not supposed to happen overnight. But, against my will, glands conspired to pass me off as someone else. And just then, Bradley's copy-cat chemistry got the idea. His same system of vats and ducts lurched and knuckled into action. And I could feel him breathing down my neck, the new him, right behind me, respiration loud and clear, waiting for the straightaway, a roadhog who is definitely going to pass even if the unmarked curve ahead is very dangerous.

I opened our bathroom door and he was standing right there, fresh from the shower, drying his hair with a towel, a black one, wound in turban round his head, the yellow ringlets, wet to brown, popping out like decorations, and he was otherwise attired in absolutely nothing but the waist-high results of having to wear gym shorts through a tanning summer. Into our mirror, he grinned at my reflection, not seeming to note how nude he was, not seeming to recall that no one in our family had seen him in the altogether since he was chubby and maybe eleven. My image showed a skinny blur, but he was focused. He'd rubbed clear one port-hole wide enough to hold his shoulders, face, and head-dress. His confidence ricocheted from shower-steamed mirror to me. Brother's grin simply said, ''Oh. It's you.''

I slammed the bathroom door. I jaunted to my room, knocked books out of my desk chair, and sat. Having seen his smirk, I thought I understood the kind of rowdy grown-up loudmouth he was going to be. I knew, for instance, how he'd probably act in gym classes. I knew from kids in mine who strode around like ads for their own brand-new nakedness, popping one another with wet towels, genitals aswing matter-of-factly, boys noisy and shameless as young chesty iridescent bantam roost-ers. I was not like them. Half-immobilized by modesty, I wore the towel double-knotted at my waist, and when I dressed, it was behind the locker's door. Blushes, I'd discovered in gym showers, commence not at the chin but with a burning all across a person's shoulders, ris-ing to his face as the very thought ''I'm blushing'' brings a whole barrage of extras, till your ears are ring-ing with the headstrong blood.

Thanks to silken brunette bristlings on my upper lip, I now looked somewhat dingy. People kept telling me this, out loud, and in front of others. Mother insisted that severe regular scrubbings would take care of everything. In her philosophy of life, nun-strict hygiene always loomed large. The poor could at least *wash*. I looked poor now.

Bradley got taller than I quicker than anyone ex-pected, considering the childhood allergies. No one was surprised at my size itself, only how it became less and less than Bradley's, whose chin and shoulders got squared and solid faster. He stayed blessedly blond, and his was not the grimy ghost of a mustache. The lip under his snub nose grew only the palest down. And, in direct sun, as a sort of bonus, this shone golden.

They planned to ship me off to boarding school the next September, the school my father had graduated from, the one my grandfather, self-made, would have chosen to attend. I imagined the place as some rambling landscaped hospital where doctors and patients all wore, not robes, but crested double-breasted blazers. Bradley planned to follow. He spent the summer he turned fourteen getting into shape for the St. Matthew's Preparatory track team. He took to running around our neighborhood without a shirt or shoes, just white shorts. Young housewives, coming home with groceries, climbed out of sedans, a bag under each arm, and watching him jog flashily past wearing gym trunks he'd outgrown, these women who'd witnessed his recent unruly upsurge, would simply shake heads back and forth and say, in sighs, such husky girlish things as, "My my my."

Meanwhile, I stood half-hidden by a hedge, big-eared, observant and embittered. At grandmother's house, relatives poked my lower back, uttered the hateful word "Posture." Distant cousins who had no right, kept telling me to stand up like a soldier. Our Aunt Cecily, who'd been twice married, twice divorced by handsome semigigolos from Florida, thought herself a pretty good judge of manly form, and she said young Bradley was Greek, almost. Like someone hurling discus on a vase, almost.

It was easy to see his total posture since, from May till October, he rarely wore more than shorts. Sundays were exceptions. And, in coat, shirt, pants, tie, cufflinks, he seemed choked as someone active who's been sealed up in a body cast for months. After benediction, he'd gallop to our station wagon, claw off his tie, wrestle himself free of his own jacket. He sat there, half-dressed, staring out at scenery.

Cure means the extinction of your illness, right? That should be good, such health.

Once asthma rattled in my younger brother. Breathe out, breathe in for him. Once they told me that one thing only stood between his dying and his not and that seemed me. And I felt ready to stay on guard like that forever.

How he became our state's singles junior tennis champion is anybody's guess. The wind it took! I attended the finals, half expecting an attack on the court, half prepared. Instead I had to sit up in the overheated bleachers with others. I had to watch him—oblivious to anything but winning—win.

He's over thirty now. Our Bradley is the father of twin boys. He gave up his early partnership in a Georgetown firm and moved west, where health is. My parents sold their house with its yard big enough for baseball and tentworms. They shipped off to Bermuda of all seemingly inviting but actually deeply uninviting places. Dad had a touch of prostate trouble but is better now. My mother plays sharklike bridge four days a week with the wives of retired IBM vice-presidents and English military brass, and she's as contented as I've seen her. That makes Father happier, he says.

Ardelia retired from ironing for us, attended junior college. Dee got certified as a teachers' assistant, grades one through six. She now wears conservative suits to work. She uses contact lenses. She improves the world for thirty kids per year, not just my brother and me. Bradley, set up with some money from his wife, Elaine

(good person, Elaine, a relief, a surprise), now manu-
factures water-skiing equipment. He says he's allergic
to nothing that he knows of. We see each other once
every two or three years and he's just wonderful company. With his wife and twins, he lives in Venice (California)—a big home, a Labrador, a vegetable garden,
hollyhocks, bees, what have you.

There, in Venice, Bradley has a dock. We sat on it
one year ago, just at sunset, admiring sky as an extension of his real estate. He smokes some, Bradley, and
that worries me but I say nothing, of course. I was,
after all, his houseguest. Laughing a bit, we sat discussing our parents, now called "them." We jawed
about them with the same wry fond concern once overheard in private talks when their "them" meant us. The
wine was running low. I volunteered to head back to
the kitchen for a refill. He asked if I'd bring out more
goat cheese too. I rose, a bit unsteady, I lifted the platter, took three steps uphill toward his low-slung lighted
house, his boys playing in the yard.

"I burned your models," I told a quiet seated smoking man.

"Yeah I pretty much guessed that."

"When?"

"I must've been, oh about twenty-seven, in there.
I'm slow about these things. —What'd, you set them on
fire one by one, or what? The paintjobs were all I really
cared about."

"Remember the hole where we buried club dues in
the Maxwell House can? I chucked them all in there.
Let them have it with Dad's charcoal lighter fluid. They
sort of fused—great smoke, these whining sounds. You
would've been proud. They're probably still out there
with our club dues underground. Actually, the planes
would've looked great in your twins' rooms. Those

planes would have an added period appeal by now. Sorry. —How about some more endive with that goat cheese, bro?''

"Sure. Super. —It's okay. You took everything to heart. We're grown now, remember?''

"Yeah. Please keep reminding me, all right?'' Then I trudged uphill toward my brother's lovely home.

And myself? I'm in Manhattan. A bachelor again, and not unhappily. I support myself by ad-copywriting, doing occasional magazine opinion pieces. I'm still a review stringer for one dance magazine that was kind to me early on. I don't forget these things. I lost my actor friend to an early illness, unexpected, unexplained. For reasons of my own, I subsequently married—a woman somewhat younger than myself, and then a woman considerably older. Versatile, I've proved. A good provider. Lately alimony mostly. But, turns out, I like taking care of people, actually. I do.

So, let's see, Bradley just turned thirty-four. What does that mean I am? Bradley's thirty-four, and thriving; that makes me thirty-six.

1975–76

America Competes

For John L'Heureux and Richard Scowcroft,
and for Dolly Kringel

THE NATIONAL FUNDAMENT OF THE ARTS—ALL TOO aware of its jeopardized fiscal standing at this time of increased government scrutiny—announces what may be its final competition.

At their recent news conference, Fundament director Dorothy McPhee repeatedly stressed the need, at this moment of world crisis and sharp cutbacks, for continuing optimism among American Artists.

The prominent west wall of a large Washington D.C. office building will be given over to the provocative design theme "America, Where Have You Come From, Where Are You Bound?" The space in question is windowless, 555 by 310 feet (see attached diagram).

If you are a non- or semi-, or fully professional artist of American citizenship, over eighteen years of age, you qualify to enter. Written proposals should accompany the drawn-to-scale renderings. Winner (one only) will be announced May 5 and the mural will be completed in time for a nationally televised July 4 unveiling by the First Lady.

Due to the number of expected participants, applications cannot be returned. We refuse responsibility for any entry's loss or damage. Ours is an Equal Opportunity competition. Nonetheless, the judge's decision will be final.

Dear Miss McPhee and other Fundament Folks,

Would you kindly mail the first mural packets to my Massachusetts studio instead of the Manhattan address I gave you before? I expect to be up here on our little farm for three luxurious months. I'm planning to paint in the mornings and spend evening poring over the proposals. As the final authority in all this, I *think* I'm game and capable. I do take it seriously and am eager to see the first responses. So is Lucia, my wife. She'll be here for a few more weeks and has agreed to help.

Today we cleared off two plank tables in the kitchen. Lucia carried back issues of magazines to a chicken coop we use for storage. I've dusted and polished both tabletops and so we stand braced, Miss McPhee. Bombard us with that first batch of America potential. I sign myself

More enthusiast than judge,
Kermit Waley

Dearest Sirs (or Madame[s]),

I had the distinct good fortune to serve on the Beautify America Committee a few years back. I've done a little research, and, I believe, of Mrs. Lyndon Johnson's select group, I am the only one still actively planting on the civic level.

What you've got is a long wall with a westerly facing. In Oct. 1916, my late mother and her head gardener planted forty boxwoods and lots of English ivy sprigs around our local branch post office. All forty shrubs still thrive, and every inch of the build-

ing's outer walls is now nicely ivied. Meanwhile, inside, murals done during the Thirties by three New
Yorkers (painted twenty years *after* Mother planted)
are now water-stained and flaking like some rash.
They weren't all that great to begin with. The farm
children depicted have huge necks on them and are
smelting iron (on a farm?) and surveying with equipment that is absolutely inaccurate, even for back then.
Each time I go to mail a letter, I come out more
angry. Then, luckily, I see the English ivy plus those
stately boxwoods—always so soothing. Time cannot
wither nor custom stale *their* infinite variety.

In the greater D.C. area, wisteria will do nicely for
you as a wall climber. Its perfume would offer a
lovely bonus to passing office workers.

Pyracantha can eventually be espaliered, and orange autumnal berries provide a visual feast, then a
literal one for migratory cedar waxwings forced to
lay over en route to haven in the South.

Think in terms of perennials. Don't settle for fast-
fading painting fads. When you and I are pushing up
daisies, my suggestion will go right ahead without us.
The miracle of photosynthesis remains as up-to-date
as tomorrow's newspaper and a whole lot more comforting. What better symbol of our national hope than
a plant—well chosen, expertly maintained, grounded
in native soil but straining upward, always upward?

> Mrs. Frank A. Parrish
> Astabula, NC, zip 27801

Dear Judge Artist of National Distinction,
I've always thought one art carries right over into
another and that really sensitive people can spot true
quality in other similar type artistic persons. For this
reason, I am sending not a mural but a children's

book, one of my best, ''Jenny the Wren's Vienna Misadventures.''

I also illustrated it. Some people have said my book's wren is sketched much more realistically than the Viennese buildings—but how many English-speaking kids care that much about Austrian architecture anyway? What they love is Jenny the Wren herself!

Jenny has sure been to lots of publishers lately. I'm still trying to get her into the right hands. Suggestions? Anyway, enjoy, enjoy. Here is ''Jenny the Wren's Vienna Misadventures.'' I am

>Interdisciplinary,
>Ms. Mirabelle Braith
>Rte. 3 Blackfoot Hghy.
>Billings, Montana

Dear Contest,

My Dad he did good drawings. He work out at Moss Furniture evenings and the Grave Yard shift Kenilworth Byproducts. He finished forty pictures of Eagles holding the branch in one hand and the arrows. He love that Eagle. Please send these back if they don't win it. My Dad died. He did Eagles on placemat menus from where our Momma worked waitressing.

Miss Martin the teacher she told my wife to inter this. Dad was 74 and never sick a day in his life. He was born at West Virginia but come out here when Momma needed to for her breathing.

>Rollo Krause
>Phoenix, Arizona

Miss McPhee,

There was no return address on this bundle. Our posters said we wouldn't send back applications but this seems an exceptional case. Can you trace this Krause fellow, maybe through the teacher the poor guy mentions? Lucia studied every one of these menus, all yellowed and obviously used before the old man drew eagles on them. Somhow, when I agreed to do this judging, I expected perhaps a higher degree of "professionalism," whatever *that* is. To tell the truth, it's hard to recall just what I expected. Reading some of these "essays" becomes a humbling experience. Many of the drawings are done in Crayola, Bic pens, even fingerpaints. One was sketched in homemade charcoal and had not been sprayed with fixative. By the time our mailman lugged it up the front stairs with two dozen others, nothing remained in the envelope but a smudged piece of cardboard and a handful of crumbly black powder.

So many people want this commission so much. Lucia keeps telling me I'm far too empathetic a person to make this kind of decision. But she's the one who laid the eagle menus all over our kitchen counter and spent a whole rainy afternoon shaking her head and repeating, "Do you relize how *lucky* we are, Kermit?" Anyway, Miss McPhee, we're wading knee-deep through the heartbreakers, trudging onward in search of an undiscovered genius from Utah or some such place. Full speed ahead, I remain,

Yours,
Kermit

Committee dear!
Stand by, have cheer!
My every fifth-grade boy and girl
Would simply *love* to do that mural.
After a vote, we picked a theme,
A happy one, a cheering scheme.

We chose the subject of "Balloons!"
In poster paint, bright as moon-doubloons
We'll soon splash up a pretty grouping
To keep those bureaucrats from drooping.
Ballons of every size and color,
An interracial cure for dolor.
A paint contractor, my husband is.
He'll build our scaffolds. (*Such* a whiz!)
He says he'll do it all for cost.
Four floors is high, but no kid'll be lost!
He'll spray our mural with clear acrylic
After they're done, my class angelic.

They're daily bussed right past this spot,
Against their will, like it or not,
So why not give them some say-so,
In how this country's going to grow.
If chosen, they will simply glow.
If not, they'll think Democracy
Smells oddly like Hypocrisy.
If you guys shatter such high hopes,
They'll call *all* judges corrupt dopes.
When fifth-grade ideals hit the skids
We're talking about Dead End Kids.
It's up to you, you Judge, you Pontius,
It's up to you. It's not *my* conscience.

> I hope selecting will prove merry,
> I sign myself, Clarissa Cherry
> C.A. Arthur Elementary
> Washington 20009 D.C.
> M.A. (with 18 hrs. twd PhD)

To the Art Money Handout People:
Consider a documented fact—of the 101 settlers on

the *Mayflower*, only eleven were members of any church. You still think they came over here for religious freedom? Ha.

This kind of Federal spending really irks me no end. And why do these expensive projects always get put up on the *East* Coast? But if you intend to go through with this giveaway show, there's something I must say, loud and clear.

As an atheist, I now tell this committee not to hint that so-called divine inspiration had anything to do with our nation's founding. Any picture that even touches on the Godhead will bring cries of outrage from this taxpayer and others like myself. I will be watching this wall. If you people choose something like Pilgrims on their knees, or some ethnically mixed group all looking up while their hands are pressed together, I cannot be held responsible for what my organization might do. This should be said, this should be stressed. Forewarned, forearmed.

> McNulty
> 30 Foy St.
> L.A.

Dear Dorothy and her helpers at the Fundament,

A progress report: well, it's slow going at best. My wife left this afternoon. She returned to her job at an art auction house in the city. She waited three years for this position and I'm glad she's happy with it, but I already miss her. Lucia tried her hand at the mural entries but soon got very morose. She began blaming the National Fundament for how sad these things are. So I took her by the wrist and literally led her away from the growing mounds of evidence.

Now I'm alone just as the sun sets. Me, and what

has suddenly become another real presence here, all those envelopes stacked along our kitchen wall. All the artistry gummed into all those packets, mostly manila brown. Some are white. One of today's came wrapped in red construction paper, bound with gold clips, like a gift. Our foyer is already jammed. The long-suffering postman daily stacks them higher, neat as firewood. Maybe *I* should have become a postal clerk instead of this—this, whatever I am. My job, I recognize, is simply to choose one winner from the hundreds. Obviously, that's what competition is about.

Could you please send me your phone number? Your home phone. That way I can reach you in the wee hours. This farmhouse always starts creaking just before dawn. I think I'm going to maybe need some encouragement.

Kermit

To Giveaway People:

Let's face it. The *Mayflower* was a hotbed of foment and atheism. The sooner we admit this to ourselves, the better off we'll be. Americans would sleep easier if they realized that our nation wasn't settled by saints. Who *were* our forefathers? Europe's overflow of malcontents, that's who. The excess nuts and cranks and failures. Riff-raff who shot their bolt early on, drifters who were miserable elsewhere.

Stick that in your mural. Or else.

MacNulty
L.A.

Dear Miss McPhee,

Kermit says we met at that big embassy party last August in Washington. He tells me that you're attractive and conversant and that you graduated from Smith

So did my sister (Pepie Bainbridge McCloud, Class of '61, the choreographer). My memory for faces is notoriously bad but, from all I've heard about you, from the fact that you chose my husband as the one American painter to judge this mural business, I feel I can speak frankly.

Ten days ago, I left Kermit in our little nineteenth-cent. farmhouse in the Berkshires. I now have a part-time job as an art buyer and, since my official vacation was over, naturally I came back to NY. Now I wish I'd given up this whole idea and stayed in the country. I call him twice daily and he assures me that things are fine, but he sounds so vague and tired. Miss McPhee, nothing you told Kermit prepared him for the ordeal of judging. There should be a least three jurists.

When I left, packets were stacked on every available surface. The few I managed to flip through just about broke my heart. I'm *still* depressed. Some ladies' craft guild from Ocala, Florida, wanted to macramé a "Snood-type Shawl" for the entire building. One man sent his dead father's pencil sketches, done on the backs of perfectly filthy Howard Johnson's menus. A fifteen-year-old girl mailed us all her writings, a steamer trunk full. She'd done "paraphrases of Emily Dickinson." The child had been through each Dickinson poem and reduced it to a pat moral lesson. For instance, poems about death (a quite large percentage) she often summarized: "You only come this way once, so while you're at it, grab for all the gusto you can get." Her accompanying note said, in a demure handwriting, if she didn't win, she guessed she'd just go out and drown herself.

What kind of superhuman can withstand this? Certainly not Kermit. You hired him as an aesthetic authority, not a human-relations counselor. Kermit, despite my years of coaching, has never really learned to say No. His own painting has been going not all that terribly well lately. The last thing he needs is this extra burden of guilt concerning others' pitiful problems. Three weeks ago, for the first time since he was nineteen, since his Socialist days, Kermit began to stammer again. Just as before, on words beginning with M. He was also becoming dreadfully insomniac. I'd get up and find him downstairs in the kitchen, drinking milk, standing before a table heaped with amateurish drawings. His critical eye, as you—of all people—must know, is usually incredibly acute. In NY, gallery owners seek him out for advice. He can spot the slightest clumsiness or slickness. But when I was there with him, it frightened me to see how Kermit's discrimination was slipping. He'd bring in some totally trashy sketch of a wood duck viewed from three angles. Sub-calendar art, really. He'd say, Of course, it was rough, but what energy the thing had, a primitive purity all its own. I told him, Kermit, what on earth are you talking about? If one of your students had done it, you'd flunk the kid for sure, and here you're going to award *this* a national gold medal? He admitted I was probably right but he shuffled out still studying the ducks, tilting his head as he does only when looking at something first-rate.

Well, I've gone on too long, Miss McPhee. I'm sure you see my point by now. Kermit is simply the wrong man for this job. I *know* him. Essentially, he's a child; he has a child's simple faith that there is one right and honorable response to all situations. In what I often regard as a fairly sleazy world, Kermit is that oddity, a moral person. Or at least someone trying to be, which is rarity enough.

For nine long years, I've sheltered Kermit Waley. His fame is certainly deserved and since the start, I've enjoyed it with him. He was sickly as an adolescent. His early political days—handing out leaflets on windy street corners, sleeping in basements—nearly killed him. Kermit's dealer and all our friends give me credit for keeping him so productive. Now I find him embracing this disaster. He doesn't know (and must *never*) that I casually asked a congressman in my family to submit my husband's name for this job. I thought it might be fun for Kermit, somehow relaxing and good for his work. I assumed that only other professionals would apply; I didn't count on these strangers from the Midwest with their pathetic obsessions.

Please, Miss McPhee, be responsible. It's like some disease you're mailing to our farm. I don't even know if my uncle's influence had any effect; but however Kermit got martyred with this awful task, it's a mistake and it must cease.

Many other distinguished painters, equally eminent, really do need the money. They would be honored to take over, even this late. Please find someone with a little more distance on human misery, someone less emotional than my over-conscientious husband.

> I thank you,
> Lucia McCloud-Waley

Most Honorable Art Jurists:

Quilts are definitely where it's at in this big land of ours right now. I was knocked dead by the Whitney's quilt show some years back and have been a madman collector ever since. I threw over my job as an investment banker and just immersed myself in folk art. Questing for choice examples, I've made treks to Canada, Wales, and Iowa. Here, after months of loving work, is my design. You see it meshes and blends so many mellow American folk motifs: the star, eagle, flag, log cabin, etc. Alongside the wall in question, on the lot now used for parking, I would set up a huge circus tent (see Itemized Budget, enclosed). I'd fill this big top with sixty West Virginia mountain craftspersons. (These women now work for me—at decent wages—making quilts and one-of-a-kind slipcovers for my three N.Y. and two London shops.) Many of these gals have never left the mountains. Think of the human-interest-news-coverage angle. Talk about "Where have you come from, Where are you bound?"!

I'd construct a huge quilting frame (three lowest bids enclosed). In our tent, the ladies would commence stitching as only they can. Their quilt will be made from Grade A nonfading fabrics to offset weather and the ravages of aging. The finished product will be hoisted, totally covering the westerly exposure. It would, you might say, give this bleak steely government building a security blanket of the homey kind long lost and, I think we'd all agree, pretty badly needed just now. During rain or snow, we'll draw the quilt up on a massive roller like a windowshade, only enormous and more reliable. Ours will be the hugest such comforter-coverlet ever made by mankind. (The Guinness Book of Records doesn't even *list* quilts. That's how unprecedented my idea is.)

My seamstresses are a sight. Some wear sunbonnets (for real!) and their faces are eroded like you cannot believe. We're talking mega-America here. Small replicas of "The Official US Security Quilt" (like it?) will be sold as collector's items. I've established contacts for major nationwide distribution in your finer stores. How am I sounding? A big fat percentage will get plowed right back into the ailing National Fundament itself.

During this last gasp of Cold War conditions, what, I ask, could be more reassuring than a many-colored patchwork quilt, handcrafted by women so American it hurts, a warm quilt plenty big enough for one and all?

> Eager,
> Sid Green
> Offices: New York,
> London, Wheeling
> (W. Va.)

Dear Famous Artist-Judge,
Have you read "Jenny the Wren's Vienna Misadventures" yet? I sure hope so. In your opinion, what should I *do* with Jenny? She is quite eager for thousands of little readers. I've gone through so much with her. Sometimes I feel we're the same person. They won't let me read to the kids at the library here anymore. The lady said I was too prolific for my own good. But, on the street three weeks ago, the littlest Ralston child asked me what Jenny the Wren was up to *now*? She asked which kids in what country Jenny was helping these days? A good sign, Sally Ralston asking about Jenny the Wren!

I certainly don't want to overuse your precious time. So, for your enjoyment, I've enclosed only three more of the real Jenny "classics":

"Jenny the Wren, the Eskimo Twins, and the Yukon Dogsledding Disaster"

"Jenny the Wren Visits (And Learns To Like) the People's Republic of China"

"Jenny the Wren, the Santa Fe Dude Ranch, and the Morris Boys' Aunt's Missing Jewels"

How about a little Jenny the Wren "feedback"? How do *you* think her character could be enriched? Setting suggestions? I'm no prima donna and can take constructive criticism. Have you read "Jenny the Wren's Vienna Misadventures" yet?

As before,
Yours,
Mirabelle

Miss McPhee,

I sent that last letter registered mail. Your secretary signed for it. You've chosen to ignore my request and my repeated calls. Kermit answers his phone only occasionally now. He says the postman is still bringing applications, whole cartons full. My sister remembers you as captain of the lacrosse team at Smith and, frankly, she says you were "hard as nails," "a very tough cookie, indeed."

Let's look at it this way, Miss McPhee. I'm the favorite niece of Carlton McCloud, vice-chairman of the House Ways and Means Committee. If, in four days, you have not named another judge for "America, Where Have You Come From, Where Are You Bound?," I think you'll find yourself abruptly unemployed. Uncle Carl knows nothing about art but he is inordinately fond of Kermit.

I don't usually resort to this kind of string pulling. I'm averse to it on principle. But I'm fighting here for my husband's safety. There is nothing really personal, Miss McPhee, in my wanting to see your head on a platter.

Concerned,
Lucia McCloud-Waley

You,

In addition—any steeple, any kids praying at bedtime while their parents look on, any cross or cross-shaped structure, the star of David, any and all angels. Allusions to the so-called Holy Eucharist, any group of singing persons holding what might be missals or hymnbooks. Anybody wearing miters, starched collars, rabbinical getups or choirlike garments. Anything even faintly touching on what I've mentioned. If I find this stuff up on that wall come July, stand by for retribution. We all know who picked.

McNulty
L.A.

Dear Dorothy at the Fundament,

Did I tell you that our farmhouse was built in 1819? A first cousin of Herman Melville lived here. Supposedly, Melville himself cut the tin weathervane, a prickly mermaid. My wife's family gave us this place. Lucia has an inheritance. Her great-grandfather McCloud made his money through cotton mills back before unions and child labor laws. Lucia is very protective of me. She thinks I'm somewhat sickly and unstable. Maybe I am. Would you consider advancing the deadline so I won't get more? I seem to be falling behind. The stacks certainly do grow. The mailman now takes the packets straight to our chicken coop. I've taped copies of the contest rules over the kitchen sink and near our four-poster and alongside the toilet. I'm so glad it says "Not responsible for others' loss or damage." That's some relief, anyway.

You told me that my being the judge would be kept strictly secret, Dorothy. You promised. I've begun getting phone calls here. Only two of our best N.Y.

friends have this unlisted number. We've intentionally stayed somewhat aloof from the villagers (Lucia's idea and probably a good one). So it's always an event when the phone rings. Last night, I had three long-distance calls from some crazy man in Los Angeles who's sure I'm going to put up another Sistine ceiling. (If one were submitted, I'd leap at the chance.) This person growled about the pope's "nephews," a whole fleet of Vatican callboys. I said I didn't want to know and I hung up. I was afraid Lucia would phone and be worried so I put it back in the cradle and it rang right then. Some woman from Billings, Montana, reversed the charges. I've always loved that name Montana. Dakota, Montana: words so dry and beautiful. I accepted the charges. I don't know why. She was calling from a bar. I could hear country and western music in the background and sometimes war whoops like in Wild West saloons. She whispered. She told me that a wren had good feelings about me. The jukebox was still blaring when, over and over, she started whistling bird imitations into the pay phone. I hung up, then took the receiver off. It whined so I slid some socks over it, wrapped it in an Army blanket and stuffed it into a desk drawer. I'm scared, Dorothy.

The mailman arrived again this morning. I've started giving him five or ten dollars a day. This is a sleepy town and he's never worked so hard. He came in with three new boxes and said, "Tippie Wilkins is my niece." I told him, All right. I went in and found Tippie's application right on top. Her idea concerns an endangered species: whales. Tippie's just thirteen. She sent me her school photo. Tippie says there are fewer survivors each year. Extinction, I've found, is

a favorite theme among our younger contestants. I'm
keeping notes on trends in applicants' ages and ge-
ography. Our country is so vast. Regionalism will
never die, will it? My notes are around here somewhere. How much longer do I have to judge? I'll
level with you, Dorothy. My reputation as a painter
is mostly based on one rave review, one show of seven
paintings in 1969. I've been gliding on that ever since.
I teach part-time but really live on Lucia's money. I
haven't sold a large painting in four years. If this
makes you feel I'm unfit to judge a national competition, I understand.

But please keep me a secret, Dorothy. Why don't
you call me (let it ring twice then hang up and call
again)? You haven't written me since this judgment
began. I've only seen your handwriting on the check
you sent. Tell Lucia to call the same way, in our
code.

I didn't know there *were* so many Americans over
eighteen. Dorothy, send me an assistant. It's getting
lonely up here.

                                                        K.

Kermit dear,

I'm sorry our splendid phone talk was cut off just
now. I'll repeat the details for good measure. I arrive
by Greyhound at Northampton, Mass., on April 2, at
2:30 p.m., your time, Eastern time. I'm not sure how
far from Northampton your farm is, but during the
drive we can get even better acquainted. From the
tone of your sad gentle voice, I feel I know you so
well already. You've been too too kind. I wonder if
you even understand what a terrible thing isolation
is. Especially isolation in Montana.

This town made me its laughingstock when I was just eleven. You know what they say when I go by? "Look who's *loose*." They all say that. I know it's hard for an established artist such as yourself to believe. How does it happen that I, the one person for miles who loves Art, who aspires to create, should be their favorite victim? Now I'm over thirty and it still goes on. Every day another little slight or humiliation. You can hardly shop. Luckily, we'll have time to talk things over, my new friend. Thanks to your encouragement I won't ever have to come back here again. Someday, they'll all regret these years they've taunted and hurt me. Oh well, see you very soon now,

> All the love on earth, from us,
> Mirabelle *and* Jenny the Wren

Judge of It,

Still we wait for Daddy Eagles. Every day at the mailbox I don't find them yet. Miss Martin the teacher says you all have plenty of time by now to pick. If you mess up the only Eagles he sketch down on place mats I mighty upset. My boys are big as I was then. They say to say they will come looking for the one that failed to send their grandads only Eagle drawings back here. Like I said my dad he died. There will never be another Eagle drawing done at the counter while he waited for Momma to finish up her last customers. My boys get mean sometime. They all have pickups and will really come to find the missing Eagles no matter how far. I cannot control my boys when they get the idea I been treated wrong or that my dead dad gets treated bad either. I just ask you to respect a persons property and also our feelings. It is within my rights to ask back what is really mine.

Somebody dead drew those ones. There can be no new ones from someone who dead. I should not of mailed the only ones of something. I just wanted somebody outside our family to say his Eagles had something extra. Everytime that mailtruck leaves us nothing I feel that much more low and the boys they get madder.

Just please.
Rollo Krause
Phoenix Ariz.

Dorothy, Fundament,

Yesterday morning, I decided to answer the phone. I wanted Lucia to call so I put it back on the hook. I wanted you to call. Jenny the Wren reversed the charges, this time from Cleveland. I was smart and wouldn't accept. I could hear the train or bus departures being announced and, over the operator's voice, Jenny kept chirping at me. Then it was an atheist shouting something about graven images and firebombing the wall.

Around three, little Tippie got on the phone. She played me a whole phonograph record of whale voices. Tippie held the receiver near the speaker. Have you ever heard whales singing, Dorothy? Have you ever heard anything so sad? It was like an echo of an echo of a human cry. The Russians and Japanese slaughter them for face cream. They shouldn't. Tippie told me step-by-step how they do it. She started to whimper. I hung up, then yanked the phone out of the wall. I hope everyone will understand.

All afternoon I've worked on my own application. I've decided to apply. My entry would incorporate all the worthiest aspects of those who have no chance at all. What *is* our country if not pitching in to help the other person less fortunate? I went for a nice walk just now all over our land. My breath showed blue. It's chilly here now and nice. There were berries on some trees yesterday but not now. I think the cedar waxwings ate them. The moon came out early, it was silver over our weather vane. I wandered home and crawled under a quilt my grandmother made me. It's done in shades of pink and is comforting. My mother took elocution lessons as a girl. She also studied scarf dancing and poise. She learned this and every time she got the least bit drunk she'd say it with real expression as they'd taught her to:

> There's so much good in the worst of us
> And so much bad in the best of us
> That it doesn't behoove any of us
> To talk about the rest of us.

Right?
K.

Miss McPhee,

I'm sending this to your former place of employment, hoping they will forward it. I wanted you to know what I found in Massachusetts. The phone went out of order and I rushed right up there. Just two nights before, when my call finally got through, he sounded tired but otherwise quite lucid. I want you to know what you're responsible for. I walked into an abandoned house. The place was absolutely filthy. I won't bother with details but I saw that Kermit had lost control of his hygiene and faculties. All the applications were missing, every one. I'd had the good sense to bring along someone from the village, a handyman who's done work for us. Mr. Bryce went into the bedroom first and came out with a strange

expression. He said, "It should be covered up." A
cardboard suitcase blocked the doorway. I stepped
over this, and there, curled up in our bed, was a tiny
elderly woman asleep and naked. She wore only high
heels and a feathered hat. When I woke her, she
looked around so startled she began whistling for
help. She kept doing it, so shrilly, these bird imitations that were absolutely credible and absolutely
horrifying. Finally I convinced her I meant no harm.
I asked where Kermit was. I begged her to use words.
At last, hiding completely under sheets, she whispered in English, Today he's gone off to decide.

Mr. Bryce and I rushed out and wandered all over
the farm calling Kermit's name. Bryce went down by
the pond since I was too frightened to look there. I
tramped around for an hour or more, still in my city
heels, still holding my purse, screaming his name
hysterically. Then at the edge of the woods, I saw our
red wheelbarrow. A few drawings were in it, and
beyond that, uphill, in a little clearing under the evergreens, Kermit had hidden himself among the applications. He'd piled all those packets neatly into
four-foot stacks. Stacks stood like columns and, as a
roof over these, he had placed a large stretched canvas, as yet unpainted. Draped across this was a
patchwork quilt he'd inherited from a relative. I struggled up the hill in my ridiculous shoes. He seemed
pleased to see me, he beckoned me into his little
shack. I squatted on the spruce needles and crawled
in. He needed a shave but otherwise looked all right.
He looked wonderful, in fact. Very animated.

He'd torn one corner off each of the hundreds of
drawings. These lay spread before him, like a puzzle.
He kept trying to fit all these colored shards together.
I sat there, crouched beside him, watching. I could

hear Bryce's voice echoing across the pond, calling Mr. Waley, Mr. Waley. Kermit told me quietly, "This is our winner, Lucia. What do you think?" He went on contentedly arranging the torn pieces. He was humming. I put my hand on his shoulder, so soothed to see him alive. The strangeness of this hut we were in, of his activity, didn't strike me till much later.

Bryce took the woman to a nearby bus station. I never found out who she was or how she came to be in our bed. I'm not at all sorry that you've lost your job, Miss McPhee. We sold the farm. We had to. For now, we're living at my uncle's retreat on Bimini. We sit in the sun a lot. Kermit is beginning to talk again. He hasn't gone near a paintbrush in over ten weeks. I've had to hide all the art books in the house, even books on decorating. When we venture out to dinner, I do detours to avoid even the hotel's postcard racks. Anything might remind him. Anything could set him off. He's beginning to make jokes again, though he still looks so fatigued. Just after it happened, he kept repeating, "We are one big unhappy family, and poor, aren't we, Lucia?" To appease him, I said, "I suppose we are, dear." He has been stunted as an artist and a man by what this competition has shown him, Miss McPhee. I hope you are satisfied. Since all of this occurred, I have felt a great need to write down these details for you.

Lucia McCloud-Waley

The National Fundament of the Arts regrets announcing cancellation of its mural design competition. Appropriations formerly earmarked for the Humanities have, in this time of international tensions, been deemed more urgently needed in areas crucial to our national defense.

The newly appointed Fundament director is Randolph Gleason, till recently Senior Vice-President of Boeing Aircraft. Gleason stated that, should rerouted funds ever be returned to the Fundament, future contests will probably offer themes far more specific, far less open-ended and inflammatory than that of this year's competition.

When asked if art jurists revoked the mural competition due to a lack of national interest, the new director commented that, on the contrary, if anything there had been an excess of response. The entries, Gleason explained, tended to be "highly individualistic and single-issue oriented." Questioned further, Gleason would not elaborate beyond his prepared text. He then stood and pronounced the mural competition dismantled and—in turn—official withdrawal of its all-too-provocative theme question, "America, Where Have You Come From, Where Are You Bound?"

Applications cannot be returned.

1976

Adult Art

*For George Hackney Eatman
and Hiram Johnson Cuthrell, Jr.*

I'VE GOT AN EXTRA TENDERNESS. IT'S NOT LEGAL.

I see a twelve-year-old boy steal a white Mercedes off the street. I'm sitting at my official desk—Superintendent of Schools—it's noon on a weekday and I watch this kid wiggle a coat hanger through one front window. Then he slips into the sedan, straight-wires its ignition, squalls off. Afterward, I can't help wondering why I didn't phone the police. Or shout for our truant officer just down the hall.

Next, a fifty-nine Dodge, black, mint condition, tries to parallel park in the Mercedes' spot (I'm not getting too much paperwork done today). The driver is one of the worst drivers I've ever seen under the age of eighty. Three pedestrians take turns waving him in, guiding him back out. I step to my window and hear one person yell, "No, left, sharp *left*. Clown." Disgusted, a last helper leaves.

When the driver stands and stretches, he hasn't really parked his car, just stopped it. I've noticed him around town. About twenty-five, he's handsome, but in the most awkward possible way. His clothes match the old

129

Dodge. His belt's pulled up too high. White socks are
a mistake. I watch him comb his hair, getting present-
able for downtown. He whips out a handkerchief and
stoops to buff his shoes. Many coins and pens spill from
a shirt pocket.

While he gathers these, a second boy (maybe a
brother of the Mercedes thief?) rushes to the Dodge's
front, starts gouging something serious across its hood.
I knock on my second-story window—nobody hears.
The owner rises from shoe-polishing, sees what's happening, shouts. The vandal bolts. But instead of chasing
him, the driver touches bad scratches, he stands—
patting them. I notice that the guy is talking to himself.
He wets one index fingertip, tries rubbing away
scrawled letters. Sunlight catches spit. From my second-
floor view, I can read the word. It's an obscenity.

I turn away, lean back against a half-hot radiator. I
admire the portrait of my wife, my twin sons in Little
League uniforms. On a far wall, the art reproductions
I change every month or so. (I was an art history major,
believe it or not.) I want to rush downstairs, comfort
the owner of the car, say, maybe, "Darn kids, nowadays." I don't dare.

They could arrest me for everything I like about myself.

At five sharp, gathering up valise and papers, I look
like a regular citizen. Time to leave the office. Who
should pass? The owner of the hurt Dodge. His being
in the Municipal Building shocked me, as if I'd watched
him on TV earlier. In my doorway, I hesitated. He
didn't notice me. He tripped over a new two-inch ledge
in the middle of the hall. Recovering, he looked around,
hoping nobody had seen. Then, content he was alone,
clutching a loaded shirt pocket, the guy bent, touched
the spot where the ledge had been. There was no ledge.

Under long fingers, just smoothness, linoleum. He rose. I stood close enough to see, in his pocket, a plastic caddy you keep pens in. It was white, a gift from WOO-TEN'S SMALL ENGINES, NEW AND LIKE-NEW. Four old fountain pens were lined there, name-brand articles. Puzzled at why he'd stumbled, the boy now scratched the back of his head, made a face. "Gee, *that's* funny!" An antiquated cartoon drawing would have shown a decent cheerful hick doing and saying exactly that. I was charmed.

I've got this added tenderness. I never talk about it. It only sneaks up on me every two or three years. It sounds strange but feels so natural. I know it'll get me into big trouble. I feel it for a certain kind of other man, see. For any guy who's even clumsier than me, than "I."

You have a different kind of tenderness for everybody you know. There's one sort for grandparents, say. But if you waltz into a singles' bar and use that type of affection, you'll be considered pretty strange. When my sons hit pop flies, I get a strong wash of feeling—and yet, if I turned the same sweetness on my Board of Education, I'd soon find myself both fired and committed.

Then he saw me.

He smiled in a shy cramped way. Caught, he pointed to the spot that'd given him recent trouble, he said of himself, "Tripped." You know what I said? When I noticed—right then, this late—how kind-looking he was, I said, "Happens all the time. Me too." I pointed to my chest, another dated funnypaper gesture. "No reason." I shrugged. "You just *do*, you know. Most people, I guess."

Well, he liked that. He smiled. It gave me time to check out his starched shirt (white, buttoned to the collar, no tie). I studied his old-timey overly wide belt, its thunderbird-design brass buckle. He wore black pants, plain as a waiter's, brown wingtips with a serious shine. He took in my business suit, my early signs of graying temples. Then he decided, guileless, that he needed some quick maintenance. As I watched, he flashed out a green comb and restyled his hair, three backward swipes, one per side, one on top. Done. The dark waves seemed either damp or oiled, suspended from a part that looked incredibly white, as if my secretary had just painted it there with her typing correction fluid.

This boy had shipshape features—a Navy recruiting poster, forty years past due. Some grandmother's favorite. Comb replaced, grinning, he lingered, pleased I'd acted nice about his ungainly little hop. "What say to a drink?" I asked. He smiled, nodded, followed me out. —How simple, at times, life can be.

I'm remembering: During football practice in junior high gym-class, I heard a kid's arm break. He was this big blond guy, nice but out of it. He whimpered toward the bleachers and perched there, grinning, sweating. Our coach, twenty-one years old, heard the fracture too. He looked around: somebody should walk the hurt boy to our principal's office. Coach spied me, frowning, concerned. Coach decided that the game could do without me. I'd treat Angier right. (Angier was the kid— holding his arm, shivering.)

"Help him." Coach touched my shoulder. "Let him lean against you."

Angier nearly fainted halfway back to school. "Whoo . . ." He had to slump down onto someone's lawn, still grinning apologies. "It's okay," I said.

"Take your time." I finally got him there. The principal's secretary complained—Coach should've brought Angier in himself. "These *young* teachers." She shook her head, phoning the rescue squad. It all seemed routine for her. I led Angier to a dark waiting room stacked with textbooks and charts about the human body. He sat. I stood before him holding his good hand. "You'll be fine. You'll see." His hair was slicked back, as after a swim. He was always slow in class—his father sold fancy blenders in supermarkets. Angier dressed neatly. Today he looked so white his every eyelash stood out separate. We could hear the siren. Glad, he squeezed my hand. Then Angier swooned back against the bench, panting, he said something hoarse. "What?" I leaned closer. "Thank you," he grinned, moaning. Next he craned up, kissed me square, wet, on the mouth. Then Angier fainted, fell sideways.

Five days later, he was back at school sporting a cast that everybody popular got to sign. He nodded my way. He never asked me to scribble my name on his plaster. He seemed to have forgotten what happened. I remember.

As we left the office building, the Dodge owner explained he'd been delivering insurance papers that needed signing—flood coverage on his mother's country property. "You can never be too safe. That's Mother's motto." I asked if they lived in town; I was only trying to get him talking, relaxed. If I knew his family, I might have to change my plans.

"Mom died," he said, looking down. "A year come March. She left me everything. Sure burned my sisters up, I can tell you. But they're both in Florida. Where were *they* when she was so sick? She appreciated it. She said she'd remember me. And Mom did, too."

Then he got quiet, maybe regretting how much he'd told.

We walked two blocks. Some people spoke to me, they gave my companion a mild look as if thinking, What does Dave want with *him*?

He chose the bar. It was called The Arms, but whatever word had been arched between the "The" and the "Arms"—six Old English golden letters—had been stolen; you could see where glue had held them to the bricks. He introduced himself by his first name: Barker. Palms flat on the bar, he ordered beers without asking. Then he turned to me, embarrassed. "Mind reader," I assured him, smiling and—for a second—cupped my hand over the bristled back of his, but quick. He didn't seem to notice or much mind.

My chair faced the street. His aimed my way, toward the bar's murky back. Bathrooms were marked kings and queens. Some boy played a noisy video game that sounded like a jungle bird in electronic trouble.

Barker's head and shoulders were framed by a window. June baked each surface on the main street. Everything out there (passersby included) looked planned, shiny and kind of ceramic. I couldn't see Barker's face that clearly. Sun turned his ears a healthy wax red. Sun enjoyed his cheekbones, found highlights waiting in the wavy old-fashioned hair I decided he must oil. Barker himself wasn't so beautiful—a knotty wiry kid—only his pale face was. It seemed an inheritance he hadn't noticed yet.

Barker sitting still was a Barker almost suave. He wasn't spilling anything (our beer hadn't been brought yet). The kid's face looked, back-lit, negotiable as gems. Everything he said to me was heartfelt. Talking about his mom put him in a memory-lane kind of mood.

"Yeah," he said. "When *I* was a kid . . . ." and he told me about a ditch that he and his sisters would wade in, building dams and making camps. Playing doctor. Then the city landfill chose the site. No more ditch. Watching it bulldozed, the kids had cried, holding onto one another.

Our barman brought us a huge pitcher. I just sipped; Barker knocked four mugs back fast. Foam made half a white mustache over his sweet slack mouth; I didn't mention it. He said he was twenty-nine but still felt about twelve, except for winters. He said after his mother's death, he'd joined the Air Force but got booted out.

"What for?"

"Lack of dignity." He downed a fifth mug.

"You mean . . . 'lack of discipline'?"

He nodded. "What'd I say?"—I told him.

" 'Dignity,' 'discipline,' " he shrugged to show they meant the same thing. The sadder he seemed the better I liked it, the nicer Barker looked.

Women passing on the street (he couldn't see them) wore sundresses. How pretty their pastel straps, the freckled shoulders; some walked beside their teenaged sons; they looked good too. I saw folks I knew. Nobody'd think to check for me in here.

Only human, under the table, my knee touched Barker's, lingered a second, shifted. He didn't flinch. He hadn't asked about my job or home life. I got the subject around to things erotic. With a guy as forthright as Barker, you didn't need posthypnotic suggestion to manage it. He'd told me where he lived. I asked wasn't that out by Adult Art Film and Book. "You go in there much?"

He gave me a mock-innocent look, touched a finger-tip to his sternum, mouthed Who, me? Then he scanned around to make sure nobody'd hear. "I guess it's me that keeps old Adult Art open. Don't tell, but I can't help it, I just love that stuff.—You too?"

I nodded.

"What kind?"

I appeared bashful, one knuckle rerouting sweat beads on my beer mug. "I like all types, I guess. You know, boy/girl, girl/girl, boy/boy, girl/dog, dog/dog." Barker laughed, shaking his fine head side to side. "Dog/dog," he repeated. "That's a good one. *Dog/dog!*"

He was not the most brilliantly intelligent person I'd ever met. I loved him for it.

We went in my car. I didn't care to chance his driving. Halfway to Adult Art, sirens and red lights swarmed behind my station wagon. This is it, I thought. Then the white Mercedes (already mud-splattered, a fender dented, doing a hundred and ten in a thirty-five zone) screeched past. Both city patrol cars gave chase, having an excellent time.

We parked around behind; there were twelve or fourteen vehicles jammed back of Adult Art's single dumpster; seven phone-repair trucks had lined up like a fleet. Adult's front asphalt lot, plainly visible from US 301 Business, provided room for forty cars but sat empty. This is a small town, Falls. Everybody sees everything, almost. So, when you *do* get away with something, you know it; it just means more. Some people will tell you Sin is old hat. Not for me. If, once it starts, it's not going to be naughty, then it's not worth wasting a whole afternoon to set up. Sin is bad. Sex is good. Sex is too good not to have a whole lot of bad in it. I say, Let's keep it a little smutty, you know?

Barker called the clerk by name. Barker charged two

films—slightly discounted because they'd been used in the booths—those and about thirty bucks in magazines. No money changed hands; he had an account. The section marked LITERATURE milled with phone linemen wearing their elaborate suspension belts. One man, his pelvis ajangle with wrenches and hooks, held up a picture book, called to friends, "Catch *her*, guys. She has got to be your foxiest fox so far." Under his heavy silver gear, I couldn't but notice on this hearty husband and father, jammed up against workpants, the same old famous worldwide pet and problem poking.

I drove Barker to his place; he invited me in for a viewing. I'd hoped he would. "World premiere," he smiled, eyes alive as they hadn't been before. "First show on Lake Drive anyways."

The neighborhood, like Barker's looks, had been the rage forty years ago. I figured he must rent rooms in this big mullioned place, but he owned it. The foyer clock showed I might not make it home in time for supper. Lately I'd overused the excuse of working late; even as Superintendent of Schools there're limits on how much extra time you can devote to your job.

I didn't want to miff a terrific wife.

I figured I'd have a good hour and a half; a lot can happen in an hour and a half. We were now safe inside a private place.

The house had been furnished expensively but some years back. Mission stuff. The Oriental rugs were coated with dust or fur; thick hair hid half their patterns. By accident, I kicked a chewed rubber mouse. The cat toy jingled under a couch, scaring me.

In Barker's kitchen, a crockpot bubbled. Juice hissed out under a Pyrex lid that didn't quite fit. The room smelled of decent beef stew. His counter was layered with fast-food takeout cartons. From among this litter, in a clay pot, one beautiful amaryllis lily—orange, its mouth wider than the throat of a trombone, startled me. It reminded you of something from science fiction, straining like one serious muscle toward daylight.

In the dark adjacent room, Barker kept humming, knocking things over. I heard the clank of movie reels. "Didn't expect company, Dave," he called. "Just clear off a chair and make yourself at home. Momma was a cleaner-upper. Me . . . less. I don't *see* the junk till I get somebody to . . . till somebody drops over, you know?"

I grunted agreement, strolled into his pantry. Here were cans so old you could sell them for the labels. Here was a 1950s tin of vichyssoise I wouldn't have eaten at gunpoint. I slipped along the hall, wandered upstairs. An archive of *National Geographic*s rose in yellow columns to the ceiling. "Dave?" he was hollering. "Just settle in or whatever. It'll only take a sec. See, they cut the leaders off both our movies. I'll just do a little splice. — I'm fast, though."

"Great."

On the far wall of one large room (windows smothered by outside ivy) a calendar from 1959, compliments of a now-defunct savings and loan. Nearby, two Kotex cartons filled with excelsior and stuffed, I saw on closer inspection, with valuable brown and white Wedgwood place settings for forty maybe. He really should sell them—I was already mothering Barker. I'd tell him which local dealer would give top dollar.

In one corner, a hooked rug showed a Scottie terrier chasing one red ball downhill. I stepped on it, three hundred moths sputtered up, I backed off, arms flailing before me. Leaning in the doorway, waiting to be called downstairs for movietime, still wearing my business clothes, I suddenly felt a bit uneasy, worried by a famous thought: What are you *doing* here, Dave?

Well, Barker brought me home with him, is what. And, as far back as my memory made it, I'd only wanted just such guys to ask me over. Only they held my interest, my full sympathy.

The kid with the terrible slouch but (for me) an excellent smile, the kid who kept pencils in a plastic see-through satchel that clamped into his looseleaf notebook. The boy whose Mom—even when the guy'd turned fourteen—*made* him use his second-grade Roy Rogers/Dale Evans lunchbox showing them astride their horses, Trigger and Buttermilk. He was the kid other kids didn't bother mocking because—through twelve years of schooling side by side—they'd never noticed him.

Of course I could tell, there were other boys, like me, studying the other boys. But they all looked toward the pink and blond Stephens and Andrews: big-jawed athletic office holders, guys with shoulders like baby couches, kids whose legs looked turned on lathes, solid newels—calves that summer sports stained mahogany brown, hair coiling over them, bleached by overly chlorinated pools and an admiring sun: yellow-white-gold. But while others' eyes stayed locked on them, I was off admiring finer qualities of some clubfooted Wendell, a kindly bespectacled Theodore. I longed to stoop and tie their dragging shoestrings, ones unfastened so long that the plastic tips had worn to frayed cotton tufts. Math geniuses who forgot to zip up: I wanted to give them dating hints. I'd help them find the right barber. I dreamed of assisting their undressing—me, bathing them with stern brotherly care, me, putting them to bed (poor guys hadn't yet guessed that my interest went past buddyhood). While they slept (I didn't want to cost them any shut-eye), I'd just reach under their covers (always blue) and find that though the world considered these fellows minor minor, they oftentimes proved more major than the muscled boys who frolicked, unashamed, well-known, pink-and-white in gym showers.

What was I *do*ing here? Well, my major was art history. I was busy being a collector, is what. And not just someone who can spot (in a museum with a guide to lead him) any old famous masterpiece. No, I was a detective off in the odd corner of a side street thrift shop. I was uncovering (on sale for the price of the frame!) a little etching by Wyndham Lewis—futuristic dwarves, or a golden cow by Cuyp, one of Vuillard's shuttered parlors painted on a shirt cardboard.

Maybe this very collector's zeal had drawn me to Carol, had led me to fatherhood, to the underrated joys of community. See, I wanted everything—even to be legit. Nothing was so obvious or subtle that I wouldn't try it once. I prided myself on knowing what I liked, and going shamelessly after it. Everybody notices grace. But appreciating perfect clumsiness, that requires the real skill.

"Won't be long now!" I heard Barker call.

"All *right*," I hollered, exactly as my sons would.

I eased into a messy office upstairs and, among framed documents and pictures, recognized Barker's grandfather. He looked just like Barker but fattened up and given lessons. During the Fifties, the granddad served as mayor of our nearby capital city. Back then, such collar-ad looks were still admired, voted into office.

A framed news photo showed the mayor, hair oiled, presenting horse-topped trophies to young girls in jodhpurs. They blinked up at him, four fans, giggling. Over the wide loud tie, his grin showed an actor's worked-at innocence. He'd been a decent mayor—fair to all, paving streets in the black district, making parks of vacant lots. Good till he got nabbed with his hand in the till. Like Barker's, this was a face almost too pure to trust. When you observed the eyes of young Barker downstairs—it was like looking at a *National Geographic* close-up of some exotic Asian deer—you could admire the image forever, it wouldn't notice or resist your admiration. It had the static beauty of an angel. Designed. That unaffected and willing to serve. His character was like an angel's own—the perfect go-fer.

I heard Barker humming Broadway ballads, knocking around ice trays. I opened every door on this hall. Why not? The worse the housekeeping got, the better I liked it. The tenderer I felt about the guy downstairs. One room had seven floor lamps in it, two standing, five resting on their sides, one plugged in. Shades were snare-drum shaped, the delicate linings frayed and split like fabric from old negligées.

I closed all doors. I heard him mixing drinks. I felt that buzz and ringing you learn to recognize as the sweet warning sign of a sure thing. Still, I have been wrong.

I checked my watch. "Ready," he called, "when you are." I passed the bathroom. I bet Barker hadn't done a load of laundry since last March or April. A thigh-high pile made a moat around the tub. I lifted some boxer shorts. (Boxers show low self-esteem, bodywise; my kind of guy always wears them and assumes that every other man on earth wears boxers, too.) These particular shorts were pin-striped and had little red New York Yankee logos rashed everywhere. They surely needed some serious bleaching.

* * *

There he stood, grinning. He'd been busy stirring instant iced tea, two tall glasses with maps of Ohio stenciled on them. I didn't ask, Why Ohio? Barker seemed pleased, quicker moving, the host. He'd rolled up his sleeves, the skin as fine as sanded ashwood. The icebox freezer was a white glacier dangling roots like a molar's. From one tiny hole in it, Barker fished a gin bottle; he held the opened pint to one tea glass and smiled. "Suit you?"

"Gin and iced tea? Sure." Seducers/seducees must remain flexible.

"Say when, pal." I said so. Barker appeared full of antsy mischief.

For him, I saw, this was still his mother's house. With her dead, he could do as he liked; having an illicit guest here pleased him. Barker cultivated the place's warehouse look. He let cat hair coat his mom's prized rugs; it felt daring to leave the stag-movie projector and screen set up in the den full-time, just to shock his Florida sisters.

I couldn't help myself. "Hey, buddy, where *is* this cat?" I nodded toward the hallway's gray fluff balls.

"Hunh? Oh. There's six. Two mother ones and four kid ones. All super-shy but each one's really different. Good company."

He carried our tea glasses on a deco chrome tray; the film-viewing room was just ten feet from the kitchen. Dark in here. Ivy vines eclipsed the sunset; leaf green made our couch feel underwater. I slumped deep into its dated scalloped cushions.

Sipping, we leaned back. It seemed that we were waiting for a signal: Start. I didn't want to watch a movie. But, also, I did. I longed to hear this nice fellow tell me something, a story, anything, but I worried: talking could spoil whatever else might happen. I only half knew what I hoped for. I felt scared Barker might not understand my particular kind of tenderness. Still, I was readier and readier to find out, to risk making a total fool of myself. Everything worthwhile requires that, right?

I needed to say something next.

"So," is what I said. "Tell me. So, tell me something . . . about yourself. Something I should know, Barker." And I added that, Oh, I really appreciated his hospitality. It was nothing, he shrugged then pressed back. He made a throaty sound like a story starting. "Well. Something plain, Dave? Or something . . . kind of spicy?"

"Both," I said. Education does pay off. I know to at least ask for everything.

"Okay." His voice dipped half an octave. The idea of telling had relaxed Barker. I could see it. Listening to him relax relaxed me.

—"See, they sent my granddad to jail. *For* something. I won't say what. He did do it, still, we couldn't picture prison—for him. My mom and sisters were so ashamed that, at first, they wouldn't drive out to see him. I wanted to. Nobody'd take me. I called up Prison to ask about visiting hours. I made myself sound real deep, like a man, so they'd tell me. I was eleven. So when the prison guy gave me the times, he goes, 'Well, thank you for calling, ma'am.' I had to laugh.

They'd put him in that state pen out on the highway, the work farm. It's halfway to Tarboro and I rode my bike clear out there. It was busy, a Saturday. I had to keep to the edge of the Interstate. Teenagers in two convertibles threw beer cans at me. Finally when I got to the prison, men said I couldn't come in, being a minor and all. Maybe they smelled the beer those hoods'd chucked at my back.

I wondered what my granddad would do in the same spot (he'd been pretty well known around here), and so I started mentioning my rights, *loud*. The men said 'okay okay' and told me to pipe down. They let me in. He sat behind heavy-gauge chicken wire. He looked good, about the same. All the uniforms were gray but his was pressed and perfect on him—like he'd got to pick the color of everybody else's outfit. You couldn't even hold hands with him. Was like going to the zoo except it was your granddaddy. Right off, he thanks me for coming and he tells me where the key is hid. Key to a shack he owned at the back side of the fairgrounds. You know, out by the pine trees where kids go park at night and do you-know-what?

He owned this cottage, but, seeing as how he couldn't use it—for six to ten—he wanted me to hang out there. Granddad said I should use it whenever I needed to hide or slack off or anything. He said I could keep pets or have a club, whatever I liked.

He said there was one couch in it, plus a butane stove but no electric lights. The key stayed under three bricks in the weeds. He said, 'A boy needs a place to go.' I said, 'Thanks,' —Then he asked about Mom and the others. I lied: how they were busy baking stuff to bring him, how they'd be out soon, a carful of pies. He made a face and asked which of my sisters had driven me here.

I said, 'Biked it.' Well, he stared at me. 'Not nine miles and on a Saturday. No. I've earned this, but you shouldn't have to.' He started crying then. It was hard, with the wire between us. Then, you might not believe this, Dave, but a black guard comes over and says, 'No crying.' I didn't know they could do that—boss you like that—but in jail I guess they can do anything they please. Thing is, Granddad stopped. He told me, 'I'll make this up to you, Barker. Some of them say you're not exactly college material, Bark, but we know better. You're the best damn one. But, listen, hey, you walk that bike home, you hear me? Concentrate on what I'm saying. It'll be dark by the time you get back to town but it's worth it. Walk, hear me?' I said I would. I left and went outside. My bike was missing. I figured that some convict's kid had taken it. A poor kid deserved it more than me. Mom would buy me another one. I walked.''

Barker sat still for a minute and a half. "What else?" I asked. "You sure?" He turned my way. I nodded. He took a breath.

"Well, I hung out in my new cabin a lot. It was just two blocks from the busiest service station in town but it seemed way off by itself. Nobody used the fairgrounds except during October and the County Fair. You could smell pine straw. At night, cars parked for three and four hours. Up one pine tree, a bra was tied—real old and gray now—a joke to everybody but maybe the girl that'd lost it. Out there, pine straw was all litterbugged with used rubbers. I thought they were some kind of white snail or clam or something. I knew they were yucky, I just didn't know *how* they were yucky.

I'd go into my house and I'd feel grown. I bought me some birds at the old mall with my own money. Two finches. I'd always wanted some Oriental type of birds. I got our dead parakeet's cage, a white one, and I put them in there. They couldn't sing, they just looked good. One was red and the other one was yellow, or one was yellow and one was red, I forget. I bought these seed balls and one pink plastic bird type of toy they could peck at. After school, I'd go sit on my man-sized sofa, with my birdcage nearby, finches all nervous, hopping, constant, me reading my comics—I'd never felt so good, Dave. I knew why my granddad liked it there—no phones, nobody asking him for favors. He'd take long naps on the couch. He'd make himself a cup of tea. He probably paced around the three empty rooms—not empty really: full of cobwebs and these coils of wire.

I called my finches Huey and Dewey. I loved my Donald Duck comics. I kept all my funny-books in alphabetical order in the closet across from my brown sofa. Well, I had everything I needed, a couch, comics, cups of hot tea. I hated tea but I made about five cups a day because Granddad had bought so many bags in advance and I did like holding a hot mug while I read. So one day I'm sitting there curled up with a new comic—comics are never as good the second time, you know everything that's next—so I'm sitting there happy and I hear my back door slam wide open. Grownups.

Pronto, I duck into my comics closet, yank the door shut except for just one crack. First I hoped it'd be Granddad and his bust-out gang from the state pen. I didn't believe it, just hoped, you know.

In walks this young service-station guy from our busy Sunoco place, corner of Sycamore and Bolton. I heard him say, 'Oh yeah, I use this place sometimes. Owner's away a while.' The mechanic wore a khaki uniform that zipped up its front. 'Look, birds,' a woman's voice. He stared around. 'I guess somebody else is onto Robby's hideaway. Don't sweat it.' He heaved right down onto my couch, onto my new comic, his legs apart. He stared—mean-looking—at somebody else in the room with us. Robby had a reputation. He was about twenty-two, twice my age then—he seemed pretty old. Girls from my class used to hang around the Coke machine at Sunoco just so they could watch him, arm-deep up under motors. He'd scratch himself a lot. He had a *real* reputation. Robby was a redhead, almost a blond. His cloth outfit had so much oil soaked in, it looked to be leather. All day he'd been in sunshine or up underneath leaky cars and his big round arms were brown and greasy like . . . cooked food. Well, he kicked off his left loafer. It hit my door and about gave me a heart attack. It did. Then—he was flashing somebody a double-dare kind of look. Robby yanked down his suit's big zipper maybe four inches, showing more tanned chest. The zipper made a chewing sound.

I sat on the floor in the dark. My head tipped back against a hundred comics. I was gulping, all eyes, arms wrapped around my knees like going off the high-dive in a cannonball.

When the woman sat beside him, I couldn't believe this. You could of knocked me over with one of Huey or Dewey's feathers. See, she was my best friend's momma. I decided, No, must be her identical twin sister (a bad one) visiting from out of town. This lady led Methodist Youth Choir. Don't laugh but she'd been my Cub Scout den mother. She was about ten years older than Robby, plump and prettyish but real real scared-looking.

He says, 'So, you kind of interested, hunh? You sure been giving old Rob some right serious looks for about a year now, ain't it? I was wondering how many lube jobs one Buick could take, lady.'

She studies her handbag, says, 'Don't call me Lady. My name's Anne. Anne with an E.' She added this like to make fun of herself for being here. I wanted to help her. She kept extra still, knees together, holding onto her purse for dear life, not daring to look around. I heard my birds fluttering, worried. I thought: If Robby opens this door, I am dead.

'Anne with a E, huh? An-nie? Like Li'l Orphan. Well, Sandy's here, Annie. Sandy's been wanting to get you off by yourself. You ready for your big red dog Sandy?'

'I didn't think you'd talk like that,' she said.

I wanted to bust out of my comics closet and save her. One time on a Cub Scout field trip to New York City, the other boys laughed because I thought the Empire State Building was called something else. I said I couldn't wait to see the Entire State Building. Well, they sure ragged me. I tried to make them see how it *was* big and all. I tried to make them see the logic. She said she understood how I'd got that. She said it was right 'original.' We took the elevator. I tried to make up for it by eating nine hot dogs on a dare. Then I looked off the edge. That didn't help. I got super-sick, Dave. The other mothers said I'd brought it on myself. But she was so nice, she said that being sick was nobody's fault. Mrs. . . . the lady, she wet her blue hankie at a water fountain and held it to my head and told me not to look. She got me a postcard so, when I got down to the ground, I could study what I'd almost seen. Now, with her in trouble in my own shack, I felt like I should rescue her. She was saying, 'I don't know what I expected you to talk like, Robby. But not like this, not cheap, please.'

Then he grinned, he howled like a dog. She laughed anyway. Huey and Dewey went wild in their cage. Robby held both his hands limp in front of him and panted like a regular hound. Then he asked her to help him with his zipper. She wouldn't. Well then, Robby got mad, said, 'It's my lunch hour. You ain't a customer *here*, lady. It's your husband's silver-gray Electra parked out back. You brought me here. —You've got yourself into this. You been giving me the look for about a year. I been a gentleman so far. Nobody's forcing you. It ain't a accident you're here with me. —But, hey, you can leave. Get out. Go on.'

She sighed but stayed put, sitting there like in a waiting room. Not looking, kneecaps locked together, handbag propped on her knees. Her fingers clutched that bag like her whole life was in it. 'Give me that.' He snatched the purse, and swatting her hands away, opened it. He prodded around, pulled out a tube of lipstick, said, 'Annie, sit still.' She did. She seemed as upset as she was interested. I told myself, She *could* leave. I stayed in the dark. So much was happening in a half-inch stripe of sunshine. The lady didn't move. Robby put red on her mouth—past her mouth, too much of it. She said, 'Please, Robby.' ' ''Sandy,'' ' he told her. 'You Annie, me Sandy Dog. Annie Girl, Sandy Boy. Sandy show Annie.' He made low growling sounds. 'Please,' she tried but her mouth was stretched from how he kept painting it. 'I'm not sure,' the lady said. 'I wanted to know you better, yes. But now I don't feel . . . sure.' 'You will, Annie Mae. Open your Little Orphan shirt.' She didn't understand him. ' ''Blouse'' then, fancy pants, open your ''Blouse,'' lady.' She did it but so slow. 'Well,' she said. 'I don't know about you, Robby. I really don't.' But she took her shirt off anyhow.

My den mother was shivering in a bra, arms crossed over her. First his black hands pushed each arm down, studying her. Then Robby pulled at his zipper so his whole chest showed. He put the lipstick in her hand and showed her how to draw circles on the tops of his—you know, on his nipples. Then he took the tube and made X's over the dots she'd drawn. They both looked down at his chest. I didn't understand. It seemed like a kind of target practice. Next he snapped her bra up over her collarbones and he lipsticked hers. Next he threw the tube across the room against my door—but, since his shoe hit, this didn't surprise me so much. Robby howled like a real dog. My poor finches were just chirping and flying against their cage, excited by animal noises. She was shaking her head. 'You'd think a person such as myself . . . I'm having serious second thoughts here, Robert, really . . . I'm just not too convinced . . . that . . . that we . . .'

Then Robby got up and stood in front of her, back to me. His hairdo was long on top, the way boys wore theirs then. He lashed it side to side, kept his hands, knuckles down, on his hips. Mrs. . . . the lady must have been helping him with the zipper. I heard it slide. I only guessed what they were starting to do. I'd been told about all this. But, too, I'd been told, say about the Eiffel Tower (we called it the Eye-ful). I no more expected to have this happening on my brown couch than I thought the Eye-ful would come in and then the Entire State Building would come in and they'd hop onto one another and start . . . rubbing . . . girders, or something.

I wondered how Bobby had forced the lady to. I felt I should holler, 'Methodist Youth Choir!' I'd remind her who she really was around town. But I knew it'd be way worse for her—getting caught. I had never given this adult stuff much thought before. I sure did now. Since, I haven't thought about too much else for long. Robby made worse doggy yips. He was a genius at acting like a dog. I watched him get down on all fours in front of the lady—he snouted clear up under her skirt, his whole noggin under cloth. Robby made rooting and barking noises—pig, then dog, then dog and pig mixed. It was funny but too scary to laugh at.

He asked her to call him Big Sandy. She did. 'Big Sandy,' she said. Robby explained he had something to tell his Orphan gal but only in dog talk. 'What?' she asked. He said it, part-talking part-gargling, his mouth all up under her white legs. She hooked one thigh over his shoulder. One of her shoes fell off. The other—when her toes curled up, then let loose—would snap, snap, snap.

I watched her eyes roll back then focus. She seemed to squint clear into my hiding place. She acted drowsy then completely scared awake—like at a horror movie in the worst part—then she'd doze off, then go dead, perk up overly alive, then half dead, then eyes all out like being electrocuted. It was something. She was leader of the whole Methodist Youth Choir. Her voice got bossy and husky, a leader's voice. She went, 'This is wrong, Robby. You're so low, Bobert. You are a sick dog, we'll get in deep trouble, Momma's Sandy. Hungry Sandy, thirsty Sandy. Oh—not that, not there. Oh Jesus Sandy God. You won't tell. How *can* we. I've never. What are we *do*ing in this shack? Whose shack? We're just too . . . It's not me here. I'm not *like* this.'

He tore off her panties and threw them at the birdcage. (Later I found silky britches on top of the cage, Huey and Dewey going ga-ga, thinking it was a pink cloud from heaven.) I watched grown-ups do everything fast then easy, back to front, speeding up. They slowed down and seemed to be feeling sorry, but I figured this was just to make it all last longer. I never heard such human noises. Not out of people free from jail or the state nuthouse. I mean, I'd heard boys make car sounds, 'Uh-dunn. Uh-dunn.' But this was like Noah's ark or every zoo and out of two white people's mouths. Both mouths were lipsticked ear to ear. They didn't look nasty but pink as babies. It was wrestling. They never got all the way undressed—I saw things hooking them. Was like watching grown-ups playing, making stuff up the way kids'll say, 'You be this and I'll be that.' They seemed friskier and younger, nicer. I didn't know how to join in. If I'd opened my door and smiled, they would have perished and *then* broke my neck. I didn't join in but I sure was dying to.

By the end, her pale Sunday suit had black grease handprints on the bottom and up around her neck and shoulders. Wet places stained both people where babies get stained. They'd turned halfway back into babies. They fell against each other, huffing like they'd forgot how grown-ups sit up straight. I mashed one hand over my mouth to keep from crying or panting, laughing out loud. The more they acted like slobbery babies, the older I felt, watching.

First she sobbed. He laughed, and then she laughed at how she'd cried. She said, 'What's come over me, Sandy?'

'Sandy has.' He stroked her neck. 'And Annie's all over Sandy dog.' He showed her. He blew across her forehead, cooling her off.

She made him promise not to tell. He said he wouldn't snitch if she'd meet him and his best buddy someplace else. 'Oh no. No way.' She pulled on her blouse and buttoned it. 'That wasn't part of our agreement, Robert.'

' "Agreement"?' I like that. My lawyers didn't exactly talk to your lawyers about no agreement. Show me your contract, Annie with a E.' then he dives off the couch and is up under her skirt again. You could see that he liked it even better than the service station. She laughed, she pressed cloth down over his whole working head. Her legs went straight. She could hear him snuffling down up under there. Then Robby hollered, he yodeled right up into Mrs. . . . up into the lady.

They sort of made up.

After adults finally limped from sight and even after car doors slammed, I waited—sure they'd come back. I

finally sneaked over and picked the pants off my birds'
roof. What a mess my couch was! I sat right down on
such wet spots as they'd each left. The room smelled
like nothing I'd ever smelled before. Too, it smelled
like everything I'd ever smelled before but all in one
room. Birds still went crazy from the zoo sounds and
such tussling. In my own quiet way, Dave, I was going
pretty crazy too.

After that I saw Robby at the station, him winking at
everything that moved, making wet sly clicking sounds
with his mouth. Whenever I bent over to put air into
my new bike's tires, I'd look anywhere except Robby.
But he noticed how nervous I acted and he got to teasing me. He'd sneak up behind and put the toe of his
loafer against the seat of my jeans. Lord, I jumped. He
liked that. He was some tease, that Robby, flashing his
hair around like Lash LaRue. He'd crouch over my
Schwinn. The air nozzle in my hand would sound like
it was eating the tire. Robby'd say, real low and slimy,
'How you like your air, regular or hi-test, slick?' He'd
made certain remarks, 'Cat got your tongue, Too-Pretty-
By-Half?' He didn't know what I'd seen but he could
smell me remembering. —I dreaded him. Of course,
Dave, Sunoco was not the only station in town. I worried Robby might force me into my house and down
onto the couch. —I thought, 'But he couldn't do anything to *me*. I'm only eleven. Plus, I'm a boy.' But next,
I made pictures in my head, and I knew better. There
were ways, I bet . . .

I stayed clear of the cabin. I didn't know why. I'd
been stuck not nine feet from everything they did. I
was scared of getting trapped again. I wanted to just
live in that closet, drink tea, eat M & M's, praying
they'd come back. —Was about six days later I remembered: my birds were alone in the shack. They needed

water and feeding every other day. I'd let them down. I
worried about finches, out there by their lonesomes.
But pretty soon it'd been over a week, ten days, twelve.
The longer you stay away from certain things, the harder
it is, breaking through to do them right. I told myself,
'Huey and Dewey are total goners now.' I kept clear of
finding them, stiff—feet up on the bottom of the cage.
I had dreams.

I saw my den mother uptown running a church bake
sale to help hungry Koreans. She was ordering everybody around like she usually did, charming enough to
get away with it. I thought I'd feel super-ashamed to
ever see her again. Instead I rushed right up. I chatted
too much, too loud. I wanted to show that I forgave
her. Of course, she didn't know I'd seen her do all such
stuff with greasy Robby. She just kept looking at me,
part-gloating part-fretting. She handed me a raisin cup-
cake, free. We gave each other a long look. We partly
smiled.

After two and a half weeks, I knew my finches were
way past dead. I didn't understand why I'd done it. I'd
been too lazy or spooked to bike out and do my duty.
I belonged in prison—Finch Murderer. Finally I ped-
aled my bike in that direction. One day, you have to.
The shack looked smaller, the paint peeled worse. I
found the key under three bricks, unlocked, held my
breath. I didn't hear one sound from the front room, no
hop, no cheep. Their cage hung from a hook on the
wall and, to see into it, I had to stand up on my couch.
Millet seed ground between my bare feet and the cushions. Birds had pecked clear through the back of their
plastic food dish. It'd been shoved from the inside out,
it'd skidded to a far corner of the room. My finches had
slipped out their dish's slot. Birds were gone—flown up
a chimney or through one pane of busted window glass.

Maybe they'd waited a week. When I didn't show up and treat them right, birds broke out. They were now in pinewoods nearby. I wondered if they'd known all along that they could leave, if they'd only stayed because I fed them and was okay company.

I pictured Huey and Dewey in high pines, blinking. I worried what dull local sparrows would do to such bright birds, hotshots from the Mall pet store. Still, I decided that being free sure beat my finches' chances of hanging around here, starving.

Talk about relief. I started coughing from it, I don't know why. Then I sat down on the couch and cried. I felt something slippery underneath me. I wore my khaki shorts, nothing else, it was late August. I stood and studied what'd been written on couch cushions in lipstick, all caked. Words were hard to read on nappy brown cloth. You could barely make out 'I will do what Robby wants. What Sandy needs worst. So help me Dog.'

I thought of her. I wanted to fight for her but I knew that, strong as the lady was, she did pretty much what she liked. She wouldn't be needing me. I sat again. I pulled my shorts down. Then I felt cool stripes get printed over my brown legs and white butt. Lipstick, parts of red words stuck onto my skin—'wi' from 'will,' the whole word 'help.' I stretched out full length. My birds didn't hop from perch to perch or nibble at their birdie toy. Just me now. My place felt still as any church. Something had changed. I touched myself, and—for the first time, with my bottom all sweetened by lipstick—I got real results.

Was right after this, I traded in my model cars, swapped every single comic for one magazine. It showed two sailors and twin sisters in a hotel, doing stuff. During the five last pictures, a dark bellboy joined

in. Was then that my collection really started. The End,
I guess. The rest is just being an adult.''

Barker sat quiet. I finally asked what'd happened to
his grandfather. How about Robby and the den mother?
"In jail. My granddad died. Of a broken heart, Mom
said. Robby moved. He never was one to stay any place
too long. One day he didn't show up at Sunoco and that
was it. Mrs. . . . the lady, she's still right here in Falls,
still a real leader. Not two days back, I ran into her at
the Mall, collecting canned goods to end World Hunger. We had a nice chat. Her son's a lawyer in Marietta,
Georgia now. She looks about the same, really—I love
the way she looks, always have. Now when we talk, I
can tell she's partly being nice to me because I never
left town or went to college and she secretly thinks I'm
not too swift. But since I kept *her* secret, I feel like
we're even. I just smile back. I figure, whatever makes
people kind to you is fine. She can see there's something extra going on but she can't name it. It just makes
her grin and want to give me little things. It's one of
ten trillion ways you can love somebody. We do, love
each other. I'm sure. —Nobody ever knew about Robby.
She got away with it. More power to her. Still leads the
Youth Choir. Last year they won the Southeast Chorus
prize, young people's division. They give concerts all
over. Her husband loves her. She said winning the prize
was the most fulfilling moment of her life. I wondered. I
guess everybody does some one wild thing now and then.
They should. It's what you'll have to coast on when you're
old. You know?'' I nodded. He sat here, still.
"Probably not much of a story.'' Barker shrugged.
"But, back then it was sure something, to see all that
right off the bat, your first time out. I remember being
so shocked to know that—men want to. *And* women.

I'd figured that only one person at a time would need it, and they'd have to knock down the other person and force them to, every time. But when I saw that, no, everybody wants to do it, and how there are no rules in it—I couldn't look straight at a grown-up for days. I'd see that my mom's slacks had zippers in them, I'd nearabout die. I walked around town, hands stuffed deep in my pockets. My head was hanging and I acted like I was in mourning for something. But, hey, I was really just waking up. —What got me onto all *that*? You about ready for a movie, Dave? Boy, I haven't talked so much in months. It's what you get for asking, I guess.'' He laughed.

I thanked Barker for his story. I told him it made sense to me.

''Well, thanks for saying so anyhow.''

He started fidgeting with the projector. I watched. I knew him better now. I felt so much for him. I wanted to save him. I couldn't breathe correctly.

''Here goes.'' He toasted his newest film then snapped on the large and somehow sinister antique machine.

The movie showed a girl at home reading an illustrated manual, hand in dress, getting herself animated. She made a phone call; you saw the actor answering and, even in a silent film, even given this flimsy premise, you had to find his acting absolutely awful. Barker informed me it was a Swedish movie; they usually started with the girl phoning. ''Sometimes it's one guy she calls, sometimes about six. But always the telephones. I don't know why. It's like they just got phones over there and are still proud of them or something.'' I laughed. What a nice funny thing to say. By now, even the gin and iced tea (with lemon and sugar) tasted like a great idea.

He sat upright beside me. The projector made its placid motorboat racket. Our couch seemed a kind of quilted raft. Movie light was mostly pink; ivy filtered sun to a thin green. Across Barker's neutral white shirt, these tints carried on a silent contest. One room away, the crockpot leaked a bit, hissing. Hallway smelled of stew meat, the need for maid service, back issues, laundry in arrears, one young man's agreeable curried musk. From a corner of my vision, I felt somewhat observed. Cats' eyes. To heck with caution. Let them look!

Barker kept elbows propped on knees, tensed, staring up at the screen, jaw gone slack. In profile against windows' leaf-spotted light, he appeared honest, boyish, wide open. He unbuttoned his top collar button.

I heard cars pass, my fellow Rotarians, algebra teachers from my school system. Nobody would understand us being here, beginning to maybe do a thing like this. Even if I went public, dedicated an entire Board of Education meeting to the topic, after three hours of intelligent confession, with charts and flannel boards and slide projections, I knew that when lights snapped back on I'd look around from face to face, I'd see they still sat wondering your most basic question:

Why, Dave, why?

I no longer noticed what was happening on screen. Barker's face, lit by rosy movie light, kept changing. It moved me so. One minute: drowsy courtesy, next a sharp manly smile. I set my glass down on a Florida-shaped coaster. Now, slow, I reached toward the back of his neck—extra-nervous, sure—but that's part of it, you know? My arm wobbled, fear of being really belted, blackmailed, worse. I chose to touch his dark hair, cool as metal.

"Come *on*," he huffed forward, clear of my hand.

He kept gazing at the film, not me. Barker grumbled, "The guy she phoned, he hasn't even got to her *house* yet, man."

I saw he had a system. I figured I could wait to understand it.

I felt he was my decent kid brother. Our folks had died; I would help him even more now. We'd rent industrial-strength vacuum cleaners. We'd purge this mansion of dinge, yank down tattered maroon draperies, let daylight in. I pictured us, stripped to the waists, painting every upstairs room off-white, our shoulders flecked with droplets, the hair on our chests flecked with droplets.

I'd drive Barker and his Wedgwood to a place where I'm known, Old Mall Antiques. I bet we'd get fifteen to nineteen hundred bucks. Barker would act amazed. In front of the dealer, he'd say, "For *that* junk?" and, laughing, I'd have to shush him. With my encouragement, he'd spend some of the bonus on clothes. We'd donate three generations of *National Geographic*s to a nearby orphanage, if there are any orphanages anymore and nearby. I'd scour Barker's kitchen, defrost the fridge. Slowly, he would find new shape and meaning in his days. He'd commence reading again—nonporn, recent worthy hardbacks. We'd discuss these.

He'd turn up at Little League games, sitting off to one side. Sensing my gratitude at having him high in the bleachers, he'd understand we couldn't speak. But whenever one of my sons did something at bat or out in center field (a pop-up, a body block of a line drive), I would feel Barker nodding approval as he perched there alone; I'd turn just long enough to see a young bachelor mumbling to himself, shaking his head Yes, glad for my boys.

After office hours, once a week, I'd drive over, knock, then walk right in, calling, "Barker? Me."

No answer. Maybe he's napping in a big simple upstairs room, one startling with fresh paint. Six cats stand guard around his bed, two old Persians and their offspring, less Persian, thinner, spottier. Four of them pad over and rub against my pant cuffs; by now they know me.

I settle on the edge of a single bed, I look down at him. Barker's dark hair has fallen against the pillow like an open wing. Bare-chested, the texture of his poreless skin looks finer than the sheets. Under a blue blanket, he sleeps, exhausted from all the cleaning, from renewing his library card, from the fatigue of clothes shopping. I look hard at him; I hear rush-hour traffic crest then pass its peak. Light in here gets ruddier.

A vein in his neck beats like a clock, only liquid.

—I'm balanced at the pillow end of someone's bed. I'm watching somebody decent sleep. —If the law considers this so wicked—then why does it feel like my only innocent activity? Barker wakes. The sun is setting. His face does five things at once: sees somebody here, gets scared, recognizes me, grins a good blurry grin, says just, "You."

(They don't want a person to be tender. They could lock me up for everything I love about myself, for everything I love.)

Here on the couch, Barker shifted, "Look *now*, Dave. Uh oh, she hears him knocking. See her hop right up? Okay, walking to the door. It's him, all right. He's dressed for winter. That's because they're in Sweden, right, Dave?"

I agreed, with feeling. Then I noted Barker taking

the pen caddy from his pocket, placing it on the table before him. Next, with an ancient kind of patience, Barker's torso twisted inches toward me; he lifted my hand, pulled my whole arm up and around and held it by the wrist, hovering in air before his front side as if waiting for some cue. Then Barker, clutching the tender back part of my hand, sighed, "Um-kay. *Now* they're really starting to." And he lowered my whole willing palm—down, down onto it.

I touched something fully familiar to me, yet wholly new.

He bucked with that first famous jolt of human contact after too long, too long alone without. His spine slackened but the head shivered to one side, righted itself, eager to keep the film in sight. I heard six cats go racing down long hallways, then come thumping back, relaxed enough to play with me, a stranger, in their house. Praise.

Barker's voice, all gulpy: "I think . . . this movie's going to be a real good one, Dave. Right up there on my Ten Favorites list. And, you know? . . ." He *almost* ceased looking at the screen, he *nearly* turned his eyes my way instead. And the compliment stirred me. "You know? You're a regular fellow, Dave. I feel like I can trust you. You seem like . . . one real nice guy."

Through my breathing, I could hear him, breathing, losing breath, breathing, losing breath.

"Thank you, Barker. Coming from you, that means a lot."

Every true pleasure is a secret.

1986

It Had Wings

For Bruce Saylor and Constance Beavon

FIND A LITTLE YELLOW SIDE STREET HOUSE. PUT AN older woman in it. Dress her in that tatty favorite robe, pull her slippers up before the sink, have her doing dishes, gazing nowhere—at her own backyard. Gazing everywhere. Something falls outside, loud. One damp thwunk into new grass. A meteor? She herself (retired from selling formal clothes at Wanamaker's, she herself—a widow and the mother of three scattered sons, she herself alone at home a lot these days) goes onto tiptoe, leans across a sinkful of suds, sees—out near her picnic table, something nude, white, overlylong. It keeps shivering. Both wings seem damaged.

"No way," she says. It appears human. Yes, it is a male one. It's face up and, you can tell, it is extremely male (uncircumcised). This old woman, pushing eighty, a history of aches, uses, fun—now presses one damp hand across her eyes. Blaming strain, the luster of new cataracts, she looks again. Still, it rests there on a bright air mattress of its own wings. Outer feathers are tough quills, broad at bottom as rowboat oars. The whole left wing bends far under. It looks hurt.

The widow, sighing, takes up her blue willow mug

of heated milk. Shaking her head, muttering, she carries it out back. She moves so slow because: arthritis. It criticizes every step. It asks about the mug she holds, Do you really need this?

She stoops, creaky, beside what can only be a young angel, unconscious. Quick, she checks overhead, ready for what?—some TV news crew in a helicopter? She sees only a sky of the usual size, a Tuesday sky stretched between weekends. She allows herself to touch this thing's white forehead. She gets a mild electric shock. Then, odd, her tickled finger joints stop aching. They've hurt so long. A practical person, she quickly cures her other hand. The angel grunts but sounds pleased. His temperature's a hundred and fifty, easy—but for him, this seems somehow normal. ''Poor thing,'' she says, and—careful—pulls his heavy curly head into her lap. The head hums like a phone knocked off its cradle. She scans for neighbors, hoping they'll come out, wishing they wouldn't, both.

''Look, will warm milk help?'' She pours some down him. Her wrist brushes angel skin. Which pulls the way an ice tray begs whatever touches it. A thirty-year pain leaves her, enters him. Even her liver spots are lightening. He grunts with pleasure, soaking up all of it. Bold, she presses her worst hip deep into crackling feathers. The hip has been half numb since a silly fall last February. All stiffness leaves her. He goes, ''Unhh.'' Her griefs seem to fatten him like vitamins. Bolder, she whispers private woes: the Medicare cuts, the sons too casual by half, the daughters-in-law not bad but not so great. These woes seem ended. ''Nobody'll believe. Still, tell me some of it.'' She tilts nearer. Both his eyes stay shut but his voice, like clicks from a million crickets pooled, goes, ''We're just another army. We all look alike—we didn't, before. It's not what you expect. We miss this other. Don't count on the next. Notice things here. We are just another army."

"Oh," she says.

Nodding, she feels limber now, sure as any girl of twenty. Admiring her unspeckled hands, she helps him rise. Wings serve as handles. Kneeling on damp ground, she watches him go staggering toward her barbecue pit. Awkward for an athlete, really awkward for an angel, the poor thing climbs up there, wobbly. Standing, he is handsome, but as a vase is handsome. When he turns this way, she sees his eyes. They're silver, each reflects her: a speck, pink, on green green grass.

She now fears he plans to take her up, as thanks. She presses both palms flat to dirt, says, "The house is finally paid off. —Not just yet," and smiles.

Suddenly he's infinitely infinitely more so. Silvery. Raw. Gleaming like a sunny monument, a clock. Each wing puffs, independent. Feathers sort and shuffle like three hundred packs of playing cards. Out flings either arm; knees dip low. Then up and off he shoves, one solemn grunt. Machete swipes cross her backyard, breezes cool her upturned face. Six feet overhead, he falters, whips in makeshift circles, manages to hold aloft, then go shrub-high, gutter-high. He avoids a messy tangle of phone lines now rocking from the wind of him. "Go, go," the widow, grinning, points the way. "Do. Yeah, good." He signals back at her, open-mouthed and left down here. First a glinting man-shaped kite, next an oblong of aluminum in sun. Now a new moon shrunk to decent star, one fleck, fleck's memory: usual Tuesday sky.

She kneels, panting, happier and frisky. She is hungry but must first rush over and tell Lydia next door. Then she pictures Lydia's worry lines bunching. Lydia will maybe phone the missing sons: "Come right home. Your Mom's inventing . . . company."

Maybe other angels have dropped into other Elm Street backyards? Behind fences, did neighbors help earlier hurt ones? Folks keep so much of the best stuff quiet, don't they.

Palms on knees, she stands, wirier. This retired saleswoman was the formal-gowns adviser to ten mayors' wives. She spent sixty years of nine-to-five on her feet. Scuffing indoors, now staring down at terry slippers, she decides, "Got to wash these next week." Can a person who's just sighted her first angel already be mulling about laundry? Yes. The world is like that.

From her sink, she sees her own blue willow mug out there in the grass. It rests in muddy ruts where the falling body struck so hard. A neighbor's collie keeps barking. (It saw!) Okay. This happened. "So," she says.

And plunges hands into dishwater, still warm. Heat usually helps her achy joints feel agile. But fingers don't even hurt now. Her bad hip doesn't pinch one bit. And yet, sad, they all will. By suppertime, they will again remind her what usual suffering means. To her nimble underwater hands, the widow, staring straight ahead, announces, "I helped. He flew off stronger. I really egged him on. Like *any*body would've, really. Still, it was me. I'm not just somebody in a house. I'm not just somebody alone in a house. I'm not just somebody else alone in a house."

Feeling more herself, she finishes the breakfast dishes. In time for lunch. This old woman should be famous for all she has been through—today's angel, her years in sales, the sons and friends—she should be famous for her life. She knows things, she has seen so much. She's not famous.

Still, the lady keeps gazing past her kitchen café curtains, she keeps studying her own small tidy yard. An anchor fence, the picnic table, a barbecue pit, new Bermuda grass. Hands braced on her sink's cool edge, she tips nearer a bright window.

She seems to be expecting something, expecting something decent. Her kitchen clock is ticking. That dog still barks to calm itself. And she keeps staring out: nowhere, everywhere. Spots on her hands are darkening again. And yet, she whispers, "I'm right here, ready. Ready for more."

Can you guess why this old woman's chin is lifted? Why does she breathe as if to show exactly how it's done? Why should both her shoulders, usually quite bent, brace so square just now?

She is guarding the world.
Only, nobody knows.

1985

A Hog Loves Its Life
Something About My Grandfather

For Herbert E. Gurganus (1889–1965)
and W. Ethel Pitt Gurganus (1889–1963)

1. ONCE . . .

L ANGUAGE, LIKE LOVE, STARTS LOCAL.

My grandfather called me deep into the big house.
We hid. While powdered aunts and freckled cousins
yammered on his front porch, one old farmer scolded
me. I was scared but liked it.

"Willy? Just heard you lipping-off to your mother—
close to tantrum, you were. Keep doing that, you got
no future. I won't have a grandson of mine carrying on
like Lancaster's mule."

"Like *who*?"

This antique stared at me. (I might've asked if Jesus
was the Father, Son, or Holy Ghost—if South Carolina
didn't outrank our native North Carolina.)

"Like Lancaster's mule." First Grand doubted my
hearing. When I still shrugged, he closed both eyes,
pinched the bridge of his nose, and, sighing hard, mo-
tioned me up into his lap. The sigh smelled of medicine, baking soda, and leaf mold, of bread and years.

"Since wireless came in, seems like nothing on this
earth is *grounded*. My own flesh and blood especially.
You sure don't know much. Where you *been*, boy?"

167

"I guess I'm young yet." This got me one respectful frown.

"Seems Lancaster dealt livestock. Boo-coo hogs and horses—that being French for 'heaps of.' (With you, son, I'm taking nothing for granted.) A jumbo size of a man, this Lancaster, all jaw was he, hair parted in the middle, the very middle. Animals were gods to us in the eighteen and nineties—and Buck, he *sold* them. Now, Willy, this I'm trying and tell you, it came previous to autocars, tractors, exhaust, all such mess. Maybe you think you're lucky being born so recent? Ha. Ha *ha*. More the fool you. You believe sputniks are worth writing home about? *Ha* ha. People wanted to get around the country in my time, people either bought something four-legged or else used good old shoe leather. Ever heard of it, you-in-all-the-car-pools? A person needed their field plowed, person either borrowed a hand hoe or got a good mule, one. As for Lancaster, his morals might've been the short end of nothing, but the man knew every confidence trick going, was just his nature to.

"Buck's been dead since '31. They all are. Most everybody's gone except your grandmother, wonderful woman, testy as she sometimes acts toward me. Last person alive knows to call me Little Bobby Grafton. Nowdays in this town, I'm held to be Mr. Grafton or Old-timer or Pops Grafton. But a body needs a few souls who remember he was Little Bobby Grafton. 'Ears,' the boy that lived in trouble. But wait, I'm wandering. One evening, closing time at Buck's stockyard, here comes a young hayseed. One born every minute—plenty to keep Buck busy and his daughters between satin sheets. 'You're seeking, don't tell me'—Lancaster touches one temple—'an exceptional . . . mule.' The mouth-breathing farmer blinks, asks how Buck knew.

'Simple, son,' Buck says, 'little something we call genius. Ever hear of it? Follow me.' Which ends this part.''

My teller paused, his shoulders jiggling, readied. He talked the way binge drinkers, finally on vacation, drink. Bobby was considered tight-lipped. He saved his lurid best for me. I sat staring at the man.

Us grandkids called him Grand for short. He was semifamous, the county white man with the record-largest ears. We are talking giant here. In those times in North Carolina, ears grew bigger. Especially farmers'. I studied cartilage sturdy as roofing shingles: Hinge-long, rust-colored—any hound could envy his. And I'd inherited the things. My mother wept about this. Literally wept. You can see how—all these years later—I've resisted having mine surgically subdued, a tribute.

''Buck did not know fear. Buck loved money the most. Buck was not exactly ugly—you can't call a bag of *ce*ment ugly—just there. Flashy dresser he was, though his linen pant cuffs tended to stay the color that a-man-who-owns-a-stockyard-and-wades-everywhere's pant cuffs will.''

''Brown?''

''Now, as a mule salesman, Lancaster was known to fudge a bit. A bit! Did I say a bit?''

''Yes.''

''Don't correct me here, Will. Because I won't sanction insolence. Not even from my best-looking grandchild. Boo-coo questions cannot be answered. Mine especially. Lancaster didn't fudge just some, oh no. He was a horse trader. You expected those to try and bilk you. Means 'cheat,' Willy. You went ready. I've always had a soft spot for the fellows can't resist but to drive a deal. I'm not so hot at it myself, pushover. Ask your grandmother, Ruth reminds me often enough. But Lancaster? Give such a gent fifteen hundred pounds of surplus steel wool, he'll knit you a hotel stove. Then he'll try and *sell* it to you. And, son, know what?''

''You'll buy it?'' Grand squinted down at me, impressed with my quickness, bored by my character. ''Willy? What'd I just tell you? *Just?*''

''Quiet?''

''Quiet. No wonder you know jack-nothing—way you keep busting in on a person. Look, do you want this or not? Ask me for it.''

''I do.''

''Do what?''

''Want. I'll keep still. I promise. It's just . . . I . . .''

''You're goddamn right you will. Should've seen *me* back then. One thing sure, could've beat *you* up, both hands tied behind me. Scrappy. We had to be.''

''But, Grand, know what? I bet I'm probably smarter.'' Inner corners of forty wrinkles tightened, that ashamed: a boy had admitted that another boy might trounce him.

''Smarter'n me? I didn't hear that. Buck Lancaster owned a fine three-story house, had four overly average-looking daughters. Sundays you'd ride by, Buck's girls'd be lined up along his porch, one softer than her baby sister. Did I say, 'You'd *ride* by . . .'?''

(This time, a quick study, I knew to say nothing.)

''More like walk by. Our farm was five miles out, and I oftimes hiked to town wearing my one Sunday suit. Faked errands all over a neighborhood where not a soul knew me, was studying Lancaster's beauty girls in pastel dresses. 'Ears' was all eyes then, boy. To and fro went Little Bobby Grafton, the boy that lived in trouble, hoping to get into a better class of Bobby trouble than Bobby's usual. You think those girls couldn't guess who I was staring at! Ha. I might not've been as quick as you in a *book* way—with Poppa snatching me out of Lower Normal every time something got ripe enough to pick or cut—but I could've told you to Shut Up and you would've.

"Lancaster's girls had a parrot on the porch with them. A parrot in this town then, it really meant something. Showed sparrows weren't the half of it. And not one Lancaster girl ever married is how hard a bargain Buck drove. No governor was fat, rosy, or rich enough to get in good with *Buck's* girls.

"So anyhow, the mule of it—along around closing time, near sunset on a slow week night, barn swallows probably went skimming over tin roofs (though I couldn't swear to it), and into Buck's dragged that same slow-moving young farmer from out Pitt County way. (Your grandmother was a Pitt and she will tell you in a minute if you don't stop her. Pretty much a snob, but she sometimes seems to fancy me—so I can't find total fault with her.) Young fellow craved a serious working mule. Buck happened to have one. Office was already padlocked, but Buck could smell a pocketful of bills, damp from this plowboy's clutching them clear to town. So Buck swings into his friendliest style, hands our dirt farmer one fine cigar—the first that boy'd ever had, I bet you. Just to get a fellow's *con*fidence, don't you know. Leads our boy around back where not one street lamp burns. And here in a dark corral stands the matted-eyed knock-kneed mule, all by its lonesome and acting real homesick for *some*thing.

"Lancaster might have said, 'Stranger, you are doubtless wondering—clever operator such as yourself—why I chose to separate this creature from its own born kind.' Buck talked like that, only way worse. Trust me to talk like they talked. To try. Now we're getting near the real part, part where I come in. Now we're near knee-deep in it.'' And gazing before him, Grand literally rubbed his leather palms together.

The rest of our family still jabbered on the bright porch. Jaw jaw jaw, gas gas gas. A waste. Out front, my grandmother's clear tone straddled three conversations, governing them. Family talk sounded like one church organ's many pipes and tubes—flute- to chimney-sized—all alive with a single feeding breath.

I worried: my weight might be hurting Grand's arthritis. But in Falls, N.C., then—if you were ten years old, grandfathers invited you up onto their laps, even if it really pained them. They practically had to, some grandfatherly union regulation. Grand's easy chair was a huge orange leatherette slab. He'd bought it at some cut-rate store; its ugliness daily grieved my grandmother. The matching footstool steadily leaked sawdust onto her inherited Aubusson carpet. ''It molts,'' she said.

I watched narrow lips move, silent, as Grand carpentered our next part. He studied air directly before his face. He was one of those people that, like a dog or mule, lets you stare. They hardly notice till, with you an inch away, your saying ''Hey'' can make them jump like something shot. This man owned four stores, ten rental homes, and the most broken-down dirt farm you ever saw. I admired how much property he'd piled up from total scratch. Little Bobby Grafton's folks had mostly worked as sharecroppers, their lives spent improving others' fields. As a day-labor kid, Grand got sun-cooked across his neck and over both hands' leathery backs (*roofs* of his hands, I considered them). His skin seemed lidded like the old-timey thick-topped butterscotch pudding my grandmother served. She called this favorite dessert ''commonplace but comforting.'' His was the face of a small-time landowner, accustomed to squinting with slit-eyed pride at mortgaged

horizons. During summer, when he gimped in from a
burning day outdoors, his stately wife met him on the
porch. She held a jar of Nivea, as blue as the future.
"Sun seems to consider these poor ears perfect tar-
gets." Ruth stationed herself behind his chair; she removed her ruby ring, slathered up either hand and,
focusing on the mammoth flanges, started daubing.

(Whenever *my* first wife feared losing one of our ar-
guments, she hinted I should go and have my ears surgically "pinned." Hideous word, "pinned"—especially
when the features are yours and visibly inherited. I had
confided Grand's early nickname: "Bi-plane Grafton."
And do you know she used this against me, in front of
two other couples and in a good New York restaurant?
She did. She hinted we were presently getting such poor
service because of a certain rustic somebody's ear size.
"Obscene," she once called these units you've occasionally glanced at. Go ahead—hey, no offense, really.
My first wife's inappropriateness finally stuck out even
more than do these Willy flaps. They're still with me,
she is not.)

"Now—buddy-ro for which I'm trying to spell what
'like Lancaster's mule' means, young as you are, and
as lost in the modern world as everybody seems now,
do *you* figure it's too good of an idea, buying yourself
a mule—or, for that matter, a little runabout motorcar—
at nighttime? Huh, Willy? I'm asking this one straight
out, so go ahead and answer if you can."

I stalled. With Grand, I kept my favored standing by
avoiding the porch (its gossip was considered beaucoup
more entertaining than his). He loved my admitting
what I didn't know, he loved the way I pleaded for his
Sunday installments. He let me take out his pocket
watch and fidget with its chain's three toy brass horseshoes (they came with penny candy in the 1890s, when

animals were still the gauge of distances and dollars).
But if Grand offered me direct questions, I could not
be wrong twice in a single visit. My mother explained
I need not humor the old man. She considered her
father-in-law sweet, well-meaning, reasonably pathetic.
While I sat indoors with him, I missed some good porch
rumors, ones my folks and kid brother would mention
in our station wagon bound home to the suburbs. But I
was hooked on his fierce attention, on weekly news
from one gent literally rednecked. Sundays I rushed
toward his chair. "Okay, start me off with 'Carlton's
Wren,' then do 'Lessie Poland's Boot' the long way. I
mean, please, sir, *please* do those ones first."

Mention any creek from Pitt to Nash counties, you'd
siphon a tale. The awful flood of '89; the beautiful sisters who left a note, then drowned on purpose; the fellow who swapped Indian Creek for a diamond brooch,
then lost it to his wife at poker. When our station wagon
zoomed home from Grand's and over a bridge, I looked
down on Legend. My loved ones saw just weeds and bilge.

Our *Compton's Encyclopedia* showed Egyptian murals:
Pharaohs were giant athletes—their helpful midget com-
moners came knee-high. For Grand, the dead of Falls
were royally huge. They towered over all us present pyg-
mies of the 1950s. (Ours was an age of sleekest tail fins.
A big war had just been won—by my father; Falls's stores
sold smooth, good, streamlined things. Each year at the
State Fair, we saw U.S. Army rockets displayed, but
mules? They were already scarce in suburban Falls. If
some hold-out farmer led one down our street, people
swarmed outdoors, smiling, aiming Kodaks, calling,
"You kids? Unglue yourself from that TV set. Come look
for once. You'll thank me later. It's historical.")

My own secret interest in the future changed the way I
heard Grand's yarns. He weekly binged forth a gallery of

good-sized hucksters, men brilliant as my *Superman* comics' space masterminds. At ten, I was a glum little comic-book pedant (such kids are now computer whizzes). I listened to the muddy landscape Grand described, but sent it light-years forward into chilly mineral space. I pictured crystal tower residences so tall, spotlights shone up top warning away rocket ships. Grand often mentioned hogs; I reshaped even these: rooting carnivorous robot units, stainless steel as Mother's weekday flatware. Here and now, alive and in secret in modern life, I'd found a talking map. He stayed hushed around others, semidignified; but with me in lap, Grand sketched a space frontier: vigilantes, potent animals, robberies, feuds. His past unrolled a fresh (free) Marvel Comics. Soon, our own Indian Creek—wagered for diamonds, lost at cards—seemed mythic as some Mars canal traded for hunks of white-hot Kryptonite.

Grand's mission? Explaining Falls's deceased to Falls's more newly born. Who new cared except his single scrawny disciple, the one kid willing to stay indoors, to shut up for a change, and just sit here big-eyed, positively floppy with hearing equipment? The old man told and told—unaware of giving me a future, not a past.

I finally risked: "No, sir. It's not really all that good of an idea, buying stuff at night and everything. Because, see? it's dark and they could . . . put something over on you."

Which got me one raw assessing look. Praise might be hid in it; I couldn't yet decide. So, taking a chance, I added, "Lancaster especially."

A shudder ran through runty knobbled shoulders. Grand stared. For a second I feared I needed to blow my nose, so rarely did he gape right at a person's face. Then hard hands slipped under my arms, he turned me (roughly) toward window light, he checked my freckles, coded like star charts or our genes. "I know whose grandchild *this* one is. Folks, how *about* our Willy here?" But looking around the parlor, Grand found everybody'd wandered to the airier front porch. Even so, he held me inches up in air, showing me off to absolutely nothing. " 'Lancaster especially,' says this one, like he was there. I like that. 'Lancaster *espec*ially.' " He set me down harder and ·sooner than I wanted.

"So Buck says to our farmer, says, 'Sir, what you're studying is the smartest single mule currently alive in our continental America, meaning, fellow patriot, the world generally. Please greet the Mule of Your Dreams, why, the mule of *anybody's*. But first tell me how you heard about him. You waited till closing time when all the earlier bidders got dragged away, right, you dog, you?' Buck was not above nudging a fellow's ribs. Whatever works. The poor farmer grinned—sucker was slow, Willy. I've heard your mother talk about somebody's children having reading problems and all like that. There is—your present-day liberal hates admitting—such a thing as plain D–U–M. And this clodhopper *was* it. What can you do?

"Goes Buck, 'Certain mules kept torturing this paragon, actually biting him. I'm ashamed to admit: some kicking was involved. So we hid our rarity. Reason? I caught him trying to plow, sir. Kept digging ruts, using nothing but his hoof. At the time, it was all he had *on* him. Pulling said hoof back and forth, making little furrows, steady as a Singer. By noon, my front paddock could have been the start of a decent truck garden. Of course, the other mules hate this one for being so work-loving. Makes *them* look bad. So here it is, banished from its shiftless kind, the workingest damn animule I have laid eyes on in my fifty years of com-

munity service from one single convenient location.'
Buck adds that if all this is not true, may his lovely
daughters suffer chilblains, gout, and facial warts right
. . . this . . . *sec*-ond. He stands still, like listening.
One slow grin proves honesty's won out again, his girls
are yet smooth as satin sheets. Buck tells the customer
to go freely peruse yonder mule. But our farmer cannot
get a real clear look-see, and why, Willy?''

''It's still night.''

''You're goddamn right, it's still night. And by now
it's pitch-black coal-bin midnight dark. Lancaster's
moving faster. 'Young sir, I love dealing with gents who
so *know* mulekind. Heck, *let* those other bidders duke
it out come morning. For a price our dream mule is
yours alone.' Now, say the beast cost eighty dollars.
Might sound cheap to a pip with an allowance big as
yours (your daddy told me what he pays you for doing
nothing). But back then, money was still a law unto
itself. Why, you could get you a whole motorcar for
under three hundred dollars, new.''

''Naw.'' I slapped the leather roof of his hand. ''Naw.
New?'' (I pictured a rocket ship, all my own and as
silver as Reynolds Wrap.)

''Truth. Sure. Brand-new. Tires inclusive. (Means: it
comes *with*, Will.) So that farmer'd shelled out his
whole life savings. Boo-coo bucks. And don't you
know, his wife and kids were waiting up by lantern light
to see what hero-animal they'd got. Maybe they patted
it, probably they named it. We named everything back
then. My daddy's favorite plow was called Atlas . . .
be one example. I still know the names of certain hogs
I personally ate most of. I'm saying this to feed the fire
of our story till I tiptoe in with what I eyewitness-saw.
Plus I'm hoping to put off going out on the porch, having your grandmother tell me in front of everybody that

I'm wearing one too many plaids again—how do people know? Come dawn, our poor farmer was probably up before the larks—if we *had* any round these parts, well, meadowlarks, I guess we do—he hit a snag once the harness was oiled, plow-sharpened, ready to start life over behind the Mule of His Dreams—behind the mule of anybody's, Willy o' mine . . .''

(Since I turned four, Grand had ignored my faintly suburban first name. ''Bryan is somebody's *last* name. And not *ours* either. No, here we got a person called Willy . . . it's as solid of a Willy as I've ever seen.'' Since then I have tried becoming the pure shrewd decent country ''Willy'' Grand considered me. Even in my present spreading urban middle age, I work at being worthy of the name.)

''Now we finally strike my own patch of it, a relief. Good clean fun, Buck's hog sales. Free. What us poor kids had instead of wireless or these new television sets. Maybe I was only your age and yea-high to nothing, but 'Ears' Grafton was all eyeballs in the front row. Here comes Little Bobby Grafton who lived in trouble and missed nothing and got punished even for things he didn't do, but never snitched on who did. A boy like you, only maybe keener, if not so book-smart. Your daddy went to Harvard College—though *I* paid for it. He swears you will. Go there. *He'll* have to pay. I don't know as I approve. Your dad's still rotten with Cambridge this and that. If you go, you'll probably forget everything Grand here ever tried telling. But I plan to anyhow. Nobody can say *my* Willy never learned what 'Lancaster's mule' means. Sure I was scrappier and smarter than you are now—but not by much, so don't pout so.

''Was the morning after last night's mule sale, was during a hog auction, with Buck conducting bidding at forty miles a minute (who *else* would he trust to do it?).

Say Buck was making regular waltz music and a sermon from his morning's shoat sale, when in blunders our young hayseed. Boy's definitely gnawing his lower lip, dark in the face, hat pulled low, leading the selfsame mule (all dusty now, limping bad, one eye closed). The farmer also totes a huge aught-aught shotgun, old-fashioned even for then. Quite the hush falls over everything, hogs included. Hogs are smart, Will. A hog loves its life.

"Soon as Buck spots that musket, which just *looks* loaded, he signals everybody to please hold still, not run for cover. Not yet. Using eyebrows only, he hints how his hirelings should sneak behind the customer, disarm him. And you can wager that during all of this, Buck kept the last and highest hog bid in his head. Didn't his very *name* have a 'Buck' in it? He grins. 'So, my agriculturally minded young friend, returned to the scene of earlier glories, I see. What, sir, can we do for you today?'

"At this the farmer gets to breathing funnier, hiccuping, little stray burps roll out—uncontrolled, we're talking here. 'What can *you* do? What can you *do*?' His red face under the straw brim goes toward purple. "More like *un*do, you double-dipping jackal. You might could give me my durn money back with interest and travel expenses. Is one thing you might could do. To save your hide. I'm here to announce before every other fool present, Mr. Lancaster, that me, my precious wife and six children—we consider you a . . . flesh-eating liar and a thief.'

"Certain murmuring rises. Even hogs squeal some, like whistling. A hog knows a insult when he hears it; a hog is so smart that he can . . . Hogs are smart. But not *that* smart, Will. What is it about you makes me tack on extra stuff?

" 'Those'—Lancaster stands taller—'constitute strong words, stranger.' (He's secretly signing his hog gaffers to sneak up from behind.) Meantime, Lancaster stalls by checking his famous pocketwatch. The case chimes open, its usual hymn 'Work for the Night Is Coming.' Buck rolls eyes through barn roof and heavenward.

"Hirelings whip off their hats to prove how religious Buck is. Lancaster does a silent 'Amen,' grinning down the gun's very barrel. 'Come, let us reason together. As says the Book. Take it you had a bit of trouble managing your new animal?'

" 'Trouble? Trou-ble? Mr. Snake, I'm up before sunrise, planning to get a full day's work from this critter I paid way too dear for. Broke out the new harness. Even combed my *own* hair. Overdid, I admit it. My wife and young ones line along our fence, smiling, half asleep. Well, our noise wakes the new mule. Seems a good sign. He trots out of the barn. He takes him a deep breath. Well, that strikes us *all* as a pretty good sign. A lot of nodding from folks on the fence to me, from me back to them at the fence, then back to . . .'

" 'Get *on* with it,' Buck snaps, bold—even at gunpoint. That Buck! We should all be more like him.

" 'My new mule breaks into a full trot (extra good sign). Mule heads straight toward the only oak tree in my paddock. Mule knocks hisself clean out. Lays there, cold-cocked, panting in the dust. Well, me and my family eyeball each other. Mule finally comes around, shakes his head, picks hisself up, leans on the tree for help. I'm thinking: Could happen to *any* creature, just overeager is all. Pounds into the side of my barn. Hits so hard—half the hay I spent all Saturday getting up there drops. Not real good of a sign. Every time he came to, got his bearings, he'd gallop slap into some fence, wagon, barn, tree, barn, barn, tree, fence. *Lan-*

caster—I don't mind telling you and all these fellow suckers, my wife and babies just stood at our fence crying. They acted disappointed in my *judg*ment. And I'm man enough to admit: made me cry, too. So, you latrine-mouthed coyote—I am here to get a total refund or your life, one. Because, Lancaster, you done went and sold me a blind mule!' ''

''Now, Willy, Lancaster rocks back on his heels, sizes up the moment like it is for sale. 'My good man,' Lancaster says, thumbs crooked into vest pockets, watch chain dangling, and him staring out at the auction crowd, getting folks ready. '*My good man, that mule ain't blind. That mule just don't give a damn.*'

''Well, everybody fell out. In such hooting, somebody yanked the rifle off the unhappy customer. Buck offered him a new seeing-eye mule, plus let him keep the first one. But the poor fellow's Pitt County reputation was ruined, permanent, because he'd tried to buy a mule . . . help me out here, Willy, who from?''

''Lancaster especially!''

''And at when . . . ?''

''At pitch-black dark night!'' My eyes nearly popped, that cooperative with the story. I breathed deeper, as if we'd just come a great distance at a hard gallop, which we had.

''Why, I should say *so*. Anyhow, from that very minute forward, all around here for three counties easy, folks just fell in love with saying that. Found it . . . useful, as a story. And ever since, whenever people my age and your daddy's speak of anybody doing crazy and being wild and trying whatever strikes them and not *minding* banging their heads against whatever's in the way—well, we call them what, Willy?''

Solemn, I answered.

''And odd part—even though that poor mule *was*

blind—what caught on was Lancaster's turning its being blind into a joke that saved his neck. So, see, Will, a good story, if it comes at just the right second, adds up to something. Slips into folks' everyday talk. And this whole one I've told—to keep you from ending up crazy-mean and by your lonesome, plus because you're young yet and have missed so much good stuff that came before you, stuff that surely won't strike ever again—it all stays crated up forever in those four words.''

Silently I practiced.

"Moral being today—you'd best straighten up and do right or you'll quit being *my* pick of the litter. Plus, nobody'll ever come near you. You don't want to end up corraled all *alone*, do you, son?''

I wagged my head *No, sir*. I turned then—my back fitted against Grand's front. I shifted my weight to his opposite hipbone. That way, maybe I wouldn't hurt one arthritis place so much. Speckled arms locked around me matter-of-factly. The chair wheezed. We both seemed heavier now his tale was done. Sawdust probably trickled onto Grandmother's inherited rug, an hourglass-spill running straight out of us. From the porch: voices of women and men (political fighting), bickering grandkids (contested toys).

One of my heavier aunts now bounded past our chair, rushing toward the bathroom. (She always waited till the last moment, afraid she'd miss something good, then she had to gallop. Family joke—one of many.) "Oh,'' Auntie said, startled. "Oh, you all. It's *chil*ly in here. I don't know why you don't come outside like sociable people.'' I planned scoffing at her when I heard Grand, asleep already. Farm sinew thrummed, two short questioning snores. To avoid talking back to Auntie or apologizing, I shut my eyes (an old man's trick).

The bathroom door double-locked. One uncle outside

laughed. "Says who? Where's that law written?" Shocking, how many others still jabbered out there, ignorant, unsteady, too up-to-date. Poor pygmies-of-the-present—offered nothing but shrinking crawl space. The future alone would allow us decent headroom. Thanks to vitamins and rocket travel, we'd be bigger-headed but heroic. Each our own car pool, flying out safe in front.

From my throne within a farmer's ropy arms, I found I really pitied the weak, the living. Our Dead were giants who'd done battle. The last word stayed theirs. Grand had filled me up with them. My gossip was the gossip of the dead. At ten, I saw it as prediction. At ten, I still believed in the future.

This shadowed house felt cool and blue, full of ticking clocks I hadn't noticed while he talked. Ten Swiss mantel clocks—wound every single American Monday morning since 1911. A front porch blazed, ice-tea glasses clinked. Another endless sneezy summer afternoon.

Grand breathed beneath me. He seemed to breathe for me. I thought, Us two, we've just picked to be dis-*guised* as earthlings a while, see.

Earthlings for now. I nodded, sleepy. My ambitious ears lightly touched Grand's cotton shirt sleeves. His front felt spongy, gigantic underneath me. Mulch and trampoline—my past.

Auntie finally prissed back by us, then turned, tugging at her hemline, centering her belt. She'd smudged on lipstick. As I watched with one eye, she gummed red marks onto a doubled Kleenex, then studied her own mouth-track. She read it like some love note from the future. "So [blot] which one's he been [blot] trying to tell you today, Bryan? He always exaggerates, honey, don't you believe a third of what he says." My eyes pressed shut so tight they quivered. Then Grand and

me were left alone, somehow more male for the inter-
ruption.

His chair was orange and under him—ugly, comfortable. He was mottled pink and orange and under me.
He was a crank. I was a crank in training. He was shy
around others. He saved his best for me. He had big
ears. I had huge ears, grand ones.

And I believed the man: I'd better straighten up, fly
right. Otherwise I might get stuck alone in some future
cold-as-space. (Boy, what a waste *that'd* be, especially
considering my straight-A record and how basically nice
I was!) I practiced mumbling the new term many different ways. It'd prove useful up ahead. "The future"
would be lots better than just "later on." Wouldn't it?
I now reached down, I touched the roof of one cracked
hand.

I was ten years old. I didn't know: the future would
do *any*thing. "Crazy as Lancaster's mule."

2. EVENTUALLY . . .

The old man enjoyed few great local successes. He
prospered in a small-time way. Little Bobby Grafton
was the hero of no story but my own, which this partly
is. I found his tales entertaining till I turned thirteen,
suddenly too old for them, for him. His favorites always
featured other slickers in the leading roles. Maybe my
grandmother's fondest stories put her Bobby front and
center. She's dead, of course. But I'm not.

Grand was a steady, half-religious, usually quiet fellow, a major buyer of Kiwanis Club peanuts and Brooms
by the Blind. He let himself be dragged to church on
Christmas and Easter only. He was a great one for crime
magazines and subscribed to three. Bobby considered

these superb bathroom reading. My grandmother bought chintz book covers to improve his latest "numbers."

Grand stayed one of those gentler sideline small-town guys who're always there when it happens, expert witness to others' triumphs. "Hey, Bobby? Come over here and tell these people how I told off that rude waitress that time, remember?" And he would: he'd block it out at his own farming pace, promoting the cad to a regular hero. People loved "Ears" Grafton for his skill at making them look bigger.

Though ridiculously and unprofitably honest himself, he admired the scams of strangers. He collected lore concerning folks who walk to the corner store for a newspaper and are never seen again and who've embezzled millions. "Untold millions," I once heard him dreamily say. In 1962, Grand drove as far as Cary, North Carolina, just to see a Wachovia bank that'd been held up the previous Friday. He spoke about one bullet hole in a plate-glass door; he mentioned it so often that Ruth, his dignified wife, took to screaming and covering her ears and running from the room. A mild person, he lent cash to many souls in town. Who soon forgot. Bobby hated cruelty but loved pure nerve. In others. From behind his *Raleigh News and Observer*, he would chuckle, "That Mickey-the-Mouse-Mask robber has sure pulled a good one *this* time. Listen up, honey."

My grandmother's gall was just the kind that Little Bobby admired.

The august former Ruth Eder Pitt was ingenious as any Buck Lancaster, though fitted for more genteel purposes. She was a finely made woman with big incongruous jolly breasts. Her hair must've been nearly four feet long come morning before she again wove it against her head, tight as a beautiful basket you might buy. Bobby could sit all day on the porch rereading back-issue *True Detective*; Bobby entertained chums who stopped to hear enlarged versions of their own tired early exploits. "Yeah," they smiled. "I guess I *was*, I guess I *did*."

Ruth interrupted, aiming Bobby toward whatever profit he ever earned. The young Miss Pitt, in 1909, enjoyed some money of her own. She forever after called this "Bobby's seed money." She mentioned it fairly often. She saw her nest egg gained or lost in Grafton's every business deal. (My family's recent joke about our Ruth: "She was from *the* Pitts.")

When I was ten, Grand still owned six rental homes on a street nobody would choose but where many lived anyway. Bobby collected the rent himself. "Only seems fair." If a tenant's excuse for this month's lack of cash got stated in a vivid, well-told tale, Grand might just let him slide. For a month or three.

"Mr. Grafton, sir, you're never going to believe this but I swear it on a stack of Bibles, and if you don't trust me, ask my Wanda (Wanda, haul your sweet carcass out here, sugar). My foreman down to the mill has got it *in* for me. Just does. Large-boned fellow, sir, and on Thursday—was it Thursday, Wanda? so I suspected—in he comes big as life, one serious grudging look in his eye, that if looks could kill—and they *can*, Mr. G., for a person half as sensitive as I unfortunately am—bring the coffee, Wanda, bit of white-lightning sweetener in that for you, Mr. G.? So here my foreman comes, saying 'I just hate your *face*, son,' at which point I, being a proud man—poor, sir, but proud—just *had* to carry that sledgehammer out toward his fancy new Studebaker. Well . . . so then things sure heated up quick . . ."

Grand leased two corner groceries in Falls's black

district along Sunflower Street. Few black merchants sold on long-term credit. But at stores Grand owned, if some debtor happened to be on hand the day Mr. Grafton arrived (folks hung around like attending some audition)—and if the debtor could then play a handy blues guitar for the boss man and his best-looking grandson—breaking an Orange Crush bottle against a nearby brick and using its neck to mute and sift sounds till you heard a train whistle getting nearer—and at night!—well, that man's bill was permitted to coast for another little while.

When Grand drove his black Packard home from some rent-collecting trip, arriving empty-handed (except for a string of gamey sunfish, one new tune, and three excellent almost-new hard-luck stories), his bosomy, beautifully appointed wife stood waiting by the front door. "Where *is* it?" Ruth held out her hand. She belonged to that generation where the wife was often depicted clasping her single weapon—a rolling pin. I haven't *seen* a rolling pin since 1960.

Ruth said, "It's like slave days for Little Bobby Grafton here. Only without anybody's being required to actually work for us. Slave owners fed their slaves—and that part he remembers. Meanwhile, we can't even get the front yard mown, and here he is off feeding and clothing half of our Negro community just for the pleasure of their charming excuses. I've never seen anything like it. If it weren't for my poppa's money, we'd have long since been dragged di*rec*tly to the poorhouse."

(Grand once told me, top secret, the full inventory of Ruth's 1909 dowry: a good rawhide suitcase, the French rug, two pig-iron bedsteads, a fifty-dollar gold piece, one ruby-chip ring, a couple of cloisonné lamps and flower vases, plus the monogrammed linens. Period.)

Grandmother often mentioned her husband's way with

clothes: "It's not so much poor taste. Bobby has *un*-taste. I can send him to the finest store in driving distance, one you'd think has stocked nothing but charcoal gray for thirty-five years. But he'll *make* them go to the cellar—force them, beguile them, you know how he is—and they'll scare up some houndstooth horse-blanket thing—a mat, I won't call it a coat, it was a sort of *mat* with armholes. He comes to the car holding the thing, and I promise this: *you can see it through the paper bag*. Admit it, Bobby. Tell them. It's still in one of the closets in the guest room. Go get it, Bobby. Show them. Admit you chose it. If it's not upstairs, that's because I sent it to the vet's and had it put down. Which would, I daresay, be the only way you could get it out of the house and prevent its actually baying at a full moon! Or something. You see, now he's got *me* sounding like him. I won't have it, do you *hear* me, Little Bobby? I just won't, sir. *You* over there, wipe that smirk off those ears, hear?"

When he left for work, Ruth daily scanned him by their front door. She often ordered him—looking down at himself, huffing, mystified—right back up to his room, to change, this very instant.

Ruth and Bobby, en route to Florida by car in 1949, stopped at a tourist camp. Around 4 A.M., they smelled smoke, sat up to find the motel mostly on fire. A stunning wordless teamwork took over as she ran left, he adrenalined right—as they pounded and kicked on each door, waking every guest. Only later, by the glow of flames, by the fire trucks' raking red lights, did others (then my grandparents) slowly recognize: one old ribby gent and his bosomy partner were and had been totally naked all during. Bobby grinned. "Well, what do you know?" Blankets embroidered with the motel's name

settled over himself, his wife—a Pitt and therefore un-
perturbed by flames, strangers, frontal nudity.

Unusual for their generation, these two slept bare-
assed and bragged about it. When, years later, Ruth got
rushed to the hospital, her daughters-in-law ransacked
dresser drawers, then phoned the best store in town,
ordering what might've been the old woman's first
nightie ever—ivory-colored satin worthy of a bride.
"Romeo and Juliet," my father said of his own parents;
but under his irony ran an envy we all felt—even the
kids did.

My parents hated Grand's calling their Bryan
"Willy." Ruth shamed Grand for it. "People will think
you don't *know* better, Little Bobby, and him your own
flesh and blood." She considered this a possible first
hint of galloping senility. She seemed to revel in Grand's
early memory goofs. "I'm afraid you're really slipping
now. What shall we *do* with you?" and she touched his
splotchy hand. Mentioning her husband's several faults,
Ruth would corner anybody, black or white, friend or
stranger. He sat right there all during, sat still and smiling. Little Bobby looked up at her, raucous with squint-
eyed love as she admitted his frequent lapses. Ruth
claimed he'd once owned every fashionable section of
Falls, till roughly two months before it *became* fashionable, at which point he sold it at a dreadful loss. "Didn't
you?" A gentle blinking nod. "Also, what's far worse,
I fear—you all see that gentleman over there, the one
with the exceptional hearing? in 19 and 19 he went and
peddled our 650 shares of Coca-Cola stock for something like a dollar forty per share. Now, *did*n't you,
Bobby? Fess up and get this part over with," and she
wandered to his chair, brushed white hair off his forehead. He nodded, grinning, scratching at sunburned

cartilage. "Ruth, honey? Believe it was—dollar *ten* a share."

I am thirty-nine years old. (I can't accept how aged I've become. My mother, who'll turn seventy this May, is glad, since misery loves company—my ex-wives are probably unsurprised and might consider my being upset as just more typical vanity. Only *I* feel stunned and lonely, hearing the Niagara of forty roaring just ahead.) Now, in trying to recall the few perfect couples I have known, my grandparents seem about the most contented. At best, it's a fairly short list. Around 12:15 A.M., after an evening of whining about our love lives, my friends sometimes say, "Well, who-married do we even *know* that's really happy?"

"Now, when you say 'happy,' how do you mean it? I guess you mean . . . ?"

"Happy. Just really *happy*, ever heard of it? . . . It used to be a concept."

My grandfolks were. What they mostly did: buttonhole anybody nearby—service-station men, hotel maids, family—and bad-mouth one another.

He called her a Gibson girl debutante run to seed; she said he was the most shiftless thing still half alive. And all during, they aimed sleepy, narrowed smiles at one another. I know it's now unfashionable, one person saying, "I own you and you own me." But I swear, theirs was the curt dreamy look of sovereign ownership. Maybe such love can occur only during the heyday of a rustic capitalist society.

In their household crowded with kin, you'd see the pair retreat to some corner, conferring about supper. Speaking, faces hovering unsentimental inches apart— one of them would idly lift a white hair off the other's gray-worsted shoulder; next, a straightening of the other's overbright tie. Soon their fingers were all over each other, efficient. Watching, you understood: they didn't even *know* they were in contact. If you pointed this out, they would loudly deny it. After sixty years of married days, their separate bodies had become that mutual, that pooled. Fondest strokings always started as sharpest criticism.

"Just *look* at you," she'd say, he'd say.

Ruth died before he did. I can tell you, she never meant to. Among the few wishes Ruth Eder Pitt Grafton was not granted: outliving Little Bobby. I once heard the woman, alone in the kitchen, cutting a first large piece of cake for him, explaining to no one, "Should anything ever happen to *me* . . ." Many spouses say this. We heard her but never quite believed till later.

The day before Ruth died, Grand drove a Packardload of grandkids to the hospital. Nobody under twelve was allowed to visit. Our grandfather led us up a fire-exit side entrance, pausing for breath on each landing. Grand quietly told us he would take the full official blame. We just had to see her a last time. If the rules aren't fair—he said—if there's no time left to change the rules, a person broke them, a person had to.

I was twelve, the oldest kid present. (I later discovered that many of Bobby's grandkids felt *they* were his all-time secret favorite. This actually upset me briefly, but I still believe I was and am.) The batch of us, ages five to twelve, kept silent for a change. A hospital stairwell echoes so. I remember somebody's terry-cloth slipper (one only) was resting on a landing. It had three drops of blood across its top, like a design. "Yisch," my youngest girl cousin whispered, prodding it with the toe of her blue Ked.

We were herded toward a doorway. We felt pretty nervous at maybe being caught on the third floor, nervous about seeing Grandmother. It would be our very first viewing of Mrs. Ruth, our lifetime hostess, as somebody out of control. I stood in her half-opened doorway surrounded by curly blond younger cousins, mostly girls. I felt scared by this hall's alcohol smell, by two different kinds of serious coughing nearby. I dreaded stepping into the room but felt I couldn't hold back now and disappoint Bobby Grafton.

She looked strangely small in a large, high bed. I'd never seen her with her hair unbraided. It uncoiled long as a witch's, and though I hated myself, to me it looked obscene all over the pillows like that. No discipline.

Even then, modern medicine was working those miracles that jab tubes into every outlet of the dying. Such help renders departing souls just conscious enough to be aware of this foreground indignity, it annoys them just enough to distract from Last Things. Right in my wallet here I've got a card telling authorities to withhold any such assistance from me, no way. I'm not forty but have learned from my poor loved ones' polluted exits.

"Come in," Grand called. I didn't want to step into that room. I saw clear hanging sacks and tubing. But I was scared that if I didn't cross the threshold, my little cousins might mutiny, turn back. So, dutiful, I took a breath, I stepped right in. I have always been dutiful. It is the thing about myself I hate the most. It is the thing about myself I love almost the most. How do you figure it?

Grand wanted us to see this woman dying. Another form of story-telling, showing her now—Bobby, born middleman at other people's dramas. This happened in winter. The heating system beat throughout the ward. One radiator against her room's far wall now rocked in place, clanging like a metal seizure chained near the bed. I stood, my thin arms drooped over the shoulders of plump little cousins gathered against, around, below me. "Uck," one whispered. "What'd they *do* to her? *That's* not her."

"Come closer." The old man waved, smiling from the bed, "Ruth's hair, look, her hair has always been this long. So fine. Brown when I met her. It got blonder before turning silver, then white, like it is now. Happened in less than six months. There's still a lot of brown in it if you know what color to look for. Started out the shade of clover honey. Look at her. Come on in, do." Our group's spoiled youngest just said, "No." She stomped one foot, she wouldn't budge.

Some kids had edged nearer the bed, most remained half huddled in the hall, holding on to the doorjamb as if the sight of our grandmother might make a great gust that'd blow us all back down the stairs. Nurses began noticing us here. Nurses didn't want to be bothered. They'd surely seen other grandchildren file into the hall for other enforced death watches. To keep officials from trudging down here and complaining, I must now get my cousins into this room.

Grand acted upset over the little ones' hanging back. But he turned our way, grinning anyhow. "You're scared is all. And you're damned smart to be. Still, I guess you can see her okay from out there. Here's your grandmother. She's why you're here."

I watched him try to help the woman. He lifted a glass and water pitcher; he poured some, spilling. She was beyond drinking from a glass; he tipped wet against her lips anyhow, it ran all down her chin, darkening her ivory nightie. He did this with the heavy-handed earnestness his stories showed.

Grand touched her forehead, pressed the hair back.

"You kids want to leave, probably. And who can blame you, seeing her like this?" The corners of his mouth went up for a smile, but it wasn't one. His hand tested her for fever. Grand acted possessive even of Ruth's dying.

He just shook his head. "You children don't like it now, but you've seen enough so you'll pretty much remember. Yeah, this woman here, this old woman here . . ."

And he picked up a hairbrush from the bedside table; he made a few swipes at her yard-long hair. The man grinned like a salesman demonstrating. "Ever seen such hair?"

Maybe he hoped to show us that this was beautiful, that she was still beautiful. But to me, it was not. She was not.

I can't bear recalling this next part but—as Grand predicted—I do . . . do remember. Some white hair lifted by his brush got tangled in the clear tubes leading to her nose. Then I reached for some support not there, I had to lean against the doorjamb. My cousins noticed. Since I was the oldest, dutiful and all . . . I didn't—but I'd come close to fainting. It was the smell of her room, the scorched steam heat; it was seeing how long a person's hair had always secretly been. It was all the sweetish flowers everywhere. I told myself, Grown-ups use flowers to mean this, *too*.

At a red light three blocks from the hospital, he reminded us, already bickering in back, glad to again be loud spoiled Grafton brats, "Your grandmother came from money. Not like my people. Money always made her particular. She scolded me something fierce, remember? Yeah, I could always count on Ruth for that. Merciless, she was. Merciless, hard, lovely woman. You

had to admire her. I never stopped admiring her to
pieces. She always *kept* herself so nice . . . Ruth.''
Then we watched Grand fall across the steering wheel.

At first I thought, He is having an attack. You are the
oldest. Run. A hospital's just blocks away. Go fast.
They'll help. ''Attack''—that was all I knew about old
people dying: attacks so often got them. Hers'd happened in the garden, then she crawled, on all fours, up
toward the porch; but her attack, it found her there.

Us kids slowly figured: Grand was only weeping. We
probably felt more embarrassed about the man's sobbing than if he'd perished at the wheel. ''He's *crying*,''
our fussy youngest said. ''He's crying like *you* would,
Sandy.'' ''Would not.'' ''Would so.'' But nervousness
soon hushed them.

He made sounds like a child doing poor animal imitations. The traffic light changed three times. It being
un-rush hour in downtown Falls, North Carolina, only
four cars had gathered behind us. The first tried pulling
around without even honking (it was that long ago), but
the car needed more room. So finally the driver hit her
horn once, wincing, lifting her shoulders.

My youngest, sulkiest girl cousin—who'd said ''No''
and ''Yisch'' at the hospital—now sulked. ''We're
blocking things. We're messing up everything. I hate
this part.'' Though her sassiness shamed me, I understood: its bossy tone (inherited?) might just reach him
now.

''Well.'' Grand struggled to sit, wiping his eyes on
the roof of either hand. ''Mustn't do that. Don't want
anybody complaining about their Little Bobby.'' Us kids
looked at each other. Four child hands touched his
shoulder, touched the lined, glazed neck. Our Packard
lurched forward just as the light turned red. A screeching bread truck swerved to miss us. Sidewalk shoppers

covered their upper faces. ''Joyride,'' Grand explained
to the dashboard. His eyes were locked straight ahead.
In back, we kept very still, not exactly holding hands
(it was not that kind of family) but feeling comforted
by all the cousinly little legs and shoulders pressing
against our legs, our shoulders.

With her gone, everybody saw how much she'd really
done for him. Meaning: everything. It was just unbelievable. Things you couldn't even name except by saying, ''Something's off, *some*thing's wrong. Did he have
two shoes on today?—probably, but something . . .
else.'' His driving grew wilder. It got so when locals
saw his Packard Skipper in motion, their cars pulled
right to the roadside, as if honoring a funeral. People
new to town complained, not having the full history.
Our sheriff's parents had once enjoyed six months' free
rent in 1931 in a toolshed behind my grandfather's garage. Sherriff Wilks refused to give Grand so much as
a warning. ''Mustn't embarrass Mr. Grafton,'' half our
two-man police force told strangers. ''Mr. Grafton has
a lot *on* him just now.''

Folks new here snapped back, ''Your Mr. Grafton is
a menace to society and I dearly hope it's your squad
car he totals.''

The dark Packard now seemed everywhere, in sudden need of washing. It quickly filled with litter, proof
that Grand ate, against his daughters-in-law's wishes,
fast food out on the strip by our mall. ''You mustn't let
him go *near* that highway,'' Mother scolded my father.
''Once he's on 301, it'll probably mean instant death
for him and many others.''

''But how can *I* stop him? A court injunction, what?''
Dad asked us all. ''He's my father. How can I stop
him?'' We heard: Dad really wanted advice, even from

us kids. We all sat quiet at dinner, thinking of the world's hazards, traps set everywhere for babies, animals, old people.

You started wondering. Had *she* washed the Packard all those years, a woman so intent on not knowing how to drive? "You think Mother went out there at 2 a.m. with a hose and sponge? Maybe she wore some of his flashier old clothes. Can't you just picture her?" Dad smiled. I could. (I'd felt so shamed by Grand's weeping in the car, I never told my folks.) To me at twelve, his relying so on Ruth seemed unmanly, disappointing. Scary how a man can need one woman. Ruth had warned us all those years. We thought it was just another part of their cross-with-each-other routine.

For the first time in memory, my own mother began to speak fondly of my bossy, edgy late grandmother.

Father hired a cleaning woman to live in and cook for Grand. Three quit in one month. Two ladies claimed he followed them around all day, they felt observed. Even while they vacuumed as loudly as possible, Grand shouted gory Falls sagas their way. Bank robbers, understandable hangings, infant lockjaw. One woman complained, "The old gentleman keeps hounding me with stories about the dead, and they don't *go* anywhere, they're just endless. Besides, he made certain . . . I think they were . . . advances." By now I was being sent away to school. I remember marveling that anybody would quit to avoid Grand's tales. But then, of course, I was safely someplace else. I was a year past thirteen; I now resisted Sunday visits to Grand's. If forced to go, I stayed on the porch with my opinionated aunts and suddenly-not-bad-looking girl cousins. He shuffled out and gave me wounded, amused looks—made more unbearable by their basset-hound forgiveness.

Older, safe at school, I could afford to be sentimental about the man's repeated "good ones." I felt myself to be more sophisticated than he and so decided Grand was, like the folk music then in vogue, colorful.

My Northern roommate grilled me, Wasn't Little Bobby really just your basic "slum lord?" Didn't he lease to the white merchants who overcharged blacks?

At school, around 2 a.m., stoned illegally, I tried ignoring this, tried telling my suitemates the story about Lancaster's mule. Before I even got near the punch line, my pals walked out. "Guess . . . you had to've been there," I explained to an empty dorm room. Maybe turns-of-speech involving mules didn't cut the mustard after 1962, didn't translate beyond Falls's city limits. Maybe Little Bobby Grafton would remain an acquired taste. *I* now considered him remarkable, but my own reasons might be genetically determined, too simple to quite name or recognize. Maybe Grand's charms could never be explained by a college-bound "Bryan"? Only some Willy could tell the plain and salty truth of "Ears" Grafton, loving witness to others' wit, the not-pretty poor kid who lived in trouble, who met and wooed a dowried lady worthy of satin sheets. A sharecroppers' kid who, though often crossed, never ever snitched, not once.

For the month after her funeral, he refused to leave their house. He seemed afraid Ruth might return and not find him waiting. Then we heard how Mr. Grafton had paid unannounced social calls on two recent widows. These handsome women were confused when he sat beside them on settees, saying little while glaring hard at their wrists, their necks. Maybe Bobby planned to appear amorous. He first looked peeved, then dangerous. He slid onto one knee, tried kissing a lady's hand the way some foreign baron might. She yelped, set her pug dogs barking, showed him out. Hoping to lighten things, Grand smiled. "I guess *you* know why everbody says 'tighter'n Lessie Poland's boot,' huh?"

"Why you say *what*?" (She was new here.)

When he turned up at my folks' place, Grand wasn't wearing mourning black. He arrived in plaids-over-stripes. Knotted around his neck, one unclean polka-dotted bow tie. Most of a piece of blueberry pie was crusted on it, the archaeology of a good meal. My mother first tried teasing him, hoping the indirect approach might work. "What?" He stared at his own rag-amuffin outfit. "Myself, I can't see it, Helen. To me it's all just clothes. Lucky to have them. They cover you, they come in different colors, so what?"

Mother said she really should take his bow tie off and go out in our backyard and bury it as a dog would bury a bone. Then, hearing herself, Mother laughed, adding, "I'm beginning to sound like . . ." but she hushed, quit smiling. He looked up then. "Like who? *Say* her name. I want to hear you say her *name*, Helen."

"Like Ruth," Mother said. "I was going to say I sounded like Ruth complaining she was sounding too much like you."

He grinned, nodding, jaunty. "She was merciless, okay," and tears, sudden amazing amounts, came pouring down a face the color of boiled ham.

This business about the mixed-up clothes might sound like nothing, really. But you'd be surprised how strange and funny it can look, how disturbing. With Ruth alive, Bobby usually wore white shirts, dark trousers, black business shoes, and semi-loud ties (his wife's one con-cession to the taste of a man who admired carny-barker types like Buck Lancaster). Grand loved having young-bloods around town call, "Mighty flashy hand-painted

tie you got there, Mr. Grafton." "*I* thought so," he'd
wink.

But now at the mall, Grand appeared a sad hick
farmer arrived to purchase some item expensive as a
tractor, some guy fearful of being taken, maybe thinking he'd blend in better if hidden by the right number
of city plaids.

When I came home from school, my folks drove
Grand and all of us to a new restaurant. The organist
was playing, the place was dark, Grand was offered a
large black leatherette menu. Finally he leaned across
the table, whispered to me, "Where are the *numbers*
of the hymns listed, Will? She always marks my hymns
for me."

Others heard. My father offered the benefit of the
doubt. "Like church, Daddy? 'Good one.' " The old
man's face changed; he grabbed my father's wrist, hard.
Grand then checked around and—world's worst liar—
forced a grin. "Don't *I* know? Didn't I plan that? My
own flesh and blood, and it can't even take a joke?"

We laughed. Yes. Oh, *ha* ha ha.

My father was at his law office meeting with six bigwig clients come to file a class action; Grand popped
in unannounced. The secretary had just adjourned to
the bathroom, Grand passed her desk and shuffled
through double doors into the conference room. Little
Bobby hadn't shaved for a week. He wore red bedroom
slippers, a tasteful windbreaker, and a striped shirt, but
he'd put the windbreaker on first. He carried, for some
reason, a can of 3-in-1 oil. "How *about* this weather?"
He settled at the long teak table. When people stared,
he smiled. "Hot enough for you?" Soon as my dad got
the conference uneasily restarted, Grand nodded off,
sitting upright, snoring tenderly. Since the six clients

were not from Falls, it all proved harder to explain.
These were the kind of high-powered folks who
might've called a sheriff if they saw some vintage Packard weaving lane to lane. New people.

Such business-hour visits happened often after that.
My father was too shy or kind to tell Grand his turning
up uninvited was not exactly . . . convenient. When the
old man barged in on meetings with locals, Dad could
say, "You've all met my father." But with important
out-of-towners, Dad shrugged. "A relative," adding,
quieter, "period of grieving here." Dad confessed at
dinner, "Listen, you all, it might get worse. I'm one
step away from 'I've never seen this man before in my
life.' " We laughed. What else could you do? Grand
had stayed too lucid for locking up in some home. But,
interrupting another legal meeting, Bobby told one
Yankee client, "Yeah, brought Arthur downtown with
me today." "Really?" The woman looked around for
help; Father sat rubbing the bridge of his nose. "Yeah."
Grand winked, "Arthur-*it*is."

"Ah-ha."

Sheriff Wilks, a man of principle, refused to revoke
Grand's license, even when Mother drove down with
some brownies, then begged. Two days in a row Grand
was found patrolling our county courthouse. He had
come, he told some carpenters working on office par-
titions, to buy the title for a twenty-acre farm five miles
southeast of town, the old Redmond place, please.
Grand knew the soil there very well. He had decided
it'd be perfect for soybeans and now wanted to buy it
as a little family spread. He needed it at once. He had
the money on him. He was walking around showing
strangers this great wad of hundred-dollar bills.

The county registrar, a family friend, noticed him
and was very patient and helped him look up the deed.

She phoned my parents only on finding that Redmond had died in 1880 and that Grand's own father had bought the tract at auction, had fallen behind with payments, and, in 1912, lost it. These twenty acres were zoned for business around 1946. The old mall had stood right there since late '62.

I was home from school. I planned mailing a turquoise bracelet and some philosophy paperbacks to my girlfriend, stuck at home on vacation with *her* parents. At the Falls post office I spied one old-timer flipping through Wanted posters. He wore green fishing boots, coveralls, a seersucker suitcoat. The same Wanted signs have hung on the wall since I was a kid. Other people noted the old guy; they slowed for a second, then maneuvered gingerly around him. People seemed to consider him harmless—but also about as crazy as . . . as an I don't know what.

I have to say this on my behalf. I was sixteen, a delicate age for enduring public scenes and family embarrassments. I headed toward my grandfather. He would be glad to see me. I could make a joke: "Found any good bank robbers lately?" "Got Arthur along?" something. Then I noticed that, at a table marked with today's date, he was using the chained ballpoint. He'd got some paper towels from the bathroom (when I was sixteen, clean restrooms were still open to the public in all U.S. post offices!). The towels appeared covered with finely printed notes. He must've lingered here all morning, transcribing. A Styrofoam cup of cold-looking coffee waited on one marble ledge. He slumped forward, jotting, muttering, secretive. I still felt I could handle this. I took a few steps closer, when I saw the drawings. He was copying one criminal's face. He was trying to.

He'd done other portraits. Some of these sketches were weirdly good, carefully shaded with blue ballpoint. His being able to actually sort of draw made it all seem worse to me and weirder. Since early morning, he'd been down here for every citizen of Falls to see. Was he trying to memorize likely fugitives? Did he want to recollect certain faces he'd known and lost, like the mug of shady, witty Lancaster? Would Grand now drive along the streets of Falls, bounty-hunting crooks? I never knew. I stared at the back of this man, his farmer's neck so deeply creased it pleated. Others stayed clear of him. One passing older woman saw me noticing. She offered the brisk eye-rolling look that sane nervous strangers give each other. It's ugly. It means: "Sad, yes. But *we're* not like him."

What I did next, I told myself, was really out of pity, gratitude, even love. After all, he seemed so happy, so busy over there.

I slipped out the side exit.

Four days before Grand died, Mother played hostess to a regional Master's Bridge Championship. I personally consider card games fairly silly, a waste of everybody's time. But back then bridge was important to her.

Over the years, five people have made it their mission to teach me the game. We endure one nice long comical evening; then they each mercifully give up on me. I urge them to. Even so, I'd played enough to know the game, and over one bored rainy Christmas vacation spent in Falls recovering from pneumonia, I saw what a genius my mother was at it. She has a mind that any captain of industry might covet. I don't know who to blame for her wasting it on cards. Society? or her? or cards themselves? She's never really seemed all that miffed about the waste.

The championship at our house mattered not at all to me, but I'd seen her planning it for months. And so, though I was sixteen and though this proved hard, I stayed out of her way and, for once, kept my irony to myself.

The limo of our governor's wife was double-parked out front. A uniformed driver buffed its chrome—a cake-decoration-sized state flag rode each fender and looked fairly absurd there. I was a kid. So much of the world then looked ridiculous to me, but these flags, I think, still would.

Our house held eighty-eight distinguished white women. Card tables were arranged everywhere, ash-trays and chairs borrowed from the caterer. I'd retreated to my room upstairs but could hear a musical chatter-natter. It already sounded like a great chummy success.

I remember the next part in this order: I came sneaking down the back stairs, eager for a secret lunch snitched off canapé trays. I knew from other parties how twenty-two tables of visiting ladies love catching sight of the household's big-eared if not-unhandsome teenaged son. They really checked you out, shameless, giving you the once-over from the feet up. I hated that. I hated acting polite to grown-ups I didn't respect. I didn't respect many adults then. I did not yet understand what-all they had to put up with.

So I'm dodging down our back stairs when I hear two State Bureau of Investigation detectives drag in a whimpering man. They had him by his wrists. He thrashed between them in the foyer, pleading loud, "You're *hurting* Arthur." His pants were covered with sticky seed-pods from some walk through some woods. He wore a shirt with buggy races occurring all across it. His fly was unbuttoned and a goodly number of the printed racing buggies tufted out there as at some finish line.

He wore a rolled knitted sailor's cap from the Army-Navy outlet; he sported a green clip-on bow tie. There was about him the look and scent of a fellow too smart, absentminded, or aggrieved to bathe very often.

Two young men wrestled him from the living room, where our governor's wife had just ceased dealing. They pushed him more toward Mother. She rose, gone ash-white, frowning as at some difficult eye chart. "Smarts," the old man stated. "These boys are big and they keep *hurt*ing me." My mother and I hollered it at the same moment: *"Let him go!"*

Since she hadn't seen me on the stairs, my voice made her jump. She spun my way, gave a long, freighted look up the steps, a look that might be freely translated *"Oh, shit. Darling, what are we to do here?"*

"Ma'am, we caught him hiding under your neighbor's carport. When he spotted us watching, he got down on all fours behind a hedge, then made a break for your house. Calls himself Arthur. Claims to know you, ma'am."

My mother nodded. "He did . . . does." She was fairly panting now. Her fixed, mournful smile slayed me. I eased down the stairs, hoping to be of use, still her dutiful eldest. In silence, Mother's face told me, Darling, if you get him out of here right now before it's even worse, I'll give you anything in the world, *any*thing.

But as I stepped toward my grandfather, now released and massaging his thin reddened wrists, he noticed eighty-eight women. Some gazed down from the stair landing. They'd gone dead quiet on the sunporch. Grand toured a crowded, frozen dining room; he stalked the living room, progressing rubber to rubber. The old man frowned at a house suddenly paved with card tables, four well-appointed women settled at each, all holding cards like geisha hand fans in the air before them. The women were quite correct to gape back at him. His arriving between two state agents was reason enough, but the clothes drew a little extra attention.

Then Grand smiled over at Mother. He'd got it. His sun-cooked face spread, wonderful with pleasure. "Helen, why, you sly dog you! You've gone and opened a rest-aurant. That's a good one. Always did claim you were smart, I don't care what Ruth said. Now every inch of your place is a little moneymaker, right? You little thief. And still pretty as a speckled puppy, too. Just look at all the suckers you've stuffed in here. Hi, ladies! Why, it's right cozy. You kept it *like* a house, but you're not leaving your customers too much extra legroom, packing them in like sardines, eh, you operator? You got it all over that son of mine. He still háving a hard time making a go of the office? I hope you two don't *need* a restaurant. But, sugar, tell Little Bobby something off-the-record-like—how'd you get around the *zoning*?"

And he winked.

Mother was far too stunned to hush him as he wandered. It was too late. There could be no future. He free-associated aloud, pausing to half-stoop, admiring whatever showed of nyloned legs on certain younger bridge enthusiasts.

I cannot describe to you the silence in our house just then.

Mother, using eyebrows only, swinging her head, hinted: I should maybe take him to the backyard, maybe? Very quickly, maybe? But first she did something I will always love her for.

By now he was entertaining ladies in the living room, gabbing about his constant companion Arthur. Mother walked up behind Grand. When his face turned toward hers, Mother's—oval, cordial—went instantly serene. The farmer grinned back, entranced with her beauty and business sense. These two people stood for one second, face to face. Watching, I forgot everything unpleasant. (There's a moment when every itchy sixteen-year-old boy suddenly *sees* his mother, sees her whole, and when he knows for the first time, "Hey, my mother is 'a brunette,' " when he understands that she's a not-at-all-unattractive woman, ripened by years, and is desirable and good, and when he really really wants to run away with her forever. This, for me, was that moment.) What she did: she put one palm on Grand's shoulder and—while he smiled back at her simply, so simply—her free hand touched his stubbled cheek. Then Mother said loud enough for everyone downstairs to hear, "Ladies, I want you to meet my father-in-law. A dear man."

Then I led him out.

The party chugged on, but its tones now sounded clogged; it would end early. I've always hated her guests for leaving so soon. I mean, doesn't everybody have a family? Shouldn't they have understood? And my mother never got over it, either. This sounds trivial, I know, but the things that shave the years off everybody's lives are often just this slight. —No fair.

I kept my hand on the small of Grand's back and, exiting through the kitchen, grabbed a fistful of trimmed sandwiches for us. I squired him to a group of lawn chairs in the sun; I settled at the foot of his chaise. He had gobbled four sandwiches before really noticing me. Then half-standing, reaching into his pants' pockets, he pulled out the little can of household oil, one uncut plug of Sweet Peach chewing tobacco, and a ruby-chip dinner ring now missing four stones.

"How do *you* like my bow tie?"

I smiled. "What, are you taking a poll?"

"It's just . . . nobody seems to . . ." and Grand held on to both ends of it the way a clown would. I felt he was putting me on, he'd been tricking all of us, hoping to unload faulty goods at top dollar, at night. For a second, it seemed Bobby'd finally become the kind of flimflam artist he'd always admired. But the moment passed. I saw he hadn't pulled a thing; there was no "good one." Instead, here in direct sun—a forelock of white hair, ears seriously testing the rolled cap—sat one very old and cruelly healthy senile man. He'd once been so charming. He could no longer regulate it.

"Yes, sir. Quite a tie. 'Seriously groovy,' some people'd say." (It was 1968, not that it matters.) He shifted toward our house, frowning, maybe guessing he'd just made a mistake. Toilets flushed upstairs and down—ladies discussing recent events clear of their hostess's hearing. I thought: Poor Mother. Then decided: But poor Grand here, too. Poor all of us eventually and now.

Touching the items spread before him, he shifted these, a shell game. Grand stared at me, as if trying to recall something. Yesterday I'd avoided him at the post office; I blamed that for today's embarrassments. He pointed my way, saying to nobody, "Look, a boy. What is he, about eighteen?"

"I'm almost seventeen. *I* am. I'm *here*. Say it to *me*. It's Willy, Grand."

"You seem older. Than that. And know what, buddy? You definitely look like somebody. Seems like I should know you."

Breath failed me for a second. (A civic thought: And they're letting him drive around in a car like this?)

Slowly I explained who I was, via my connection to him. I skipped being Bryan, I stuck with Willy.

"That a fact? Well, you know, one look at you and I someway said to myself, I said . . . I went . . . went . . ."

" 'Little Bobby' . . . ?' "

"Little Bobby! The very name. You're smart, aren't you? Not as smart as . . . Little Bobby, but smart."

I noticed secret service men watching us from around the house. I felt furious. I considered flipping them the finger, then remembered dodging this very gentleman downtown.

So I decided to tell him a story. It was all I could think of. Keep him occupied. If he trotted back into the house, we'd have to move from Falls. I started with one of his that you know, one about a local livestock dealer.

Afterward, he sat rearranging the can, tobacco, and ring—like hoping to sell them. Soon as I finished "Lancaster's Mule," Grand nodded. "You must've told me that one before. Why's that so familiar?"

"Because it's yours. I mean it *was* yours, first. And see, you told me so if you ever forgot it or didn't care about it anymore or whatever—then *I'd* remember it and tell it back to you, see?"

"Oh," he said. "That lady is smart. She's put about thirty tables in her front rooms and the hall, even on her landing. She's soaking them good, I bet. (Why didn't I think of it at *our* house that's so empty?) Say four women eat at every table, and if she charges them, oh, maybe five bucks a head . . ." Grand leaned nearer suddenly, voice gone stupid, manly, matter-of-fact. He said, "I bet I can beat *you* up."

I scouted for the detectives, suddenly glad that they were near. I bet he could. I'd have a rough time hitting him back.

But Grand had already coasted past his challenge. I sat looking at him. I could. He always let you. I hated

how I'd denied him in a public place. He might've hinted
what he was doing there, copying convicts' photographs. Maybe he'd finally found some scam, a "good
one." Now I'll never know what Grand had in mind.
And I only needed to ask. He would've told me.

The next Thursday, just after dawn, seeing a Packard
parked sideways at the far edge of our oldest mall's huge
lot, Sheriff Wilks found Bobby Grafton in the backseat,
dead. My grandfather was wearing—my parents explained later by phone—his best gray suit, one they'd
forced him into for Ruth's funeral. He'd parted his hair
in the very exact middle. He had on a white shirt and
blue tie, and his shoes weren't bedroom slippers and
were shined, and they matched.

It was just what Ruth once loved her Bobby to wear,
and now he'd picked the outfit by himself and—as
planned—on a site adjoining hers—was buried in it.

The old mall is a fairly good mall as malls go. But I
really wish he hadn't died there. I wish Little Bobby
had made it out to some countryside he'd owned before
selling cheap on the brink of its prospering. But then
Dad reminded us how Grand's boyhood farm—the
twenty acres that his folks could not afford for long, a
truck farm with its early-blooming hollyhocks—how
that rested right beneath where Big Elk Browse 'n' Buy
Mall got built in '62. Grand's Packard found the spot,
but not the place.

3. SOON . . .

The day I learned the meaning of Lancaster's mule,
I overheard a local woman use the term downtown. Odd
how that happens. You wonder what else you've steadily
missed. I had long since left home and settled else-

where—first Cambridge, then here in New York. I now plan to hurry toward our story's end. I rush, compensating for an inherited tendency toward storytelling longwindedness. This is the part where you find out what Time did to everybody left alive. This is the part where you see how Stories maybe offer us a little deal-making revenge on Time.

My parents and aunts unloaded Bobby's house four weeks after his well-attended funeral. A major selling point was the fine porch on three sides. Suddenly it'd become "the old Grafton place." It sold for under fifteen thou. North Carolina real estate always seems a bargain compared to Manhattan's, but twelve-five for such a roomy, boxy home is—even by local standards—a deal and a half.

Bobby'd let the place slide at the end, and it did look fairly bad and needed paint. But, as we grumpy grandkids pointed out, it had stayed structurally sound. Why sell, and so cheap? Ruth's good furniture was divided up. Her Aubusson carpet caused the only ugly feud. (In-laws behaved much worse than did blood relations. "I want *none* of it," my mother said.) Nobody claimed a hideous orange chair and footstool, but everybody said somebody really should. "Though, of course, where would you *put* it?"

A young couple expecting twins bought the place. He's chief DJ at Fall's Easy-Listening Rock station. This made us grandkids moan the louder: Little Bobby's heirs feel that rock should be hard, money is to enjoy, children should be seen and heard. Even a hog is wise enough to love its local life. The new owners had every right to paint our holy shrine that overly tart Williamsburgy blue—a gift-shoppe color. Driving past, I feel literally nauseated. On the front porch, near where Ruth frisked an incoming Grand for rent checks or criticized his outgoing outfits, one tastefully white plaster burro now stands, mopey, almost life-sized. Why a burro in Falls? It supports saddlebags, sprouting geraniums that might or might not be real geraniums. I've never walked far enough into these perfect strangers' yard to check.

For twelve-five, maybe *I* should've bought the place. But why? To do *what* with?

When Dad retired, my parents got rid of their own suburban house. They chose Bermuda, of all places, but soon admitted feeling half homesick among the hibiscus. They returned to Falls and bought a little cabin down by Indian Creek. Now they spend three months a year in our hometown, nine in Bermuda. This pleases me very much. I visit them, but only in Falls; I never set foot in dull gorgeous Bermuda. None of my New York friends can understand this.

My spoiled girl cousins have prospered and scattered; they enjoy serious careers and have kids who're nearly done with college. Hard to believe. My spirited girl cousins all turned out fairly great-looking. They've withstood the usual serial marriages. For some reason, as a group, they're just unbelievably foul-mouthed. They remain the blond family members who look the way I think I should, but don't . . . yet. They keep their hair long, professionally full around the ear area. (Our family joke and family shame.) These cousins phone me when they're passing through New York. We meet for drinks at overpriced places, where we talk about our adored low-rent grandfather and prudish grandmother, and get positively shitfaced and cry sometimes. Round by round, our Southern accents grow humid as bad actors', till we reel onto the sidewalk, are hit in the face by Yankee winter, then holler for taxis, our tones gone suddenly harsh as any Bronx truck drivers'. Gentility will not snag you that cab during a snowstorm at 3 A.M.

Sir, your brood is finally sophisticated enough just to enjoy you to pieces. Where are you, now we're ready, "Ears"?

I suppose that every county in our nation once enjoyed its own terms based on famous-for-around-here characters. These phrases are like most of us in being well-known and useful but within fairly strict local limits. Language *is* like love. Whatever phrase shows the rawest life, that finds its way into our speech. Whatever terms grow ossified and fussy get chipped away. If something means enough to enough people, if it really clarifies, feels accurate, then it catches on, spreads. If our poisoned world still matters enough to enough people, then I guess they'll keep it continuing. If not . . . well, not.

When I return to Falls for summer visits or Christmas, I begin to see exactly who Bobby Grafton was and wasn't. A very homely hick kid, he longed to own nice town things; and he got some, too. He let his renters slide if they talked as well as he did. His funeral was attended by 110 black people. The guy was loved. But a crusader? Moral beacon? Ha! Quite early, I'd started seeing him whole. I drove up and down one weedy street where no soul cared to live but many did. Roofs leaked, missing windowpanes sealed shut with tinfoil and Scotch tape. The landlord of all? My ex-tenant-farmer Grand was at home on his porch rereading *True Detective*. At age fourteen or so, I and my girl cousins secretly mailed part of our allowance money to Dr. King's civil-rights campaign. In plain brown envelopes (at the donor's request) we got back leaflets asking "Where Are the South's White Leaders? To Whom Shall We Speak?" In Falls, I sometimes still hear the phrase Grand taught me at age ten. Experts claim the National Nightly News might homogenize regional quirks out of our national language. I'm glad that's not true quite yet. I've heard Falls citizens apply "crazy as Lancaster's mule" to myself as a part-time radical graduate student, to myself during a brief intense early partnership with a woman who wanted my heirloom ears "cosmetically pinned"; I've heard it describe my second marriage to a person "rich enough to start a foundation, old enough to be your mother." I'm comforted, knowing that a term coined mid-hog auction in 1890 still pertains.

Lately, the phrase grows more and more appropriate. Maybe, like me, you read the papers. I sometimes look up from a particularly rancid front page; I scan the air packed before my face. Say I've read about some group blowing up a plane with passengers and the terrorists themselves inside it. I shake my head the way Little Bobby would. I go, "People now . . . the world now—I swear to God, crazy as Lancaster's mule."

I know my tone might seem that of someone fairly provincial, somebody well over thirty-nine. But here in the city, many nights I feel like a perpetual outlander. To Bobby, this city—its onyx towers, crystal towers—might look as alien as Mars. My apartment is on the fortieth floor. I sit watching skyscraper lights come on. I sometimes feel very old here. Especially at the end of an office day, with tonight's news smudging my hands.

I'm not the first to notice: it's dangerous, what's happening. I mean, something's wrong, so *off*. We must all be very very careful.

What can a person do? Well, you stuff the offending newspaper into the trash, you get a night's sleep and, come morning, decide to make an excellent omelet. You do what you can. (An omelet for one. Between marriages, childless, I sometimes wish I'd got custody of something, somebody. In this, I am like many of my friends: I seem to manage the career thing pretty much

okay, but I've never ever really got the hang of the love
part. Not yet, anyway.)

During breakfast I can't help noticing—this milk car-
ton is coated with Wanted posters. Posters no longer
seek the hurters. The hurt ones are now shown. Missing kids. Lost to what? To maniacs, or black holes, or
a new child-slave trade? Where've they all *gone*?

People do get used to this, right? Tell me people get
used to this.

I think about Falls in 1962. I know I'm being an
escapist. Thanks to Little Bobby, I remember a hometown of ladies' bustles, genius crooks, gold watches big
as three-egg omelets. Falls 1962 might've been Falls 18
and 62. I picture mules, not Packards. Boy, would I
love to have that Packard now.

In present-day New York, my first name is mostly
only "Bryan." Sometimes, with certain attractive young
strangers, I do try changing. "You know," one told me
recently, "even from across this bar, you somehow
looked like a Willy." "I thank you, ma'am," said
Bryan.

Oh, to resurrect Little Bobby Grafton. Even for one
night. Willy here would surely throw around the plastic.
Maybe it's a sign of our times, my wanting to spend
big on my honored guest. I'd wine and dine him all
over high-tech Manhattan, squiring Grand everywhere—to hear café singers, to see punk clubs downtown. Once back from rabble-rousing, I'd keep him
awake for the 6 A.M. news. Imagine what he'd say about
this place, this moment.

Home, I'd settle Little Bobby near my choicest window in my favorite chair. It's upholstered in pigskin. I
won't turn on any lamps; the city's commercial glare is

trapped (an oxblood color) under low clouds. In here, there's light enough to read by. I imagine Grand staring out at the skyscrapers opposite; I imagine him wondering aloud if the renters on top pay less than those more grounded. Bobby asks where city people wash their cars. He wants to know if, all along, I *planned* to live alone like this. My answer: "Well, sir, yes and no."

Tired, he'll hunker deep into my Scandinavian easy chair, his ankle-high black shoes propped on the matching footstool. I'll go and warm a little low-fat milk for him. From the kitchen, I can ask things. I mostly see his chair back, one hand curled on the armrest. I want to hear Grand say: Oh, it's really not so bad—the world now—and it's not too late. Maybe things just need to go back some, get fortified, a bit more local. Meaning what? I doubt that Grand will say this. But look, I can hope, can't I?

What realm did those moral tales prepare us for? Once, I had a childish silvery idea: the Future.

I stand stirring the saucepan, trying to keep his milk from scorching. I see Bobby by the window, a dark silhouette against the crossword puzzle of bright windows, neon names of Japanese computer firms. He appears so small and wizened in the high-backed glove-leather chaise. (For some reason, it cost me two thousand dollars, plus tax.) Grand manages to tilt the whole thing back a notch, he praises the apartment buildings opposite. They're tall enough to wear blinking red lights, warning away low planes. He calls how I sure do have boo-coo neighbors, don't I? Are they mostly nice? He's already loosening his tie, fumbling through pockets, preparing for bed.

His chair's beside a Formica cube, one sold not as a "table" but as a "freestanding modular unit." Onto this, Bobby empties each linty pocket. I see the busy knotted hand; calluses have quilted it into a catcher's mitt. Out he fishes the gold watch, its chain dangles the little brass horseshoes once considered lucky. Stub fingers wind the watch, a fringe of white hair tips into view, one substantial ear presses against gold casing. His head half nods—the watch is put to one side. Pocket change gets piled into neat columns by denominations. A small pocketknife emerges, shy in the city (but no self-respecting county man would leave home without one). The stained driver's license, then half a pound of landlordly keys: access to rental homes, livestock barns, red Allis-Chalmers tractors.

Finally, on top, thumb and forefinger place the keepsake ring, some rubies left (if just in chips). Done, the hand slides back toward its counterpart; they join over the lap, and before I can pour Grand's milk into my best mug, slow snoring unfolds. I shake my head and grin some, muttering. I step into the room, I lean against one wall, studying the back of his chair, my chair. So much to ask and him asleep. *Is the world blind or does it just not give a damn?*

Between my own smooth hands, this hot cup feels so good. Automatically both eyes close. I hold on for dear life—I live here now.

Stuck in the present on the fortieth story, Willy is still interested, but waiting. I keep listening. I stay primed for something extra.

Yeah, it's just me here—me, all ears.

1986

Reassurance

For David Holding Eil (1981–)
and for Robert Langland Eil (1983–)

1.*

DEATH OF A PENNSYLVANIA SOLDIER. FRANK H. Irwin, company E, 93rd Pennsylvania—died May 1, '65—My letter to his mother.

Dear madam: No doubt you and Frank's friends have heard the sad fact of his death in hospital here, through his uncle, or the lady from Baltimore, who took his things. (I have not seen them, only heard of them visiting Frank.) I will write you a few lines—as a casual friend that sat by his death-bed. Your son, corporal Frank H. Irwin, was wounded near fort Fisher, Virginia, March 25, 1865—the wound was in the left knee, pretty bad. He was sent up to Washington, was receiv'd in ward C, Armory-square hospital, March 28th—the wound became worse, and on the 4th of April the leg was amputated a little above the knee—the operation was perform'd by Dr. Bliss,

---

*Section 1 quotes, unchanged and complete, Walt Whitman's letter titled "Death of a Pennsylvania Soldier" from "Specimen Days"—first published in his *Complete Prose Works* (Philadelphia, 1892), reprinted in *Whitman: The Library of America's Complete Poetry and Collected Prose* (1982).

one of the best surgeons in the army—he did the whole operation himself—there was a good deal of bad matter gather'd—the bullet was found in the knee. For a couple of weeks afterwards he was doing pretty well. I visited and sat by him frequently, as he was fond of having me. The last ten or twelve days of April, I saw that his case was critical. He previously had some fever, with cold spells. The last week in April he was much of the time flighty—but always mild and gentle. He died first of May. The actual cause of death was pyaemia, (the absorption of the matter in the system instead of its discharge). Frank, as far as I saw, had everything requisite in surgical treatment, nursing &c. He had watches much of the time. He was so good and well-behaved and affectionate, I myself liked him very much. I was in the habit of coming in afternoons and sitting by him, and soothing him, and he liked to have me—liked to put his arm out and lay his hand on my knee—would keep it so a long while. Toward the last he was more restless and flighty at night—often fancied himself with his regiment—by his talk sometimes seem'd as if his feelings were hurt by being blamed by his officers for something he was entirely innocent of—said, "I never in my life was thought capable of such a thing, and never was." At other times he would fancy himself talking as it seem'd to children or such like, his relatives I suppose, and giving them good advice; would talk to them a long while. All the time he was out of his head not one single bad word or idea escaped him. It was remark'd that many a man's conversation in his senses was not half as good as Frank's delirium. He seem'd quite willing to die—he had become very weak and had suffer'd a good deal, and was perfectly resign'd, poor boy. I do not know his past life, but I feel as if it must have been good. At any rate what I saw of him here, under the most trying of circumstances, with a painful wound, and among strangers, I can say that he behaved so brave, so composed, and so sweet and affectionate, it could not be surpass'd. And now like many other noble and good men, after serving his country as a soldier, he has yielded up his young life at the very outset in her service. Such things are gloomy—yet there is a text, "God doeth all things well"—the meaning of which, after due time, appears to the soul.

I thought perhaps a few words, though from a stranger, about your son, from one who was with him at the last, might be worth while—for I loved the young man, though I but saw him immediately to lose him. I am merely a friend visiting the hospitals occasionally to cheer the wounded and sick.

W.W.

2.

Dear Mother, It's Frank here, hoping a last time to reach you, and doubting I can but still I'm really going to try, ma'am. I want you to put your mind at rest about it all, Momma. That is why I am working hard to slip this through. You must really listen if this gets by the censors and everything, because I have limited time and fewer words than I'd like. I would dearly love to be there soon for breakfast and see that cussed little Wilkie come downstairs grumping like he always does till he's got a touch of coffee in him. I would even like to hear the Claxtons' roosters sounding off again. I remember Poppa, God rest him, saying as how other men kept hens for eggs but the Claxtons kept roosters for their noise and it was our ill luck to draw such fools as neighbors! The old man that wrote you of my end had the finest gray-white beard and finest-speaking voice I ever met with, finer even than parson Brookes we set such store by. The man who wrote you was here most days after lunch, even ones I now recall but parts of. He brought ward C our first lilacs in late April, great purple ones he stuck into a bedpan near my pillow. Their smell worked better on me than the laudanum that our Army chemists were so sadly out of. He read to us from Scripture and once, my hand resting on his safe-feeling leg, I asked him for a ditty and he said one out that sounded fine like Ecclesiastes but concerned our present war, my war. I told him it was good and asked him who had wrote it and he shrugged and smiled, he nodded along the double row of cots set in our tent here, like showing me that every wounded fellow'd had a hand in setting down the poem. He was so pleasing-looking and kind-spoken and affectionate, I myself liked him very much. Ice cream he brought us more than once—a bigger vat of it I've never seen, not even at the Bucks County Fair. Him and our lady nurses kept making funny jokes, bringing around the great melting buckets of it and the spoons and he himself shoveled a good bit of it into my gullet, grateful it felt all the way down. "Now for some brown." He gave me samples. "Now pink, but best for you is this, Frank. You've heard Mrs. Howe's line 'in the beauty of the lilies Christ was born across the sea'? This vanilla's that white, white as your arm here. Makes vanilla cool the deepest, my brave Pennsylvania youth." How I ate it. Cold can be good. If you hurt enough, cold can be so good. Momma? I do not love Lavinia like I forever said. I do not know how I got into being so mistruthful. Maybe it was how her poppa was Mayor and I liked the idea of pleasing you with our family's possible new station or how everybody spoke of Miss Lavinia's attainments and her skills at hostessing. It is my second cousin Emily I loved and love. She knew and knows, and it was just like Em to bide that. Em met whatever gaze I sent her with a quiet wisdom that shamed and flattered me, the both. Once at that Fourth of July picnic where the Claxtons' rowboat exploded from carrying more firecrackers than the *Merrimac* safely could, I noticed Emily near Doanes' Mill Creek gathering French lilacs for to decorate our picnic quilt later. You were bandaging Wilkie's foot where he stepped on a nail after you told him he must wear shoes among that level of fireworks but he didn't. I wandered down where Emily stood. She had a little silver pair of scissors in her skirt's pocket and I recall remarking how like our Em that was, how homely and prepared and how like you she was that way, Momma. She was clipping flowers when I drew up. I commenced shivering, that fearful of my feelings for her after everybody on earth seemed to think Lavinia had decided on me long-since. "Frank," Emily said. I spoke her name and when she heard how I said hers out, she stopped in trimming a heavy branch of white blooms (for, you know that place by the waterwheel where there are two bushes, one white, one purple, grown up side by side together and all mixed?). Emily's hands were still among the flowers when she looked back over her shoulder at me. Tears were in her eyes but not falling, just held in place and yet I saw the light on their water tremble with each pulse from her. It was then, Momma, I understood she knew my truest feelings, all.

"Why is it we're cousins and both poor?" I asked

her. ''Why could it not be just a little different so
things'd fall into place for us more, why, Emily?''
And she lifted one shoulder and turned her head
aside. She half-fell into the sweet bushes then, white
and green and purple, but caught herself and looked
away from me. Em finally spoke but I half-heard with
all the Roman candles going off and Wilkie bawling.
She said quiet, looking out toward water through the
beautiful branches, ''We will always know, Frank,
you and me will. Hearing as how you understand it,
that already gives me so much, Frank. Oh, if you but
guessed how it strengthens me just to say your name
at night, Frank, Franklin Horatio Irwin, Jr., how I
love to say it out, sir.'' Lavinia was calling that same
name but different and I turned, fearful of being
caught here by her, me unfaithful to the one that loved
me if not strongest then loudest, public-like. ''Excuse me, Cousin Emily,'' said I, and walked off and
then soon after got mustered in, then snagged the
minie that costs the leg then the rest of it, me, and
no one knowing my real heart. Mother? I never even
kissed her. Momma? Treat her right. Accord my
cousin Emily such tender respects as befit the young
widow of a man my age, for she is that to me, and
not Lavinia that made such a show at the funeral and
is ordering more styles of black crepe from a Boston
catalogue even now, Momma. Have Emily to dinner
often as you can afford it, and encourage her to look
around at other boys, for there's not much sense in
wasting two lives, mine and hers, for my own cow-
ardly mistakes. That is one thing needs saying out.

I used to speak to my bearded visitor about brother
Wilkie and all of you and I thought up things I'd tell
my kid brother who has so bad a temper but is funny
throughout. I'd want Wilkie to be brave and not do

what the town said he should, like pay court on a girl who's snooty and bossy just because of who her kin is and their grand home. I would tell Wilkie to hide in a cave and not sign up like I did, with the bands and drums and the setting off of all fireworks not burned up in the Claxtons' calamity rowboat—but, boy, it sure did look pretty going down, didn't it, Momma? My doctor took some time and pains with me and, near the end, got like Lavinia in telling me how fine a looking young man I was. That never pleased me much since I didn't see it all that clear myself and had not personally earned it and so felt a little guilty on account, not that any of it matters now. The Lady from Baltimore combed my hair and said nice things and I am sorry that she never got the watch and the daguerrotypes to you. She is a confidence artist who makes tours of hospitals, promising to take boys' valuables home but never does and sells them in the shops. Still, at the time, I trusted her, her voice was so refined and hands real soft and brisk and I felt good for days after she left, believing Wilkie'd soon have Poppa's gold watch in hand, knowing it had been with me at the end.

Just before they shot me, Momma, I felt scared to where I considered, for one second, running. No one ever knew of this but I must tell you now because just thinking on my failing cost me many inward tribulations at the last. "I could jump out of this hole and run into that woods and hide and then take off forever." So the dreadful plan rushed forth, and then how I stifled it, choked practically. I never in my life was thought capable of even thinking such a thing, and here I'd said it to myself! Then, like as punishment, not six minutes after looking toward that peaceful-seeming woods, I moved to help another fellow from Bucks County (Ephraim's second cousin, the youngest Otis boy from out New Hope way) and felt what first seemed a earthquake that'd knocked the entire battle cockeyed but that narrowed to a nearby complaint known just as the remains of my left leg. It felt numb till twenty minutes later when I seriously noticed. It takes that kind of time sometimes to feel. It takes a delay between the ending and knowing what to say of that, which is why this reaches you six weeks after my kind male nurse's news, ma'am. I asked him once why he'd quit the newspaper business to come visit us, the gimps and bullet-catchers, us lost causes.

He leaned nearer and admitted a secret amusement: said he was, from among the thousands of Northern boys and Reb prisoners he'd seen, recasting Heaven. Infantry angels, curly-headed all. ''And Frank,'' said he, ''I don't like to tease you with the suspense but it's between you and two other fellows, a three-way heat for the Archangel Gabriel.'' I laughed, saying as how the others had my blessings for that job just yet. He kept close by me during the amputation part especially. They said that if the leg was taken away, then so would all my troubles go. And I trusted them, Momma. And everybody explained and was real courteous and made the person feel manly like the loss of the leg could be his choice and would I agree? ''Yes,'' I said.

My doctor's name was Dr. Bliss and during the cutting of my leg, others kept busting into the tent, asking him stuff and telling him things and all calling him by name, Bliss, Bliss, Bliss, they said. It helped me to have that name and word drifting over the table where they worked on me so serious, and I thanked God neither you nor Emily would be walking in to see me spread out like that, so bare and held down helpless, like some boy. Afterwards, my friend the nurse trained me to pull the covers back, he taught me I must learn to look at it now. But I couldn't bear to yet. They'd tried but I had wept when asked to stare below at the lonely left knee. It'd been "left" all right! Walt (my nurse's name was Walt) he said we would do it together. He held my hand and counted then—one, two, three . . . I did so with him and it was like looking at what was there and what was not at once, just as my lost voice is finding you during this real dawn, ma'am. He told me to cheer up, that it could've been my right leg and only later did I see he meant that as a little joke and I worried I had let him down by not catching on in time. I have had bad thoughts, lustful thoughts and evil. I fear I am yet a vain person and always have been secretly, Momma. You see, I fretted how it'd be to live at home and go downtown on crutches and I knew Lavinia's plan would change with me a cripple. Lavinia would not like that. And even after everything, I didn't know if I could choose Emily, a seamstress after all, over so grand a place on Summit Avenue as the Mayor'd already promised Lavinia and me (it was the old Congers mansion, Momma).

It seems to me from here that your Frank has cared way too much for how others saw him. It was Poppa's dying early that made me want to do so much and seem so grown and that made me join up when you had your doubts, I know. You were ever strict with me but I really would've turned out all right in the end . . . if it hadn't been for this.

Momma, by late April, I could feel the bad stuff moving up from the leg's remains, like some type of chemical, a kind of night or little army set loose in me and taking all the early lights out, one by one, lamp by lamp, farm by farm, house by house it seemed. The light in my head, don't laugh, was the good crystal lantern at your oilclothed kitchen table. That was the final light I worried for—and knew, when that went, it all went. But, through chills and talking foolish sometimes, I tried keeping that one going, tried keeping good parts separate, saved back whole. I felt like if I could but let you hear me one more time, it'd ease you some. Your sleeping so poorly since . . . that's just not like you, Ma, and grieves me here. Dying at my age is an embarrassment, on top of everything else! It was just one shot in the knee, but how could I have stopped it when it started coming up the body toward the last light in the kitchen in the head? You told me not to enlist— you said, as our household's one breadwinner, I could stay home. But the braided uniform and the party that Lavinia promised tipped me over. Fevered, I imagined talking to Wilkie and all the younger cousins lined up on our front porch's seven steps, and me wagging my finger and striding to and fro in boots like our Lt.'s beautiful English leather boots, such as I never owned in life. I talked bold and I talked grand and imagined Emily was in the shady house with you, and beside you, listening, approving my sudden wisdom that'd come on me with the suffering, and on account of the intestine cramps, and after the worst convulsion Walt got me through, still that lead was coming up the thigh into my stomach then greeting and seizing the chest and then more in the throat and that was about all of it except for the great gray beard and those knowing eyes that seemed to say Yes Yes, Frank, even to my need to be done with it, the pain (the last white pain of it, I do not mind telling you, was truly something, Momma). I couldn't have held

out much longer anyway, and the idea of choosing
between my two loves, plus living on a crutch for
life, it didn't set right with vain me.

This I am telling you should include that I hid the
five-dollar gold piece I won for the History Prize at
the Academy commencement up inside the hollowed
left head-post of my bedstead. Get Wilkie to go upstairs with you and help lift the whole thing off the
floor and out the coin will fall. Use it for you and
Emily's clothes. Bonnets might be nice with it. But
nothing but what's extra, that is how I want it spent.
I should've put it in your hand before I left, but I
planned to purchase my getting-home gifts out of that,
and never thought I wouldn't. Selfish, keeping it
squirreled back and without even guessing. But then
maybe all people are vain. Maybe it's not just your
Frank, right?

If you wonder at the color you are seeing now,
Momma, the pink-red like our fine conch shell on
the parlor's hearth, you are seeing the backs of your
own eyelids, Momma. You will soon hear the Claxtons' many crowers set up their alarum yet again and
will catch a clinking that is McBride's milk wagon
pulled by Bess, who knows each house on old
McBride's route. Your eyes are soon to open on your
room's whitewash and July's yellow light in the dear
place. You will wonder at this letter of a dream,
ma'am and, waking, will look toward your bedside
table and its often-unfolded letter from the gentleman
who told you of my passing. His letter makes this
one possible. For this is a letter toward your loving
Franklin Horatio Irwin, Jr., not only from him. It is
your voice finding ways to smoothe your mind. This
is for letting you get on with what you have to tend,
Momma. You've always known I felt Lavinia to be

well-meaning but right silly, and that our sensible and deep Emily was truly meant as mine from her and my's childhoods onward. You've guessed where the coin is stowed, as you did ever know such things, but have held back on account of honoring the privacy even of me dead. Go fetch it later today, and later today spend it on luxuries you could not know otherwise. This is the rich echo that my bearded nurse's voice allows. It is mostly you. And when the pink-and-red opens, and morning's here already, take your time in dressing, go easy down the stairs, let Wilkie doze a little longer than he should and build the fire and start a real big breakfast. Maybe even use the last of Poppa's maple syrup we tapped that last winter he was well. Use it up and then get going on things, new things, hear? That is the wish of your loving eldest son, Frank. That is the wish of the love of your son Frank who is no deader than anything else that ever lived so hard and wanted so so much, Mother.

Something holy will stand before you soon, ma'am. Cleave to that. Forget me. Forget me by remembering me. Imagine what a boy like me would give now for but one more breakfast (ever my favorite meal— I love how it's most usually the same) and even Wilkie's crabiness early, or the Claxtons' rooster house going off everywhichway like their rowboat did so loud. I know what you know, ma'am, and what you doubt, and so do you: but be at peace in this: Everything you suspect about your missing boy is true. So, honor your dear earned civilian life. Nights, sleep sounder. Be contained. In fifty seconds you will refind waking and the standing light. Right away you'll feel better, without knowing why or even caring much. You will seem to be filling, brimming with this secret rushing-in of comfort, ma'am. Maybe like some bucket accustomed to a mean purpose—say, a hospital slop pail—but one suddenly asked to offer wet life to lilacs unexpected here. Or maybe our dented well bucket out back, left daily under burning sun and daily polished by use and sandy winds, a bucket that's suddenly dropped far beneath even being beneath the ground and finally striking a stream below all usual streams and one so dark and sweet and ice-cream cold, our bucket sinks it is so full, Mother. Your eyes will open and what you'll bring to light, ma'am, is that fine clear over-sloshing vessel. Pulled back. Pulled back up to light. Be refreshed. Feel how my secrets and your own (I know a few of yours too, ma'am, oh yes I do) are pooling here, all mixed now, cool, and one.

I am not the ghost of your dead boy. I am mostly you. I am just your love for him, left stranded so unnaturally alive—a common enough miracle. And such fineness as now reaches you in your half-sleep is just the echo of your own best self. Which is very good.

Don't give all your credit to your dead. Fineness stays so steady in you, ma'am, and keeps him safe, keeps him lit continually. It's vain of Frank but he is now asking: could you, and Wilkie and Em, please hold his spot for him just a little longer? Do. . . . And Mother? Know I rest. Know that I am in my place here. I feel much easement, Ma, in having heard you say this to yourself.

There, worst worrying's done. Here accepting it begins.

All right. Something holy now stands directly before you. How it startles, waiting so bright at the foot of your iron bedstead. Not to shy away from it. I will

count to three and we will open on it, please. Then
we'll go directly in, like, hand-in-hand, we're plung-
ing. What waits is what's still yours, ma'am, which
is ours.

—Such brightness, see? It is something very holy.
Mother? Everything will be in it.
It is a whole day.
—One two three, and light.
—Now, we move toward it.
—Mother? Wake!

1989

Blessed Assurance

A Moral Tale

*In memory of James Zito
and for Grace Paley*

I SOLD FUNERAL INSURANCE TO NORTH CAROLINA black people. I myself am not black. Like everybody else who was alive fifty-nine years ago, I was so young then, you know? I still feel bad about what went on. My wife says: telling somebody might help. Here lately, worry over this takes a percentage of my sleep right off the top.—So I'm telling you, okay?

See, I only did it to put myself through college. I knew it wasn't right. But my parents worked the swing shift at the cotton mill. We went through everything they earned before they earned it. I grew up in one of those employee row houses. Our place stood near the cotton loading ramp. Our shrubs were always tagged with fluff blown off stacked bales. My room's window screens looked flannel as my kiddie pajamas. Mornings, the view might show six white windblown hunks, big as cakes. You didn't understand you'd steadily breathed such fibers—not till, like Dad, you started coughing at age forty and died at fifty-one.—I had to earn everything myself. First I tried peddling the *Book of Knowledge*. Seemed like a good thing to sell. I attended every

232

single training session. This sharp salesman showed us how to let the ''T'' volume fall open at the Taj Mahal. Our company had spent a little extra on that full-page picture. In a living room the size of a shipping crate, I stood before my seated parents. I practiced. They nodded. I still remember, ''One flick of the finger takes us from 'Rome' to . . . 'Rockets'!'' Before I hiked off with my wares, Mom would pack a bag lunch, then wave from our fuzzy porch, ''Jerry? Say 'Please' and 'Thank you very much.' They like that.''

Other saleskids owned cars. I had to walk from house to house lugging my sample kit: twenty-six letters' worth of knowledge gets heavy pretty fast. My arms and back grew stronger but my spirits sort of caved in. Our sales manager assigned me to the Mill district—he claimed I had inside ties. The only thing worse than facing strangers door-to-door is finding people you knew there.

Grinning, they'd ask me in. Mill employees opened their iceboxes, brought me good things. I chattered my whole memorized routine. Neighbors acted proud of me. But I felt like a circus dog and some stuffy teacher, mixed. Like a crook. When I finished, my hosts sighed, said this book set sure sounded great. Then they admitted what we'd all known all along: they just couldn't afford it. I'd spent forty minutes ignoring this. They looked troubled as I backed out, smiling. ''Hey,'' I called. ''It's copacetic, really. You'll save for the down payment. You'll get *Knowledge* on time—it'll mean more to you.'' Then I knocked at the next door. I stood praying for an empty house.

One day I came trudging over the Mill's suspension bridge—the weight of world knowledge was giving me a hernia. My third week of no sales. One middle-class kid had already won a trip to Mexico. "This boys' going places," our sales manager said. "Whereas Jerry's going home and napping every afternoon, right, Jer?" I threw my whole kit in the river. The case flew open. Out volumes shot: "Cat" through "Graph." "Uterine" through "Xanadu." All human learning (illustrated) lay sogged and ruined on the rocks below. And I loved it. I stayed to watch the current wash every book over the dam that ran the cotton mill that made the cloth that fattened accounts of the owners who'd kept my parents broke and wheezy forty years. Bye bye, *Knowledge*. I couldn't afford it.

(In here, I tried selling a vegetable shredder. "Make a rose out of a radish and in no time." This is all I'll say about those two weeks of bloody fingertips and living off my demonstration salads.)

Here comes Funeral Insurance. Okay, I answered an ad. The head honcho says, "Son, I'm not promising you the moon." I loved him for that. He was so sad you had to trust him. On his desk, a photo of one pale disappointed-looking wife. There were six pictures of two kids shown being sweet but runty at three different ages in three different ways. I felt for the guy.

He kept his shoes propped on a dented desk. A bronze plaque there spelled *Windlass Insurance for Funerary Eventualities, Cleveland.* My new boss flashed me a nonpersonal salesman wink; he offered me a snort of whiskey from his pint bottle. I said No. I was under legal age. With Sam's legs crossed, with his eyes roaming the ceiling's waterstains, he rocked back and told. Admitting everything, his voice grew both more pained and more upbeat.

"Black people come from Africa. No news, right?

But all Africans are big on funerals. It's how your dying tribe-people announce the respect they deserve in their next life, see? *I'm* not buying into this, understand— just laying out why a person who's got no dinner will cough up fifty cents to three bucks per Saturday for a flashy coffin and last party.

"Now, times, you might get to feeling—nice boy like you, college material—like maybe you're stealing from them. You take *that* attitude, you'll wind up like . . . like me. No, you've got to accept how another type of person believes. Especially when there's such a profit in it. And remember, Our Founder was a black man. Richest colored family in Ohio, I'm told. Plus, for all we know, they could be right, Jerry. If there *is* the so-called next world, they'll turn up in it, brass bands to announce them. And us poor white guys who sold them the tickets, we'll be deep-fat-frying underneath forever. That'd sure get a person's attention, wouldn't it? Coming to in Hell? For being Bad here?

"What I'm saying: You've got to work it out for yourself, and quick. Here's your premium book. Take plenty of change. Four bits to three bucks per week might sound like nothing to a crackerjack like you. But, with most of Colored Town paying, it adds up. And, Jerry, they *do* get it back when they break the bank. Soon as some next-of-kin comes in here with a legal death certificate, I pay off like clockwork. So, yeah, it's honest . . . I see that look on your face. Only thing, buddy, if they miss two weeks running, they forfeit. They lose the present policy and any other Windlass ones they've paid up. I don't care if they've put in thousands, and several of your older clients will have: if they let one, then two (count them) two big Saturdays roll by, their pile becomes the company's.

"You getting this? See, that's the catch. I warned them during my own feistier collecting days, I'd go,

'Hey, no remuneral, no funeral. No bucks, no box.'
They'd laugh but they got my meaning. Your client
misses two back-to-back Saturdays, it's hello potter's
field. Could be worse. I mean, *they* won't be around to
suffer through it.

"And listen. Jer. No exceptions to our two-week rule,
none. Because, Jerry, they'll beg you. Hold firm. Way
I see it, anybody who can't come up with fifty cents a
week on this plane, they don't deserve the four-star
treatment in the next, you know?—No, I lied. That's
not the way I see it. The way I see it is: I wish I hadn't
washed out of dental school. The Organic Chemistry,
Jerry. The goddamn Organic Chemistry, I had a sick
feeling about it from the first. Like a drink? That's right,
you said No. So here's your book, names, addresses,
amounts paid to date. See—our clients they've got nothing else—they're hoping for a better shot next go-round.
Your middle-class black people wouldn't touch funeral
insurance with somebody else's ten-foot pole.

"Jerry, I recommend a early start on Saturday. They
mostly get paid Friday night. They've mostly spent
every penny by Sunday morning. And, son, they *want*
to pay. So, do everybody a favor, especially yourself,
grab it while it's in their hot hands. And if you need
leverage, mention . . . you know."

"What?" I had to ask. "Please."

"It. A beaverboard box held together with thumb-
tacks. No flowers but what the neighbors pick. Not a
single whitewalled Packard graveside. One attention-
getter is—saying their hearse'll be from the City Sanitation Department. Face it: we've got a heartless
business going here. And, Jer? the minute they smell
heart on you, you're down the toilet, Jerry. They'll let
Number One week slide by. Then here goes Numero
Dou, and they'll start blaming you. And you'll believe

them. Next they'll try and bribe you—homebrewed liquor, catfish, anything. I had one woman promise me her daughter. Girl couldn't have been older than twelve. I'm a family man, Jerry. But these people are fighting for their souls in the next life—you can understand, it matters to them. They'll do anything, anything, if you won't squeal and cut them off from their picture of heaven. But Jerry?—cut them off.

"The minute I got promoted from door-to-door, I swore I'd tell each new collector the whole rancid truth. You just got it straight-up, kiddo. Now head on out there. They'll love your argyle sweater vest—new, is it? Me, I plan to sit right here and get legless drunk. Hearing the deal spelled out again, it breaks me fourteen ways, it does. When I think of what a decent dental practice can net per year for a hardworking guy, when I remember certain pet clients who almost got the full treatment on the next plane, but . . . hey, this I'm giving you is a pep talk mostly. This is our business here. It's the food in our mouths. —Go, Jerry, go."

My territory was a town of shacks. With dogs at every one. Dogs trained to attack Whitie. I, apparently, was Whitie. I bought a used car on credit. Had no choice. I couldn't walk for all the hounds—spotty small ones, ribby yellow lion-sized things—each underfed, many dingy—all taking it extra personally. Under my new J.C. Penney slacks, I soon wore three pair of woolen knee socks. I hoped the layers might soften my share of nips. I sprinted from my black Nash up onto a rickety front porch. I knocked, panting, whipping out the book. One very old woman seemed to peek from every door. Toothless, blue-black, her shy grin looked mischievous, a small head wrapped in the brightest kerchief. At some doorways, her hands might be coated with flour. At others she held a broom or some white man's half-ironed white business shirt. She wore male work boots four sizes too large, the toes curled up like elf shoes. Sometimes she smoked a pipe (this was in the Forties). Her long skirt dragged the floor, pulling along string, dustballs. She asked, "What they want now. You ain't the one from before—you a young one, ain't you?" and she chuckled at me. I smiled and swallowed.

I mentioned her upcoming funeral, its expenses, the weekly installment due today. Overdressed for my job, I admitted working my way through college. This had melted hearts among my parents' Milltown friends. But in this zone called Baby Africa, it didn't help.

"Working through a what? Well, child, we all gots to get through something, seem like."

Some customers asked if I owned the Funeral Home. Others asked if my daddy did. I tried explaining the concept of insurance. I failed. For one thing, my clients called it Surrance or Assurance or The Assurance I gently corrected them. One woman frowned. "That what I *say*. . . .'Assurance.' " These old ladies seemed to be banking on a last sure thing. Assurance meant heavenly pin money. Shouldn't it have tipped them off? Buying certainty from a confused, fresh-faced kid, nineteen, and about as poor as them?

"Fine morning," I kept grinning even in a downpour.

"Who you supposed to be?" Some giggled, pointing at my snappy-dresser's getup, then toward a pack of mongrels waiting, patrolling the mud yard. In the seam of a half-opened door, my clients' eyes would narrow. "Oh, is you . . . the Assurance?" It was our password and secret.

"So they tell me, ma'am." I smiled hard. "Yep,

looks like we've got ourselves another winner of a Saturday morning going here, hunh?''

The insured snorted, then eased me into a dark room I didn't want to know about.

''Seem like it always Saturday,'' my customer mumbled and shook her head. I followed her in. It was my duty to.

The same stooped old lady led me through sixty-five overheated homes. Even mid-July, a fire burned in the grate. White picket fencing was stacked, neat, her kindling. In bare wooden rooms hot as the tropics, rooms with shades drawn, a kerosene lamp helped. Some rooms were poor and filthy, some poor and tidy, but each held this ancient woman surrounded by two dozen grandkids. Children sometimes hid when I knocked but, slow, once I was inside, they seeped from behind doors, wiggled out from under beds. Their bellies looked swollen due to lacks. They swarmed around their grannie, tugged at her long skirts, begged for treats she didn't own and couldn't buy.

The roadsides of my route bristled with zinnias, with sunflowers thirteen feet high. To my eyes, these bright jagged hedges looked African. They seemed cut by a hand-crank can opener out of tin. When I later learned that our white ladies' Garden Club had done the planting, I couldn't believe it. I always figured the seeds of these plants had crossed the ocean in warm hands of slaves chained deep inside ships.

I bought new clothes, trusting these might spiff up my errand. But Saturday after Saturday stayed the same blur: me kicking at my dog escort, me admiring the stiff flowers running defense along dirt roads, me knocking on the door, me sporting my brush-cut hairdo and mail-order bow tie, me grinning out my winning wasted good manners on people manners couldn't save.

It only made me smile the wider. My mouth stayed full of spit.

The door moaned open two inches. Heat, escaping like a sound, pretty much wilted me. Older children squinted in a stripe of daylight. Behind the largest kids and not much taller, easing onto tiptoes, the funeral's guest of honor, her face weather-beaten/permanent as any turtle's. She cupped a hand over her eyes. Sun hurt her. From so shadowy a hut of the sun itself must've seemed just another big blond Caucasian visitor, come to collect.

"Oh, it you. It the boy back for Assurance." I got squired indoors then. I didn't want this. Into shacks, lean-tos, Quonset huts, through the smell of frying fat, toward backrooms of Mom and Pop grocery stores (mostly only Moms present). Through shanties, former stables, leaky bungalows no bigger than my parents' company dive. In I went—ducking under low door-ways—in against my better judgment. The nervier farmed-out grandkids and great-grandkids touched my pale hands ("They *hot*!"). Others trailed me, stroking my new shirt: our latest miracle fabric, rayon ("It *look* squeaky"). I let myself be led as kids commented, "Ain't he pink?" For a Whitie, I was sure a shy Whitie. Did they believe I couldn't understand our mother tongue? Did they think that, even understand-ing, I wouldn't care how others saw me?—Downtown I'd overheard redneck white men speak loud about some passing black girl of real beauty. "Roy, is that the most purple dress you ever seen in your life, boy? My, but that'd be a fine little purple dress to take home late tonight, hunh, Roy?"

Now I stood in a dark hall and listened as children

discussed Assurance's hair color, his two-tone shoes and rosy size. Trapped, I did what any embarrassed nineteen-year-old would do: grinned till the ears hurt. I pretended not to hear. It was what the beauty in the purple dress had done. It was all I could think of.

My customers feared me. I tried acting regular, I said Please and Thank you very much. But, given our setup, I couldn't be just regular. Fact is, from the start, this job scared me so bad. I couldn't afford to quit it yet. But, boy, I tell you I was already counting the Saturdays.

Windlass Funerary Eventualities Inc. had been founded in Cleveland some ninety years before. It seemed that several of my collectees had been paying since the outfit's opening day. Behind some names, four completed policies'd piled up. I found amazing shameful dollar totals.

One month into the job, nobody knew my name. I'd stayed "Assurance." And my clients still looked pretty much alike to me. Maybe it sounds bad but, hey, they *were* alike. Me: their Saturday white boy. Them: all one old black woman. People started having names when I deciphered the last collector's rotten handwriting. One morning, it yielded like a busted code. Then the ladies began standing out from one another. Oh, man, I couldn't believe some of the tallies!

"Vesta Lotte Battle, 14 Sunflower Street— commenced payment on policy #1, Mar. 2, 1912, four policies complete, collected to date: $4,360.50."

During a major rainstorm, my old Nash had its first blowout. My parents had never owned a car. I didn't know how to change a flat. When I bought the used sedan, I'd been feeling cocky, grown, too vain to ask the salesman for instructions, please. Everybody else knew. I figured ownership itself would teach a guy. After all, new babies don't get lessons in breathing—it's something you pick up—on-the-job experience.

So this particular Saturday morning I'm trying to collect during what seems the start of a respectable hurricane. I'm tooling along Sunflower when here comes a bad bad thumping. My Nash gimps, then tilts. I was near Mrs. Battle's house but hardly knew her then. This early in my coin-collecting days, she still seemed like all the others.—The good old days.

Out loud, hoping to sound like an expert, I said, "I believe your problem is in the front-right-tire area, Jerry." "No lie," the live-in cynic answered. I climbed out, immediately kicking at the curs. Blinded by driving wet, dogs still lunged my way. Some now hid under the chassis where—safe and dry—they snapped at soggy passing argyle ankles. I took an umbrella from the trunk, lost it to wind, watched it disappear over a hedge of sunflowers whipping every whichaway. "So," I said, already drenched. I unclamped the spare and a trusty jack. Now what?

I should mention being watched. Four dozen black faces lined up on many porches, faces interested in weather, willing to look at anything and now all aimed—neutral—my way. I should admit: I don't think Mr. Laurel and Mr. Hardy could've filled an hour with more stupid accidents than I managed in this downpour. The car fell off its jack three times. People on porches didn't laugh outright, no, it was a deeper kind of pleasure. They fairly shivered with it and I couldn't blame them. I noticed how one of my clients, an obese widow, had huffed up onto an iron milk crate. She hoped for a clearer view of my misfortune above her peonies the wind kept scalping.

I knew that if I walked up to any of the dry people on their cozy porches and asked for help, I'd get help. That was the deal. But I couldn't ask. I was too young a man, too car-proud to admit being broken down on a street of walkers who mostly owed me money. So I just kept at it, on my hands and knees. I settled in mud— flat on my back under the Nash—trying to hold off attacking dogs by swinging a tire iron badly needed elsewhere. Once I struggled to my feet again, my own umbrella swooped back over sunflowers and hit me in the neck. I'm still not sure somebody didn't throw it. Spectators now lifted their babies. Old people in wheel-chairs were being rolled out to see. I'd turned the color of the mud, then the color of the tires and was standing here considering sobbing.

"Get out the way, you." A husky voice spoke loud enough to outlive the gale. I looked behind me at this dark old woman, scarecrow thin, hands pressed on hips, acting furious with me. She'd been watching from a porch and was not amused. She seemed to hate incom-petence and the pleasure my incompetence was giving to her neighbors. Seven blinking kids, black and white, surrounded her. They also seemed to be clucking, dis-gusted, shaking their heads. "Don't want any favors," said I. "Just show me how." Kids snatched my tire iron and lug wrench. Kids jerked the spare away from me like planning to roll the thing off and put it up for adoption after years of my mistreating it. Children worked around me like trained elves, the old woman snapping orders, pointing to a porch where I should go wait. Kids had just slipped the flat into my trunk when I noticed the spare already locked in place. I studied this through slanting blue water. Dogs, tails wagging, now sniffed at kids, forgetting me. "How can I thank you?" I hollered over the squall, wondering if I should offer money, all while following my helpers. Then I was going up some porch steps. I worried for this old woman, soaked at her age. But she ordered, "Get out them soggy clothes, you." Everybody else disappeared into the house. I was handed laundered flour sacks. I saw I should use these as towels. Kids brought me a stained silk maroon dressing robe—antique, some hand-me-down. I changed, in one corner of a small front room. It was stacked with consignment ironing. I dared not strip on the much-watched front porch. Next, hot tea appeared. Then we were all settled on this strange woman's porch, we were dry. We all sat sipping similar green tea from cups, no two alike. Everybody was silent. We could watch the rain let up or continue, it didn't much matter now. My car out there looked clean and new. My clothes had been spread to dry in the kitchen's open oven. Sitting in this borrowed robe, I smelled like an old house.

To be here with this group of helpful strangers—kids lined like a choir, plus the old woman—to see how all the neighbors on their porches, especially the fat one next door, now gaped, not at the car, but over here at our congregation staring straight out, sipping warm tea on this cool blue day, well, I felt rescued. It was a strange pleasure of the sort that makes you shudder at the time. When rain slacked some, I dashed inside, dressed fast and, half-apologizing, backed off her porch with an overload of talky etiquette that makes me cringe now to recall. Soon as I got in my car, I grabbed the premium book, checked her address, found the name, Vesta Lotte Battle.

The next Saturday I turned up to collect her regular fifty cents, nobody mentioned lending me a hand. Of course, with me being such a kid (one whose sin was and is the Sin of Pride), *I* never brought up my clumsiness, their help. No. Just let it pass. Soon everybody forgot this favor. Everybody but me.

From then on, forever, 14 Sunflower Street was *Vesta Lotte Battle, $4,360.50*. This woman now looked quite specific while passing me ten hand-temperature nickels at a time. I wanted to tell her, "Look, ma'am, it's going on 1950. For the amount you've laid by, you could hire Duke Ellington's orchestra. You might get your own parade, the Goodyear blimp. Maybe even Mrs. Roosevelt."

Like other homes on my list, Vesta L. Battle's had its fair share of religious pictures; some were decaled onto varnished conch shells. But here I started noticing the unlikenesses. Mrs. Battle's place was furnished with fine if ruined furniture. Possible leftovers from some great plantation house. Her andirons were life-sized bronze greyhounds. The huge horsehair loveseat had a back of pretty jigsaw curves, but one cinder block and many bricks held up its crippled end. Vesta Lotte Battle was the first of my insured to start looking different from all others. I never forgot her. Times, I still try.

She always wore a used amethyst necklace—four of its six stones missing. Early in our acquaintance, I boldly asked her age. She shrugged. "Courthouse burned. Someplace uphill of ninety some, I reckon." She had cataracts. These meant that her whole head gleamed with the same flat blue-gray color. Like a concord grape's—that beautiful powdery blue you only find on the freshest ones. Greeting me, she stood so straight. But her face hung loose off its moorings, drooping free of her like more unpressed hired-out laundry, needing work. She always aimed her front toward my voice, not me. She seemed to pay me too much attention. Only slowly did I understand how blind she was.

Her house milled with stray kids, poor whites mixed with darker Sunflower neighbors. First time I visited after my flat tire, fifteen kids were making taffy in her kitchen. They wore whole gloves of pale sticky stuff. They kept saying "Yukk" and "Oogh." Two, happy with strands slacked between them, did a little dance. They backed apart—then, palms forward, rushed each other.

Mrs. Battle led me into this taffy workshop. "Look, you all, it the Boy come for Assurance." Her voice crackled, seeming even less stay-press than her shriveled face. Mrs. Battle's tone sounded smoked, flaky and layered, like the pane of isinglass I noticed glowing in her kitchen stove. She'd left off ironing a white shirt. It rested, arms drooping from a board, flattened by a set of irons she heated on her wood stove. To hold the sprinkling water, she used a Coke bottle plugged with a red celluloid-and-cork nozzle bought at Kress's for ten cents. Momma had the same one. The old woman now offered me hot tea. I nodded, wondering how much she earned per shirt. Candy makers cleared counter space for her.

I worried: accepting tea might be my first client-collector mistake. I hadn't asked for her tire help, either. Sam warned me: "Take nothing from anybody." But a person can't consider every kindness a form of bribe, can a person? Maybe I was a night-school Business Major, but I wasn't *always* counting. "Tea sounds great, ma'am." I watched her—slowed, so old—go through the ritual. Her hands knew everything's whereabouts. This lady, I told myself, trying to keep things logical, she's in too far to ever back out of her Insurance now. She can't live much longer, can she? Vesta Lotte

Battle had entered that oldness beyond plain old age. She'd hit the part where you dry out, you've become a kind of living mummy sketch of who you were. They've stopped checking your meter. You've gone from Rocket back to Rome. Everything you could lose, you have. Lost.

Only stubborn habits keep you moving. Like this making tea. I watched her hands. They went right to each decanter, no nonsense, no waste. She'd started paying for her funeral decades before I got myself born. All those slow years, all these quick-arriving Saturdays.

She handed me a sky-blue teacup, then scuffed deeper into her narrow home, searching for my fifty cents. Should I follow a client into her bedroom or wait out on her porch? I figured: any place but the yard. Sixteen dogs were waiting in the yard. —Now, as ever in these small houses, I felt huge and I was. Sparrow-sized black ladies kept handing their coins up to me. In a tiny wizened hand, one quarter can look almost saucer-sized and made of mirror.

"You children so rude," the old voice hollered back. "Give Assurance some eats."

Kids surrounded me, their clownish mouths caked with sugar, egg whites. "Every kindness is a form of graft," I heard Sam's voice. But smiled. Kids held their hands up toward me. Candy *was* their hands, taffy wrapping to the wrists. One dark girl took my teacup, set it down then touched my hand. Over and under my ruddy right paw, she pressed her hands, mittened in white goo. I laughed, it felt odd, but good. I made a face. Kids hooted. I saw they'd been waiting. "How do it taste?" a cracked voice asked behind me. I really jumped. Vesta Lotte Battle made a sharp gasping sound I later guessed to be a laugh. I smiled, held one finger to my mouth, nibbled my knuckle, "Mmm. Thank you. It's taffy all right."

"We knows that," the dark girl stepped forward, ready to give me a teasing shove. Fearing for my new cardigan, I hopped back fast. They all roared. I laughed too. Somehow I didn't mind. I knew I looked ridiculous to them.

They showed me the pleasure in the joke—the joke of me, I mean. Then things felt easier. "More," I said, "please, I want more." Up hands shot. I faked munching on ten kids' extended palms, I grazed along fingers. Then everybody seemed satisfied, even bored. They went back to work. "*Now* can I wash?," I turned toward my client. My client was Mrs. Vesta Lotte Battle. By then I surely knew her name. She nodded, pointed me to her sink. It had no faucets, just a well you pumped. I pumped. I scrubbed hard, taffy still under my fingernails.

My hostess had returned to seeking her money, my money. I waited in the front room. This was taking forever. I heard two drawers open, a jar got shaken, some furniture was moved. Then, posture spoiled, Vesta Lotte Battle came creaking back toward me. She was bent nearly end-to-end, shrimp-wise. Her white hair grew in mossy coin-sized lumps under the headcloth. Both her hands were lifted, cupping nickels, pennies, and the one dime laid—proud—on top.

Every toasty coin she dropped into my big clean college hand, I counted aloud for her and with some cheer. Seemed the least I could do. But the brighter I sounded the worse I felt. Older children stopped to watch this payoff. I felt ashamed. "It's no popularity contest," Sam had advised me.

Since 1912, Vesta Lotte Battle had paid. While employed as a housemaid uphill, her weekly dues ran dollars higher. Now she had four completed policies, all ripe for forfeit if she missed just two current payments. She was in to Eventualities to the tune of nearly five thousand bucks. And on this particular taffy-making Saturday, she turned up twenty-one cents short. "Uh oh," I said. It was all I could think of.

"Let's see here. You had the twenty-nine but you're missing the twenty-one, correct? Look, just this time, all right, Mrs. Battle? We'll see you next week for the full amount, okay? But falling behind and all, it's just not copacetic."

"Copper-who?"

"It's just not . . . smart. No tardiness again, all right? All right."

"One thing," her voice sounded even smokier. "I ain't no 'Mrs.' "

"Fine. So, we'll see you for the makeup payment next week same time same station, okay? Okay. But, please, have it, Mrs. Battle."

Her shoulders lifted then dropped one at a time. She said, "Vesta Lotte Battle tries." It was a statement, not a promise—she made me know this.

Again she stood so straight, the clouded eyes aimed right at me. Her dignity was perfect. Right from the first, her poise just totally slayed me. It seemed some law of nature. Then she closed her unpainted door on me. Doing so, she proved: the rented hut, the tea I'd sipped, the candy nibbled, this houseful of borrowed kids, the life itself . . . insured or not—all these, she proved, were hers, not mine.

"After while, crocodile," I spoke to the door's pine planking, windblown silver as a coin. People were just starting to say, "See you later, alligator." Locally I was one of the first. I considered myself something of a pacesetter.

* * *

Part of my Windlass Insurance earnings paid night-school tuition. The rest meant grocery or doctor money for my folks. I made A's in my classes, but breathing was getting lots harder for Dad. I bought him this expensive humidifier. We got him inhalers and sprays, anything.

The folks sometimes asked about my route, they called it. They remembered my paperboy years. To them, this job seemed easy as peddling *Herald Travelers* off a bike. I couldn't explain the terrible difference. You stop delivering somebody's morning paper, they go and buy one at the store. For Assurance, my clients couldn't turn to anybody but me. I never told my parents what this job really meant. My folks fretted enough. Just recently, an old friend sent me a snapshot of them dressed for church and sitting on our porch. She is in his lap and laughing, and they're both much handsomer than I'd let them be in memory. He wears a high white collar and has long good hands, and except for the cheap porch furniture, these two people might be Lord and Lady Somebody, larking it up for a reporter. Their good looks, recognized this late, only make me sadder. They could've done *any*thing.

When I was fifteen, I presented Dad a Christmas subscription to *Life* magazine. It continued ever after, best thing I ever gave him. He wore his bifocals only once a week when sitting down with the new issue. You'd think he had just received the Dead Sea Scrolls by mail for a first scholarly look-see. He turned pages one by one from the top corner. "They've got pretty much everything in here," he'd say. And if I lumbered in from work, Mom would hush me, smiling with strange pride. "Let's be a little quiet. He's reading."

* * *

The first time one of my customers, a retired brick-layer, fell behind payment-wise, I said something semi-stern, and he wept at me, then dropped onto arthritic knees. He pressed his wet face against my creased chinos.

"Please," I pulled him back up. "Don't *do* this to yourself. Nothing's worth this." I'd started seeing that these old folks were paying me for more than fancy burials. They were shelling out for the right to go on living for another week.

I should add how the last ingredient of my Saturdays was—along with old ladies (like Mrs. Battle herself) and many grandkids in hand-me-downs and cornrow braids (like Mrs. B's clan)—about a million Jesuses.

Every ashtray, each souvenir candy dish, the baby rattles, all hand fans (compliments of the three leading black funeral parlors), spoon rests, pillow covers, and, once, a whole couch—showed pastel pictures of a mild-looking soap-faced shepherd. He wore clean, pressed 100% cotton-looking robes. He had the sugar-water stare of a bad actress dolled up to play some fairy god-mother. In Kress's frames, he held several sheep and one crook. I figured, maybe he gave my clients hope; whatever helped them, I was for that. But I worried: candle-white himself, he was shown clutching multi-colored kids. From lithos and oleographs, he knocked on castle doors, he lifted lanterns, he carried blond infants over rickety footbridges. Promises, promises. He always turned up, central, in each rental box. Sometimes alongside His picture, I'd find one of President Roosevelt, a cleaner-shaven and plumper gent but still looking like some Jesus second-cousin, worthy.

I waited, half on clients' porches, partly in their front rooms, not wanting to seem too interested, hoping not to seem jaded either. I counted front rooms' Jesuses. I pretended not to notice my clients fishing fifty cents to three bucks out of nut-brown face powder or from behind clocks, from underneath the tubular legs of heavy beds where people who'd been sired and born, later died. Out coins came, wedged between the heel and sole of a work shoe. Quarters were egged into daylight from deep private panels of mended bras worn by my insured. Right in front of me, slack bodices got plundered. Old ladies didn't seem to mind my seeing where they squirreled their cash. (Maybe they knew I'd get it anyway?)

Their most regular hiding spots, of course, were Jesus places. Coins got taped behind tea-towel resurrections, tucked back of window-sized calendars that showed Christ walking the waters, sandaled footprints denting foamy whitecaps. I felt seasick, waiting for my money, waiting.

Already I'd started picturing my own hands putting all of Vesta Lotte Battle's redeemed funds—a chef's salad worth of crisp green—into her outstretched leather palms, bony hands that, so glad, trembled.

But instead it was me back at her orderly shanty, smiling, "Now, you see, you've fallen three weeks behind. We can't have this, ma'am. Really. *Three*."

She'd brought me tea in a mended bone-china cup with goldfish handpainted on it. The saucer (whole) was a different pattern but yellow bone-china too. I kept standing. So did she. Her French mantel clock, marble gilt and stopped years ago, showed a bronze blindfolded woman holding up a scale. All Mrs. B's furniture was missing limbs or spines or cushions—bricks and broomsticks were busy being everything's crutch—but the room looked beautiful anyhow. Especially if you squinted some. Vesta Battle had spent her life working for the owners of the cotton Mill. It showed in how she handled the tea things, how she asked, "You wanting one lump or two, Assurance?"

"I was *saying*, 'You're three weeks overdue.' No sugar. One—maybe one—thank you, but listen, Mrs. Battle. Seriously. You've paid in so much. I just can't have you lose it. You let the latest policy go, they'll grab all your others. You signed, you agreed to this. I mean I've already absorbed that first twenty-one cents from a month back. Okay. I'll let that slide—I wasn't exactly overjoyed about advancing you that but I did. Since then I've paid your last three weeks my own self. Look, I'm poor too or else I wouldn't keep this job, believe me.—Now, maybe that dollar seventy-one doesn't sound like much to you . . . (no, I'm sorry, of course it's a lot to you or else you'd have paid. I see that). But, think, here I am, already lying to my boss. I'm paying out of my own pocket. And for your funeral, ma'am. I'd rather give you food money any day. Let's reason together, all right? It can't go on, can it. Are you even listening? I mean this. Can you hear me?"

Reserved, blue-brown, old the way trees are, she settled, hunched across from me and stated facts. Her eldest daughter, living in Detroit, usually mailed checks home. The last postal money order was five weeks overdue. Mrs. Battle admitted to worrying: maybe something bad had happened. Plus, she'd never much liked her daughter's man. He fought with the line boss at Ford. He hit Pearl way too much. Didn't seem much hope of finding what'd gone wrong.

"Now we're getting somewhere!" I said. "We can *do* something now, see? Action's always best. Just *phone* her."

No telephone here and no number in Detroit. Besides, Vesta Lotte Battle said she didn't trust phones, never planned to touch one; if lightning hit a wire any place between Detroit and here, the shock rode wires into your ear or mouth. Phones were still too new.

"Oh," I said. "Well then *write* her, for God's sake." My advice was growing loud. Kids peeked out of the kitchen then went back to chattering. I smiled noplace. Mrs. Battle sat studying her palm's worn lines.

"Look," I said. "Do you have her address, Pearl's? Let me jot it down. I'll write the letter myself. You mind? My eyes are better than yours." She went for it but had no paper in the place, none that wasn't either a Bible page or some form of printed Jesus. I'd started feeling ill at the sight of Him, meek and mild Saturday-to-Saturday from home to home. FDR seemed lots likelier to offer my clients a fair shake and a moment's assurance. I tore a back page from my ledger. I copied the Detroit address. Mrs. B didn't offer me a stamp or envelope. Okay, I had my own. That same Saturday I mailed the letter. My tone tried balancing the business-like with a tenderer jokey type of human lightness. Even at my age now, I still feel superstitious about mailing certain things. Back then, too. Before dropping Pearl's letter into the slot, I remember kissing all four corners of it—for luck. I waited and hoped.

Insurance was just one of my three part-time jobs. Mrs. Battle was only one of my insurance customers. Like her, others'd stopped seeming all that much alike now. That was just it: the more vivid each dark person became, the blanker, blander, and whiter I felt. A plug of stray cotton: cake-sized. Again I knocked at buckled doors, once more I answered challenges from inside: "It's Assurance. Open up. Hi. Just Assurance back again, ma'am." I'd stopped pointing out the difference between in- and as-surance. They only let me in if I spoke our word.

My ninth week on the job, all clients permanently broke down into themselves. There was the one missing two fingers, the one who always tried to give me geranium clippings for my mom, the plump one in the bed, the pretty young one in the wicker wheelchair, the old one in her metal wheelchair who wore a cowgirl hat, the one with the wig, the one who told the same three easy riddles each week, the one, the one . . .

My rounds sure felt easier when people had the decency to stay blended. Now I started worrying over payer and nonpayers too. You know how it is, once a crowd splits into separate faces, nothing can ever mash them back into that first safe shape.

I was now reading books on ways to cultivate a positive manner, how to make strangers sort of do what you wanted. I learned many innocent jokes by heart. I grinned even more, I switched to plainer clothes—black and white—trying to prove I wasn't all that flush myself. I shook the hands of bashful kids at all my Saturday homes. I taught these kids to holler—when I closed their front door—"After while, crocodile." Somehow it sounded joyless. I perspired a lot. It was a scorching September. You can't imagine the heat in some of my clients' homes.

Once, a drunk husband, wanting the surance money for his booze, tried to take it back. His wife helped fight him off me. "Run," she shouted my way. Pounding on her man's shoulders, wedging herself between him and my getaway, she sobbed at his chest, "No! It for our funeral, baby. Don't you hurt one flower on us two's funeral. Do, baby, and you done seen the last of me."

(I asked myself: If life insurance is you betting on your own death—how much worse is the funeral kind?)

* * *

Mrs. Battle owed. A lot now. Owed me a lot. So did four others. By Christmas she was in to me for the most, to the tune of six dollars and some already. I'm sorry but during the Forties, to a kid in my bracket, six dollars meant something. I was getting in over my head. I knew it, but couldn't seem to stop. I considered whining to Sam. But that would mean ratting on several of my older clients. The ones who'd paid the most over time, they had the most to lose. I felt I should protect her, especially. Mrs. Battle. I don't know why exactly. Maybe because she never explained, never thanked me. She wouldn't consider apologizing. A real aristocrat. Visiting her was like going to see some fine old Duchess in a book. At other homes I refused dandelion wine (in gallon jugs), five free wire-wheeled tires, one lewd offer from this old man in a kimono!, two dozen wonderful-smelling home-cured hams. I only accepted Mrs. Battle's conversation and her green China tea. These soon seemed drudgery's one dividend. I looked forward to her face at the door. We still waited for Pearl's answer to my letters, we looked forward to Pearl's checks. Some Saturdays I'd save Mrs. B's house for last, like a reward, my commission.

Sam had tipped me off. "Once they smell heart on you, kid, you're lost." I wondered how heart would smell to a half-blind old woman. Like beef? Or bread. Or beer? Maybe vanilla extract. How?

One windy Saturday, walking through Mrs. Battle's yard, I heard a creaking in her roadside sunflowers—I found a signboard hid among the leaves. The wooden plaque was teapot-shaped, two feet across. It'd been enameled pink, then painted over with many black crack-marks and the words "Can Fix."

I wondered, What literate person had written those two words for her? Some child maybe. When I asked about the sign, she pointed to a red table set at the back of her kitchen. It was propped with glue pots, masking tape, brushes and—at the center—a little scaffolding of toothpicks, twigs, and Popsicle sticks. Some miniature ship seemed under construction but, holding my account book against my chest, I bent nearer and saw a fine old soup tureen. The thing looked imprisoned in its own splint. Hundreds of fissures had recently spoiled it, but each was now caked with white powdery stuff like a denture cream. Mrs. Battle, again startling me at how close she'd got so silently, explained: the porcelain paste, once dried and set, would wipe off with solvent. Someday, good as new. On the tureen's side, an old woodland view was daubed, done fast but with great skill. Mrs. B. had set little support brads into its bowed porcelain. She'd hid metal clips right in the painted landscape; one paralleled a brown tree trunk. The brad's blue metal looked just like the tree's own shadow. You couldn't separate VLB's mending from the little ideal glade itself. I saw the beauty of the *fixed* tureen clearer than I would've noticed it, whole.

"It *looks* copa . . . terrif, really," I said, standing. "But will it ever hold soup again?"

"What good'd it be otherwise, Assurance? Ain't this *for* the soup?"

She seemed to consider mending a parlor game, said she'd learned it in a henhouse-workshop. A lady missionary, returned from China, taught local black girls this skill in the 18 and 70s. Final exam: You personally chose one hen's egg and jumped on it, then you personally rebuilt it so it looked unbroken to the picky naked eye. Excellent training for the world.

As I sat having tea with Mrs. B, an overdressed white

lady appeared, apologizing for "having barged in." She handed over the dust of a ruined teacup. How ruined? It was in one of her husband's letter-sized business envelopes!

"Ooh my my," Mrs. B laughed dry but deep. "Somebody must've fell on this with both they boots." "Yes," the woman smiled my way. "I'm married to a man who doesn't, shall we say? have the lightest touch on earth?—What would we do without her?" and nodded to our mutual friend who ignored this. I did too.

Mrs. Battle sat shaking the envelope. Listening to crumbled porcelain rattle, her face went dreamy as somebody eavesdropping on a conch shell's pulse. "One big mess," she said with relish. "Yes, well"—the customer turned to leave—"I admit as how this may finally be beyond even your skills, my dear. Even so, do have a go at it. Otherwise, I fear Mother's service for twenty-four is totally useless. You'll try? Good day, young man." She nodded, maybe wondering if I'd brought VLB *my* busted fingerbowls. (Fat chance.) The lady stared like asking why a sternly dressed young gent should be here sipping tea midafternoon. But I saw she didn't disapprove a bit. If anything her glance seemed jealous of VLB. So, we understood each other. Every Saturday for weeks after, I asked to see the progress of Mrs. Fancy Schmantsy's cup.

First there were heaps of grit—then handle grit, side grit, bottom grit. Soon it became separate Wedgwood blue and white nuggets. Shaping from the bottom up, a roundness started showing—at its lower edges—the calm little sandals of picnicking gods and goddesses. I'd sometimes find Mrs. B using a magnifying glass big as Mr. Sherlock Holmes's. She'd hold the cup not just near but practically against her face—pressed over her best eye the way you mash beefsteak there to prevent swelling. She had so little eyesight left, she seemed to feel this last amount might squeeze out as a bonding glue. Once, I planned to surprise her and I stole up from behind. I heard her whisper into the cup's hollow like down some microphone, "Captain Wedgwood? Coming back to you senses? I setting up a meeting between you and Marse Earle Grey late next week. Won't be long now."

Uneasy, I tiptoed back out, lunged in again. "Assurance!"

The more relaxed I felt with her, the harder my job got. Friday night before collection mornings, I started having regular bad dreams. I saw myself turning roses into radishes. I kept shoving people off a high bridge. Mrs. Battle had fallen further and further behind. Three long-distance calls finally got me the Employment Office of the Ford Motor Co., Detroit. I asked after one Pearl Battle. They found four on their payroll; what was my Pearl's middle name? I didn't know but, wait, yes I did. "Vesta—either Pearl Vesta or Vesta Pearl. After six minutes of crackling long-distance time, (me paying, naturally, me sweating bullets), they came back, No Vesta Pearl or the other. "Did I say Vesta? Must be slipping. I meant 'Lotte' Pearl Battle or else 'Pearl Lotte' Battle. Hello?" The line was dead. Not sure why, I went out and got drunk for the first time ever and, knee-walking smashed, considered driving to Michigan to find my favorite's favorite daughter.

One evening, pitifully sober, headed home after my last Saturday collection (some nights it took till ten), I motored along Summit Avenue, our town's richest white street. Boys I'd known at high school were out playing basketball. They were my age, lawyers' and dentists' sons home for Christmas break, back from freshman year at Duke, Carolina, Princeton. One goal was mounted over the big home's back door, another hung above its three-car garage. This morning when I rode by, bound for Baby Africa, the same guys had been playing.—Now parked nearby, I slunk low in my car, headlights doused, my windows down. I sat listening to their ball pinging in that clean trusty way basketballs do. It was so dark you wondered how players could see the goal but you still heard the swish of the net, point, point. Guys horsed around; one yodeled, "Glad I back in de land ob cotton, your feet stink and mine is rotten, look away . . ." They called each other butter-fingers, cross-eyed, air-brain. I just sat. Lamps were being lit inside the three-storied house. Then the mother of the place turned on a back-porch light and appeared carrying sandwiches and bottled sodas on a silver tray. She left this and—without a word—slipped indoors. All day these guys'd been here doing this.

I rolled up my window. I envied them but pitied them but mostly envied them. I drove off, slower than usual. I felt like crying. I wouldn't let myself. It seemed a luxury people like me couldn't afford.

I visited my night school's tuition office. I asked for a payment extension. Six weeks only. It wouldn't happen again. I blamed family problems. That seemed true. I was paying Dad's extra medical bills, paying for household food, plus funding the upcoming funerals of four black strangers, along with one ninety-some-year-old near-stranger. ("If they'd just hurry up and keel over while I'm supporting them, they'd all get the red-carpet treatment.")

I lied for them. I paid. And this stupid generosity made me feel ashamed, not good like it's supposed to. I told myself, "You're just too weak to give her up. No

Princeton pre-law ballplayer would be such a sap. You're helping losers, clod, because you are one.''

The Wedgwood cup, week to week, healed like a stupid perfect little garden vegetable on her second kitchen table. Then one day it was gone. I missed it. Back it went to its home set, and another white person's porcelain disaster took its place. I wondered what Mrs. B charged these country clubbers. Not enough, I guesssed. She needed a manager.

Payment-wise, she had slipped further behind, no word from Pearl. I wondered if she'd made Pearl up. I knew better and felt ashamed, but even so . . . And yet, grouchy as I felt, I still sort of leaned toward having my tea with her. The kids at VLB's place usually behaved and often seemed funny, noisy in a good way. I decided not to mention how much Vesta Lotte Battle owed, not till the end of today's visit. That'd spare us both some embarrassment. While driving to her place, I'd mapped out my speech and tactics. But once arrived, there was something about her emptied necklace, the brocade bolsters sewn shut with clear fishing line. There was something about how the children at her house tried cleaning up after themselves and looked out for each other and her. Some Saturdays when she called me ''Boy Assurance,'' I believed her. I wanted to. I called her ''Vesta Lotte Battle'' to her face and in my head. The name started sounding classic and someway fertile. But, hey, eventually, I *had* to bring it up—I mean the money.

''Look, did Pearl let you know yet? I told her to write you here.''

Mrs. B sat rocking somebody else's sick baby. Seven older kids—all quiet, groggy-acting, maybe with fevers?—rested in sweet lost heaps around the room. My client hadn't answered me.

"Well? Are you planning to speak? I'm sorry but I'm getting cross here. I am. And who can blame me? It's January already. No word from Detroit?"

The blue-black head wagged sideways.

"Mrs. Battle, with all due respect, I earn about two dollars and eighty cents per Saturday doing this. A lot of it's going to you. I've cut off some of the others. You not. But it's plain. I can't keep this up much longer, right? I mean I've carried you—week by week, I have. It hurts me but I can't . . . much longer."

"You ain't got to."

Rocking the borrowed baby, she just looked at me. She said this. The thing was, she meant it. Maybe that's what always made me feel so bad. If I did drop her from the rolls, she wouldn't hold it against me. That was the absolute killer.

"Well, I know I don't *have* to. Not by law, I don't."

I stood before her chair, hoping she might at least offer me some tea. "But, Mrs. B, you'd lose your life savings. And that's taken you your whole life to save up, right, ma'am?"

She sat rocking, eyes aimed past me.

She seemed so unlike the others, unlike any person I've met since. How can I explain it to you? I want to. My other clients often faked long hunts for coins they knew weren't there. (Try and imagine the agony of standing before a wheelchair where an old lady in a cowgirl hat is going through every pocket of her house-dress ten times while you wait, looking hopeful—trying to.) Clients would hide inside their homes. I'd peek through a window and notice six adults and two children lying face-up on the floor. Caught, they'd grin, then all fake napping. "Hi. I see you," I'd say.

"Please." You would not believe the hassles, sob stories, and runarounds I got each Saturday.

It's why I loved coming here. Mrs. Battle never blamed me for inventing the rigged setup. If all five of her policies got revoked, I knew she wouldn't fault me. (She hadn't even blamed me when I chose to take her payments on myself.) Today I understood, it was, from the start, my own doing, not hers.

Odd: standing before her chair, furious at our situation—meaning furious at *her*—I found myself wondering how Mrs. B must have looked when she was, say, my age. By now she had nothing left but this unexplainable . . . power, I'll call it. (Where do such put-upon people *learn* such pride?) Was it something time had done to her? Did it come because she knew so much, or did she understand very little but in a deep deep way? I have never bought the stuff about all old people being wise. You don't get Wisdom with your first Social Security check. I mean, here I am, near the brink of sixty and still waiting for the old light bulb to snap on overhead. That day, I saw: nothing was left her but a raw, quiet sureness. Mostly blind, stripped down to vitals, she could now take anything that came. Ninety-some, she'd finally got fairly limber. She could dodge it all. She could even take losing everything on my account. For that reason, I just would not permit it. No.

There was something about the old woman—I'm not sure that I can explain it or, if I do, that you'll believe me. Mrs. Battle had some kind of stature or something. I mean, aren't there people—maybe Churchill or Roosevelt maybe—who're lit up with a cranky kind of genius that everybody, even their own enemies, respects? True, I'd never seen Vesta Lotte Battle *do* all that much. She never saved the Free World or anything like that. Yeah, she once gave me shelter during a downpour, she mended collectors' item china practically for free, she let neighbor kids hang out at her house and make candy. She knew how to change a tire. So what? Most days she just sat in this rocker, rocking, looking out at a view on noplace. It galled me, standing here, waiting: I thought, almost envious, why should it be *one old black woman?* Aren't I crazy to consider that she knows this much? I must be insane to feel so much because of her. I must be making this up.

Still, right along, I was positive about it. I still am. That's why I'm bothering to tell this. Her? she knew. It was less anything she did or said, more who she was, I guess. She'd never seen the ocean, a hundred and ten miles from Falls. And yet, you just felt her life. Felt it go right into your own. You were helpless. Instantly you couldn't separate. You walked into the room and it was like that stove of hers burning when I met her in July. Her life stayed closer to the skin than most people's.

Part of what I'm saying is: It seemed unbelievable that such a woman couldn't come up with fifty cents a week.

She now asked would I go make our tea? Today she had a lapful. I did. I found I knew where she stored everything. I noted a ruined gravy boat, trying to re-group itself inside her toothpick bracings. For a second, putting water on to boil, I closed my eyes, imagining blindness—imagining *her* blindness. I admired how she managed to fake vision. She really looked right at you. Odd I'd never noticed any food in her kitchen, nothing but sugar and cream for my tea, nothing past candy makings for her kids. Did she live on tea, on whatever nourishment seeped into her mended cup from all the glue that held the thing together?

I brought Mrs. B her own best one-of-a-kind cup, laurel and nasturtiums painted around it. I was pouring tea as she started talking about slave days. Uh oh. I saw her start relaxing back back into being blind. She finally trusted me enough to let me see she couldn't see. "This is a trick!" something told me. I knew I shouldn't listen. I imagined Sam scolding me, "Jesus, kid, you just ask for trouble, you know that? Rule Numero Uno is: always think of your assigned list as the group. Group life, ever heard of it? Then everything'll go down easy as Jack Daniel's. But when you start slipping, start thinking, 'There's this man and that woman,' then they'll really nail you, son. They know this, they plan it." I shouldn't pay attention. History'd only make me feel worse, her history would. And yet here she was, cradling the kid in one arm, using her free hand to hold a teacup to her mouth. (*It* now seemed blind too). Between sips, she slowly told. (What was I going to do? mash my hand over her three-toothed mouth? What, was I going to run away or what?) Despising my own politeness, I settled cross-legged on plank flooring beside her busy rocker; the brocade and cinder-block chaise was too far off. OK, but I'd just fake listening.

She'd been born the property of our local mill-owning family. She said she'd got freed while still a child. The day after Sherman marched through our county, burning things, freed slaves killed all the plantation's livestock. The old groom cut the throats of two white Arabian horses he'd curried and exercised daily. Then, knife in hand, he stood over them, crying, "What *else* do I got?" She remembered everybody's dancing by torchlight in the Quarter. Ex-slaves raided their mistress's closets, wore all her gowns. Some of the funny little boys dressed up, tripping on hems. Freed slaves held a Harvest Ball in April, a candlelight party like

ones that'd lit the big house before the War. That first
night of freedom, three older men asked Vesta Lotte to
marry them. Freed, she now felt free to say No three
times running. She was eight.

Vesta Lotte, old, rocked on, telling me of huge forest
fires that Sherman's troops had set. She'd watched our
town's first cotton mill burn. She rambled, saying,
"Then, right after it surrendered . . ."

I'd heard other older black people say "After It Surrendered." They seemed to speak about some octopus
"it" that'd once had ahold of them. They never said
"after Lee surrendered"—just this "It." I wanted to
explain to my beloved client—Maybe General Lee did
finally bow out in '65, but it, old it, had not surrendered yet. It still held her, still had us all.

Down here, I studied her men's work boots, the stick-
thin black ankles. On she rocked. Her dignity irked me.
I'd paid Eventualities Mrs. B's last nine dollars and fifty
cents. *I* should be in the position of control here, right?
But, just by holding still, by aiming her cataracts straight
out toward the roadside's browned sunflowers (were they
blurs to her? were they even visible?) she put me
through these hoops of bad feelings, gave me moral
insomnia. —In my night-school philosophy course, our
teacher had read one line from an Eastern religious
book: "Seventy-five righteous men carry the world."
Considering what I imagined soon doing to Mrs. B, I
muttered under my breath, "Today . . . marked down
to seventy-four."

"Why?" I asked her now, interrupting. I got up onto
my knees beside her chair, I set my cup down. I felt
tempted to place my butch-waxed head into her lap beside the sick child panting there. "Why *funerals?*"
Rude as it sounded, I couldn't help asking. How could
anybody so smart sink all her money into last rites?

What—I half-hollered—did she imagine for herself after death? Hunh? —The morticians' perks would get her into the next world; okay—then what? How did she picture this Heaven?

I wondered, did Saturday coins seem installments on some future boat fare? Did VLB think of her own afterlife as a long-awaited china mending, or maybe as Old Africa itself? Waiting for her answer, I imagined a jungle shore of flowers seen from some rocking boat: Home. I sat straighter, readying myself for her answer. Since I was bankrolling this voyage, I felt I had a right to hear. Pumping her for news of after—death kind of thrilled me. I figured, ''Hey, if anybody knows the score, it's Vesta Lotte Battle here.'' I was nineteen. I admired her. She owed me.

I almost thought of her as mine.

I kept still, poised on my knees beside an active rocking chair. This was happening one quiet January Saturday on a side street in Falls, NC's worst possible neighborhood. The only steady noise: squabbles among the large black-owned dogs moping near my Nash, peeing on its whitewalls, waiting to chase me. ''Roses,'' Mrs. Battle answered, husky, without hesitation. ''Dozens. Roses. Thousands maybe.''

(Somehow I'd pictured her paradise blooming shields, zinnias, spears, sunflowers. The beauty of roses seemed patented as Whitie's.) ''So,'' I rushed her. ''Roses for starters. What else?''

Time passed as youngsters curled into deeper napping. The baby in Mrs. B's lap made suckling noises, dreaming.

''And plane tickets for all my grown children so's they can come on back down here for it. Around-trips, too. A lined red casket be nice. Oh, and some big white

town cars . . . I wouldn't mind.'' Hearing this, I felt
sickened some, and slowed. I understood: For her, the
funeral itself was a kind of heaven. She hadn't dared
picture anything more glamorous than a decent middle-
class send-off. ''And marble markers with two rock
lambs on top, or, if they out of lambs, maybe a couple
baby angels'd do.'' Bobbing back and forth, clucking at
the sick child, Mrs. Battle kept mulling over her list of
funeral needs. She stared out a bright window and finally shrugged. In a voice too resigned to sound bitter,
she said nowhere, ''I ain't asking much.''

I wondered aloud how many children would be heading south. ''I mean 'eventually' of course.'' (I've always been more tactful than was needed, a disease.)

''Nineteen. Plus them ones what they lives with or
be married to. It mount up.''

I nodded. You had to admit: the transportation costs
alone could really set a person back.

We just kept still for twenty minutes more. First I felt
real gloomy, and next, slow, I got extra mad. Not at
her now. But for her. For us. Resting by her creaking
rocker, sipping lukewarm tea, it struck me: Vesta Lotte
Battle's former owners still mostly owned my own
broken-down wheezing parents. I wanted to kill somebody then, to go kill the people put in charge of us all.

''Okay.'' I finally stood, stiff, feeling old myself. I
cleared her tea things, brushed at the seat of my pressed
pants. ''Okay,'' I sounded huffy, wronged. ''But I warn
you I'm only good for one more week. I know you
understand how much I think of you. But, look, I've
carried you, I've covered for you. I'm doing this fast-
and-loose bookkeeping so my boss won't nab you. Finally, even for people like us, there are limits, you
know. You know?'' She gave me one dry shoulder-
heave. The dark voice went, ''I reckon you'll do what

you wants.'' (Sam had told me, ''There's always one that gets you. Really gets you.'' Odd, the worse I am at describing the power of Vesta Lotte Battle, the surer I am of it, the deeper I still feel it—right up under the rib cage.)

That very week I sent a telegram to Detroit: ''Mother's funeral in jeopardy STOP of default STOP act quickly please STOP a friend STOP.'' I promised myself this'd have to be the final Christian act for soft-headed non-pre-law really un-Princeton Jerry. My sleep was suffering, gone spotty and shallow. I did well in my night-school business courses. I aced Philosophy but started feeling sneaky about my unnatural straight A average. For somebody nineteen, somebody American and intending to be self-made, I was growing pretty cynical pretty early. Funerary Eventualities had started eating me alive. On a night-school pop quiz, one question asked, ''Define 'Business Ethics.' '' I wrote, '' 'Business Ethics' is a contradiction in terms.''

Then I erased this.

So I'd pass.

Life did an article about the heir to the Funerary fortune. Dad saved it for me, ''You think this magazine is just pictures but they cover most everything, Jerry, what've I been telling you?'' The heir, a Shaker Heights resident, was shown wearing his bathing suit. A coffee-and-cream-toned gent, he looked plump and sleek as a neutered seal. He was a millionaire many times over, his daughter sang opera, he'd been photographed beside his Olympic swimming pool. It was shaped like a clock—diving boards at the 12 and 6! Well, that helped me be firm. This week was it.

I rushed off to knock at Vesta Lotte Battle's door. I'd brought along a jar of my mother's excellent blackberry

jam. I hoped this might sweeten and sort of humanize
my bad news. I'd prepared a little speech. It incorpo-
rated a quote from Plato—one memorized for my *Book
of Knowledge* spiel.

I planned to tell Mrs. B: her dignity seemed so safe,
really, so beyond me or anybody, it was something that
Time had given her and nobody could take away. This
royal quality of hers consoled me and, in my remarks,
I planned to mention it as praiseworthy. I'd add: since
she seemed so secure about her long life, why this worry
over burial? Why sweat the small stuff? I would point
out necessary facts. Superstition seemed to me Vesta
Lotte Battle's single fault. Maybe my nineteen-year-old
perspective would finally help the woman see her life
more clearly? Maybe it'd help her mind this less—being
cut off and so forth.

I pushed open her door. No one had answered. There
she stood, poking her own rocking chair idly to and
fro. She'd been waiting for me. She'd sent her usual
kids home. I grinned. I held out her jar of world-class
jam. I'd bought a nice plaid ribbon, I'd tied it around
the lid. "I'm afraid," I started, "I'm afraid this'll have
to be your last free week. I believe we both knew this'd
have to happen, right? From the day we met, even with
our getting to be friendly and all, we've basically known
it, right?"

"Word come," she fixed her ruined eyes on me, she
offered me one yellow bit of paper. "Pearl dead."

Then Mrs. Battle pretended to reread her telegram.
She was holding the thing upside down. She was hold-
ing the goddamn thing upside down. "No," I said.
"You made it up. No."

I rushed over and flopped into her rocker. I clutched
the jam against my chest, arms crossed over it, head
down, chair bobbling back and forth, panting like my

one job was to guard this gift I'd brought, this bribe.
"No," my eyes wouldn't focus right. "A trick," I said,
"I mean: a trick on both of us."

I heard Mrs. B step nearer, she touched my shoulder,
trying to cheer me. Then her right hand crooked under
my arm, she coached me into standing. Her palms
pressed the small of my back, leading me toward her
overheated kitchen for our usual tea. Her head came no
higher than my elbow.

I stood beside her scrubbed oak table. I set down the
jam, then leaned here, my hands flat, my full weight
tilted forward. On her mending table, somebody's gold-
rimmed fruit bowl dangerous in three hundred pieces.

I listened as, blind, efficient, she filled the teapot at
her pump, doing everything so well. I kept staring at
the scoured tabletop, saying, "What are we going to do
here? Pearl was our only hope. Now I bet we're going
to lose it. Help me, Mrs. Battle. Help me think this out
for us. Really. Oh boy, what are we going to do here?
God, what are we going to *do* with you?"

A dry brown hand pushed one mended apple-green
cup into my vision, a scrap of steam, a perfect cup of
tea.

"Something's wrong," Sam said. "Black circles
creeping under your eyes. You're not taking this to
heart? You *are* keeping the old heart well out of this,
right, Jer?"

" 'Heart'?" I looked up, trying to grin. "What's a
. . . 'heart'? I never heard of one of those. 'Heart'?
What, is it something like a flashlight?"

" 'Flashlight'! Got to remember that." He showed
me his kids' new school photos: the girl wore thick
white hair ribbons that made her thin hair look transparent. Sam kissed her picture. "And this boy of mine's

going to set the world on fire. You watch.'' Sam needed
my opinion about a paint color—he planned improving
his office here in maybe two or three years' time. Nursing the bourbon bottle, he said he only drank during
our appointments. He didn't know, something about me
got him. Sam asked how *I'd* done in organic chem? I
sat looking at this man, he might've been speaking
Latin, his face looked orange, solid orange to me.

Now I see I was in the middle of something like
what's known today as a mini-breakdown. Then we
called it the blues. We called it Having Black Circles
Under Your Eyes For A While. The Whiteboy-With-
Blackness-Under-His-BabyBlues-Blues. (And the whiter
the person is, the more deadly his case can be. Cotton
starts out white but if you breathe white cotton for years
enough, it gives you something called Brown Lung. You
figure it.)

Here I'll hurry what happened next. Sometimes you
rush stories because you don't have sufficient info. In
this case, a person's maybe got too much. You know
those memo pads with ''While You Were Out . . .''
printed at the top, yellow pages maybe four inches by
four? Well, inside my tweed windbreaker's breast
pocket, I'd recently placed just such a piece of paper.
Names were written on it in my own admirable forward-
tilting Palmer script. I'd arrived at Sam's office building
early. While waiting in the weedy park across the street,
I chose a sunny bench. Bored, working from memory,
I copied nine offenders' names (plus their dollar
amounts in arrears). To the cent, I knew. I wrote just
to soothe myself, I told myself. I've always been big
into lists.

How carefully I inscribed each name. Lovingly almost. One example, I traced ridges like gutters over the
TT in the middle of one name. I extended those cross-

bars to shelter the whole name LoTTe. That list, now hidden in my jacket pocket, crackled when I fidgeted, talking to Sam. The square of yellow paper burned me like a mustard plaster.

Everybody's superstitious. About money especially. "If I clear this figure by March, I'll give X amount to charity, really." "Like it or not, I'll only eat what's in the house till we go out and splurge on Friday." The folkways of the wallet. Pretty strange. Consider our nervous computerized stock market: It still uses a bull and a bear to explain itself to itself. Animals? Now? See, it's homemade magic. Where money comes in, we're all primitives. And, like that, I'd carefully copied a list so I'd *prevent* myself from saying out loud any name on that list. Got it? Logic, it's not—heartfelt, it is.

See, even as I made those two T's spread like a porch roof and guardian umbrella over the name beneath, I was giving myself one teentsy loophole. If, and only if, Sam smelled this list on me, if he asked for it point-blank, then and only then might I consider maybe possibly letting him just peek at it perhaps. And for one sec.

It's just, I'd been so silent for so long. Nine old people felt they owed me their lives. Once Sam read the thing, I knew I'd feel better, I'd find the stamina to sustain Group Life a little longer.—I was, after all, legally responsible to Sam here and if a person's boss actually *orders* that person to hand over an inventory of backsliding wrongdoers, well . . .

What can I say? I was nineteen years old. I'd been buying my own clothes since I was eleven. Other guys my age and half as smart, a tenth as driven, were already off at college, lounging around, sleeping in till 11:30 a.m.

Early March, Sam's office overheated, but I couldn't take my jacket off because the list was in it. He'd see. Paper crackled if I didn't sit real still. Fiduciary voodoo.

My wife says: for somebody like me, somebody with a strong head for facts, it's even more important to empty out that head from time to time. So I am, okay? Clearing the books.

"Buddy? Something's off, right? College material like you, and with bags down to here. I'm seeing a wear-and-tear beyond the normal wear of raking in their coins come Saturday. Know what Sam here's starting to think? Somebody's holding out on you, kid. You definitely got moochers. More'n one, too. Your face gives it away. You're too young to know how to hide stuff yet. In time, you'll get that right—but now your kisser is like neon practically, going bloink blink blank. And this particular neon tells Sam, says 'Sam? Certain moneys are coming directly out of young Jerry's personal bone marrow.' You got parasites, Jer. It shows. Draining you.

"You're shielding them but who's looking after *you*? Your folks? Naw, you're on your own. *I'm* here for you. You were handsome when I hired you. *Now* look. Your pantcuffs are frayed, the boy can't even sit up straight.— Jerry, who you covering for? Let me help, son. I swear it won't get past this desk. You know their names, you maybe even wrote names down. Yeah—probably got those tucked somewheres on your person. Look, kid, trust me here. You want Sam to step around his desk, ease you against that wall and frisk you, Jer? You're a good-looking kid, Jerry, but not that good. Spare us both. Pass your uncle the names. I'll need the exact dollar amount each leech has sucked out of my favorite. Jerry? Tell your Uncle Sam.''

Tears stood in my boss's eyes. That's when I knew I had to let him save me. Yellow is such a beautiful positive color, isn't it? *While You Were Out* . . .

I slept so well that night! Why lie about it? I dropped off saying things like "Figures don't lie." It was a sleep too deep to let one single dream come tax it—just blackness so pure I woke up sweaty, half-panting. Getting true rest seemed the most exerting thing I'd done in months. One room away, Dad coughed, Mom promised him it'd be all right, she pounded his back, Dad thanked her, he said it'd passed, he choked again.

The Friday after, I was driving toward the night-school business office to make my overdue payment. I'd got certain bonuses and could again fund my education. I still collected for Windlass but now avoided the two hundred block of Sunflower Street. I called on that block's paying clients only after dark. It was a gusty March afternoon, dust devils spun along the roadside. Winds rocked even the biggest trees. One wad of cotton, large as a hassock, came tumbling down the center line, rolled up onto my car hood and snagged one windshield wiper. I braked, cussed, got out to yank it off and—two hundred yards away in Baby Africa's clay cemetery—saw a funeral in progress.

Women were hunched under shawls, men held hats against their chests. Everybody, fighting wind, kept faces turned down and aside. They all looked ashamed and—in my present state—this at once attracted me. An old woman stood surrounded by kids. "It's Pearl's," I said. "They're burying Pearl." My voice broke, but, understand I am not asking for credit. Fact is, I slunk back into my Nash, flipped down both sun visors, prepared to roar off. Then unexpectedly my car was pulling over, I was out in the air, was walking toward a familiar group. Like so much I did back then, I hadn't planned to.

I remember dry weeds snapping under my new loafers. I waited off to one side, hands joined before me. I was the only white person present.

Two weeks back, I made four phone calls to the Detroit morgue; I'd helped get Pearl's body shipped home in a railroad ice-car. The trip had taken her eleven days. Pearl's coffin was splintery pine. You could see black nail ends bent crooked under half-moon hammer dents. Must be the crate they packed her home in. Somebody'd tried painting out stenciled instructions: THIS SIDE UP. KEEP REFRIGERATED AT ALL TIMES. Near the coffin's tapering foot end, a Maxwell House can rested on the ground. It was stuffed with dried hydrangea blooms big as human heads. Alongside the jagged grave, a pile of earth waited. Wind kept flicking dirt off that and onto the mourners. Everybody stood with eyes closed, less in prayer than to protect themselves from the menace of flung grit. (I wondered why this didn't usually happen. I'd only been to two funerals but remembered that the undertakers usually spread a grass-green groundcloth over such waiting dirt to hide it, and protect the living.)

People lined up looking into the coffin a last time. I'd never seen an open coffin at the graveyard. But, having strolled over here, I felt I couldn't hold back. When I joined the line, Mrs. B's neighbor kids saw me. They suddenly closed ranks around her. Only then did she turn in my general direction. Her neck lengthened, the blue-gray head twisting my way. I knew she couldn't see me at this distance but both VLB's arms lifted from her sides, wavering noplace. She seemed to be hearing a sound or maybe scented me standing here. I felt so honored I got weak.

The woman in the box was over seventy, she wore a mostly emptied amethyst necklace. On her chest a gold pin-watch read FORD MOTORS, a perfect attendance prize. Her age shocked me. I'd always pictured Pearl as just a bit older than me. I now saw: that would've made Vesta Lotte Battle a mother at seventy-three or so.

In the makeshift coffin, Pearl's head had shifted to one side, she faced pine planks like a person choosing to look punished, refusing even a last chance at formality.

The coffin was then closed, boys nailed it shut. Nails kept doubling over and this looked so ugly it grieved me. Strong young boys lowered Pearl's crate by ropes. Mourners themselves started heaping in the dirt. Garden spades and shovels seemed brought from home, no professional gravedigger waited in sight.

The girl who'd once pressed my hand between her candied palms now led Mrs. B away, detouring to avoid me. I walked over anyway. I was helpless not to. My mouth and lips felt novocained (I later realized I'd been mercilessly biting them without noticing). I felt foolish and exposed here, *rude*. But I still needed something from the old lady. *My* old lady, I still thought of her, but knew I had no right.

She must have seen a pink blur fumble nearer. VLB resisted ten children who tried dragging her past me. When she stopped, kids eased back, but their chins stayed lifted, hands knotting into fists. I didn't blame them. I knew how I must look out here. They'd taught me. I kept swallowing to keep from smiling. I gulped down a beefy-yeasty-copperpenny taste that turned out to be blood.

Mrs. Battle—grieving like this, far from her familiar

house—seemed disoriented. Her skin had lost its grapey luster; she now looked floured in fine ash—her eyes' fronts too. Daylight showed a face composed entirely of cracks depending on splits and folds; her hands stayed out in front of her, long fingers opening and closing, combing air. She groped my way, lightly, almost fondly. Plain daylight showed her to be so tiny, malnourished maybe. Sun made her look just like . . . a blind person! Completely blind. Somehow she seemed less dignified out here and less unique. I have to say: it made things easier on me just then.—I'm telling you everything. That's our deal.

She faltered quite close, finally touching my sleeve, but jerking back like from a shock. "Ah," her voice recognized me. "You, Assurance?"

"Yes ma'am." I studied my new shoes.

"You did come. I knew it. I done told them. And we thanks you. Pearl'd be glad.—Look, not to worry bout all that other, hear? We doing just fine. Fact is, been missing you more than we miss it, Assurance. You steadily helped me to find my Pearl, get her on back here. Don't go fretting none, child, you tried.—You gone be fine. I'm gone be fine."

Then she turned and moved away from me supported by neighbor kids' spindly arms and legs.

I waited till everybody left. The wind got worse. I stood at Pearl's grave. Handprints and shoe marks had packed the earth. Wind had tipped the coffee can. Water made mud of the grave's foot end. I squatted and crammed hydrangeas back into their tin and set it upright. Last year's hydrangeas had dried brown but still showed most of their strong first blue. You know the color of hydrangeas—that heavenly blue so raw it comes close to seeming in bad taste.

I drove out into the country and passed a rural mailbox I'd always admired and meant to check on. I did that now for no good reason. It was a life-sized Uncle Sam enameled red, white, and blue—meat-pink for his face and hands. The eyes were rhinestone buttons salvaged off some woman's coat. His vest buttons were dimes glued on and varnished. While I stood looking, the proud owner stepped out of a tractor shed, then headed over to tell me how he'd got the idea and to accept my compliments. I panicked, saw myself as one of those guys, like Dad, who'll jaw for forty minutes with complete strangers over nothing. I hopped back into my Nash and squalled away.

I drove to Lucas' All-Round Store, needing staples for my folks. Mom loved angel food cake. With a little teasing encouragement from me, she could sit at our kitchen table and pull off a bit of white fluff at a time till she'd eaten it, whole. The embarrassment was part of her joy. "I *ate* that? *I* ate it?" And somehow she never gained. So I got her a big Merita angel cake and, for Dad, the giant economy size of Vick's Vap-O-Rub. (On his worst coughing nights, he sometimes dipped one finger in and swallowed gobs of it till I had to leave the room.)

Here recently, dredging all this up, I've decided: if a person's emotional life were only rational—if it just "came out" like algebra does—then none of us would ever need good listeners or psychiatrists, would we? We'd do nicely with our accountants. We'd bring our man a whole year of receipts, evidence, and pain. We'd spend two hours together in a nice office and, at the end, our hired guy could just poke the *Tally* button and we, his client, would feel clean again and solid, solvent. Nice work if you can get it.

After Pearl's burial, I dropped off my folks' supplies,

explaining I was headed for our Public Library to hit the books. Instead—pretending I didn't know what I was up to—I drove along Sunflower, switched off my ignition and headlights, coasted to a halt three houses down from Mrs. Battle's.

I sat screened by dried sunflower stalks rustling in the breeze, I looked toward her kerosene-lit home. I heard kids in there talking loud, once a wave of laughing broke. Her narrow body, half-doubled, crisscrossed the room from ironing board to stove and back, for tea, for hotter irons. I knew hers was just a little bent black nail of a body, but she threw such large blue shadows. I slumped out here feeling like a spy or a spurned lover, like some hick planning a stepladder elopement. I knew if I walked up and knocked at her screen door, she'd greet me, "Look children, our Boy Assurance's back." Kids might act snooty but she'd go make me tea in a mended cup so fine you could hold it up and—even against a kerosene lantern's glow—read imprinted on the bottom, its maker's name.

I watched her shack, pretending to guard it. Dumb thoughts: What if it caught fire? Then I'd carry her out, lug all the kids to safety. I was big: I could, I could carry most of them at once.

Why was I waiting? Did I hope she'd sense me here and suddenly pop up like when my tire blew? Maybe I could take her for a car ride tonight, go find her and the kids ice cream someplace. On me, of course. Maybe have two cords of firewood sent? I soon disgusted myself and drove home. I stayed up extra late, studying. Days, I didn't get much time for schoolwork. I think I told you I was working a couple other jobs. Managing a soda fountain and, after hours, cleaning two laundromats for this hermit bachelor who owned much of Falls while spending absolutely nothing. Plus I had the four night-school courses a week.

Working late that night, I heard Dad hacking in a new way, more shrill, yappier. I stood up from the card table that was my desk. I eased along our short hall and waited outside my folks' room. The cough came again. Only, it was my mother coughing. Her case had never seemed as bad as his. Whenever Momma got to hacking, she always laughed, claiming it was just a kind of sympathy vote for *his* shortwindedness. They'd worked cleaning the same looming machines for thirty-some years. What made me believe she'd found a purer air supply than his? Did I think Justice made things easier for the ladies? I leaned there in our dark hallway— beaverboard paneling bowed under my weight. I'd always understood that Dad, after thirty-seven years, had pulled enough fiber into his plugged lungs so you could maybe weave a long-sleeve shirt from it. But Mom? That night, I started knowing she'd inhaled enough to make one lacy deadly blouse. I stood here listening, though this just meant asking for more trouble. It seemed to me then: Staying alive is learning to make meals out of setbacks. Eating them, eating them up.

So it's six weeks after the Detroit police wired us news of Pearl's death, two weeks after Pearl's burial and I'm driving Sunflower, still collecting. I'm half past Vesta Lotte Battle's clean shanty when I see this fresh white wreath nailed to her front door. Poor Pearl, I thought. Lined along VLB's weathered porch, a dozen children, black white brown, all wearing play clothes, all sitting very still. They're eating the usual pale taffy but, today, kids gobble it like taking some group poison.

Then, slow, two blocks and a thousand sunflowers

later, I understand: my favorite, the old lady herself, is
dead.

I drove on, forgetting waiting clients—I speeded right
through town, hands choking the wheel. It felt like some
hypodermic had just wedged under my breastbone,
sucking. What'd been leached out was my breath's continuing interest in itself, breath know-how. Your wind
has to be ambitious minute to minute—has to have a
renewable *interest* in continuing. Installments.

The roadway was turning yellow from the edges inward when I finally pulled over, parked in the open
countryside. A meadowlark balanced on a cattail gone
to seed. And all at once I remembered. How. To
breathe. The gratitude. I sat in the Nash gasping like a
diver who's just found—by accident—the top, his life
again.

This much was clear: I had to do something—for the
dead Mrs. B, for my living folks, my customers, for
everybody else—meaning myself. OK. Right there in
the car, I decided to attend one. A funeral, a black
funeral. I needed to see an ideal one. I discovered:
Mrs. Battle's had been held two days before. Nobody'd
let me know.

I checked Monday morning's *Herald Traveler* for a
likely name and church. I called in sick to my
laundromat-cleaning and soda-jerk jobs. I'd never done
that before. The church I picked was just off Sunflower
Street. I had to drive right past the Battle home. A
staked 'FOR RENT' sign was already pounded into her
front yard. Browned sunflowers had been cleared, the
hanging enameled teapot was gone. I hoped Vesta Lotte
Battle's kids had claimed the thing before some realtor
removed it as an eyesore. Riding by, I grumbled: real-
estate agents sure didn't waste any time, the bloodsuck-

ers. I kept trying to forget my parents' new caliber of rattling. They now seemed to alternate the need to breathe—him then her, her then him—like taking turns, sex-wise, waiting for each others' pleasure.

Nothing reminds you of how fragile it all is—nothing like living with two mild and often funny people who, if offered any riches on earth, would choose to get one deep single breath again.

To myself, aloud, after passing her shack, I said, "Vesta Lotte Battle, Vesta Lotte Battle. Pray For Us Left Here." I am no believer . . . still, you never know. I'm a percentage player. Besides, I missed her more than seemed quite rational or possible. I was just nineteen but already knew that Mrs. Battle was only starting up for me.

When you suddenly hear news of a friend's death, you sometimes want to call up one particular person who'll listen and help you through the worst first brunt of it. And so you're rushing to the home of the single person who might really help you get through this when, en route, of course, you find: the only one you want to be with now, she's the one who died.

My '39 Nash coasted still before a ramshackle church. Off Sunflower, on Atlantic Avenue, the Afro-Baptist Free Will Full-Gospel Church appeared bandaged in three kinds of tar-paper brick. Its roof showed crude dribbled asphalt mending. Set on the highest peak, one unpainted steeple tilted. The place looked home-crafted as some three-tiered dollhouse, doghouse, or outhouse. Even in early April, church windowboxes spilled great purple clouds of petunias. From one box, a sunflower had sprouted. Though it looked totally out of place—a windblown seed—though it'd already lifted a few feet high, straining toward the rusty gutters, it'd been allowed to live.

Parked in one low Hollywoodish line, hired white limos gleamed with sunlight, hurt your eyes. An empty hearse bloomed big ostrich plumes and small American flags from either silver fender. Black morticians loitered in white suits and dark glasses. The undertakers smoked, polished their cars, stood in proud jumpy groups. They acted like Secret Service guys outside a civic building where some bigwig official is appearing. They waited, smug and antsy, for their boss: Today's highest-paying black body in Falls, NC.

Turns out I was one of three whites in a large loud congregation. I kept straightening my black tie. Elders welcomed me with great ceremony and graciousness that made me feel even more a worm, a spy. Why was I here? Respect. Paying respects, paying. Came time to view the corpse. Almost immediately it happened, people filed toward the box. All the people on my row stood. Somebody nudged me from the left. I rose, not quite meaning it. Like in drill formation, we marched toward the knotty-pine altar and a coffin propped over velvet-draped sawhorses.

This happened on a Monday. Somehow, my premium book and a few rolls of quarters had been stored in my car's glove compartment, left there from Saturday rounds. I didn't want to leave them outside: this neighborhood was dicey (being the neighborhood where I collected). I'd brought the things in with me and now took them toward somebody's open coffin. The insurance ledger was imitation black alligator, hinged so it flipped open like a paperboy's record book. It bulged now in my jacket pocket. I took it out and held it, hoping it'd appear to be some prayerbook maybe. Sweating like I was, I nearly dropped the slippery thing,

then grabbed it, gulping. Imagine my list of names toppling into the box with this stiffening stranger.

She looked to be about thirty-eight. All in lilac, a
cocktail dress. Pinkish feathers curled around her head
like some nightclub's idea of a halo. Her coffin was
lined in white glove leather, the sides were plugged with
gleaming chrome buttons; it was framed in oiled walnut—the thing smelled just like a brand-new Cadillac
convertible. Giddy, for a moment, I wanted to climb
in. I don't know why. I hadn't eaten much that day.
Since Mrs. Battle died on me without a proper good-
bye, I'd started feeling really tired, like I'd forgot to do
something important.

The stranger's chest was massed with purple orchids.
Flowers picked up the exact color of her dress. I wondered if the orchids might be painted. But, no, I could
see that they were real. Huge curling bugle-nosed
orchids seemed to crouch there on her breastbone—
beautiful but someway wicked—like they were guarding
her while feeding on the body. Above her luxurious
coffin, along the empty choir loft's edge, dozens, maybe
hundreds, of Easter lilies. Tin collection plates hid behind flowerpots. The lilies washed Afro-Baptist with so
sweet a smell it burned your sinuses and eyes.

Stepping back toward my seat, I heard quarters jin-
gling, one roll unpeeling in my pocket. I winced. Trying to tamp the sound, I grinned.

Soon as we settled, the huge choir swooped in. Lined
up like a jury, they nearly outnumbered us mourners.
Openmouthed, they arrived singing something called
"Blessed Assurance." The scary appropriateness of this
(for me, I mean) changed and deepened verse to verse.
It went from seeming a wild coincidence to feeling almost expected, natural. I sat telling myself certain

mumbo-jumbo things like: "You have chosen the right place. Today is the day you were intended to be here." I didn't really know what all this meant. I still don't.

Many small children belted out the hymn from behind spiky white lilies. Some of the kids might've been among Mrs. Battle's household regulars but I wasn't sure. (When a boy is nineteen, little kids all look alike for a while.) Over flowers you could see the dark cloudy hair of tallest children, heads tipping side to side as mouths moved:

> "Blessed Assurance, Jesus is mine!
> Oh, what a foretaste of glory di-vine!
> Heir of salvation, purchase of God,
> Born of His Spirit, washed in His Blood.
> —This is my story, this is my song,
> Praising my Savior all the day long."

When human voices' pure pure sound rushed out carrying such words, I felt drunk, half-faint. I'd settled near the back. I could only bear to watch my own pale hands. I studied wrists' yellow hair shining in daylight. I thought odd things, "Strange, how no American coin is gold-colored." I looked at my long fingers' freckled backs, I turned over wet pink palms. These hands seemed to belong to one plump and silly boy. But my eyes, staring down on hands from what felt like a great and sickening height seemed the eyes of an old man, one teetering at some cliff's brink, a tired old person considering jumping.

Music swayed the choir that sang it. Each hymn swung singers toward a wilder kind of seasick. The people were one thing, their singing was another but, combined, these jumped past making an equal third. Everything seemed swollen past proportion, quan-

tum. Some choir members turned in place—hard for me
to watch, impossible to ignore—they spun around and
around, white sleeves flaring like cheap wings. The
choir loft was stairstepped in rows. At any moment three
or four singers would be whirling, self-contained, white
robes cheerfully slapping robes of those beside them.

At football games when your team is winning, everybody in your bleachers starts leaning side to side and
shouting one thing—it was like that now. This was a
funeral but the peppy choir still considered us the winning side.

I disagreed. I fought the row's rock and sway. I considered leaving. I felt out of my depth here. But I knew
that, in climbing over six weeping strangers singing in
my pew, I'd have to say, "Excuse me. So sorry. Thank
you, oops, pardon." I couldn't bear to let manners make
a fool of me again. Not here. Instead I fought this tilting. Everybody moved but me. I now turned into some
blond Princeton boy, chilly with a vengeance. Soon the
volume grew. They sure were working on me. Everyone
nearby sang in three-part harmony—sang like conser-
vatory grads—so skilled, their diction glassy, right.
Soon it seemed the church building itself was tipping,
a screened box that pans for gold, searching for some
glint among the mud. It kept rocking us, helpless as
pebbles shifting in the sieve—it kept us rattling back
and forth, almost auditioning.

Everyone but me. Straight-backed, massive. I refused. No way. Bumped from either side, I muttered at
the woman beside me. Cheerful behind her tears, she
yelled, "Tell it, bro!" She was just encouraging me. I
explained how a person could sure use a little more
room here. She nodded. My complaints just swelled the
hymn. Everybody took me for a singer. Glum, feeling

semi-hateful, I got coached by "Blessed Assurance." On it rolled. First I hummed along just to be polite. (With me it's a disease.)

Jostled from left and right, I tested a chanting note here, a word there. A person almost had to. Pretty soon, though you still fought it (for the sake of principle), you did sort of catch on, you soon nearly liked it. But, wait, no. I stiffened my spine, wanting to prove something. What? Maybe to keep things controlled on behalf of these wild emotional people noisemaking around me. *Some*body had to stay in charge, right? It was a favor that you paid others who'd lost it. There were rules.

I asked myself what she'd advise me—what Vesta Lotte Battle'd say? ("Hey, you, un-hitch a inch. What you keeping back? You hiding something, boy?")—I soon joined somewhat in. I trusted her. I wanted to do well. Maybe I was overly conscientious at it—but, hey, after all, Whitie does what Whitie can!

My shoulders soon felt safe between others' rolling massaging shoulders holding mine up from either side. I wanted to blend in for once. I hated being the go-getter all alone out front. I longed to seem the same as everybody else.

Maybe too quick for safety, I felt enclosed, half-pardoned. I felt explained. All this was what I'd been so homesick for, and without ever having lived it!

Soon you were pretty much loving it. I was. It felt like dancing sitting down. Like fainting with your eyes open. Like singing in the shower but with others singing in their showers nearby, others who, like you, didn't sound so hot on their own, but pooled became an angel choir that exhales, not carbon dioxide, but perfect pitch. I felt like telling everybody why I'd come, like singing why.

Our group stopped in one ragged rush. I was loud—alone—amazingly off-key for a long long second.

Nobody blamed me or much noticed as I sucked air, swallowed "Fool!," curled my toes. Others were now standing one by one. Fanning themselves with Jesus fans, they talked about the corpse.

"She been a mighty good neighbor, Lila," the woman near me rose. "One time, remember when my William cut his foot so bad on that soda bottle? well, she look after all my other little ones the whole night till we walk back home from the doctor's out Middlesex way. Then Lila say, Don't you be coming in here waking up these babies in the middle of no night, you let them sleep. She kept mine over to her house till they all awake and then she fed them a mighty fine breakfast, sent them back on home to me. Too, Lila done give my momma eighty cents, one time she couldn't pay."

"Lila," one old man with two canes called. "Had the prettiest yard on Atlantic Avenue, better'n mine and you know how nice mine is. Yeah, she got her dahlias to someway grow big as you head. Used bonemeal, some says."

They told why she never married (tending her sick mother). They said she dearly loved a moving picture show. She knew the age and facts of every movie star onscreen. Lila's say-so settled every movie bet or argument in Baby Africa.

Listening, I nodded. I soon felt I knew Lila a little, then—maybe it sounds pushy—I felt I knew her pretty well. It *was* pushy. Odd, I almost missed her. But even then I understood—I'd confused Lila with certain others: a Detroit autoworker I'd never seen alive. I mixed up this Lila person with my own ailing parents. I confused Lila with a freed slave whose burial I'd missed and maybe caused.

After the testimonies, music started again and I really threw myself into the pump and swell of hymns. I let

myself go, wanting to be excellent at this. I was a silly
kid hoping, his first time out, to get straight A's in
Grief. But even while crooning the choruses, while
practicing A-plus Amens loud, I still knew: This might
be fine for today. For a change. Oh but I needed this
now, oh yeah. And I would never forget it or outlast its
uses; but, being white like me, I couldn't *live* here.

I might rant and sway, released toward the best of
Afro-Baptist, I might be today's greatest hottest pudding of emotion—but I would always remain a tourist
when it came to such display. Call me frozen, or career-
oriented. Fill in the blank by saying I'm hyper-
Caucasian. Some claim that just such hanging back has
already turned our white race into the losing side: crea-
tures that cannot take the heat and so keel over. Maybe
we've already been outranked by those more fluid, faster
moving, closer to the earth and ready to adapt, sweat,
go with things.

That day I tried, though. Oh I tried to get it right.

"We hopes our white friends will feel free and
speak." It was the preacher crooking off his varnished
perch. He smiled for the first and only time that day.
He bared his square white teeth in a fake, presented
grin I recognized as mine. The single white lady popped
up quick, then looked around and seemed to regret it.
She'd stood to force herself. I knew this and felt for her
as, stranded, she cleared her throat, alarmed but determined. The lady wore trim navy-blue, her foil-colored
hair all in a knotty permanent. I couldn't place her name
but—knowing Falls the way this ex-paperboy did—I
could've told you her street address to within one block.
She might've been sister to the owner of that resur-
rected Wedgwood.

In a girl's voice, the lady now mentioned hiring Lila-
here for many years. The lady admitted how hard Lila'd

worked, far above the call of duty. The lady sounded short of breath—maybe she gasped due to sadness or stage fright, both. Soon you could hardly hear her. Everybody tipped forward, trying. I did too. She went, ". . . Feel we never . . . understood or whatever what a fine person . . . we had . . . around our house till Lila got so . . . so sick last . . . June was it?" she asked the man seated beside her.

"June, yes. Lila'd fallen in our rec room. We came back on Monday. We found her. She'd knocked over liquid floorwax and was lying in it, it'd dried. And when my sons pulled her to standing, the sound was like the flooring coming up with her. She was embarrassed about having spilled. It was too awful. The first Monday she didn't turn up for work I felt our house was like . . ." the lady waited, standing, doubting her lungs. "Like . . . house . . . was . . . hollow. There was an echo, it seemed all our rugs had been taken out. My husband can tell you. Now it seems that . . . to be . . . our self—our best selves—we needed Lila there to . . . And since she . . ." This time the matron curved one palm around her throat, gulping, unable to find a voice. But she refused to sit. Her husband reached out, almost touched her back, decided against it—improved his own posture instead. You saw that the woman really wanted to sit—she knew people would forgive her. But she'd decided. She had to finish.

"Tell the troof," some old man called, rapping floorboards with two homemade walking sticks. "Jesus going to see that you get all the air you needs for speaking true. Jesus going to fan some cold truth-telling wind down into you. You watch."

The thin woman smiled back at him, nodding. Her fist now rapped her sternum, she shook her prim head sideways. Her embarrassment, I saw, was a country club white

person's. Social embarrassment. She feared she looked
foolish. *Being* foolish pained her less than getting caught
at it by strangers, especially these decent black ones.

Still, I felt for her. Takes one to know one.''The Black-
and-Blue About Being White Blues.'' I sat remembering
Mrs. Battle in the rainstorm, drenched for me, throwing
rocks under my car, scattering dogs that'd taken cover
there to snap at my sogged ankles. I'd never thought of
doing that. Being watched like I always was in Baby
Africa—it'd never come to me that I might just kick
dogs or chuck stones at them. Why'd I settled for their
nipping at me? Why hadn't I properly defended myself?

"Loving Lila," the white woman tried summing up.
"Might've let us love each other more, but I'm not sure
that was reason enough . . . for taking up her life the
way we did. And by accident almost, looking back. We
gave her ten days off a year. Five of those she spent at
the beachhouse with us. She cooked for us there. Which
was no vacation. I see that now. Believe me, I'm living
with this. We learned so much from her. Look, we
loved her is all. Maybe that's the best thing anybody
can teach anybody? I don't know."

She sat, face in hands then. "Amen. It'll do," somebody shouted. Heads bobbed.

The white man hopped up to remark that what his
wife'd just said sure went double for him.

Then I stood. I did. I hadn't known I would. Suddenly it's like the church had sunk and left me vertical.
I think the singing had made me light-headed. That
song "Blessed Assurance" chanted in child voices, the
white flowers' smell, white robes like makeshift wings.
Those made me.

I told everybody I felt real bad about selling funeral
insurance. I told why I'd come. I admitted seeing the
great beauty of this ceremony. I conceded: Negro fu-

nerals had it all over white ones—much more personal
and everything. But it seemed I'd never understand
enough to help me feel quite easy with the business end
of burial. I admitted: some of my most beloved clients,
they had lapsed, see? I'd let them drift from the black
into the red and then I told on them. I had. I couldn't
rescue the whole world, could I?—though, for a while,
I'd given it my level best. You try and save a drowner
but if you drown too—what good is that to anybody,
you know? I said, Sure, I wanted a college education
but not one built by walking on the heads of others. I
apologized for taking up their time with something not
exactly on the subject. Then I added—feeble, I knew—
that Miss Lila's lilac dress was about the finest-looking
lilac dress I'd ever seen. "Amen. Ain't it, though?"
two old women, maybe twins, hollered. I sat. Breathing
hard. No way would I start sobbing like a fool, no, they
were all looking. The same old man up front began
really beating floorboards with his canes, he cried back
at me, "Jesus Have His Ways, Child. Be of Comfort,
Son. You going to act right. You wait. Scales going to
fall off them young eyes by-and-by. You'll see."

Then—that fast—I knew what I would do.

Again I stood. I emptied my pockets of all rolled
quarters and loose change. I yanked out every bill. I
whipped the premium book from my jacket.

Mourners between the aisle and me kindly slid out.
They let me step free. I walked to the tin collection
plates tucked behind massed lilies. Into one plate, I
piled all my money. About eighty-nine dollars and fifty
cents, I think. Maybe more.

Then—not able not to—I dropped in the keys to my
loyal Nash. I held the key ring back up—I told everybody where my car was parked, what kind it was, what
color. "Oh Lord," somebody called. "Jesus got them

Miracle-Working Ways. He look into the whiteboy Soul. He Clean House.''

I announced I wanted some kind of college scholarship set up. It'd help some straight-A child from this church. Elders would sell my used car—that and what cash I'd left here would at least help get things rolling. The fund would be named to honor . . . Miss Lila here. I didn't want to say Vesta Lotte Battle's name. Then they'd know it was me that turned her in. I left.

Two ushers swung open the exits for me. One young man was smiling, face all wet. The older gent gave me this ''Who are you kidding?'' stare, his mouth looked big, postcard-sized and folded in on itself with scorn. *He* seemed right. But, soon as sun hit me, I felt light and wonderful. Sunflowers and zinnias seemed my African honor guard. I weighed nothing for six blocks. Though this neighborhood was rough, no dog chased me today. I felt afraid of nobody. Nothing dared to hassle or to nag me.

I hiked back to my folks' place. They hadn't heard me drive up, they asked what was wrong, where'd I parked? I told them, I tried. They sat looking at each other. Dad's latest *Life* rested open on his lap. I remember Ava Gardner was on the cover. She's also from North Carolina, from very much the wrong side of the tracks and with the face of a Contessa and I have always loved her. Neither of my folks could drive. Proud, they called my wreck ''Jerry's runabout.'' I often took them shopping in it or out to the Dairy Queen.

Now Dad laughed, removed his glasses, folded them. He had an uneducated person's respect for eyeglasses, like these were some substitute for a college degree. He set the bifocals in their little casket, snapped it shut. He kept shaking his head side to side, he told Mom, ''They give our boy free encyclopedias, he throws them in the drink. Now he's gone and handed over his road-ster to the colored people because they're poor. Who knows? Maybe if a boy acts like a rich man long enough, he turns into one? Sure hope so.''

Then Poppa's chuckling slid, like always, right down breath's stairsteps into deep and deeper coughs till you never thought his wind would surface again. Mom jumped up and stood patting his back. It never helped but he liked it anyway. Next, Momma bent toward me, bent across Dad's leatherette easy chair. She touched the top of my hair, then one side of my neck. I felt too young then, shrunken down, just like earlier I'd felt so old and high up.

''Jerry's always had him a soft streak,'' Mom said, with me standing right here. ''It's not soft,'' I snapped at her. ''It's the only part I like. It's hard—and the rest of it is sloppy and extra. Don't say 'soft.' '' She pitied me, knowing I was weak enough to pity others. I hated her for that.

I stumbled to my room, threw myself onto the bed, mashed my face into the chenille spread's nubbins, pre-tending they were Braille—I'd soon read what to do next. I just wished I hadn't left my premium book in the collection plate. I don't know. I worried what might happen to my other clients. Even with Mrs. Battle gone, I still had big responsibilities. My ledger, was it the only record for the tens of thousands that older folks had saved toward their standing on the next plane? Would they miss out on their hard-earned heaven just because I'd lost my head while feeling generous?

Two days later, the mailman brings me a package. In it, my insurance book, all the money I'd left, plus—held to a piece of cardboard by crisscrossed electrician's tape—my car keys. The cardboard said, ''Parked right where it was.'' A note read: ''We all get move some-time. Sometime we needs to think out why. If it still

the same way you felt then we start up the college thing
for one our young folk. If not then that OK too. Cause
we all Children OF God. Either way you a man of
heart. IN Christ Blood Bartered for us sinners I am Rev.
T. Y. Matthews— Free-Will Afro-Baptist (Church).''

I sat down to write a check for two hundred dollars.
Signing it, my hands shook—the largest check I'd ever
written. I kept the ledger. And, look, I kept the car.
Can you forgive me? I waited till night to go collect it.
I hated being seen. My parents applauded when they
heard me pull up out front again. ''Pile in,'' I hollered
and they came running like kids rasping from a touch
of croup. I drove them to the Dairy Queen. They sat in
back, royalty, holding hands. You'd've thought it was a
Rolls, my used Nash. We said nothing the whole way
out and home. They were back there, sighing, eating
their cones. Driving, I breathed through my mouth, not
wanting to cry. The three of us, we had been so un-
lucky, really. And just getting back what little was ours,
it seemed some great reward to us, some justice.

Next day, I drove to Sam's office, I would turn in my
book and quit. But just outside his door, I decided on
collecting two more weeks. I'm not sure why. I guess
I wanted to get things cleaned up for whatever poor soul
Windlass Eventualities hired next. Two more Saturdays.
Hounds showed no mercy. Foolish and smug of me, but
I somehow thought dogs might act kinder during these
last trips. I half-believed dogs would smell my sacrifice:
the Miss Lila Scholarship. I hoped yard dogs would finally decide I was a friend to Baby Africa. Dogs didn't.

Again I knocked. Mrs. Battle's nosy neighbor, the
hugely fat widow, peeked out. She said, ''You come for
your Assurance? Is you new? You look older than that
last one.''

"Yes ma'am, older."

From inside the darkest corner of her home, underlit by a dime-store votive candle, one Jesus grinned—dressed in powder blue and white, beard marceled just so, he had a twenty-four-carat halo that somebody really should go hock for food. He looked guilty over being so pretty on a street of such bad need. This client's payments were only two weeks overdue. She'd greeted me with a broad face so scared I didn't like to see it. Dead Lila in her box looked much more in control than this living woman. "I checks," she shook her head. "I goes and looks but I real low just now."

Watching her move, I wondered how somebody so poor could stay so mammoth.

She lumbered toward a tiny vase that showed another Jesus hammocked among clouds, arms out beside him like a diver about to leap. From here the vase sure sounded empty. She stood—eyes closed, one ear mashed against it, like listening to a seashell. Like she could hear a hundred coins trying to hatch alive in there.

"Seem like it ought to be around here." The widow moved from vase to firewood box to mantel. She shifted things. There sat an unopened jar of jam, a tartan bow topping it. A gift from Mrs. Battle? An inheritance?

"I busy checking," the woman promised.

But I stood remembering Mrs. Battle's honesty: "I ain't got no money today." "Pearl dead." "Vesta Lotte Battle tries." "I reckon you'll do what you wants." I felt I'd learned something from the old woman. I still couldn't explain quite what.

"Maybe it been stole. Yeah, stole probably," the obese woman patted around behind a sheeny Last Supper wall rug. Then she moved to a calendar that showed Christ holding out his own lit-up and dripping heart. His face looked sobered. You could see why.

"Assurance? These young boys now'll steal you blind. Ain't nobody safe. Too, I getting so I forgets. You sure it already a Saturday again? I done sunk mighty low but I still hunting. Don't you fret your pretty head none, I gone find it yet. You so pretty. Look how 'good' and yellow his hair is. Golder'n that"—and she scanned the room for her favorite picture, then pointed to the rouged Jesus who posed nearby—heartless Himself because He kept *offering* it to everybody.

Such flattery always sickened me. I really couldn't abide it. "Here," I bent, kicking over one corner of her rag rug. Since the house was dark, since her notched swollen back was toward me, it was easy to unpocket the two quarters. I picked them up, held them out to her. "These?" I said.

She turned, she made a cry, "No!" She inched forward, blinking, her jaw slack. Each huge arm now lifted from the elbow—wobbling like udders as she neared me. The sad weight hanging off her sides and breasts suddenly seemed like a burden assigned, not chosen. In the face, surprise mixed with such fear. Fear that I might take these back, fear I meant to trick her. I couldn't stand watching. *May this job end, and now, Amen. I am not fit to earn a living in this world.* "So let's see here, that's what?—fifty—five zero—cents, paid in full?" I fiddled with my black book. "Listen, there'll be a new fellow next week. Just to make sure you get full credit, you'll want to save these. Just give him these same two next week, okay? Okay."

I passed her fifty cents. All the hut's accidental sunlight, the shine from her red candle got snagged across two silver coins. Her callused hand itself, charcoal dark on its back, showed a pale pink copper color inside. It seemed that years of work for whites had rubbed the true black pigment off her palm.

Her face gleamed, the upper body rocking toward me. Moaning, she showed me my own coins—like these were two working eyes that some genius had awarded a blind woman, round things she could pop right into ruined sockets, and see again.

"I still on the assurance, Assurance?"

Beside her name, I read the tally, three policies complete: Two thousand three hundred five dollars and fifty cents. "Consider yourself carried, please." I backed into daylight, glad even for the posse of sunning mongrels. They rose, stretching, grumpy at their duty. We all have our jobs.

She hid both eyes behind the heavy crook of one great arm.

I heard her weeping, then explaining to the crowd of paper Jesuses, "Your Dorothy ain't lost out after all, Savior. You done carried her over into the Promised Land of another week of Surrance and for free. I still under the coverage. Your old Dot here, she still covered, Lord."

Now I'm going on sixty. It seems impossible, but years are really the bottom line, aren't they? Semi-retired, I've had the usual two heart attacks but, as with some of us who get the best cardiac specialists, I lived. Of course, as a young man, I went into business for myself. I actually did pretty well.

It came about in a strange enough way. I was working other odd jobs, saving up for law school. I'd got my BS through night courses. My parents lived to see me graduate. They were so happy about it. My father wore his reading glasses all through the ceremony. I wanted to tell my folks, "No, this is just the start . . . don't be so thrilled so early." But they were.

I sometimes wonder what they'd think if they could

see where I live now. We just built a fancy guest wing
onto our beach place. I designed it myself. It doubled
the floor space of our original cottage. These days we
don't have too much company and the addition's not
that practical. I just wanted to add it on is all. The kids
come down when they can get away from their jobs and
such. My wife calls this wing—with its white spiral
staircase, all the glass, cathedral ceilings—Gerald's Taj
Mahal. My wife is from one of *the* old families around
here. She stops short of calling my new annex that
dreaded word of hers: "nouveau." I can't explain to
her just why I had to get so flashy this time around.

Last August, she and I were on our new porch just
sitting there, reading. It was late afternoon. A young
white couple, strangers, wandered off the public beach.
Holding hands, they crossed our property, headed toward the road. They were country kids in bathing suits,
very tall, they moved well, they were as good-looking
as they'd ever be. They walked right by the entrance to
our new guest wing. I jumped up. "What's wrong?"
Millie asked from behind me. I shook my head No. I
couldn't answer for a while. In the second I'd seen one
pale man and woman come up from the ocean, slowed
by sand and tramping toward our fine glass house, I
understood I'd built it for them. For my parents, dead
these thirty-odd years, people whose idea of an annual
vacation was one spendthrift afternoon at the State Fair
outside Raleigh. For a second, in the late night, I
thought they'd finally come home to collect.

But my career so-called, I was telling you about that.
I cleaned two laundromats for a rich ill-tempered bachelor. We hardly ever saw each other. He'd leave my pay
envelopes in his rural mailbox. He must've liked my
work. His will left me both laundromats. I was twenty-
five by then. I'd been studying law on my own. This

first equity helped get me a school loan. I made Law Review at Duke. I was thirty-one when I finished.

I moved back here to Falls and bought another laundry unit. I hung up my shingle and started managing the estates of the lawyers and dentists whose widows needed help, whose Princeton sons now practiced in flashier cities. The boys'd gone off to Atlanta and New York where real fortunes could be made. Me, I stuck it out locally. In the late Fifties, I put new laundromats into the shopping centers that'd started opening nearby and all up into Virginia. Then, with our kids off in good schools, with me now spending more time managing my own holdings than other people's, I invented something.

I'd stayed polite and steady, of course—forever grateful to have a leg up in this town society-wise. To this day I follow my dead mother's advice, I still say "Please" and "Thank you very much." They still like that. And it's only now, when I no longer *have* to be polite, it's only now that people notice my manners and find them humble, touching. Odd. I got somewhat sly. I concocted (with a smart college boy's summer help) and patented (on my own) an adjustable coin plunger for commercial washers and driers. It used to be—when prices went up (as they will)—a laundromat owner had to rebuy the whole coin-activator component. With my device, the owner can just adjust his own machine's templates. He can ask whatever seems fair—and without getting soaked by the manufacturer every time he ups the load cost by a dime or a quarter. It sounds simple. It is. "Strictly a nickel and dime operation," my wife teases me. But I got there first and it has made our financial life a good bit easier.

I took over other laundry facilities. I worked all this out consciencewise: Washing helps people, right? My forty-one Carolina/Virginia locations are open to all—

all who have some pocket change and the will to stay tidy. Who can argue with the beauty and value of a clean 100% cotton business shirt, pressed, brand-new, and on its hanger, ready-to-wear? How could that cause anybody pain?

Over my years in business, I've been ethical usually, and (to be fair to myself) sometimes even when it hurt. One thing I admit I'm proud of: I volunteered as an unsalaried consultant in a local class-action against the cotton mill here. Nowadays, newspapers call my parents' disease 'brown lung.' Then we just said, They've Got What You Get From Working Too Long In The Mill. The Wages of Wages.—Owners, clever, never let anybody *title* the sickness. That meant it wasn't real, see? —Workers won this go-round. Japanese-made filters now purify the plant, replacing its entire air supply every twenty minutes. Some new insurance benefits are in place, there's back-pay for those too broken-winded to work.

Strange, though technically I'm pretty well set now, I've never really felt rich. If that's any defense! Weird that my own kids have trust funds—it's thrilling, really. Only two bothered finishing college, of course. One teaches the deaf in Savannah. Our middle daughter, Miranda, took Sarah Lawrence by storm and will enter Harvard Law this fall. Our baby girl lives in St. Louis with a black airlines mechanic who plays jazz on weekends. She says she's happy. You have to believe them. I know that her living situation shouldn't bother me. But, hey, it does bother me some, what can I say? Nobody's perfect.

Oh, and I'm not insured. Drives my estate planner absolutely crazy but, after that first experience, forget it. Insurance based on getting sick, they call Health.

The kind depending on everybody's fear of death they call Life!

You can have it.

Some Saturday mornings here lately I wake at our beach place and I'll be half out of bed before understanding I don't have to go to work. It's almost disappointing. I'm free finally. No routes left. I still remember most every house along Sunflower Street and Atlantic Avenue, my Eventualities crew.

I have a mind that holds onto such details: the one that told the same three easy riddles, the one in the metal wheelchair and wearing, for no good reason, a cowgirl hat. —A head for facts is good in a lawyer and a tinkerer like me. But you can overdo remembering. Recalling too much makes the person inefficient. As I age, early memories come clearer. I still picture many a door opening on those wizened faces. Many faces probably no older than mine now. I settle back in bed, I listen to the ocean working at reclaiming our oceanfront lot. It should soothe you, having a big white glassy house right on the beach. So I lie here looking at the patterns sunlight-on-water moves across our high white ceiling. Times, I say—low so as not to wake Millie—"That's over and done." Then I try and catch more sleep. But you know how it is, once your eyes are open, you can pretend for forty minutes but you're awake for good.

Over thirty-odd years, I've told myself to forget the insurance route. And yet, lately for no good reason, it's been coming back on me, like an overrich meal.

We all have our crimes. Right?

I remember, after Sam got hold of my list, before he rang up Cleveland with news of impounded funds, he

promised me I'd done the right thing. Sam said I'd fingered fewer Overdues than any collector he could remember, especially for a *young* collector. They were really
ruthless about turning in certain oldsters, these darned
eager-beaver kids. Sam claimed I must be good for my
clients' morale. "Thank you," I said. "Tried," I said.
Since I'd personally floated many of my old folks' funeral
payments for weeks, months—I *was* their morale.

   "You're beginning to look better already, Jerry. Know
your problem? See, you're like Charlie Chaplin or this
Paul Robeson or Mrs. Roosevelt maybe—you want to
be all things to all people, but you can't. Nobody can.
Choose maybe four, six, tops. Think of these as job
slots you've filled. You get to pick this one handful,
then you really better stick your neck out—but just for
them. The rest you let go. You've got to, Jerry. Of your
six all-time keepers, I seriously doubt one's on this list.
Don't say otherwise, Jer. —My job? I'm here to make
you feel better. You haven't got the organic chemistry
figured out yet. You're like me—just dripping virtue.
There's no percentage in taking it to heart, son. What
we're doing here is rigged, sure, but you know why,
Jerry? Because it's part of the world."

   Soon as he phoned in our nine worst credit risks to
Cleveland—a town he called The Mistake by the Lake—
Sam offered me a drink right from his bottle. This time
I took it. My eyes watered. To me the stuff'd already
started tasting like old couches, the smoky interiors of
huts, my Baby Africa route and brown clientele distilled.—I drank and drank it so I'd sleep. My homely
boss leaned back, he took his longest hardest bourbon-
pull so far. Dazed, I sat in the office's half-light, drunk.
Sam gulped; I kept watching his notched Adam's apple
hopping and hopping like some small live thing you
pity.

I quit Funerary Eventualities forty years ago. I still feel responsible for those nine who never got the warm reception they deserve. On the next plane, I mean. And, look, I don't even *believe* in the next plane, you know? Still, I understand certain basics: Everybody expects a few sure things, a bit of blessed assurance. A person wants to feel covered.

Hey, and I appreciate your listening. Really. I don't know—I've kept fretting over this, feeling it for all these years. I mean, basically I'm not all that bad of a man, am I. Am I?

I've never once credited any type of heaven. No way. But I still worry for the souls I kept from theirs. —Even now I know the names of my nine clients I squealed on. They are:

> Betty Seely
> Easton Peel
> 'Junior' Turnage
> Carlisle Runyon
> Mary Irene Tatum
> Leota Saiterwaite
> P. M. Hilton
> Minna Smith
> Vesta Lotte Battle

I still try and imagine her—on hold, rocking between this world and the next. I want to either bring her back or send her on toward her proper reward. I can't.

Vesta Lotte Battle owed me $12.50.

There, I've told you. I'll feel better. Thank you very much.

1987–1989

About the Author

Allan Gurganus was born in Rocky Mount, North Carolina, in 1947. He attended the University of Pennsylvania and the Pennsylvania Academy of Fine Arts to study painting. Following military service in the Vietnam War, he studied with Grace Paley at Sarah Lawrence College, and with Stanley Elkin and John Cheever at the Iowa Writers' Workshop. Named a Wallace Stegner fellow at Stanford, Gurganus stayed on to teach as a Jones Lecturer. He has subsequently been professor of writing at Duke and at the Iowa Writers' Workshop, and is permanently associated with Sarah Lawrence. He is a Danforth fellow, winner of two PEN Syndicated Fiction prizes, and recipient of an Ingram Merrill Award and two grants from the National Endowment for the Arts. His first novel, *Oldest Living Confederate Widow Tells All*, was named winner of the Sue Kaufman Prize for First Fiction from the American Academy and Institute of Arts and Letters. *White People* won the 1991 *Los Angeles Times* Book Prize for Fiction and the 1991 Southern Book Award for Fiction from the Southern Book Critics Circle. Allan Gurganus lives in New York City and in Chapel Hill, North Carolina.